THE VAMPIRE AND HIS STAR WEAVER

DEVON ATWOOD

Vinci Books

vinci-books.com

Published by Vinci Books Ltd in 2026

1

A CIP catalogue record for this book is available from the British Library.
Paperback ISBN: 9781036733780
The EU GPSR authorised representative is Logos Europe, 9 rue Nicolas Poussion, 17000 La Rochelle, France contact@logoseurope.eu

By Devon Atwood

Cosmic Ley Series

The Vampire and His Star Weaver

The Faie King's Mortal

Faie and Fury

Bonds and Envy

Reign and Ruin

Love and Other Jobs

Love Rx

Love MD

Love Esq.

Love JD

Love Op

Love and Other Joys

Kiss-Met

Kiss Me, Doc

Touch Me, Doc

Marry Me, Doc

Tease Me, Doc

Married to the Faie

The Prince of Salt and Sea

Trigger Warnings

Violence
Mortal peril
Explicit sexual content
Explicit language
Kidnapping

To the ones with stars in their eyes and vampires in their hearts.

You're cute, but you're filthy.

Chapter One

SAGE

Blood dripped in a steady cadence, plopping to the polished oak table in uniform splotches. I stared at the droplets, and suddenly, I had the bizarre urge to dip my finger in them and paint a clumsy picture like a carefree toddler. Instead, I snapped out of it, reaching quickly for the napkin dispenser to grab a fistful of papery, white napkins to staunch the bleeding from my nose. I used my other hand to wipe the table and sent a fast, cursory look around the quiet cafe to see if anyone had noticed. A student with bright yellow headphones glanced at me but then returned his attention to his laptop. Embarrassing crisis averted. This time, anyway.

As I held the tissues to my nose, I felt the blood seeping through the thin ply, already coating my fingers in sticky warmth. At this rate, I'd get blood on my laptop again. I grabbed another bunch of napkins and added them to the mass.

I couldn't react like normal people did to stress, lack of sleep, and lack of food. Oh, no. I had to get *nosebleeds* to signal that my body was about to throw up its arms and be done with me. *It's been real, Sage, but twenty-one years of this bullshit is about my limit. Have fun in whatever afterlife you're headed for.*

With my left hand holding the tissues to my face, I turned back to my assignment. The second semester of senior year in college was actually Hell. We were almost done, almost full-fledged adults who might have mortgages and a string of subscriptions we forgot we'd signed up for. We had internships lined up or had chosen master's programs. But before any of that, we had to pass our final classes.

And I had to survive my last semester working for the school newspaper, the *Mane Daily*, preferably without strangling the editor of the sports column. Like she was tempting that fate, Cassandra's number popped up on my phone with the name "Sam Eagle" and an eagle emoji. I answered wearily. "Hey, what's up?"

Immediately, her nasally, droning voice stuffed my ears unpleasantly. "We have a problem." Cassandra had earned her nickname from me because she wore her hair in a tight ponytail that made her look bald, and she spoke with the same insufferable mannerisms as Sam Eagle from the Muppets—though I wouldn't dare share it for fear of being kicked off the paper.

Keeping my voice low so I didn't irritate the other students in the campus coffee shop, I asked, "What problem?" I'd submitted my proofreads three days early, so it couldn't be that.

"Keagan just came down with strep. Apparently," she paused, drawing out the word like a disapproving nun, "Wylde and Foster went drinking with him." With an audible cringe she added, "And they shared cups."

I recoiled like I was facing the army of germs personally. "Gross."

"Ava has cheer practice and Miley declined, so you're all I have left."

God, it just warmed the heart to be the last on the list in our department. I was a senior, I had straight As in all my classes, I'd taken every elective in media relations imaginable, and I had a damn good writing voice if my professors were to be believed. And yet, I had been relegated to sports stats and proofreading. I saw where this was going, though. "You need someone on the field."

"The Lions have a scrimmage game," Cassandra confirmed. "Nothing *big*," she emphasized.

But my heart was already soaring with hope. "I can do it," I said quickly. "I know the media crew, so we can work together to—"

"Just get the facts," Cassandra clipped. "Nothing fancy. It's just a scrimmage."

I was finally getting my first article. My first honest-to-God *piece* for the *Mane Daily*, reporting on the *best* college soccer team in the nation. The Lions had won five NCAA championships and proven they were the best of the best year after year. People outside the college actually read our newspaper just for updates on them. My name would finally be *on something*.

I was sure she could physically hear my heart beating over the line. *Like that's even possible.* I had to calm down, or my nose was going to gush harder. "Okay," I assured her, trying to move the wad of tissues aside so I didn't sound muffled. "No worries. I got this."

Around a groan, she said, "Deadline is Friday."

That was an unfair deadline, objectively. It was Wednesday, and we wouldn't be using this story until the next issue, but whatever. Bullying me was Cassandra's second favorite hobby after jerking off to yiff porn. Probably. Actually, I really didn't know what Cassandra did in her free time for fun. I wasn't sure she was *capable* of having fun. "When is the game?"

"Kickoff is in forty minutes."

I blanched. "*Forty minutes*?"

"It *is* last minute," she reminded me.

Asshole. She'd asked everyone else first knowing full well that Wednesdays were my study days with no classes and no hours at the movie theater. She could have asked me first thing this morning.

"Thanks, bye." I hung up on her and tossed my phone in my star-pattern backpack before slamming my laptop closed and sliding that in, too. I had to keep the tissues in my left hand so that I didn't accidentally bleed on a tchotchke in the bookstore/cafe combo. They had collected all kinds of cute, quirky things like owl lamps and weird gnome statues, and I could tell the owner honestly cared about everything in here. It was my favorite place to study, and the fantastic iced herbal teas certainly didn't hurt, either.

A pang of loneliness assaulted me, whacking me over the head with a frying pan and reminding me that I would only ever hang out here alone. My time for making friends in college had long since passed. My roommates were okay, but I could never seem to connect with them fully. They had inside jokes from having lived together already, and I didn't quite fit in with them. Although, my ADHD thoughts taking up space in my brain while they were trying to tell me their—sorry, girls—horrifyingly boring stories about manicures and prom escapades did not help either. I had a thing with attention span. As in, the fake owl lamp over my head probably had a longer one than I did.

With one hand, I managed to get my things packed up, and then I dashed out of the store and over to my electric scooter I had tethered to a lamp post. Going by scooter, the stadium was a good fifteen-minute push from here, and that wasn't taking into account making my way to the sidelines and meeting up with the other media students. Cassandra had totally screwed me. I had no time for before-game interviews or eavesdropping on the coaches before the game started. I'd have to show up, take notes on the game itself, and get some after-game interviews from the star players. I was sure that was what Cassandra had intended. God forbid I get some kind of scoop at a scrimmage.

Piedmont University had practically been built into a forest, set far off from the city of Kingston, New York, it had been carved into the Bluestone Wild Forest. The result was a slightly wild, heavily shaded campus drenched in green. Fortunately, the stadium was east, downhill, so I didn't have to push myself uphill and waste time.

I coasted through the campus, and the path meandered through colonial-style architecture, brick outbuildings, lush planters, and trees that had fully bloomed at this point in April. I passed several students walking or riding bikes, and some of them looked a lot like me—wearing a sheen of sweat from the humid air and wishing AC was portable.

I had thrown my long, wavy hair into a bun this morning, but I could feel it sagging under the weight in a lopsided way. Not exactly professional, and my torn jeans and cropped T-shirt didn't help that much, either. Whatever. A piece was a piece, and even if the soccer team didn't know me, the media team did from our shared classes together, so they wouldn't care.

When I finally made it to the stadium, parked my scooter, and hightailed it inside, I found a rowdy crowd already gathered in the stadium seats and the enormous, arched entrances mostly empty. I fumbled with my bag while I walked, fishing out my wallet so I could find my *Mane Daily* ID card. It wasn't anything professional like a "press badge" I'd seen on real pros. It had been printed on cardstock and laminated, and the picture was three years old, before I'd discovered curl cream and I had looked more like the *Mane*'s lion mascot than a journalist.

I paused before the media access entrance with a blip of humor—I *still* didn't look like a journalist. Despite my mother being the most famous news anchor in the New York City Metro area, no matter what I did and how hard I worked, I always looked like a bewildered nerd instead.

Probably because I was one.

Shaking that thought off, I pushed through the heavy, metal door and into the narrow hallway lined with storage closets and equipment, and the buzz of the crowd grew to a resonating hum that I could practically feel through my feet.

I opened the field access door, and the hum became a wave of noise that only grew louder as I rushed down a flight of steps to the pitch. Then the roar of the crowd washed over me, unmuted and thrumming through my chest like I'd taken a pair of headphones off my ears. The field stretched out before me, vibrant green and perfectly pristine without the players digging their cleats into its surface. And fortunately, it looked like I had made it just in time, with both teams on the field and gathered around their coaches. I took in the Lions and their blue jerseys, white shorts, and muscular thighs, and I tried not to gawk.

I wasn't much of a sports girl, despite my position on the *Mane Daily*'s sports column. When I'd accepted the student position, I'd been willing to take any avenue I could to follow in my mother's footsteps. Even—*eugh*—sports. But although it hadn't been my first choice, I'd found some... perks along the way. It wasn't like I was a sex-crazed maniac or anything—okay, a sex-crazed *anything*—but as I made my way across the sidelines to the camera crew off to the left, I allowed myself another appraising once-over of our team. Thighs, glutes, and biceps for days. Tasty.

I wonder what Cassandra would do if I submitted an article entirely dedicated to the player's physical attributes. "In the first quarter, Saleki, 34, wowed with tantalizing glimpses of his rippling thighs, eclipsed only by the notably plump jock strap of fan-favorite player 13, Evensly."

Smiling to myself, I came to a stop by a familiar face with thick, black headphones on his ears and his eyes on a tablet. He scratched between the rows of tight, ebony braids that followed the slope of his head, his features pinched. Adjusting the mic in front of his mouth, he muttered, "Switch it to three. Yeah, that looks better. It's your feed. Check the cables." Marcus had on a black sweatshirt with the media team's name in white letters along the back, and as he looked up to check the camera to his left, he caught sight of me. His dark eyebrows lifted in surprise. "Well, if it isn't Hot Mess Express."

That had been his nickname for me during our three classes together. Marcus actually *liked* the media aspect of our major, whereas I was a little more into the journalistic side of things. I waved, out of breath and probably looking like I'd rolled in olive oil after running in this humidity. Like I always did, I focused on his mouth instead of his eyes to keep from feeling overwhelmed. It was also a trick I'd learned to keep my brain focused on the conversation and not off in la-la land. "Hey, Marc."

"What brings you to the sidelines?" He shifted a look around. "Or sports. In general."

Still completely out of breath, I pointed a thumb to my backpack, like that could show him anything remotely useful. "I got a piece. For the *Mane*."

His lips parted in surprise. "No shit. Well, finally."

"I mean, it's just a scrimmage," I panted, swallowing thickly and resting my hands on my hips to catch my breath. I tried to look cool, but I was pretty sure I missed the mark by a mile. "Nothing crazy."

"What's crazy is them not giving you more," he muttered, returning his gaze to his tablet. He gestured to the folding chairs that had been set up near the pitch. "Have at it. Make it amazing. Make them wish they'd asked you sooner."

"Yes," I agreed like a dork and a little too enthusiastically.

Marcus' mouth flatted with suppressed amusement, and he shook his head. "Mercy."

I took a seat in the black folding chair, breathing in the scent of fresh soil mixed with French fries and popcorn that wafted through the air. The Lions had fans from all over the state, and it didn't matter if they'd already played their season and placed first in the NCAA championship back in November. Lions fans showed up for Lions games. Simple as that. Piedmont University had a rich history that went back more than a hundred years, and its alumni took that seriously, from science fairs to soccer. More than half the stands were full, even for what was largely considered a practice game against the West New York Buccaneers.

Red jerseys met blue in the center of the field, and with a piercing whistle, the game began. I kept my eyes on the plays, noting assists, saves by our well-loved goalie, Brenner, and then the nasty knee a Buccaneer took to the nose near the end of the first quarter.

I hadn't known anything about sports before I'd started working at the *Mane Daily*, and I hadn't had any interest in learning, either. But it seemed like door after door had closed for me as I'd worked toward my dreams of following in my mother's footsteps. Once this one had opened at the *Mane*, I'd had to take it. Sports, obituaries, advice column—I didn't care. I just needed to try, or my mother's disappointment would cripple me. She'd raised me on her own. I was her everything and she was *my* everything. I had to make her proud.

So, I would write a stellar if informative piece on the April scrimmage between the Lions and the Buccaneers, and I'd be damned if I missed a single play. But it was so *hard* when sports had so many breaks. Someone would go out of bounds, and then they had to set up a corner throw, and my eyes glazed over. I had to snap myself back to it so many times, I wondered if people might be able to see welts on my forehead.

By halftime, my neck was cramping, and we were up two to nothing. My notes were far more extensive than they needed to be, but better that than skimming through footage post-game to come up with nonsense. Or, worse, getting lost in thought while I was trying to watch. It took all my energy, but I'd managed it for half the game. I could do this.

I stood, stretching, and Marcus loped up the field to join me. "How's it going?"

I shrugged. "Riveting. Really, this is scintillating stuff." His mouth wavered on a laugh, so I added, "I think this might win me a Pulitzer."

He laughed then, throwing his arm around my shoulders. "Hot Mess, you are wasting your talents on that stuffy black-and-white operation over there. You sure you want to be a journalist?"

"It's my dazzling wit that will win over my readers," I grinned.

"Fair enough," he conceded. With his arm still around my shoulders, he led me back to the media team where they were passing out coffee cups from a station set up behind the cameras. "Coffee?"

"If I'm breathing, I'm going to want coffee. I don't know why you even ask."

"Even if you're in a coma?" he challenged, reaching for a cup.

"Put it in the IV," I replied solemnly. He laughed again, and I took a cup from one of the freshman media team members, smiling and thanking her. After adding a packet of sugar, I followed Marcus back to his camera setup where we stood next to the expensive equipment.

I liked Marcus. He was easy to talk to, friendly, and supportive, but he wasn't anything more than that. Honestly, no one paid much attention to me anyway—I tended to fly under the radar, never belonging to one group or the other and never finding friendships that actually stuck. But Marcus was at least friendly when we were around each other, even if we weren't actually friends. Whatever positive human connection I could scrounge up with my busy schedule, I was happy to take.

We stared out at the empty field, sipping warm coffee as the sunset deepened, and Marcus turned to me. "So, any graduation plans?"

I shrugged. "Working. Then I start my internship in July."

He gave me a curious eye squint. "That's big news. Where?"

It wasn't big news because it was straight-up nepotism. "With my mom."

He nodded like he'd expected that. "Hey, it's not what you know, it's who you know. Use it."

"Yeah," I grimaced. "That's fair. Totally earned that spot."

"I'd say you did," Marcus replied mildly. "Top scores in all your classes, you're never late, you're friendly and smart." He slid another glance my way, and it was different that time. Softer. "You're cute, too. Doesn't hurt in television."

I lifted my gaze to his for the first time, suddenly transfixed by his walnut-rich eyes and the unexpected warmth in his features. Heat crept up my neck like I'd swallowed an ember. Marcus had never said anything like that to me before. He'd never so much as asked me out for coffee, but the way he was looking at me at the moment…

Breaking eye contact, I took a step back, but I wasn't sure why. Desire had actually popped its head out of the soil, looking around and wondering what was going on. I hadn't thought romance was in the cards for me, not with my work and school schedule—and, okay, overall personality. But here the opportunity was, a gorgeous, six-foot-tall media manager with lips that were spreading into a knowing smile and the self-assured posture of someone who knew I found him attractive, too.

Holy sheep, Sage. Are you about to get a date?

But as I took another step backward, my feet carrying me like I had no control over them, the heat in my face suddenly bottomed out. Searing warmth exploded across the soles of my feet, traveling up to my calves and warming my inner thighs. I gasped, looking down and expecting to find that I'd stepped in front of an industrial-sized heater.

Instead, I found a bright blue flash, like lightning, that pulsed around my feet and streaked out behind me. Marcus stumbled away from me with a cracked, "What the fuck?"

The warmth blossomed in my belly, low and disconcertingly satisfying between my legs, and as my eyes followed the streak up the stadium stairs and into the stands, it stopped with another blinding flash. A few exclamations escaped the crowd, and then the light was gone. Blinking hard, I stared at the place where the light had traveled and ended. Could lightning travel along the ground likc that? Had I been hit by it? I felt alright, though, even if that heat remained at my core and my pulse had quickened.

Where the light had vanished, a group of tall, well-built men stood on the steps with food in their hands and shocked expressions on their faces. The man closest to me, whose gorgeous facial features I could make out even from this distance, latched onto me with his shaded eyes. My heart thunked hard in my chest, and the warmth in my abdomen swirled. His dusky lips tipped into a smile, tugging at something inside of me I couldn't begin to name.

He crooked a finger and motioned for me to come to him. And for some psychotic reason, *I did.*

Chapter Two

SILAS

The augur peered at my star chart for the thirtieth time, and my patience frayed faster than the ancient tapestry beneath her padded chair. She was taking this far more seriously than she needed to for a randomly appointed, thirty-five-year-old augur in Kingston of all places. It wasn't like she was in the inner sanctum of the vampire stronghold in Geneva, Switzerland. This was a box to tick, and the faster she got her soothsaying over with, the better.

The female augur had French-braided hair of a nondescript brown color that frayed around her temples, and she pushed her thick-rimmed glasses up her nose. "The swallows have been active this week," she said as she leaned her elbows on the table and ran her finger down the star coordinates that had been present at my birth. "They follow the ley lines to the east."

"Go east, got it," I bit out impatiently. "Anything else?"

She lifted her eyes to mine with a quirked, thick brow. "You are the second oldest, are you not?"

"Technically third," I admitted begrudgingly. Behind

me, Art snorted. I didn't even deign to spare him a glare. He was a full fifteen minutes older than I was, and he rarely let me forget it.

"Ah, yes, your twin was born first," the augur smirked. "Even still, I think it would be in *all* our best interests if we gave our full effort to finding your ley socium. At your age…"

My stomach growled, and I tuned her out. We had been in the augur's cramped cabin for going on five hours now as she had read each of my four cohort brothers' star charts, compared them to the patterns of *bird watching* she had done, and given each of us advice on where we might find our eternal mates. I was last, thankfully, and all I wanted to do was go home, make an enormous plate of hot wings, and watch *House of the Dragon*. Was that too much to ask? I didn't think so. It wasn't like I was going to find my magical mate right this damn minute. Or even this century, likely. It had already been over five hundred years.

Then again, this augur had been watching the skies for a full year for us. It was a blip in time for us, but for her, it was her life's work. She took it seriously, and if she didn't, well… the Conexus of vampires who ruled and lived in Switzerland wouldn't take kindly to her failure. Gathering my centuries-honed patience, I nodded stiffly. "East ley lines."

"And a crescent moon," she added with a finger up. "The starlings gathered under Venus at lunar value one hundred thirty-six."

I could practically be an augur myself with how well-versed I was at ley line reading at this point. Except nothing —and I meant *nothing*, not even a mate—could induce me to spend my days watching bird patterns. I understood enough to know that she was asking me to walk around heavily crowded areas somewhere east of here and during a crescent moon. "Will do."

Her bland, brown eyes held mine imperiously. "It is a crescent moon now."

Alvaro snickered behind me, and since he couldn't read *my* thoughts the way he could read a human's, I shot him a middle finger behind my back. "Go mate hunting tonight. I'm on it." I would not, in fact, be doing that.

The augur nodded like she was satisfied. "The shift in ley lines will take you away from my area next year, correct?"

The ley lines shifted as steadily and predictably as the stars they were connected to. Where the ley magic flowed, we followed. It was maddening and, in my opinion, pointless, but tradition was tradition. No matter how much I liked the place we had settled in for a short time, my wishes didn't factor into things. Not that Kingston was on my list of "most liked." I had almost died of boredom this decade.

"Augur Dana, are you satisfied with your readings? Can we conclude this gathering?" Constantine asked politely, his bass voice filling the small cabin. The augur lived in the Catskill Mountains permanently, and her sole reason for existing was to chart the ley lines in this area and observe bird patterns to report changes in magical energy that might affect our kind. Her cabin wasn't unappealing, with rugs and tapestries everywhere and plants crawling along the exposed timber walls. But five hours had been more than enough time to fully appreciate its… quaintness.

"Certainly," she smiled affably.

"Thank you for your time," I said drily, and when I turned to go, I found the enormous frames of my brothers already filtering out of the cabin door and into the bright sunlight beyond. Constantine actually had to duck under the doorframe, which was a common problem for him. And that very reason was why we stuck out like blueberries in a strawberry pie everywhere we went. We were all tall, built sturdy, and hewn like classic marble statues. Constantine was the tallest and palest, like the fucking Beacon of Gondor with wavy, blond hair and ichor gold eyes, and whether he was with us or not, he drew attention. I was the next tallest, but—as the augur had pointed out—the third oldest. Art and I shared similar features with dark hair and light eyes, but mine leaned more green and his blue, and my larger stature gave away my vampiric sanguis nature. I fed on blood, and that, in turn, gave me the extra strength to kill efficiently. He fed on emotions, and he had the mercurial temperament to match.

Alvaro was the next tallest after Art, and with his perpetual five o'clock shadow and *apparently* charming demeanor, he was more likely to trick a mortal into trusting him than the rest of us—before they realized he had fed on their thoughts. The last of our cohort, Matteo, had retained much of his Italian heritage with tightly coiled, black curls and enormous eyes that belied the monster he really was. Well, to be fair, he was only a monster to a mortal who happened to have a significant charge of ley magic in their body. He fed on magic, and as the youngest vampire in our cohort, he still had his… impetuous moments.

We all crossed the small front porch and went down the front steps, and then our shoes crunched on gravel. I sucked in a relieved breath. Art, as usual, echoed my thoughts out loud by remarking, "It smelled like oregano and socks in there."

I rolled my eyes and Alvaro blew out a laugh before hitting the key fob on his sleek, black 296GTB. In Spanish, he mused, "Too bad Matteo isn't allowed to suck her dry.

We could make him watch the birds and save the annual trip."

Matteo scrubbed his clean-shaven jaw, looking like he was actually considering it. He responded in English because we had been ordered to primarily speak the language of the country we were residing in, and he was a habitual rule follower. "I'm considering what could possibly make my near immortality any more boring than bird watching, but I'm coming up short."

"Actually finding a mate and raising babies," Alvaro replied immediately, his lips turning down at the corners. We all gave him silent "what the fuck" looks. Alvaro was definitely in the minority on that one. We all hoped to find mates, as unlikely as it might be. Not only would it bring prestige to our cohort, but it would also ensure our kind lived on—a hard task to ensure when all the legends about turning humans into vampires were patently false. One could not become a vampire after being bit. Vampires were born, not made, and that could only happen with a mate, a ley socium. As he opened the car door, he spread his hands out. "What? Are we not supposed to say that out loud?"

"Not in Spanish," I reminded him. *Or ever, if you don't want your house's wrath brought on your head.* Alvaro's parents didn't live in Spain anymore, but he slipped into his native tongue often. When he fed on a mortal's thoughts, and they *happened* to speak Spanish, we had to correct him every other sentence for days after.

"Half this country speaks my language anyway," he pointed out in English.

An exaggerated but fair point. I glanced at Constantine to find him studying the sky, his hands in his pockets. Our blond giant was a vampire of few words, but I could see when his gears were turning. "Looking for bird patterns?" I asked him.

"Did you pay attention to any of that?" he asked with mild reprimand. He turned his amber eyes on me and held my gaze steadily. "The signs were better than they've been in over a century."

I resisted the urge to roll my eyes. "The last mate a cohort found was—"

"In Pakistan, eighty-three years ago," Art finished in a bored tone. He leaned against our white SUV, tossing the key fob carelessly. "Yes, brother. So you've reminded us often."

"So, chasing it, or even hoping for it," I added with a meaningful look toward stoic Constantine, "is pointless. You guys always get like this when we see an augur. You two get moony-eyed," I accused, pointing to animal-loving, innocent Matteo and our silent incubus, Constantine, "and you get cynical," I said, pointing to Alvaro.

"Right, because you aren't cynical at all," Alvaro drawled.

"What about me?" Art grinned. Art's finer bone structure and puckish, blue eyes set him apart and obviously matched his personality, especially when they twinkled with mischief like that.

"You get on my fucking nerves." I went around to the driver's side of our SUV. "Now, are we done with this shit? Can we move on? I'm starving." I wasn't *blood*-starved. I'd fed yesterday. But I could do unspeakable things to a bowl of bulgogi right now.

My cohort brothers stared at me, unblinking. Suddenly, Art smacked the car. "That's it! She told us to go east, and you're starving. Let's go somewhere with a crowd." He licked his lips. "Somewhere… emotional."

Constantine rolled his eyes and headed for his blue sports car. Matteo cocked his head, considering what Art had suggested. "A crowd? That's not a bad idea. We would be more likely to cross ley lines with her if we do."

"With whom?" I challenged. Okay, maybe I was a little grouchy about it, but having my entire life hinge on finding one frail human was maddening. After hundreds of years of war and gore—two things I was an expert at—this just seemed so *insipid*. But ley matches, or ley socium as it was officially called, had been more and more rare. Our houses, five of them that represented each faction of vampire, had all been applying pressure on their five-person cohorts. It had ramped up to eleven after eighty years had passed with no matches—and, in turn, no babies.

"With *her*," Constantine rumbled, pausing to look over his shoulder at me. His glare pinned my conscience to a wall with spiky darts of censure.

"Or even them," Art pointed out with a finger up.

We were all meant to find matches of our own. That felt even less likely than finding just one. I pinched the bridge of my nose. "Well, I'm so glad you've all been rallied to the cause again."

"Not me," Alvaro offered unhelpfully, hanging off the open door of his sports car with his white shirt half unbuttoned and his half-grin in place. Who the fuck was he trying to charm right now? It was just us.

Matteo had pulled out his phone and was scrolling through something. "There's always the movie theater."

"Not big enough," Art said automatically. Or emotional enough. People felt things when they watched movies, but it wasn't authentic feeling. It wasn't the potent emotion of humans interacting with humans and stirring up all the junk in their subconscious to the surface. It wasn't the kind of "food" Art preferred.

"Okay," Matteo said patiently. "It's a Wednesday, though. Maybe we should see what festivals are happening over the weekend."

"One hundred thirty-six," Constantine reminded us in his baritone voice. "That's today. We have to try today."

Art, Alvaro, and I gave our Turkish brother eye squints, but Matteo seemed unphased. "Okay, how about a soccer game? The Lions have a scrimmage tonight."

I perked up. "They do?"

Alvaro groaned. "I am cursed. One more soccer game, and I swear to the ley, I will end my own existence." He quickly switched over to Spanish, cursing us fluidly and wondering why it was always sports and never an art gallery or a wine tasting.

Because those didn't have enough people. We had to cross ley lines with our one true match in order to actually find them. The ley lines ran through the earth like veins, feeding it with magic, and in turn, imbuing us with its power. My match, the one who had an identical star chart to mine, who had been born under the same sky centuries after I had, needed to cross a ley line with me before I could even find her. It was not an efficient method of procreation, which was why there were so few of us vampires left. The more people who populated the earth, the harder it got to catch the right one born under the correct sky. Charting and following the ley flow helped narrow it down, but only by a slight margin.

"Stop bitching," I advised. "There will be ample thoughts in a stadium."

"Neanderthal ones," Alvaro shot back. "This play, that play, the ball is here, did I remember to renew my FansOnly subscription," he listed off fast. He waved a hand despondently. "I am not in the mood to eat stupid tonight."

"Harsh," I muttered.

"Sometimes, I wish I could drain you just a *little*," Art said, his voice going higher and his thumb and forefinger pinching close together. "You never stop feeling, you know that?"

"It's called passion," Alvaro glared. "Something none of you—" he paused, eyes falling on Constantine. "Most of you lack."

Constantine's lips tipped up a fraction, and it was because he knew *we knew* his true nature. He looked like an emotionless block of granite on the outside, but if you got him in a bedroom with a willing partner, he was a warm-blooded incubus.

I tried to pull us back on track. "Soccer game. Matteo, you lead the way. And then," I emphasized with a hard look around the group, "I'm getting several pounds of fast food, and you will all leave me the fuck alone for at least a month."

"Except me," Art amended, sliding into the passenger seat.

I gave him a side eye, still standing outside our car. "Especially you."

The stadium reeked of people. Even in the open air, I caught whiffs of body odor, blood, and… well, humans had all kinds of unsavory smells. The concession food slightly masked it, but I had to resist hiding my nose in my jacket collar.

This wasn't the kind of place I could feed like Matteo,

Art, and Alvaro. Matteo usually got lucky in crowds this size; if a human had been born on a strong ley line on a full moon, they usually possessed an inordinate amount of magic that made them "lucky." Or skilled. We all knew the ones—unusually talented, irritatingly lucky, or uncanny with their intuition. That wasn't human evolution at work, it was magic. And if Matteo found someone with a good enough supply, then all he had to do was convince them to kiss him, which for him, was laughably easy. Then, he would steal a generous portion of their ley magic, and he would be full for a few days, at least. The person's magic would eventually replenish, much like blood when I fed on humans. *If* I fed on humans. Blood bags were a lot less dramatic.

Art would be feeding off whatever emotions were strongest, and Alvaro on thoughts. Neither of them even had to touch a human to do that. And as we made our way down the stairs with concession food in hand, I watched with some amusement as Art paused by a bickering couple. He inhaled, a smile playing on his lips. The couple suddenly stopped, staring at each other like they couldn't remember what they'd been arguing about.

I took a bite of my hotdog, devouring half of it in one go and chewing slowly as I looked around. The tang of blood was stronger here, but I suspected that was due to injuries on the field. It wasn't uncomfortable enough to want to leave, not when there was a soccer match halfway over and the promise of a little violence in my future. It wasn't the underground brawls of London in the eighteenth century, but it was something, at least. God, I missed the days when gentlemen were assholes by day and savages by night. A vampire hadn't really lived until they'd beaten the shit out of a burly boxer and then sucked him dry.

Those things were frowned upon these days. The

Conexus was changing with the times, and the hold my house, Sanguis, had held over the other four houses was slipping. People didn't want bloodthirsty warriors anymore. They wanted… peace.

Abhorrent.

We made our way down the steep stairs, and I kept my eyes peeled for free seats. It wasn't a full house during off-season skirmishes, so anywhere would do. Alvaro paused, his eyes on a curvy woman with her attention on the pages of a book. He inhaled like Art had, running his thumb under his lip. "Dostoevsky," he moaned.

I curled my lip. "Get a room or keep it to yourself, Jesus."

The girl looked up, blinking, her silky, raven hair falling down her back and her eyes going blank. Alvaro licked his lips. "She thinks he's melancholy."

"He was obsessed with suffering," I pointed out wryly.

"As are you," Alvaro countered smoothly.

I caught his pointed look. "Causing it. Not ruminating over the consequences of it."

He shrugged, his rakish Mediterranean looks catching the interest of a nearby gaggle of girls, and as he moved on, the girl he'd fed from shook her head and went back three pages, likely assuming she had been spacing out while reading. Pro vampire tip: when that happened, it was the work of a mentem vampire nearby.

I took another step down the stairs, but as I did, my knees locked and my heart clenched hard in my chest. Before I could even inhale in surprise, a flash of blue ley lit the air. My eyes tracked it, zeroing in on the halo of pure magical energy as it rose up around a startled human woman.

I took in her appearance with a microsecond-long evaluation and found her oddly… disheveled. Even at this distance, my eyes could see her just as clearly as if she was a meter away. Her hair was falling out of a messy bun, her jeans had dried blood stains on them, and her expression was comically shocked. With a crack that rent the earth's crust, the magic zipped from her to me, so fast even my eyes had trouble tracking it. And when it hit me, I swore my heart stopped altogether.

With a painful rush, my blood pumped hard in my veins, drowning my ears with my pulse, and heat scorched from my feet straight to my groin. It should have hurt—It had to hurt, right?—but the ley strike only filled me with intoxicating warmth. It was the kind of warmth I had never known and would never truly understand. Only, I was feeling it now. Mortal warmth. It buzzed through my veins for one moment, one second in time, and I realized with a shock, it was *her*. It was the messy little human's life force joining with mine and giving me a taste of who she was.

And then it was gone. The light receded just as quickly as it had come. I only looked down at myself for a moment, just to confirm that I hadn't actually lost my lower half to a ley line explosion, and then my gaze sought her again. And this time, I had a second to see her, to really *see* this mortal, with her thick, chestnut locks, her pink lips full and made for kissing, and the pert, round ass that swiveled as she turned to face me, her eyes locked on mine from across the distance between us.

Beside me, Art sucked in a breath. "Holy shit. Holy shit."

Her eyes were enormous. Fringed with thick lashes and almond-shaped, they widened even further, giving me a clear view of their intricate rust and cinnamon hue. Her nose was turned up on the end, giving me the impression that she had a fair amount of sass in her gorgeous brain—and *my God* did I want to know what she was thinking. Because she was staring at me, in that half-breath moment the ley line had been crossed, and she had felt the connection between us.

My ley socium.

My mate.

Chapter Three

SAGE

My feet were carrying me up the steps, one foot and then the other, robotic and mechanical, like the internal screaming in my brain was having no effect on my wayward legs. What the hell had just happened? I thought I remembered reading something about lightning being able to travel along the ground, but it wasn't even overcast, let alone stormy. Which meant that had been some kind of electrical phenomenon, some tweak in nature that had hit me just right, and for whatever reason, it had scrambled my prefrontal cortex, and now I was walking closer to a group of five men who, the more I climbed, the more I realized were inhumanly handsome.

And, *shit, I rambled my way right to him.* I stopped on the stairs, just below the dark-haired stranger, and his eyes, green like a spruce forest, traveled from my startled expression, down to my worn sneakers and then back to my face.

"Hello."

His voice was dark chocolate. It was melted fudge and oozing lava cake, and I could practically taste his words on my tongue. I couldn't find my own words, though. Where had my words gone? My thoughts were here. Chaotic and unruly as ever, but the *words* to look *normal*...

A man to my stranger's left stepped away suddenly, chuckling with giddy glee and bringing up his phone to take a picture of his friend. Or was he his brother? They looked like brothers. My stranger was wider, more muscular than his counterpart, but they both had square chins, aquiline noses, and classically handsome features. Also, the man currently eating me with his hungry gaze looked fucking *scary*. Gladiator scary. Predator scary.

"Look at your face," the brother goaded, clicking the camera button in rapid succession. "Vampie's first ley mate."

What on God's green earth was a ley mate? Or a “vampie?”

A tall blond man behind the camera guy smacked him on the head. "Knock it off."

My man—Why did I keep calling him that?—spared his brother an irritated glance but then returned his full attention to me. "Are you alright?"

See, that was a normal question to ask. Lightning had just struck us both in broad daylight with several witnesses, so of course he would wonder if I'd been hurt. And a human, not awkward-as-hell response would be...

Nothing came out. I stood rooted to the spot.

A dark-haired, devastatingly handsome man beside the blond leaned over and whispered with a Spanish accent, "Is she broken?"

The blond met his look sardonically. "You tell me."

"Don't you dare," my lightning buddy snarled over his shoulder. *Snarled*. With a growl.

"My God," a curly-haired Adonis said to the far right.

"It's true. He really found her." He glanced at the man on the other side of the blond. "Did you see that? He almost ripped your head off."

"Silas, you realize what this means, right?" the annoying brother whisper-shouted. "We get babies!"

This was, hands down, the weirdest social encounter I'd ever had. And my mom had sent me to summer camps in the Catskills. At least the crowd had their attention focused back on the game, and although a couple of them closest to us sent curious glances our way, they too returned their focus to the soccer match.

I licked my lips, trying to remind them that they did, in fact, work, and they really should do their job and get me out of this bizarre exchange. Mr. Snarl tracked the movement, his pupils dilating. Suddenly, the crowd roared, and several people in the stands stood up, cheering enthusiastically. That snapped me out of my trance, and I gasped, whirling around to find the Lions clapping each other on the back and already jogging away from the goalpost. "Shit!" I hissed.

I missed an entire goal! I didn't see any of the plays that got there. I didn't even see who made it. Maybe if I ask Marcus, he will give me a play-by-play. I know he tends to focus more on the production, switching between cameras and making sure everyone is in focus and prepped to follow, but I'm sure he saw—

My feet had taken only a few steps down when a hand wrapped around my upper arm and halted me. I swiveled a look up to find my dark stranger with a crease between his brows. "Where are you going, Dulcis?"

"Duchess?" I asked incredulously.

"Oh shit," the brother said with obvious glee. "He's pulling out the Latin."

"Not the Latin," the blond added in deadpan.

The stranger had a firm grip on my arm, gentle, but somehow, I sensed that he could literally squish my arm to red mist if he really wanted to. He tugged me back up a step with soft pressure. "*Dulcis*," he repeated, "I didn't get your name."

Red flag. Big, banner-length red flag. My consciousness waved it around, sprinting and making it flap in the metaphorical breeze. "Um." I jiggled my arm, testing to see if he would unhand me. "I'm a reporter. For the *Mane Daily*. I-I'm sorry. I didn't mean to be rude, but I have to get down there and record who made that goal."

His vibrant, sea-green eyes flitted to the game and then back down to me. "Don't worry about that. It's not an issue anymore."

The swarthy model slapped a hand to his face. "Dios mio."

A frown slowly pulled my eyebrows together. "Please let go. It's my job. I have to get back down there." By now, a couple of the onlookers nearest to us were finally realizing that an enormous, muscular dude was holding a girl by the arm, and in my periphery, a couple of guys stood up cautiously from their chairs.

My captor didn't let go. "We can discuss your job in a bit, but first, you need to come with me."

Discuss my job? What the hell? "I'm a student," I corrected. "And you're scaring me. Please release me." My rational brain told me to panic, but my body didn't follow suit. My heartbeat stayed strangely even, and my head and chest buzzed pleasantly like I'd taken a shot of my favorite whipped vodka.

"Is there a problem here?" one of the dudes with a backward baseball cap asked. He actually looked pretty fit, and his arms flexed like he was ready to fight.

But he wasn't anywhere near as stacked as the man currently pulling me up another step and closer to his body. "Back off," he snapped.

Forget the flags. Alarms. Red alarms. Blaring sirens and panic buttons. The concerned bro brought out his phone, and I was willing to bet he was about to call 911. How had this escalated like this? I fought against the stranger's hand, but it was a useless endeavor. His skin didn't so much as shift under my attempt. "What are you—" I started.

"Silas," the curly-haired younger guy cautioned.

"What, you want me to just let her go?" he asked the four men behind him. Indecision wavered across all their faces, and he had pulled me so close to him, we were on the same step. Even on level ground, he towered over me, his chin brushing the top of my head. He smelled like leather and cedarwood under the subtle notes of masculine soap, and against all reason, I found myself leaning into him.

What. The actual. Scud bucket. Also, what is a scud bucket, Sage? Your ADHD really needs to be medicated. I tried again for sanity, forcing myself to lean away from him and go down a step, pulling against his hold. "Get off me right now."

"This is going so well," the snarky brother said, still grinning. "You charmer, you."

Annoyance flashed across the man's face—Silas, I remembered one of the others had called him. He effortlessly tugged me back to his step. "I'm sorry, this isn't how I meant to do this, but you do need to come with us."

"Meant to do what?" I looked down at myself. Was I injured and I hadn't realized it? No, my jeans were still in place, and my feet weren't steaming or sizzling like a B-movie extra who'd been struck with CGI lightning. "And why?"

"Let her go, man," the bro said behind me. More people

were taking note of our altercation, and three more men stood up slowly.

One of the guys behind Silas muttered something in Spanish, and the wide-eyed younger man scrubbed a hand through his thick, curly black hair. The brother leaned over Silas' shoulder, catching my frightened gaze. "He's not usually like this." He paused, thinking. "Actually, on second thought, maybe he is. You'll get used to it."

"Alright, that's enough," Silas growled. Taking my other wrist in his hand, he pulled me flush against his hard body, and his eyes captured my attention again.

I hardly ever really looked people in the eyes, and normally, I couldn't remember what color someone's eyes were after I'd talked to them. But with this man, Silas—I was already memorizing the starburst of blue that exploded around his pupils, and how flecks of gold mingled with blue and green to create a deep, rich hue that was far brighter and far more alluring than the clearest of turquoise bays. He seemed just as enamored with me, which was unfathomable to me given how he looked.

But it didn't matter if he was on the front cover of a body-building magazine somewhere. He was holding me hostage, and I was losing my patience. "If you don't release me right now—"

"Matteo, Alvaro, take care of the witnesses," Silas said, not taking his eyes from me.

"Witnesses?" I asked incredulously. But he didn't explain himself or answer any more questions. Silas bent at the waist, and in one fluid motion, he had me over his shoulder. "What the fuck?" I gasped.

I dangled over him, my hair finally escaping its tenuous bun, and it swished against his calf as he turned and started up the stairs. The man with the accent grumbled, "How many? You want me to stay here all night?"

"Yes," Silas grouched.

I got a sinking feeling in the pit of my stomach, and for the first time, fear caught up with my brain, slamming through my veins and beating a painful tempo in my chest. "Wait," I got out breathlessly. I clutched at Silas' black canvas jacket, trying to leverage myself upright so I could slide off him. But then he jiggled me, and I lost my grip before flopping over his back again.

"I'm sorry, Dulcis, but this place is too public," he replied, nonplussed by my efforts to wiggle free. I glimpsed his four companions dispersing themselves through the crowd, stopping before each person, whether angry or oblivious. Alvaro—or Matteo, I wasn't sure which—stood before the angry man who was on the phone and inhaled visibly. The angry bro got a blank look on his face, and then his phone dropped.

"What are you doing?" I demanded. "What are *they* doing?"

"Don't worry about them. You're safe," he promised.

"Like hell I am!" I kicked against him, but he stopped me easily. Fear clogged my throat and climbed up to my eyes where tears gathered. "Where are you taking me?" *These guys look scary. And dangerous. Maybe they're the mafia. Maybe my mom pissed someone off and they're taking me hostage. Or maybe the lightning was significant, and I saw something I shouldn't have seen. Or—Jesus—are they kidnapping me for trafficking? In broad daylight? With* witnesses*? I'm going to end up on* 60 Minutes*. They're going to make a Netflix documentary about the random nerd who was kidnapped by a mob of swimsuit models in the middle of a college scrimmage game.*

"You're shaking," Silas said as we reached the exit tunnel. "Please calm down. I'm not going to hurt you."

"Of course, I'm shaking!" I seethed, my words breaking against my tears in a humiliating squeak. "You just kidnapped me."

"I'm taking you somewhere safe," he countered, walking past a couple of curious students with soft pretzels and drinks in their hands. He carried me with long, steady strides through the stadium, eating the distance with startling speed.

My lungs worked hard suddenly, sucking in tiny bubbles of frantic air. "Oh my God. Oh my God."

"You're panicking," he stated. "Stop that."

"I think I'm going to be sick," I said weakly, and my stomach churned like I was seasick.

Silas cursed under his breath, and suddenly, he changed direction, heading for the concessions area where a pair of college kids with Lions jerseys were serving customers fried food and sodas. When we reached the counter—What kind of kidnapper stopped for a snack?—I heard him speak to the employees, but with my head down and ass in the air, I couldn't see shit. "You closed up early, and I'm here to do an inspection. You saw nothing out of the ordinary. Go home."

His voice vibrated through my body unnaturally, buzzing through my limbs and making my head swim. And then, whatever he'd said, however he'd done it, the employees obeyed, shuffling out the side door and disappearing from behind the counter. Silas walked around the counter and through a door to the galley kitchen behind it. With his foot, he slammed the adjoining door closed, blocking off the stadium area and enclosing us in the warm, muggy room.

Then he plopped me on a stainless-steel counter, settling

his hands on my arms. I stared up at him, still fighting for a full breath and equal parts dizzy and nauseated. "What are you doing?" I asked. I wasn't even sure I wanted to know the answer. I should be fighting for my life, but I couldn't seem to find the drive. I was scared, yes, but my body refused to do anything about it.

"Your body just dumped a massive amount of adrenaline and cortisol into your liver, and now your glucose levels are plummeting. You're going into shock, and I'm going to feel *really* put out if I accidentally kill you ten minutes into getting you."

"Kill me?" I squeezed out. My rapid-fire brain latched onto the other significant thing he'd said. "Wait, *get me*?"

Ignoring me, he sifted through the contents of a cabinet. The kitchen was pretty cramped, with only one sink, a griddle, an industrial fridge, and a fryer crammed into the space. He moved further away, going to the fridge, and my heart sped into overdrive as I realized this was my only chance to escape. I had no idea what his plans were or why we were in a university stadium concessions kitchen in the middle of an attempted kidnapping, but I sure as hell wasn't going to wait around to find out.

I launched myself off the counter and toward the door. I wasn't athletic by any means, but even I was impressed with how far my push off the counter got me, and then in three bullet-fast steps, I was at the door. But just as my hands were about to slam against the painted metal surface, a strong arm shot out and ripped me away. "What—" I eked out incredulously.

Silas pinned me to his hard body, swerving us around so my back pressed against the door and his towering frame caged me in. His chest expanded against mine as he inhaled slowly, and I got the distinct impression he was gathering his patience. His bulging, muscled arms bracketed me on either side, and leaning down so our eyes were almost level, he whispered, "Don't be foolish."

Foolish. It was clearly so impossible to give him the slip, he thought I was *foolish* for trying. What was going to happen to me? Would the police show up in time? Was he going to kill me in this kitchen? Or worse? My throat felt swollen suddenly, and I sucked in a sob.

His handsome features fell. "Oh, shit."

Tears blurred my vision, and thickly, I asked, "What do you want?"

"Shit," he repeated, pinching the bridge of his nose. "I am royally fucking this up." He stepped away scrubbing his hands down his face. "The first one in eighty years and she's *mine*. Of *all* people." I wasn't entirely sure he was talking to me, but I let him continue, hoping he would talk his crazy out of keeping me here. "How am I supposed to keep you alive when I can't even explain this situation to you?"

I surreptitiously reached behind me, turned the door-knob, and eased the door open. Completely unbothered, he reached around me and slammed the door shut again, keeping his hand on the knob and resting his warm arm against mine. His eyes found mine again. "We should start over."

"No, I'm good," I croaked.

"I'm Silas," he went on seriously. I wished I didn't find him so damn attractive, but it was hard to look away when he was giving me his full attention like that. "And you're terrified of me. I can understand why."

"Okay," I replied an octave higher than normal.

He released a breath, looking away for a second. "You'd think they'd give us some kind of manual on this. They've only had a few thousand years to figure one out."

Oh yeah. This cutie was the mayor of Crazy Town, alright. "It's okay," I reassured him, wondering if I could keep him grounded long enough for the police to find us.

His attention on me hardened wryly. Alright, he might be crazy, but he definitely wasn't stupid. "Tell me your name, Dulcis. And I'll explain why I've carted you out of the stadium like a Viking."

Crazy, smart, *and* self-aware. Interesting. "Anna," I lied.

He chuckled, leaning in a little closer so his cool breath coasted over my cheek. "You cannot lie to me. Try again."

Maybe if he trusted me, he'd be more likely to let me go. And really, a name wasn't going to make much difference in this scenario. "Sage," I said.

"Hmm," he hummed, and I could have sworn that the sound infiltrated my bone marrow. "I like that. It suits you."

"Super," I managed to say, but my voice was strained.

He paused, as if thinking again. Then he straightened away from me but kept his hand on the doorknob and my body bracketed by his. "Before I explain myself, let me tell you what I already know about you. The reason I know these things is because you were just lit up like a Christmas tree in the middle of a stadium, and as weird as I'm sure you found that, it's nothing compared to *why* that happened."

Chapter Four

SAGE

I watched him quietly, my brain trying to shoot off into thirty other directions. I schooled my thoughts, focusing on his lips. Something inside of me told me I wanted to hear this.

"However old you are, Sage, I know for a fact that you struggle with relationships in your life. Whether you are friendly or surly, it doesn't seem to matter. You can only get so close to someone before *something* compels you to pull away."

My eyes widened. Had this random stranger been stalking me?

Steadily, he continued, "You feel alone, but you don't want to be with others. You want love, but no one seems right. And as a result," he said with a glint of humor in his tone, "you're a virgin."

I seized up. Now *that* was deeply personal, and even my own mother didn't know it. "Who the *hell*—" I began.

"And your sense of direction is impeccable," he finished. "They always have an innate ability to follow the stars."

"They?" I repeated.

Silas was perfectly calm, a summer lake at sunset, glassy and warm. "I suppose I mean just you. But you aren't alone in those traits, and I know this because no one ordinary finds themselves illuminated by a strange blue light in the ground. That blue light was a ley line."

I'd heard of ley lines before. Or, I'd read about them in fantasy stories. I wanted to flat-out deny the plausibility of that, but then again, it was either that or lightning had come from the ground. Neither seemed terribly likely. "Is that dangerous?" I asked. He'd said he needed to take me somewhere safe. Maybe that was why he was doing this. Though that was probably too much to hope for.

"No," he replied, dashing that theory on the rocks. "But as I'm sure you noticed, it formed a path between us."

It had been rather hard to miss, actually. "And?" I prompted.

"And that is because we are… connected." He seemed to chew on his own words and then think over the next ones carefully. "Call it a supernatural phenomenon."

Vampie's first ley mate! The brother's taunt echoed through my mind. With the word "supernatural" on the table, my brain whizzed to life, conjuring implausible possibilities and nauseating nightmares out of the things his companions had said. "You can't be serious."

A ghost of amusement crossed his features. "My brothers would say I am always serious."

"Is that who you were with? Your brothers?" *Are they going to kill me? Are you?*

"Only one is my blood brother, Arthur—we call him Art. He's the one who looks like me but… smaller." I thought back to the brother and nothing about that guy was small, but I supposed in comparison to Silas, he might be.

"The other three are Alvaro, Matteo, and Constantine. Alvaro is the one with a beard who prefers speaking in Spanish, Matteo is the Italian with curly hair, and Constantine is that tall, blond guy who looks like he's the life of the party."

I had to hold back a blip of amusement. "Party animal."

"So wild. We can't contain him." He waited, humor lighting his eyes, but I refused to give him another inch, so he added, "Alvaro, Matteo, and Constantine are my cohort brothers. No blood relation." I frowned in confusion, so he bobbed his head to the side once, thinking. "Kind of like a fraternity."

Crazy, smart, self-aware... *frat boy*? This made no sense. "You're too old to be in college," I pointed out with a squint of my eyes.

That tugged his smile wider. "You have no idea."

"So, a magical something exploded from the ground, and we're connected," I supplied, hoping his insanity had some logical conclusion we could reach. "How are we connected?"

He waved that away. "Let's get to that in a minute. I know you don't believe me, and you seem like an intelligent woman, so let me present my facts to you."

I blinked rapidly. "APA or MLA?"

An actual laugh escaped him, dancing over my skin and leaving goosebumps in its wake. He eased away from me, apparently believing that I had tabled my escape attempt for now. Maybe I had. Some part of me couldn't resist his voice, his presence. And against all logic, I couldn't deny that it did feel eerily supernatural. "May I *please* get you some juice while we talk? Without you trying to bolt? I believe I've just shown you it's not going to work."

"You're holding me hostage so you can feed me juice and convince me ley lines are real?" I clarified.

Silas hooked his thumbs in the pockets of his black jacket. He had a white T-shirt underneath, and it showed off his pecs and broad shoulders. Not that I noticed. Shit, I was noticing. "Glad you understand the situation."

I mean, as long as he wasn't feeling stabby. I eased away from the door, my attention on him warily, and I crab-walked past him and back to the counter. But Silas gave zero fucks for my personal boundaries, and as soon as I reached it, he planted his hands on my waist and lifted me to the counter so I could sit with my legs dangling. Surprised, I braced my hands on his shoulders.

A charge zapped between us, stealing my breath and igniting that strange ember of warmth low in my stomach. It seemed Silas had been affected too because he froze, staring at me like he was just as surprised. Softly, he said, "Stay here. Yes?"

My heart had already slowed to a more even rhythm. I nodded.

Silas returned to the fridge, his posture relaxed. "In defense of what you must surely find the ramblings of a madman, I present to you the employees who were working in this kitchen. Did you hear me tell them to go home?"

"Yes," I replied cautiously.

"I compelled them." He found a stack of paper soda cups under one of the counters, and after retrieving some orange juice, filled one of the cups. He also said "compelled" with a completely serious face.

"Like, you're their boss?" I asked hopefully.

"No." He slid me a knowing glance. "Sorry. It's nothing as mundane as that."

"If you can control people with your magic voice, then why didn't you just order me to go with you?" I challenged. Probably stupid to give him tactics.

Silas returned to me, a tall cup filled to the brim with orange juice, and his expression held a wealth of emotions I rapidly cataloged. Amusement, yes, but also a softness that melted my insides, limned with serious intent. "I would never do that to you, Sage."

I took the cup, but my fingers felt weak. "Why not?"

"Because," he said slowly, resting the tips of his fingers on the counter on either side of my hips, "we are connected."

"Right." I eyed him mistrustfully. "Well, any other evidence? Because you look like you can kill someone with your pinky toe. I'd follow your instructions, too, if I were them."

"Drink that," he ordered, drifting toward me again.

My throat bobbed. "I'm nauseous."

He clicked his tongue. "And here I thought I was so scary, you'd do what I said. Disproving your own arguments. If you sip that, I'll give you another piece of evidence."

My mouth did feel extraordinarily dry. I took a cautious sip, and the sweet sourness rushed over my tongue, soothing some of the thirst. Alright, so I might have taken a *few* sips. It was pretty refreshing. I licked my lips, and his eyes tracked the movement, like he was fascinated.

"Second point," he went on calmly. He reached over to my right where the griddle took up a good three feet of the wall space. He grabbed it, and not by the handle, either. He literally dug his fingers into the metal at the front, crumpling it like aluminum foil, and like he was lifting a grocery bag, he hefted the stove clean off the floor. He didn't even strain. It groaned and sizzled, crackling as metal scraped against the counters and the electrical cords stretched. And the whole time, he held eye contact with me.

My jaw unhinged. "Uh."

Silas lowered it again, still holding my gaze. "I'm not human."

Chapter Five

SILAS

Sage blanched, and I worried that the glucose dump I could smell in her blood was going to overwhelm her system and make her pass out. Her fingers twitched around the cup of juice, and her chest rose and fell rapidly. Her heart had kicked up again, too. I'd just gotten her calm, dammit, but the sooner I helped her understand, the better.

Although, it was shockingly hard for me to focus, too. I should be putting all my effort into easing her into this reality, but instead, my instincts had gone berserk. My first instinct had been, *do not let her get away*. And the second one had been... *mine.* I didn't want anyone else remotely near her.

And now, I was confined with her in a small kitchen, overwhelmed by her scent and dangerously close to making an even bigger fool of myself. Sage wasn't like the tasty morsels I'd indulged in over several centuries. It was funny how my heightened senses worked. Things without a discernable scent usually entered my brain and got filtered through known aromas so my mind could catalogue them.

Usually, women smelled and tasted like sugar—like the vampire equivalent of sweetened coffee. But Sage smelled like cinnamon and wild pine, and the nearer I got to her blood, the sweeter it became, cut with a citrus and nutmeg fragrance that made my mouth water. I imagined if she was less afraid, that sharp pine smell would be replaced with something like cardamom. I wanted to bury my nose in the curve of her neck and feel her pulse on my lips. I wanted to wrap myself in her scent and never emerge.

No matter what my parents had taught me growing up, no matter how they had imparted the gravity of finding one's mate, it never could have prepared me for *this*. I was enamored with everything about her. The way her soft waves fell to her waist like hanging ivy or the way her expressive, brown eyes drank me in and sized me up, clearly conjuring and storing away facts, plans, and possibilities for her to digest. I was fascinated with how thick and dark her eyelashes were, and I wondered how they would feel fluttering against my skin.

Focus, Silas. Keep the pretty girl alive, first. I wrapped my hands around hers, lifting the cup to her lips. "You smell like you're about to crash into a glucose coma, so please, for the love of ley, drink your juice."

She did, her throat sliding and her enormous doe eyes watching me in terror. I wasn't sure what she was thinking—what I wouldn't give to have Alvaro's abilities in this situation—but she appeared to have been shocked into silence. When she finished about a quarter of the large glass, I took it from her and set it on the counter to my right. Her eyes followed me like prey caught in a snare.

I sighed. "Technically, you aren't human, either, if it makes you feel any better."

Her lips went bloodless. "Excuse me?"

Wrong factoid to throw her way. Noted. "Never mind. I didn't mean to scare you, but it was the most obvious way to show you who I am. My brothers are different than I am, but that's my… thing."

"Bench-pressing ovens?" she asked weakly.

God, she was quick. It was a miracle the ley wards around her had held and she hadn't fallen in love with a lucky mortal. It had been known to happen, especially if we took too long to find them. "Among other things," I quipped lightly.

She glanced down at the oven, and then back to me. "So, what do your muscles have to do with the lightning thing?"

I bit down another smile. She reminded me of Art, using humor to diffuse difficult situations. "It's the connection I mentioned. There are some beings in this world who operate differently than mortals. I'm one of them. And we don't just fall in love, fuck freely, and create offspring when we feel like it." Blood tinted her cheeks rosy, and I had the intense urge to lick her skin and *almost* taste that delightful blood of hers. "We are beholden to an ancient system that runs through the earth and even the universe itself."

"Ley lines," she guessed.

I nodded. "When I cross a ley line with exactly the right person, the phenomenon you saw is the result. And it tethered us."

Understanding pulled her features taut. "When you say connected, you mean…"

"Mates," I confirmed.

She grimaced, clearly horrified at the idea. "That's a disgusting word."

I rubbed my mouth, giving in to a slight smile. "Socium is the official term."

"That's worse."

"Well, it's what you are," I shot back softly, leaning into her and resting my fingertips on the counter again.

A normal human would have leaned away. She leaned in. "I'm trying to be nice so you don't kill me, but that's really absurd."

"More absurd than a guy lifting an oven?"

She stole a look down at the oven again. "Yes."

I didn't bother declaring that I would never hurt her. She'd only think I was creepy. "Alright, so it's absurd. Doesn't make it untrue."

She considered me, and as she did, I heard her heart slow again. That cardamom I thought I'd detected before perfumed the air, drawing me to her blood and her body. "Alright, I believe you. Let's exchange numbers, and you can… text me sometime."

A chuckle shook my chest. "That's not how that works."

Her mouth scrunched to the side. "Figured." She sat up a little straighter, and I had to give her some space so we didn't bump noses. I wasn't sure my restraint could survive accidental contact. My dick was already straining against my pants and the need to positively bury myself in this woman was physically painful. "Let's say I believe you. Your evidence is still flimsy, and I'm being generous with that term."

I nodded in acquiescence. "Alright." There were other things I could show her, but I just got her body to stop pumping pure adrenaline and cortisol into her poor liver. In my experience, humans could accept the impossible, but they needed to be introduced to it slowly. One inch at a time into the pool of the metaphysical.

"So, assuming you're not full of nut sauce, then *what* are

you?" She hooked me with those innocent, cinnamon eyes, and I could barely breathe.

Here it was. I reached over and handed her the orange juice. "Drink that first please."

She eyed me over the cup skeptically. "That's disconcerting."

"Right, hence the juice. Drink it."

She did, slowly, draining about half of it, and then set it down again. "Okay, I'm ready. Hit me with it."

My phone rang suddenly, buzzing in tandem with my wristband. I turned my wrist to peer at the inside of my forearm, and Art's name and picture appeared on my skin like a tattoo. I swiped the picture and it disappeared, sending the call to voicemail. Sage's eyes landed on my wristband, round with surprise. "Hold up, I thought those were prototypes."

My wristband had the capability to project my phone's display onto my forearm with limited capabilities, and she was correct, it was supposed to be a prototype. "I own the tech development company. They send me presents sometimes."

"Wait, wait, wait," she held up her hands. "You're *rich*?"

I rubbed my jaw, thinking. That was one way to ease her into what I was. "If you want to quantify it, I've been making about a million dollars an hour, twenty-four hours a day, for about four hundred years."

"*What*?"

My wristband buzzed again, this time from Constantine. Reluctantly, I tapped the button on my forearm. His voice over the speaker was perfectly clear as he intoned, "We attracted too much attention. Get home. Now."

Ah, hell. I shouldn't have dragged her out of there. But what else was I supposed to do? Let her go? The thought made my insides wrench. "Alright. We're coming."

"We?" Sage challenged with an arched eyebrow.

"Sorry, beautiful." I allowed myself another intrusion of her space by taking her by the waist and setting her on the ground again. "I've made a mess, apparently. Time to go."

"Probably because you kidnapped a woman in broad daylight," she pointed out.

"You're awfully insouciant about that fact at the moment," I reminded her. "This way, please. I'm happy to answer your questions further, but maybe not in the concessions kitchen." She hesitated, not moving. I huffed a breath through my nose. "You saw me lift an oven. You think I can't force you into a car?"

She glared. "I can't believe you're still doubling down on the abduction thing."

"I can't believe you haven't heard a single word I said in the last twenty minutes," I volleyed back. "Once the ley match is activated, that's it. Fate is at work."

"What fate?" she insisted. "Whatever it is, I'm not interested." *So* fucking feisty. This woman really was made for me. All her emotions played on her face so clearly, I could practically read her mind, and she had a tendency to blush on her cheeks and nose, which only made me want to bite her. Lovingly. Maybe.

Also, this wasn't working. All the stories I'd heard about ley mates were so simple. They connected, the vampire and human were ecstatic, they fell deeply in love, and they made an adorable vampire baby or two. I had never heard of a ley match fighting back. I needed to revise my tactics. I hadn't been born during the Roman Empire's rule, but my parents had, and they'd imparted those strategies to me well. Feigned retreat and a solid defense in-depth strategy appeared to be in order, here.

I knew enough about her to keep an eye on her now. Her name was Sage, she was a student here at Piedmont, and she worked with the sports column of the *Mane Daily*. That was enough to at least make sure she stayed safe, and in the meantime, I would have to trust that our bond would draw her to me. Eventually. Hopefully, sooner rather than later.

I held my hands palms up. "You know what, you're right. I'm sure this has been a lot for you."

She blinked. "What."

I closed the distance between us slowly, cautiously. "Let me present my last piece of evidence for you, and then you can go where you wish."

She turned her head at an angle, eyeing me askance, and her feet carried her back two steps toward the door. "Okay."

A smile slid up one side of my face. "You probably should have asked what it was before agreeing."

She backed up another step, passing the utility sink and reaching the door she'd attempted to escape from the first time. This time, I would let her go. But not without elucidating some of her conflicted thoughts. She watched me, and I paid close attention to her body language, to her expressive eyes and the way her heart fluttered. Her eyes were curious, if a bit guarded, and although she'd backed against the door, her shoulders were relaxed, and her heart had an anxious rhythm to it.

She threaded her bottom lip through her teeth, and my dick throbbed painfully at the gesture. "You're acting awfully predatory."

"At the risk of giving you more palpitations—" I began.

"You're a predator," she finished. She looked me up and down. "I think I caught onto that. Are you going to tell me werewolves are real?"

"Real? Sort of. But I'm not a vertos." I reached her finally, and my hands found her hips. She sighed, and my heart echoed the sound. She felt the same longing I did, and relief coursed through me that my instincts had been right.

"Alien?" she whispered. Her eyes were soldered to mine, a galaxy of gold and rust shimmering in her irises.

I shook my head again, and this time, I leaned down to hover my lips over hers. "What I am isn't half as important as who I belong to."

She lifted her chin just a fraction, her breath stalling in her lungs and her eyes flickering. "The mafia?"

"You." I breathed in her scent, all cinnamon and cardamom now, sweet and earthy, like she belonged to the ley and pulsed with its power. "My last piece of evidence," I murmured, watching her for any signs that she was afraid or might not want this. But she did. We both did. "It's a feeling. And when I let you walk out of here, I want you to consider the possibility that it's real."

She'd stopped breathing, and her lips relaxed. I hoped I wasn't dead wrong about my intuition and brought my lips a breath from hers. With a puff of an exhale, her sweet breath skimming over my lips, she closed the distance between us. Elation soared through me, and I brought one hand up to cup the back of her head so I could deepen the tentative kiss she'd pressed to my mouth.

My chest nearly exploded. Something deep and arcane swelled around my heart, battling for space and swirling through my body with so much joy, so much satiation, I feared I was at risk of conjuring tears for the first time in nearly four hundred years. Kissing Sage was more gratifying, more soul-rending than any epiphany searched for throughout time. Nothing compared. Nothing could *ever* compare.

She responded immediately, her body angling into me and her lips sliding over mine, soft, and then hard, searching, and then demanding. Sage brought her hands up, and the way she framed my face was almost desperate, like she didn't know what to hold onto. I slipped my left arm around her waist to ground her. If she felt even a fraction of what I did, then she might feel like she was losing control entirely.

And I was. Her scent thundered through my senses, overwhelming my logic and compelling me to move my lips and search for the pulse point along her neck. I scraped my teeth against the delicate skin. And then she moaned, and my tenuous hold on my self-control nearly snapped. With a Herculean effort, I lifted away from her, fighting the tethers that strained between us.

Sage stared up at me, her lips pink and her eyes half-closed. Her heart had fired to life again, but I didn't smell fear in her blood anymore. The delicate perfume of her arousal, on the other hand…

I took a step back, breathing hard. With my hands in fists at my side, I managed to grate out, "Now you can go."

She put her fingers to her lips, running them along the plump fullness and staring at me in wonder. "What—"

"Go," I insisted. If she didn't, I was going to do something I'd really regret. I didn't know if it was possible for a vampire to screw up a relationship with a ley match. I'd never heard of such a thing. But I didn't want to take any chances with her by pushing her away.

With another searching look, she fumbled for the doorknob. I waited patiently, allowing her to wrench open the door and then disappear through it. I glimpsed her exiting the side door of the counter, and then she looked over her shoulder one more time. Our gazes caught, and she stumbled. I jumped forward reflexively but stopped myself from going back to her just in time.

Patience. If this was more of a war than a union, then I was certainly in familiar territory. I could do this. For her, I would do this the right way, the way that made sense to Sage and eased her into her new reality. Tempting as it was to scoop her up and carry her to my house *Seven Brides for Seven Brothers* style, I had a feeling that it would only cause mistrust between us.

Glancing at the oven, I made a mental note to anonymously donate a hefty sum to the university stadium, and then I made my way out of the kitchen with forced calm. My cohort materialized in the archway, and a stream of spectators rushed around them. I must have been standing in that kitchen alone a little longer than I thought. That tended to happen when I'd lived for centuries. Hours were mere minutes if I wasn't paying close attention.

Art ducked his head, looking for something in my face. "Wait, where is she?"

Even Constantine looked mildly alarmed. "You lost her?"

"I didn't lose her." I typed up instructions to our security detail with Sage's name and information and requested as much information on her as they could dig up. "She wanted to go, so I let her go."

"You *let her go*?" Alvaro repeated. His eyes widened and he lifted his face away from me. "Who are you?"

Matteo rubbed his chest, clearly uncomfortable. "I don't think we do that. Let them go."

"Definitely against protocol," Alvaro agreed with an eye squint.

Art watched me, his mind already tuning itself to mine as we had done for hundreds of years. "Already, you care for her that much?"

Discomfort tugged at me, pinching my pride. "It was tactical," I muttered. I slid my phone into my jacket pocket and headed to the car at a fast clip. "Women are different now. This isn't eighteenth-century France. You can't just rescue the milkmaid with your lands and titles."

"Those were the days," Art sighed. "So much pussy, so little time."

Ignoring Art, Matteo followed me, his features concerned. "But she's mortal."

"Breakable," Constantine cut in.

"Stupid," Art added flippantly.

We joined the crowd as they exited the stadium into the dark parking lot, and I did my best to ignore the incessant, internal alarm bells that shouted for me to find Sage and make sure she hadn't died in a freak accident. "If the mother hens are done clucking," I drawled, hiding my rising panic, "we have work to do."

"What could be more important than keeping the first ley match in eighty years *alive*?" Matteo asked.

We all turned to stare at him. Our curly-haired youngest brother had been born a good hundred years after Alvaro, and he often deferred to those of us who had waited so long for him to reach maturity and join our cohort. But this time, he was scowling at me, his eyes darkened and his thick brows furrowed. I slowed, considering his reaction. "What makes you doubt me, precisely?"

"She might be a modern woman, as you say," he argued. "But this world is dangerous. Cars, guns, natural gas explosions, and not to mention the fae—"

"Stop." I halted in the middle of the moving crowd,

pinning my youngest cohort with a glare. "What you name, you summon. Be careful."

"They will show up eventually," Constantine reminded me calmly.

"If they haven't already," Alvaro muttered with a shifty look around us. It was true that the fae could already be here, could already be searching for the socium who now held more ley in her body than fae royalty. The fae considered vampires and their ley-blessed matches an abomination to the earth's balance. They were responsible for feeding the ley in the first place, so anything that drew from the well to serve their enemies did not sit well with them. Historically, the fae had fought full wars just to capture and sacrifice the socium back to the ley spring.

"I'm not leaving her alone," I relented finally. "I've alerted security to her existence, but also," I hesitated, rubbing my jaw.

"Ah." Constantine, folded his long arms over his massive torso. "You're breaking away."

"*What*?" Art and Matteo asked in synchronized outrage.

"Only until I can convince her to come to the house," I amended.

"We can't do that," Art argued like I was too simple to understand the most basic tenant of being in a vampire cohort. "You'll weaken our wards."

"And what are the wards for without a ley mate?" I challenged. "We can't all five of us go skulking outside her campus apartment, can we?"

They exchanged wary glances, except for Constantine, who, as usual, appeared to be contemplating my plan in a measured, more logical fashion. Constantine nodded thoughtfully. "Two nights maximum, and then you must return."

"Two nights?" Art asked incredulously. In his defense, we hadn't spent a single night apart since the eighteenth century. That was how bonded vampires were to one another, and especially so if they were the only pair of vampire twins born. Ever.

"We approach this with caution," I said simply. Art scowled at me, but I wasn't budging on this. Yes, my instincts were screaming at me to take off running and find her *now*, but my well-honed logic won out, thankfully.

We reached our cars, and I faced Art, who shifted a look between our white luxury SUV and the other three cars. "Oh, for fuck's sake. I have to drive my own car, now?"

Art had never liked cars. I found no reasonable explanation for it, and he couldn't articulate it, either. They weren't a danger to him at any speed and in any crash scenario, so I wasn't sure where his fear of them had come from. But he refused to drive them. I clapped him on the shoulder. "You can ride with Matteo. He has a bleeding heart."

"Funny words for a sanguis," Matteo snarked.

As I climbed into my car and read the text from my security team, giving me Sage's address on campus, I thought briefly of what Constantine wanted me to watch out for. It wasn't car accidents, that was for certain. For a vampire on his own, there were far more sinister dangers lurking in the shadows. I punched the car to life and took off for Sage's apartment. They'd be coming for her now, too.

Chapter Six

SAGE

My body crumbled before my mind did. Mentally, I had one focus—get my things, get out. And that was what I did. I ran faster than I had since the high school mandatory mile—pathetic, I know—and ignoring Marcus, the media team, and anyone else who tried to stop me and ask if I was alright, I gathered my backpack and made it back to my scooter out of breath and sweaty.

And then I was shaking. My fingers trembled on the scooter handles, and my knees wobbled so badly, I had to stop twice on the paved walkway to plant my feet and lean over the handlebars.

"Shit," I whispered to myself. Night had fallen, and I still had a mile before I made it to my apartment. There were lantern-style light posts situated along the campus walkways, giving it a charming colonial feel I usually appreciated. But tonight, as I panted and leaned on my scooter in the dark, I noticed for the first time how many dark pockets they allowed. Thick swaths of shadows stuffed the space between each gold halo. As my limbs trembled and my heart thundered, I swore I saw movement in those spaces. Slithering.

Breathing harder, and dimly aware that I was probably having a panic attack, I ramped up my scooter's speed and took off with my eyes on the light spaces. It was counter-logical the way my fear had increased the *farther* I was from Silas. Or, perhaps, it had only caught up to me just now, and before, my adrenaline had kept me calm. But somehow, I didn't think that was the case. With Silas, I had been frightened and bewildered, and then angry and irritated. But that paled in comparison to the unrestrained panic that sprinted through my veins and drenched my body in a thick sheen of sweat.

And that kiss…

Saint Joseph, that kiss. Not only had I not even attempted to stop him, I had *wanted* him to kiss me. Even more than that, I'd needed it. The closer he came, the more drawn to him my body had become, and before I knew it, I had been desperate for his hands on my body and his mouth on mine. I'd kissed a few men, but never like that. Never anywhere near that intensity.

As I rounded a corner and entered the brick apartment complex, a rush of longing hit me hard. Suddenly, the only thing I wanted was to be in that kitchen again with Silas' arm around my waist and his hard body surrounding me, his lips on mine. My lips tingled, remembering the slide of them. My skin sang, remembering the feel of him. My blood hammered against my veins for *him, him, him, more, more, more*—

I stopped again, my tires squealing against the brakes and my temper flaring. "Enough!" I shouted. A couple of security guards on bikes heard me, and they turned their heads toward me. Gritting my teeth, I tapped my closed fist against my forehead. "Fuck." *Nice work, psycho.*

I turned to greet them, kicking out the stand on my scooter and attempting to look calm rather than like a panicked jackrabbit in a coyote den. One of the campus security guards was a huge but cuddly-looking guy with a bushy beard, full lips, and a helmet that looked a little too small on his enormous noggin. The second could not have looked more different with her small frame and shock of bright blue hair. She wore her bike helmet, navy blue polo, and khakis like they belonged on the runway, and her hair streamed behind her like silk ribbons.

They came to a stop three feet from me, and the bearded guy asked, "Are you okay?"

The blue-haired guard was even more beautiful up close. She had huge, dramatically up-tilted eyes and straight, white teeth. "Your scooter broken?"

Still breathing hard like I'd run from the stadium uphill, I shook my head. "No, just—" I gulped for air, swallowing hard. "I remembered something."

They exchanged confused looks. "Oh," the girl said.

I waved weakly. "I'm all good. Thanks for checking." A buzzing started in my skull, droning and constant like radio static. My fingers trembled so hard, I gripped my handlebars with white knuckles, and every intake of breath rattled.

"You don't look great, sweetie," the girl said. She glanced at her companion. "Do you want to finish our route? I'll walk her home."

As she spoke, my head actually vibrated so hard, my vision crossed. The bearded guy nodded slowly. "Yeah. Yeah, that's… good idea. I'll see you later."

Then he was gone, and a pair of lavender eyes came

into focus while I clutched my head and tried to right my senses. "Hey, lovely. Let's get you home."

I held up a hand. "No, I'm fine. I'm good, thank you."

"I really must insist," she smiled. But as she reached for me, she suddenly halted, hands in midair and eyes drifting over my shoulder. "Oh."

"Oh?" I kneaded my forehead, pinching it hard and willing my body to go back to normal. *Please*, I begged silently. *I just want to go home to my bed. I want to sleep and maybe reset the entire world and start over.* I didn't even want to think about what had happened. I didn't want to contemplate who Silas was or what he'd told me… or what he *was*.

"I see you have things… handled," she said, her voice growing tight. With a smile that didn't reach her mesmerizing eyes, she backed away. "If I see you again, I'll be sure to check in."

"Thanks," I gritted out. A sharp pain pierced my temple and traveled to the base of my skull, but then the blue-haired guard was gone, and I found myself nearly alone. A few students walked in groups or hurried to their cars, and I watched them numbly while my equilibrium gradually righted itself.

Well, that had fit the general theme of my day: Unbe-fucking-lievable.

With arms that felt like glass noodles and a headache that pounded on the Richter scale, I forced myself the last block to my apartment building. The apartments weren't anything fancy—eight-unit brick buildings with two floors and metal stairs, and no matter which unit we got, there were thin walls and loud neighbors.

I parked my scooter at the base of our metal stairs, locking it with fingers that were working more like frantic beater attachments than actual digits, and then I ran up the stairs to our front door, which I knew I'd find unlocked in the evening with most roommates in for the night. On a Wednesday, anyway. I slipped through the front door and right into the living room. The apartment wasn't huge, with just enough room for two couches and a TV in the living room, along with the giant beanbag chair my roommate Mila had brought. The kitchen/dining room combo took up a modest amount of space at the back, with abysmal cabinet storage, and then there were bedrooms on the left and right of the main space with attached bathrooms.

My shared room was on the right, and although I hadn't eaten and I felt jittery, I walked right past where my roommates were gathered and for my bedroom. My roommates could best be described as the Powerpuff Girls, right down to their hair colors and temperaments. Mila had short, curly blond hair and a bubbly disposition, Harper wore her bright red hair long and often braided down her back, and she was the definition of an energetic overachiever, and Zoe had never outgrown her goth phase, with her natural-crop black hair, thick eyeliner, and general "fuck off" attitude.

As I hurried past them, my face slick with sweat and my heart still going a mile a minute, Mila perked up from her little nest in the beanbag chair. "Hey, Sage!" She looked me over, her disproportionately enormous, blue eyes wide. "Did you... did you hit the gym or something?"

I halted, and surprise flitted through me. My roommates never noticed me. I'd made a few attempts early in the year to get to know them, and while they were polite, they had never reciprocated my attempts at friendship. I even attended the same observatory club as Mila every week, but she rarely acknowledged my existence, "Uh, no," I panted, still inching over to the bedroom. "It's just... warm."

Zoe glanced up from her phone with a bored expression. "Marcus thinks you got kidnapped."

"Wait, you know Marcus?" I slumped against the hallway entrance, confused. Where was this sudden interest in my whereabouts coming from?

"Yeah, we're all in media relations. Obviously," she said like we'd been best friends the entire year.

I tried not to let my confusion show on my face. "Oh. Well…" Marcus had seen Silas throw me over his shoulder. How the fuck did I explain that? *"Yes, a hulking supernatural something walked off with me and fed me orange juice."* I wiped sweat off my cheek uneasily. "It was just a prank."

"Are you okay?" Harper asked, standing from the kitchen table where she had her books splayed out in front of her. "Shit, look at you. You need to drink some water."

Since when had anyone worried about my *hydration*? This entire day felt like the Upside Down from *Stranger Things*. But it was true that I needed water; my mouth felt like a dry, used kitchen sponge. "Okay," I croaked.

Harper's long, auburn braid swung as she hurried to the sink and filled a glass with tap water before bringing it to me. Her green eyes danced over me in worry. "You sure you're okay?"

"Yeah." I took a sip of water, and then suddenly, I couldn't get enough. I downed the glass, gulping bellyfuls of air along the way. With a satisfied gust of air, I said, "Wow. Okay, thanks."

Zoe cocked her head, considering me. "So, it was only a prank? Because you look like you had kind of a rough night."

"Want me to beat them up?" Mila offered in her helium-high voice.

I scratched out a rough laugh. "No, it's okay." *Good luck*

beating that guy up. "Thank you, guys. I'm going to shower and hit the mattress, though."

"Do you need dinner?" Harper asked. "I have leftovers from what I made."

Another first. They'd never so much as eaten at the table with me, let alone offered to have me eat *with* them. "I'm good," I hedged, backing up a few steps. Then I realized I had the glass still, and Harper stepped forward to take it from me.

"Hey, we're your roomies," she smiled softly. "Let us help if you need it, okay?"

What in the parallel universe? Did I fall down a rabbit hole? "Right," I replied, no longer able to mask my confusion. I inched away from them and into the short hallway that led to my bedroom. Although I knew Zoe could come in at any moment, I shut the door and leaned against it. My legs finally gave out, and I sank to the brown carpet weakly.

My room was dark, lit only by the steady blink of Zoe's charging laptop on her bed, and in the quiet shadows, my labored breaths filled my ears like a rushing tide. I sat there, feeling my heart, hearing the air fill and leave my lungs, and clutched my knees to my chest. I felt like the apocalypse had just jumpstarted and no one else had noticed. Like the world had flown off its axis, and only I had reason to panic.

I know for a fact that you struggle with relationships in your life. Whether you are friendly or surly, it doesn't seem to matter. You can only get so close to someone before something compels you to pull away.

How could he possibly have known that? And for that matter, how had Silas done *any* of the things he'd done? The compulsion on the students, the inhuman strength, and then that kiss…

I dug my fingers through my disheveled hair, leaning my forehead against my knees. "This isn't happening," I whispered to myself. "You agreed to take shrooms with Marcus. Or hit your head. This isn't real."

Silence greeted that statement. For some reason, I'd expected Silas to show up and answer. But, as I lifted my head, I could only make out the two twin beds on the left and right of the room, the small desk between them, and the window in the middle of the wall. I spotted my eight-inch Dobsonian telescope set up on the desk and pointed at the open window. Although Zoe had never been overly friendly, she'd also never minded all my equipment on the desk or my late-night star searching. Beside my telescope, my DSLR camera rested.

No matter what was happening to me here on Earth, I could count on the stars to be consistent. It didn't matter if my mother hadn't called me in three weeks. It didn't matter if I was a lonely star in my own solar system with no planets or moons to orbit my solitary existence. None of it mattered when the stars were wondrous all year long. When I lost myself in the stars, I drifted in a Milky Way of comforting isolation, and sometimes, it was hard to force myself to stay here in the present where I belonged. Photographing the sky had been the next logical step in my stargazing hobby, and although I was still learning the technicalities of capturing photos of the night sky, it had been the only thing to bring me joy, well… ever.

With my limbs creaking, I stood and slumped over to the desk. Even in the near darkness, I could make out the glittering photographs I had taken of the stars this year. They were attached to my side of the room with pushpins, and as a cool breeze filtered through the open window, a few of them fluttered. I touched one of my favorite photographs of the Milky Way tenderly, taking in its violet pinks and indigo blues dotted with sparkling gems.

I was sweaty. I was tired. I was thirsty and hungry. But despite all of that, I found myself carefully removing the window screen, setting it against the desk, and then bending over the eyepiece of my well-calibrated telescope. I'd been watching Orion this week, taking in the minute shift the stars made over time while I waited for the Ring Nebula to become visible later this spring. I didn't have any pictures of Vega and her surrounding stars yet, and that was the thing with watching the stars. It required patience, research, and attention to detail, and that was why I loved it.

I stared at the sweep of dusty stars, and the rhythm in my chest slowed. My shoulders relaxed, and the thoughts of monsters and mates that had been torturing my mind quieted. Sighing in relief, I kneeled on the chair in front of the desk, keeping my eye on the night sky. I knew it wasn't possible, and I knew that the stars had fixed trajectories in the universe, but sometimes I could swear I detected a different kind of sweep between the twinkling points. It looked like stardust or the faraway galaxies that made up the Milky Way cloud, but more concentrated. I had tentatively brought it up on a Reddit thread once, only to be ridiculed and called an amateur… among other things.

Still. I saw it. I knew the swirling dust changed directions from time to time, and it almost seemed to actively flow like a stream. Dutifully, I flicked on the table lamp and dragged my notebook out. Star charts littered each page, matching the seasonal patterns that drifted across our night sky. And between the points, I'd mapped out my imaginary blue lines. I couldn't explain the compulsion to do this, but it just felt right.

We are beholden to an ancient system that runs through the earth and even the universe itself. Silas' voice drifted through my mind once again, and this time, I sat up straight with a gasp. My blue coloring pencil clattered to the desk, and I stared down at my drawing like I was seeing it for the first time. Lines. Lines between the stars. I flipped back a page, and they were everywhere. Lines connecting stars, lines flowing and shifting.

Blue lines.

Why the *fuck* had I made them blue?

I didn't sleep after that. I charted stars and scoured notes, and all the while, memories of a blue light pulsed behind my eyes.

Chapter Seven

SILAS

The fae's bones creaked in my fist. Her lavender eyes bulged from her skull, and her glamour shimmered before sputtering out, leaving her as she truly was. Her teeth elongated to deadly points, and her black gums oozed blue liquid. Her skin took on the appearance of glacial rock, hard and faintly blue. Her azure hair remained the same, and it was that vanity that had alerted me to her presence in the first place.

That, and her stench. Fae smelled like rotting fruit.

I squeezed, and she shrieked, clawing uselessly at my hand. "Please!" she screamed.

I held off decapitating her. "How long have you known about her?"

"The moment it happened," she snarled. We were under a mature oak tree, shrouded in darkness on the sleepy campus. "So, what? An hour? For fuck's sake."

"And why would they station fae in Kingston, New York in the first place?" I challenged. I had the fae girl pinned to the tree trunk, my hand around her throat and my eyes locked on the minutiae of her facial expressions to detect falsehoods. Despite what some of the legends said, fae *could* lie. They lied rather well.

"Where there are monsters, there are fae," she rasped, her mouth elongating into a hideous, feral smile.

Translation: Queen Eliana knew our cohort had been getting close to a match, so she had us followed. It was a cruel irony of nature that the fae fed the ley lines with their magical rites, and as a result, were directly tethered to its events and movements. The same source that granted vampires strength and connected us to mates was the lifeblood of the one species hell-bent on eradicating us from the earth. We were just as tethered to each other as we were doomed to hate one another.

I considered my options, briefly thumbing through them like a playbook. Vampires hadn't killed any fae since the Crimean War, so beheading this one would most certainly be an act of war my father would frown upon. It wasn't that House Sanguis was opposed to violence; actually, we craved it. But it was all we could do to keep the humans from wiping themselves out to the point of extinction, and since the First World War, we had devoted most of our strategic energies to intervening in mortal disputes and keeping them from nuking each other to oblivion. Crass as it was, we needed the human population alive and well for our own survival. If I started a war with the fae, it would stretch our already taxed resources.

I squeezed the sharp-toothed creature and leaned in so close, her sickly-sweet scent almost made me puke. She recoiled as I hissed, "Deliver a message to your queen. The next fae I see within a mile of *my mate* will not be given the same mercy."

Relief stretched the fae's features taut, but only for a

moment. I reached up, grasped her elongated, pointy ear, and ripped. Blue blood coated my fingers the same instant she screamed, and beneath us, the ground trembled with her rage. The leaves overhead shivered in sync with her spindly body, and then I cast her to the side where she bounced in a heap on the dark grass. I dropped her ear into the grass, my lip curling. Gods, the fae stank.

Still screeching, she shouted, "My ear! You beast! You vile abomination!" Blue blood mixed with spittle from her open mouth, and she crouched on the ground, clutching where her pointy ear had been. Her eyes flashed like a cat's irises as she turned back to me. "Our Divine Mistress will hear of this!"

"The question is," I replied calmly, hands in my pockets, "will you? Stay a moment longer and I will take the second ear and what remains of your hearing."

The fae snarled, but then a gust of air blew through the campus' green space, and like dandelion seeds on the wind, she disappeared in a white swirl. I stared at the space she had been for a moment, and it was only then I realized how my heart rate had increased and my chest had tightened. For the first time in centuries, I had felt true fear, if only for a moment. Fear that Sage would be taken. Fear that the fae might snatch my would-be bride and drain her body of its life force.

My mouth had gone dry, and I suddenly found myself thirsty for the first time in a while. I usually kept my blood thirst well in hand—centuries of knowing my own body's rhythms and having ample access to sources of blood had kept me from being lost to the mindless bloodthirst that House Sanguis vampires were known for. Tonight, I felt like I hadn't drunk in weeks. I usually needed a pint every two or three days along with a regular, healthy diet. I'd had a glass of O-negative just last night.

Perhaps it was the memory of Sage's scent that had me craving more. Perhaps it wasn't bloodthirst, but desire. I smoothed my fingers over my forehead, turning to face the direction of her apartment. A full night with no sleep and a blood-parched throat? That was a new sort of Hell for me. But I couldn't leave Sage on her own, and my instincts still told me she wasn't ready to face the truth yet. I would have to be patient.

Sage's perfume hung in a cloud around me as I leaned against the brick wall of her apartment building. The sun had finally crested the thick foliage, peeking through in gold ribbons and illuminating the sleepy campus with a dull light. I'd been beneath Sage's open window all night, listening to the scratch of her pencil, the symphony of her distressed sighs, and the restless rhythm of her heart. She hadn't slept. I had barely blinked. My eyelids were sandpaper and my mouth a dusty catacomb. Smelling her all night, listening to her blood pump through her veins and her breath quicken with distress had almost killed me. There were actual divots in the brick wall from where my fists had ground concave patterns.

She was in the shower now after her sleepless night, and I listened to the sound of the water trickling over her body. I turned and pressed my forehead against the brick wall. Torture. Was that what mates really were? Painful, agonizing longing and interminable patience?

It's been less than twenty-four hours, I reminded myself. *"The strongest of all warriors are these two—Time and Patience." And now*

I'm quoting Bonaparte. L'audace, encore de l'audace, toujours de l'audace.

Eventually, Sage gathered her things, made herself some coffee, and ate what I assumed was toast based on the smell. I acknowledged the intense creepiness of whatever this stalking plan was, but the alternative was to leave her alone with fae hiding in her shadow and hungry wraiths growing in numbers around the world. No human with as much ley in their blood as Sage should go unprotected. I'd be damned if I let *my* human be a walking ley buffet for the supernatural.

As Sage exited her building, I kept a safe distance from her, allowing my well-honed senses to keep track of her. My phone rang, and I answered without looking at the caller ID. I knew who it would be. "Did you sleep?"

"No. Did you?" Art asked.

I lifted my eyes to the pale blue sky. "Naturally, no."

"I thought you contacted security," Art groused. "They can watch her."

He knew as well as I did that a human security detail might alert us to danger, but they wouldn't stand a chance against a real threat. "I'll have them tail her while we change shifts if necessary. But I'd rather not."

"I'd rather you just grab the chit and dash," Art countered, his dialect slipping into one of his favorite eras from our younger years during King Edward's reign in England.

"Do you want a fainting human hyperventilating in the house?" I asked calmly, walking along the campus path several meters away from Sage.

"Less than appealing," Art admitted.

"A mate happens once," I reminded him, my voice more serene than I really felt. "We can allow for some discomfort momentarily."

He grunted in agreement. "I told Mother."

Our mother had been human once, herself. Or she had mistakenly thought herself human, anyway. She would be an advantageous ally for us when easing Sage into her new life. Maybe. That had been back in the Byzantine era, so my mother hadn't exactly questioned the idea of an arranged marriage at the time. Was it possible for Sage to not feel a connection? What would happen if she denied it? "What did she say?"

"She was speechless for once, actually."

I made a sound much like Art's, wordlessly acknowledging that. "How long before they're here and want to see her, do you think?"

"I wouldn't be surprised if they're on the jet already." I didn't know why I'd asked. I'd known the answer to that question even as it left my mouth. Art added, "Best hurry this along, brother. It might be awkward to face the Dominus Sanguis without your mate at your side."

It would be catastrophically weak, was what Art meant. What kind of vampire matched with their ley mate and then just let her wander around? I picked up my pace a touch. "I have it handled."

"Brother, when I boasted once that we were history in the making—"

"You didn't mean this way. I'm aware." Art and I had made history plenty of times, even if we had never been recognized for it. What we didn't want was to go down in history as the only vampire twins ever born… who then failed to secure their ley matches. Embarrassing didn't quite cover it. "I told you. I have it well in hand."

I didn't. I had no idea what the fuck I was doing. Art's wry chuckle told me he didn't need to see my face to read my thoughts. "If you don't have her by tomorrow, you might need to go caveman again."

That hadn't gone well the first time. Although, in hindsight, what twenty-first-century woman wanted to be manhandled and carted away over a stranger's shoulder like that? None. Moron. "I'll catch up later," I promised Art. I hung up, and then Sage went into a communications building. I checked my watch. It was just after eight, and the schedule my security team had sent me said her first class wasn't until nine forty-five. I followed at a distance still, but I used the hallway corners and open doors to keep out of her line of sight. The modern building had industrial gray carpet on the hallway floors and several dozen classrooms for media education that were maybe half filled this early in the morning.

She walked down one hallway, down a flight of stairs to a basement area, and then made a right turn into what sounded like a video processing room. I went down the same stairs, keeping my ears trained on her footsteps and closing the distance between us cautiously. I passed a young kid with headphones over his thick hair, and we made momentary eye contact, so I smiled benignly. Although I aged exponentially slower than humans ever could, I still looked about thirty-five years old. Hopefully, he would think I was a professor. My predatory instincts kicked in, urging me to blend in, to remain unnoticed. He looked back down, apparently unconcerned with my presence here.

"Hey, Marcus," Sage said from the room down the hall.

A male voice answered, "Hey! There you are. You disappeared last night."

The predator in me growled low and irritated. *Who* was Marcus? And why did he sound so familiar with Sage?

"I know, I'm so sorry. I had… well, there was a miscommunication with someone," Sage explained hesitantly.

"Huh?" the guy asked.

Sage's voice calmed suddenly, and she said, "It was nothing."

My clever Sage already working her ley magic to blend in with the humans. She didn't even know she was doing it. I was down the hallway now, the basement fluorescent lights piercing my eyeballs and giving me a headache. Anytime I was underground for a long time, I felt vaguely ill. Our kind preferred to be surrounded by nature and the natural ley aura as much as we could. All the tales of vampires in coffins and graveyards had done their job of masking our existence by being the exact opposite of the truth.

"Okay," Marcus replied easily. "Well, what's up? How can I help you? Or was this about my question before the whole spotlight malfunction? That was so weird, wasn't it?"

Sickly sweet invaded my nostrils, suddenly. I paused, a meter from the door she had entered, and the hair on the back of my neck stood up. Something about that smell was off.

"No, no," Sage assured him. "It's not about—I just need footage of the game if you have it. Because I had to leave."

I inched closer, inhaling deeply and trying to place the scent. It was *almost* fae, but not quite. Marcus' voice dropped, and I heard his feet approach Sage. His scent mingled with hers, detonating a rage grenade in my chest. How fucking *dare* he—

"Yeah, I've got footage," Marcus said softly. "Would you be willing to do something for me, first?"

Then Sage made a choking sound, and her heart went wild with fear.

Chapter Eight

SAGE

Marcus had his hand around my throat, and my brain couldn't seem to comprehend it. I choked, surprised that my friend would even do such a thing, but I didn't move. I froze completely, staring at his handsome face in confusion. I had *just* been admiring the way Marcus' T-shirt stretched across his wiry frame.

But then, his voice had changed, he'd stepped into my space, and his hand had darted to my throat faster than my eyes could track it. Behind him, the dark basement room partially shrouded the several cameras, green screen box, and tables littered with camera equipment, but there was no one else here but us. Marcus pulled me close to him so his breath, like rotting apples, washed over my face. "So, it's true. You reek of ley little socium."

I choked, finally bringing my fingers to his hand. "Marc—"

Another impact rocked through me, jarring my teeth together and sending me flying away from Marcus. What little I had managed to process led me to believe I was about to go face-first into a table of camera lenses, but a strong arm stopped me, pulling me tight against an iron frame of a body. I found my feet, and from the corner of my eye I caught the strong profile of the man who had caught me. Silas.

He stared forward, mouth tight and eyes fixed across the room. "Silas?" I whispered in confusion. He didn't even glance at me, and a hissing sound, like fat hitting the pan, drew my attention away from him.

Marcus had been knocked into the flimsy green screen setup and was emerging slowly, hunched over and emitting an ominous, spitting, hissing sound. His body had changed, no longer the solid flesh and bone he had been before, but a wispy, black, humanoid shape that shifted and flicked, a midnight swath of shadows and slick oil that slipped from his tall frame only to disappear into thin air. Marcus' face had changed completely, and crawling, viscous shadows slithered over his skin and slid into his eyes, darkening them like ink drops in water before flitting across his skin again. He looked like an alien, like a ghost made of shadows and fear.

I began to scream, but Silas calmly pressed his hand to my mouth, muffling the sound and shocking me into silence. "Who are you?" Silas asked.

He doesn't know? I thought with a fresh wave of fear. Silas, himself, was unnatural. A monster, he'd said. If he didn't know who Marcus was, then who would?

Marcus straightened, grinning with a mouthful of sharpened, black teeth. "Who? Or what?" His voice hissed and whipped through the air, causing me to flinch. I'd never heard a voice like that. Like gravel and static had been jammed down his throat.

"What, then," Silas replied. His hands held me steadily,

and although his body felt tense, I didn't hear a quiver of fear or hesitation in his tone.

Marcus took slow steps to the side, a stalking nightmare, forcing Silas to angle us away from him. "What I am matters less than what I will do to you."

A shiver of fear climbed up my back, snapping my spine straight and rattling my arms. Silas held me steadily, but he lowered his hand from my mouth. "To me? I'm flattered." He shifted me so I stood behind him. "Prove it." I couldn't seem to help myself. I held onto his black, canvas jacket, noticing for the first time that this was exactly what Silas had been wearing yesterday when we'd first met. He didn't shake me off; instead, he kept one hand on my arm behind him and squeezed it in a comforting gesture.

Marcus gurgled out a mimicry of a laugh, hissing and spitting like a reptilian monster. His eyes, solid black now, found me, and his hideous smile elongated. "To hurt her is to hurt you."

I flinched away from him, but there was no need. Silas blocked me from Marcus' line of sight. "You talk too much to be a wraith. You wouldn't have waited this long to claim your prey. A fae, on the other hand…"

Marcus snickered again, curling his hands up and bowing his shoulders like Silas had told an unbearably funny dad joke. "A wraith. A fae."

"Or both," Silas finished. Curiosity tinted his voice as he asked, "But how?"

"Not how," Marcus spat out, still smiling grotesquely with his too-wide mouth full of sharpened teeth. "But why?"

"Fae riddles," Silas muttered. He seemed so calm… almost irritated. He was shielding me, yes, but I sensed no fear in him.

My body, on the other hand, had decided it was fully

stressed to the max. A warm trickle wept from my nose, and as I absently wiped at it, I realized my nose was bleeding. Silas stiffened, rotating a pained look my way.

The Marcus thing hissed, his tongue lashing out in a disgusting sweep. "She bleeds for me. Do you see? She is mine. I was promised."

Silas turned away from me but pushed me back a step. "Who sent you? And don't say it doesn't matter as much as what your teeth can do or some irritating bullshit."

Marcus licked his teeth with a long, thin tongue coated with blue and black liquid. "But who *doesn't* matter when—"

Silas suddenly chucked something at the creature. The object smashed into the creature's face, and blue spurted from his nose and mouth. As the thing screamed, stumbling back and crashing into two broadcast cameras, a black phone crashed to the floor, and glass shattered over the tiles as it landed. Had he just used his *phone* like a baseball to that thing's face?

"Sage, run," Silas commanded, his voice far more grave than he'd let on. He pushed me, sending me stumbling toward the open doorway.

I didn't even question the command. With my heart slamming painfully against my ribcage, I regained my balance and bolted for the exit. I kept my hand plastered to my nose, but the blood dripped freely, running between my fingers and staining my shirt. I only made it four steps before a wrenching pain in my chest whipped me back. I flew through the air, my world spinning and my chest squeezing so painfully, I felt sure I'd been shot with a grappling hook and yanked off my feet. I landed hard on my back, and the air expelled from my lungs in a terrifying whoosh that left me scrabbling and fighting for breath.

The insidious version of Marcus landed on me hard,

and it was only then I realized something really was sticking out of my chest. A tether made of whispering, obsidian shadow stretched from my chest above the V of my lavender T-shirt to the creature's inky fingers. With his knees on either side of my body, he tugged the tether, and my chest jerked up. Bone and tendons screamed, stretching and cracking until I found my breath. I screamed then, reaching for the oozing cable. My fingers swished through nothing. The creature's hideously long tongue darted out, swiping up the blood oozing from my nose and down my mouth. "Mine," he hissed.

Silas grabbed Marcus by the throat, lifting him easily from me, but the tether didn't disappear. The slithering shadows stretched, still connecting me to the snarling creature in Silas' firm grip. Silas glanced down at me, his verdant eyes assessing and almost cold, and then they fixed on Marcus, who vacillated between cackling and grunting, fighting against Silas' hold on his neck. Silas lifted the creature so high, his feet left the ground, and then he slammed him down to the tile so hard, the ground shook.

I coughed, the sound rattling around the place in my chest where that *thing* had impaled me. I didn't know what was protruding from my body, and my brain reeled, trying to understand that I'd been stabbed. As something sharp and burning invaded my body and slithered under my skin, I struggled to comprehend that there was a possibility that I was going to die here, and I would never even understand how.

Then Silas had me in his arms, his stormy eyes dancing over my terrified features and his body supporting mine upright. I stared at him, wordlessly pleading. *Help me. Please.* He seemed to have one moment of hesitation, and then he shifted me in his arms so my head lolled back and my breasts lifted. He bent his head to my chest, his long fingers moving my shirt aside to reveal the swell of my breast. I felt a slight pinch, which was nothing compared to the pulsing pain in my chest that crawled with every heartbeat, reaching through my veins and creeping over my torso. I felt a sucking pressure, and then the pain ebbed, leeching away like the sensation of an IV line being slowly drawn out of a vein.

I gasped, arching my back harder, and glanced down. Silas had his mouth to my breast, sucking the top slope so hard, his cheeks caved in. Red seeped out from his lips and in a thin stream over the white of my skin. That should have horrified me, but a strange numbness came over me instead. Relief coursed through me, fogging over my senses and causing my eyes to flutter. Not even morphine felt this instantaneously blissful, I was sure. My skin sang and my mind hummed, content and euphoric.

When Silas lifted his head, he turned to the side and spit out blackened blood. It landed on the ground with a heavy smack, like it was gelatinous. The black tether had disappeared, and my whole body tingled with elation. I wanted to wrap my arms around his neck and bury my nose against it. I wanted to kiss his soft skin and feel his fingers between my legs. I wanted him so badly, I was sure I would implode if I couldn't have him.

Silas raked a concerned gaze over my expression. I stared at him, wide-eyed and lips parted breathlessly. He licked my blood from his lips, and his eyes closed briefly like it was… delicious.

The phantom creature stumbled to his feet behind Silas, but with my thoughts numbed and my body shimmering with sedated calm, I couldn't find my fear. The thing looked truly horrifying now, with its face crunched and bleeding, its arm hanging at an awkward angle, and three of its pointy teeth broken and leaking thin, blue liquid. I'd expected to find it enraged, but the Marcus thing was… crying. "Mine," he sobbed, staring at me with wide, almost childlike eyes. "They promised."

It stumbled our way, but Silas had me flat on the ground so fast and so gently, I wondered if I'd imagined it. Then the creature was in Silas' grip again, and this time, I was certain the muscled, pristine God would break the Marcus looka-like's neck.

But then the monster disappeared in a puff of black smoke, dissipating into the air so quickly, he might never have been there. Silas rotated his hand, staring at his palm with his dark brows drawn together.

I released a quick breath of relief and turned my gaze to the dim fluorescent lights overhead. Strange, but my friend turning into a night terror wasn't bothering me as much as it probably should have. Silas gathered me in his arms again, kneeling on the broken tile and looking me over with quiet concern. "Sage," he said so softly, I barely missed it. "I'm so sorry."

I snuggled into him, loving how he smelled like leather and something undeniably masculine. "S'okay," I murmured. My chest felt better, and even the place where he'd drank my blood had stopped stinging. Remembering that he'd actually sucked out my blood, I sat up and glanced at my breast. A straight, deep cut wept blood, and I wiped bright red with my finger and held it up between us. "Was I poisoned? Is that why you did that? Like snake venom?"

Silas angled away from my fingers like my blood smelled bad or something. "Not quite. But close enough." His voice was strained, and his lips pressed firmly together. He used his jacket sleeve to wipe at my nose, which thankfully had stopped bleeding now.

I looked around for a place to wipe my fingers, but then Silas lifted me from the floor fluidly, settling me in his arms before carrying me to a table littered with equipment. After carefully shifting the expensive items aside, he set me down and reached for two microfiber cloths usually used to clean camera lenses. He wiped my fingers for me and then pressed the cloth against my open wound before using the other one to swipe at the blood on my chin and lips. "You'll need stitches for that cut, I'm afraid. I'm sorry. I was in a rush to get as much of the wraith's essence out of you as I could."

"Wraith," I repeated. "Is that what he was?"

Silas clenched his teeth visibly. "I'm not entirely sure what that was, actually."

I stared up at him, my head still buzzing, but some of my common sense returning to my thoughts in a slow trickle. I should ask about the wraith, I knew. But my mind shied away from the topic and settled on a more tangible one. "What did you cut me with?"

He glanced up from where he was holding the cloth. "My teeth."

I cocked my head, leaning forward. "Your..."

"Teeth," he repeated, lifting his brows a fraction. "Yes. Hold this in place, please."

I flattened my left palm against the cloth, and the cut stung again. My skin hummed a little less, and my heart kicked up in tempo. "What just happened?"

His throat shifted as he swallowed, but he held my gaze steadily. "I cannot tell you what that thing was for certain. Even in my world—the world you know nothing of—I have never seen such an aberration."

"What world?" I managed to get out.

"The one beneath your feet and beyond your sight," he replied softly. His eyes softened a touch, and he cupped my jaw, sliding his fingers beneath my long waves with a gentleness that relaxed my shoulders. "I'm sorry, Sage. I had no idea something like that would be waiting here for you."

"But," I reasoned, my head clearing enough that I remembered to be afraid, "you aren't surprised he exists."

"I did tell you," he replied steadily, his handsome, angular features set, "I am one of many monsters."

The image of him licking my blood from his lips resurfaced, and then I heard his brother's mocking tone in my memories. *"Vampie's first ley mate!"*

I clenched my jaw, leaning away from him. This couldn't be happening right now. And yet, my logical reasoning kicked in, grasping what I knew to be true and fitting the facts together to repair my fractured reality. What I thought I'd known about the world was wrong. Whatever Silas was, he drank blood. He enjoyed it. "Are you going to tell me what kind of monster you are?" I whispered.

He didn't even flinch. "You know what I am, Sage."

It was too absurd, so I didn't say it. "How did you know to suck the venom from my chest if you had no idea what Marcus was?"

"I had a theory," he replied simply. "It was right. Thankfully."

"Why did he do that?" I pressed.

Silas shook his head once. "I can't say. I need to meet with my… I must discuss it with others."

Other *vampires*. I tasted the word in my head, trying out its bitterness before I let it fall on my tongue. "Are there more of those… not-wraiths?" I scratched out softly. Whatever had happened to my body, whatever had drugged me when Silas had drank my blood, it was fading, and my hands trembled as I came down from the adrenaline.

Silas took my free hand in both of his, warming the cold digits and chafing his skin against mine in a soothing gesture. "I can't know for sure. If I had to guess?"

I nodded silently.

"Yes," he admitted. Wariness had crept into his features. "I think there might be more like him." He glanced at the door, and a couple of students walked in with backpacks on their shoulders and smiles on their faces as they joked about something. Both boys pulled up short, their gazes roving over the destroyed green screen, broken equipment, and upturned tables.

Silas' voice purred unnaturally as he said, "The video production room is undergoing routine maintenance. Your professors want you to study for finals with your class time instead."

Both of them blinked hard, one taller and with buzzed blond hair, and the other with a slight build and a messy top knot. They stared at Silas, and then their gazes glazed over. The taller student said, "I need study time. Sweet."

"Yeah, thanks, man," the wiry guy said.

When they had both backed out and left, Silas returned his gaze to mine. He didn't look embarrassed or chagrined; he watched me with an arrogant kind of patience, like he was waiting for my comprehension to overtake my disbelief. My eyebrows drifted together. "Have you ever done that to me?"

"Never," he replied evenly. "And I never will."

It was hard to deny the reality of what my own two eyes were telling me. Especially because I hadn't slept all night, studying ley lines and the very real theories around their existence. My star charts, the blue light, Silas... it all fit together in a way I wished didn't make so much sense to me.

Silas still had my smaller hand between his enormous ones, and I fixed my attention on them. "You were following me just now, weren't you?"

"Yes," he replied softly.

"And... all night?" I guessed, looking up again.

He didn't waver from my searching gaze. "Yes."

Any sane woman would balk at that. Something inside of me purred happily instead. "Because you believe this connection is real?"

"And because I fear for you," Silas said with a meaningful lift of his eyebrows. "That light show yesterday made you a glowing target."

"A target? For what?"

He released my hand to point with his thumb behind his back. "That kind of shit."

"I'm a target for supernatural monsters because I'm—purportedly," I amended with an eye squint, "your ley mate."

He dipped his chin in affirmation. "Most definitely, you are."

"You seem pretty sure about this."

Silas cupped my jaw again, and I had to fight not to lean into his touch. The drugged effect had worn off, but my desire to be near him hadn't. "I've never felt more sure about anything in my *very lengthy* life, Dulcis."

"What is 'Dulcis?'" I whispered weakly. That wasn't the right question to ask, but I couldn't help my curiosity.

"Sweet. Or darling." His lips twitched lightly into a smile. "It's a... bit old. It's Latin."

"Latin is pretty fucking old," I agreed.

That amused him, and he brought his second hand to

join the first, cupping my face gently. "You deserve time to acclimate to this. But you are also in danger. I am doing my best to straddle those two truths."

Maybe you should straddle me. The thought had come out of nowhere, and it almost shocked me more than the fact that he was touching me so intimately. I didn't know the first thing about straddling anyone. My mouth went dry, and I wet my lips, searching his face for any additional clues that would help me make sense of the world. "I'm not sure I can acclimate to something this bizarre," I admitted.

He looked away, tilting his head one way, and then the other, considering my words. "You are very young. And it isn't as though arranged marriages are commonplace these days. I wouldn't expect anything else."

"What do *you* want me to do?" I asked, almost dreading his answer.

Amusement pricked at the corners of his mouth again. God, he was gorgeous. That alone should have clued me into the fact that he wasn't *normal.* "I want you to come home with me. I want to order your favorite takeout and wrap you in blankets on my couch so you can settle down safely instead of shaking like a jackhammer on this plastic table."

I looked down at my body. Sure as shit, I was shivering violently. I glanced back up at him. "If—if I eat takeout… then do I become the takeout?"

He didn't even look offended by the insinuation that I thought he was going to eat me. "You are literally the most delectable thing I've ever tasted, Sage. But, no, you aren't dinner." His eyes darkened a touch. "I might be tempted to lick you for dessert, though."

Heat pooled between my legs. "Oh," I eked out. All of that sounded suspiciously wonderful, but my head was at war with my instincts. "And if I say I'm going to class instead?"

He considered me quietly, his forehead creased. "I won't stop you."

"But you'll follow me," I guessed. He nodded again. "For how long?"

"For however long it takes," he replied easily. There was a shift in his gaze, though, and I could tell that it didn't sit well with him.

I reached up and pulled his hands down from my face. My heart screamed in protest. Still shaking, I lowered myself from the table, careful not to move the cloth from the wound, and I backed away from him. I wasn't sure what kind of logic this was, continuing to deny what was fairly obvious now. Maybe it wasn't logic but pride. I couldn't accept this beautiful, otherworldly man crash landing into my life and dictating who I belonged to or what my purpose was. "I guess you'll have to wait a while, then."

His jaw ticked, but he didn't move to stop me. With his hands in fists, he gritted through his teeth, "You need stitches."

"I'll take care of it," I replied, still backing away slowly. I bent to the side and picked up my star-patterned backpack. "Urgent care won't ask questions."

His jaw worked back and forth. "This isn't the safe choice."

"You said you wouldn't stop me." I had reached the doorway, and I peeked down the hall as if there might be another wraith-like thing waiting at the end of it.

"I won't," he said tersely.

I held his gaze one last time. "I have a life," I said like that might explain my stubbornness. "I have… there's too much to do. I can't drop everything for whatever this is."

He rubbed his jaw, looking away for a silent beat. Then green eyes flicked to mine with a stern glint. "We'll see, Dulcis."

I backed out of the room until he was out of sight. Eventually, I turned and fast-walked down the hallway, glancing over my shoulder at the empty space. I didn't see him, but somehow I still knew.

He was there, all the same.

Chapter Nine

SILAS

"The human instinct to deny obvious truths just to protect their perceived reality is endlessly astonishing," Art said on the other end of the phone.

I sighed, nodding as I followed Sage from her second class of the day to the dining hall for lunch. "And Sage is very human."

"Except she's not," Art reminded me. "She's a socium, remember?"

"Yeah, well," I grunted, dodging behind a tree as Sage searched for me over her shoulder for the thirtieth time today, "she begs to differ."

"Maybe you should make her *beg* for something else, and then she'll worry less about her humanity."

I rolled my eyes. "Do you think it's my stalking that will get me into her panties or the vampire bit?"

"Chicks love vampires," Art replied confidently.

"You eat their fears, how do you know?" I challenged dryly.

"I've had to listen to women moan in your bed for three

centuries, brother. I think it's safe to say they enjoy your company."

I cringed, moving away from the tree and striding casually to the dining hall to find somewhere to loiter while Sage ate. "You know, I actually feel kind of… filthy about that now. Like being with other women was wrong."

"Did you convert to Mormonism? What the fuck does that mean?" Art asked with a laugh in his voice.

"I don't know," I muttered, and my hearing picked up on Sage's footsteps moving through the loud building. "I just feel gross when I think about it."

"Wow," Art drawled. "Pussy-whipped and you haven't even tasted it yet."

I scowled. "Art—"

"I know," he breezed. "I know. Don't speaketh of thine cherished in blasphemous ways. I get it. Listen, the real reason I called you, lover boy, is to relay a message from Marios in Greece."

Marios was another sanguis close in age to me, and his cohort had been hoping for mates for as long as we had. I'd asked Art to sniff around a bit, to see if anyone else had seen a half-wraith, half-fae abomination.

"He said he's never seen anything like what you described to me, but the wraiths caused a disturbance in Kuwait the Americans misconstrued as an attack by a terrorist faction, and there was some kind of scuffle out there. They've been dealing with a lot of full-blooded wraiths but they haven't noticed anything like what you fought this morning. Also, they hate you a lot for finding a mate."

I leaned against the exterior of the building, listening to Sage pick up a tray from several yards away. "Reassure him it's actually been an enormous pain in the ass."

"Happily." Art paused, and I could hear his thoughts churning even from miles away. I'd told him everything—about the wraith-like thing, about sucking its venom from Sage, about the way her blood had tasted on my lips and how I'd very nearly sucked a full pint from her just to slake my thirst. I'd told him I felt hungrier than I had in centuries, and I didn't think a cold glass of O neg was going to cure it. Finally, Art said, "I can watch her. I think you need rest."

Vampires needed as much sleep as humans did. I was beat to shit, and I felt like I hadn't had blood in weeks. "I can't," I rasped. "I thought… at first I thought I could switch out, but I can't."

"You can't leave her," Art filled in.

"Yeah." I sat down in the grass, peering up at the cloudless sky. "I can't leave her."

"Well, I hope she's suffering just a *little*—"

"Don't even joke about that," I snapped.

"Jesus, you're touchy about her," Art muttered. "Mommy texted. They're expecting you the day after tomorrow in the Goldwing Marina."

Of course, they'd settle for nothing less than a superyacht to house their royal court, even temporarily. "Alright," I sighed wearily. What would that look like to show up without Sage at my side? Actually, more realistically, what would happen when I *didn't* answer their summons because I couldn't leave Sage's side, but she had refused to acknowledge our bond? Not many things incited fear in my gut, but that certainly did.

"Go eat a vapid communications major before you go bloodlust on the campus," Art suggested.

I grunted noncommittally and hung up. I had no interest in a vapid communications major… I craved only one person at the moment, and it was tearing me apart not to have her in my arms. But I was starving, and even vampires needed real food to keep strong, so after thinking through the implications, considering possible outcomes and consequences as I always did, I stood up and joined the thin crowd of students entering the dining hall. I needed food and Sage already knew I was following her. I didn't think it would hurt anything to let her see that I was still there with her.

I got in line behind a group of volleyball teammates, ignoring their gossip about their coach's relationship with the racquetball coach, and I listened as Sage's chewing stopped completely. She'd seen me, then. A ghost of a smile played on my lips, and I accepted a plate of beef stroganoff from the lunch lady. By the time I'd gotten a salad, fruit, and a soda, Sage still hadn't started eating again, so I turned slowly and caught her gaze with mine. She was sitting alone at a table, and she stood out for that fact alone. Everyone else had someone with them, but Sage remained alone in a sea of friendly chatter.

My heart squeezed painfully for her. There were inherent wards placed on a socium when they were born under the same starry ley lines as a vampire mate. Like a ley net, magic had surrounded her at birth, and had stayed with her right up until she'd matched with me. The wards were meant to protect the socium, keeping them from being harmed by others and preventing relationships with other people—matching with someone already in love would be something of a disaster. Now that we had matched, those wards should be lifting, replaced instead by our bond. Last night, her roommates had seemed friendly enough. But clearly, the many years of magical protection that kept Sage from making friends to sit with at lunch had made an impact on her social life. Seeing Sage alone in this way only stirred anger in my chest and guilt in my gut. I had never considered what that kind of life would be like, but I could see now how terribly lonely it must have been for Sage. My instincts screamed at me to go to her, to claim her, take her home, and surround her with the love of *my* family.

Instead, I sat across the room, blending in with a group of frat boys who gave me a somewhat confused glance, but then ignored me. I ate my food, watching Sage as she resumed her meal and looked at her phone. When it rang in her hand, she answered, and I sifted through the noise in the dining hall, straining to hear the conversation.

"Cassandra, hey," Sage said tightly.

"I heard you left the game last night," a fellow student snapped. "Are you for real right now?"

I clenched my fork. *Calm. Stay calm. She's a big girl. She can handle her own business.*

"I had something come up," Sage mumbled. "I'm sorry. But I got the stats and some footage I missed from the second half, and I'll have the article in. No worries."

"This is exactly why you were last on my list for coverage," the shrill woman seethed. "I swear to God, Sage. I knew you were going to screw this up."

The fork in my hand bent in half. Apparently, someone had a death wish.

"You said yourself it's just a scrimmage," Sage replied calmly. How was she still speaking with even a modicum of respect to this sewer rat? "And you asked for basic information only. I have that, and it will be in the exact same format your other articles are in."

"I honestly don't know how you're Malon Herriman's daughter. I know you only joined the paper because of your mom, and I know you only *got* a spot because of her," the nasally, dead woman continued.

I forgot about my food, and then I crumpled the fork in my hand like a ball of aluminum foil. One of the frat boys glanced at me with wide eyes. Sage answered softly, "I'll have the article for you tonight. Sorry."

The fork lost all semblance of what it had once been, solidifying into a hardened mass of cheap metal in my fist. *Whoever this Cassandra person is, she's about to be seven quarts of blood short of another breath.*

"Just get me the facts. I'll have to rewrite it anyway," Cassandra replied. Then she hung up, and Sage pulled the phone away from her ear, staring at the screen morosely.

"Dude," one of the frat boys said, drawing my attention. He looked from my fist to my eyes and back again. "That's wild. Is that a magic trick or something?"

"Or something." I dropped the clump of metal onto the tray and stood. My appetite was long gone, and I had a thirst for something entirely different, now. It had been a long time since I'd hungered for violence, but it seemed that this Cassandra person was long overdue for it.

Sage still hadn't moved, and most of her food sat untouched. Rage roiled inside me, scalding my rational thoughts and nearly spilling over. This was the "important thing" she had to do? Be abused and rejected by low-life upstarts from a college newspaper? From the *sports section*?

Suddenly, she sat up straight and tapped on her phone before bringing it to her ear. I disposed of my food, still listening as I slid the tray on top of a stack of dirty ones.

"Hello," a cheerful, older woman's voice said.

"Hey Mom," Sage sniffed. At least she had someone she could turn to. I was beginning to think Sage really had walked through this short life of hers entirely alone. "I need to talk to you."

"Of course, but honey, I've got a big piece on the upcoming election tonight, and we're going over talking points, so I have three minutes if that's alright." The woman sounded stressed, out of breath and clearly walking while she talked.

"I'll be quick," Sage promised. "It's just... I don't think reporting is my thing, Mom. I've been thinking about it—"

"Sage, please," her mother snapped, cutting her off with a harshness in her voice that grated on my already burning nerve endings. "We've been over this. There's no reason for you to *not* follow me into the business. I've already told the producers you'll be joining us as an intern in July."

I glanced at Sage again and found her hunched at the table, her hair falling in a curtain around her slight frame. "I know, but..." she petered off.

But you hate it, I thought, nearly screaming the rest of that sentence across the space between us. I'd known Sage for less than twenty-four hours and it was clear as day that she was miserable.

"We're going to be a legacy," the mother said with forced brightness. "You'll love it. You'll see. Give it a try and no fussing. I've got to go. Keep those grades up."

Sage practically caved in on herself, hunching forward and staring at the phone as it rested on her lap. She didn't eat anything else after that, and eventually, she stood slowly, like she was so weary she could barely move, and she deposited her food in the trash before trudging out of the brightly lit cafeteria. No one paused to tell her hello. No one held the door for her or waved in polite greeting. Sage Herriman was invisible.

And it was my fault.

Chapter Ten

SAGE

Immediately following the Marcus incident, I had half-ton weights attached to each of my feet. They dragged as I made my way to the urgent care, where they easily accepted my explanation of a box cutter gone wrong incident. I should have felt the stitches more, but I was numb, and not just from local anesthetic. I was sleepwalking, putting one foot in front of the other in a mechanical haze. I had just enough time to buy a T-shirt that wasn't stained with blood from the campus store before I made it to my 9:45 class.

I managed to get through my classes, diligently taking notes so I didn't fall behind, and then I spent my afternoon writing up the article that should have taken me thirty minutes but took much longer because I agonized over word choices and struggled to make it perfect so Cassandra would have no choice but to leave it alone. The less I heard Sam Eagle droning on about my lack of assertive tone, the better for my overall morale.

By the time I made it to my job at the movie theater, my whole body ached. My stitches were sore finally, tugging every time I opened a package of soft pretzels or hefted boxes from the back area to the concessions. My coworkers ignored me as they usually did, and I could have sworn that my boss looked surprised every time I showed up for work like he'd forgotten I even existed. At least tonight, he actually remembered I was there after I'd clocked in, and he called me by name when giving me assignments. Like my roommates, it was unusual, but I didn't have the strength to question it. Silas might as well have drained all my blood this morning for all the life I had left in me now.

The movie theater was huge, with a lobby that reached up several floors to a domed ceiling painted with classic movie characters and hanging chandeliers that lit the space with soft lighting. Red carpet covered the hallways, and carpeted walls kept the acoustics perfect for the moviegoers. I mostly did odd jobs around the theater, unpacking boxes, stocking concessions shelves, and walking around with a broom and scoop dustpan to sweep up stray kernels of popcorn. Today, I felt so bloodless, I could barely manage to shuffle from one place to the next with my head up.

It was only a four-hour shift from six to ten, but by the time I untied my apron and hung it up in the small employee breakroom, my arms and legs were sore, and my energy was at an all-time low. Maybe it was the near-death supernatural experience this morning. Or maybe it was just general exhaustion.

I'd been working my ass off for four years, now, but no matter what I did, no one noticed me. No one saw me. I was half-convinced my stalker vampire was the only being on this planet who actually gave a shit that I was still breathing.

Vampire. I'd allowed myself to think that word several

times throughout the day. I'd named him when I'd spotted him in the cafeteria. I'd labeled him in my memories as I went over and over the kiss he'd given me the day before. I'd let the term roll around in my brain until it made groove marks I could trace and feel familiar with. Vampire. My stalker was a vampire.

Accepting the impossible was surprisingly easy once it became an undeniable truth. He could lift ovens like I picked up my bath towel from the floor. He had an uncanny ability to follow me, and I suspected, to only be seen when he wanted. He'd beat the shit out of a terrifying nightmare monster with almost no effort. And…

My blood. He'd tasted my blood, and he'd liked it. He'd called me delectable. A shiver of pleasure raced through me as I entered my quiet apartment. The idea of Silas drinking my blood shouldn't have thrilled me. The idea of him putting his lips to my neck and filling his mouth with my essence shouldn't have sent goosebumps of expectant pleasure over my arms. But it did.

I found the small apartment dark and empty, and I remembered that it was Thursday night. My roommates all had long weekends in their schedules, and they often went off to friends' houses or parties to kick off their weekends. Normal college student things. And I usually took the weekend to get a head start on homework and stare at the sky through a lens. Not normal college student things. As I entered my dark bedroom and shut the door, staring at the open window that let a cool spring breeze into the space, I wondered if Silas was still close by. Did vampires have to sleep?

I bumped my fist against my forehead as I threw my backpack into the corner. "You are so stupid," I muttered to myself. I tore off my simple, lavender T-shirt with the Piedmont lion on the back, queuing up the rest of my night in my head. Pajamas first, and since the night was still warm and muggy, I chose a pair of silky shorts and a spaghetti strap top that I'd gotten for myself on a whim from a lingerie store last year. I definitely wasn't choosing it in case my creepy but hot-as-fuck stalker happened to glimpse me. Yes, that was psychotic. At this point, I wasn't sure any of my life was sane, anyway.

Then I resolved to make myself relax and ignore the stars, charting, and anything vaguely supernatural. I was going to watch a baking show and eat dry marshmallow cereal from the box, and then I was going to fall into a sugar coma and get some actual sleep tonight.

But as soon as I'd gotten dressed, my exhaustion caught up with me. I couldn't even find the energy to dig out my laptop and shuffle to the kitchen for a box of cereal. My bed called to me, rumpled and unmade though it was. My comforter was made of white linen, soft and warm, and once I turned on the small string of fairy lights over my bed, I found myself lulled into a state of sleepy immobility. I snuggled under the blankets and turned to stare at the open window.

Leaves rustled beyond it, and the warm spring breeze drifted across my face. I realized I was sweating, and when I glanced down, my hands were shaking again. What the hell? My heart wasn't as calm as my mind, either. It was beating fast, tapping against my breastbone and filling my ears with the rushing sound of blood racing through my veins. My shivering grew more pronounced, and then I realized what this was. It had to be some kind of latent shock after the events this morning. I'd resolutely ignored the horror of what I'd seen and experienced, but now that I was alone and unhurried, my body was getting its chance to react to everything.

Fucking bodies. I tried to remember if I'd had anything but coffee and a few bites of lunch today, but I hadn't. Not even water. The cut above my breast burned, and although my limbs had gone suddenly gelatin, I couldn't seem to actually relax.

I glanced at my dark room, and my eyes skipped over the shadows in the corners. They shifted, swirling and flicking like Marcus' skin had. I tightened my hold on my blankets, staring wide-eyed at them. *Please, no*, I thought with a sudden onslaught of tears that pricked at my eyes. *No more. I can't handle any more today.*

The shadows shifted again, and I cried out, shoving my body into the corner where my bed was wedged against the wall. Movement in my window pulled my attention suddenly, and I screamed just as a familiar form lowered himself from the window to my desk. Silas stepped carefully around the telescope and papers before bringing his long body off the desk to stand beside my bed. The soft glow of fairy lights illuminated his sharp features, which danced over me with concern.

My body relaxed immediately. No sane person would have relaxed if their stalker had climbed through their window in the middle of the night, but clearly, I was no longer lucid. Maybe I never had been.

"Sage?" he asked cautiously. His voice was so smooth, so low and lulling, it worked like a drug to my overstimulated system. My eyes flicked to the corner of the room and back to him. I still had the blankets pulled tightly to my chin, and I had crowded my body as far into the corner of the wall and the bed as I could. Silas glanced over his shoulder at what I now saw was a completely empty corner. With an understanding look back to me, he crossed the room and waved his hands around the shadows. "There's nothing there, Dulcis."

Feeling foolish, I lowered my hands and swallowed hard. "I-I know. *You* scared me."

Silas had his hands low on his hips, and he angled his face to me, half in the shadows and half lit by warm yellow light. His eyes flashed with a trace of humor. "I see." He returned to my bed, towering over me. It didn't intimidate me. I felt safe. "You've had a long day," he observed.

How much could he tell about my body's reactions? He couldn't read minds, could he? God, I'd never even asked. I'd had him to myself twice now, and instead of asking important questions, I'd run from him. I wasn't sure that made much sense anymore. "Do vampires sleep?"

My question seemed to surprise him. But after a flare of his eyes, his mouth relaxed, tipping up. Moving slowly, like he expected me to protest, he sat on the edge of my bed. "Yes, we do."

Fucking hell. He hadn't even denied the word. "How often?" I probed.

"Every night, just like you," he answered mildly. His eyes danced over me. "Keep going."

His encouragement was all I needed. "How do you… eat?" That was the big one, and I figured I might as well get it out of the way.

"I need about a pint of blood every two or three days, depending on how active I've been. But I also need regular meals like you do. I burn about six thousand calories a day."

I blinked in surprise. His face remained clear and open, and I didn't sense one iota of dishonesty in his words. "How… where do you—who do you—" *Whose neck are you sucking on and why the hell do I care?*

His smile widened a fraction. "Blood donors. I drink from a mug, usually."

"Your morning cup of Joe?"

There was a twitch in his smile, an almost laugh. "I see what you did there. It's all perfectly above board, and our donors are fully complicit."

I released a breath of relief. "You aren't like... hunting students or whatever?"

"Only if I'm *really* bored," he joked. He didn't move, still watching me closely. The interesting thing about Silas, I was beginning to see, was that he wasn't ashamed of what he was. He didn't so much as flinch at the fact that he relied on blood to survive. Perhaps it wasn't so different from humans sustaining themselves on dead animals, really.

"How were you made?" I asked next. My body was unwinding the more I was with him. Like it sensed he was safety, my tremors had eased, and my aching muscles untwisted themselves.

"When a daddy vampire and a human mate love each other *very much*," he began with a heavy dose of humor.

I bit down a smile. "Seriously? You were *born* this way?"

He nodded again. "Yes. All vampires are born to one vampire parent and a human mate."

"So... you can't turn people into vampires by biting them?"

He shook his head, clearly amused by my curiosity. "It's not that easy, I'm afraid."

"Sunlight?"

"Love it."

I scrunched one eye. "Garlic?"

"Best with butter and preferably over fried dough," he deadpanned.

I scratched my head, trying to remember all the lore

that had been circulating around vampires for years. "Are you impossibly fast and strong?"

He released a laugh, knowing exactly which sparkling vampire I'd been referring to. "Actually, that part is true. I'm a Sanguis vampire, and my kind is known for having increased strength and speed."

I tilted my head, and my hair fell over one shoulder. "Sanguis? How many of you are there?"

"Only about half a million around the world." Silas scratched his cheek, and I noticed for the first time that he had a shadow of a beard, now. He really was more human than I'd expected from a supernatural creature. He had tired shadows under his bright, green eyes, and although he was as breathtakingly handsome as ever, he did look tired. "Our percentage compared to the human population used to be higher, but our numbers have… slowed. Recently."

A line formed between my brows, and I drew up my knees to my chest. "How do you mean?"

He hesitated, skimming a look over me with some wariness. "Not as many ley matches."

I remembered what he'd said about the ley lines matching people together. From the sound of it, it was a completely random event, and if that was the only way for them to reproduce, then that *would* complicate things. "I see."

"You don't," he added with a half-smile. "There haven't been any ley matches around the world in eighty years."

My eyebrows shot up. "Wait… no one has had any babies in your—for your…" I scowled, fumbling over the words. What was he? A species? A creature? A person?

"Vampires of all kinds have stalled in reproduction," he confirmed gently. "We don't all feed on blood, but we do all depend on human beings to survive. We feed on them in various ways, but we also match with them. Recently, an unprecedented gap in matches has slowed our growth immensely. Especially compared to the boom in human population in the last century."

There was a lot to unpack there. "You don't all feed on blood? What do you mean?"

"I drink blood," he listed, ticking them off on his fingers. "Mentem feed on thoughts, incubi feed on desire, magicae feed on ley, and adfectus feed on emotions. I'm called a sanguis."

My mouth popped open. "There are different kinds of vampires? So, you don't all need to kill?"

"None of us kill our prey," he corrected. "At least, not the mentally stable ones. Apex predators aren't the deadliest, they're the most opportunistic. We rely on the human race, and whether they realize it or not, they rely on us. We've kept them from annihilating themselves through war for centuries. We would be fools to kill when we can utilize."

He had me there. It wasn't like he was keeping thousands of humans in disease-infested CAFOs like we did with livestock. As far as I knew. "How have I never heard of this before?"

"You have. Incubus were often thought to be demons, and rakshasas have been feared in India for many generations, although they are actually called magicae, and they take ley magic, not 'life force.' We've all been noticed at one time or another, but we don't divulge our secrets to mortals lightly. They tend to broadcast information, especially these days." Silas spoke calmly, like the existence of mythological beasts was no big deal. For him, I supposed it wasn't.

"What else is real?" I whispered, my mind conjuring a hundred different possibilities. What else walked among us? Genies? Basilisks? Ghosts? Were UFOs the work of supernatural creatures? How many humans went missing because of—

"I can practically hear your thoughts, and I'm not even a mentem," he chuckled. "Vampires account for most of the human myths around magical creatures. Vertos maybe the rest—those are shifters like your werewolf tales. Witches are a pain in the ass, but they are helpful. The fae," he bit out like it was a bitter curse, "have remained largely hidden."

"Like, fairies?" I asked incredulously.

"Put aside your visions of Tinkerbell and think more... demonic." His face twisted into a disgusted sneer. "The fae and vampires have fought for eons, and it all comes down to who the ley belongs to. The fae are responsible for all the ritualistic magic that has popped up throughout history. They perform rituals that feed the ley, and then the ley, in turn, feeds the vampires, vertos, and witches."

"Sounds complicated," I frowned.

"Immensely," he agreed. Silas glanced over his shoulder at the shadows that had scared me before. "Other than those species, we have to contend with wraiths. Shadow spirits."

I shivered, suddenly terrified all over again. "Do I want to know?"

Silas snared me with a steady, reassuring stare again. "Let's focus on us, for now. You're safe with me."

Like a warm hand smoothing away worry wrinkles on my brow, my fear eased a touch. "Okay. Tell me about you, then. There are different kinds of vampires... do you all get along?"

"Vampires are divided into five houses, as I've told you. We form cohorts when we are young adults to foster continued alliance between the houses. One vampire from each house joins the cohort, and we become our own unit; we make a family."

That sounded so cozy, even if it was vampires. I leaned my cheek on my knees. "Sounds nice."

He shrugged. "The brotherhood is an important bond."

"I didn't see any sisters." I frowned. "Do they do the same?"

"All vampires are males," he corrected.

My eyebrows shot up. "So, all mates are—"

"Women," he confirmed with a nod. "Not that we can't have relationships with other vampires or humans of all gender persuasions. But mating is a rather biological affair."

"And what if a vampire mate gives birth to a little girl? Do you throw them to the crocodiles?"

Silas gave me a reproachful frown. "I am not that sort of monster. As I said, there is biology at work here. Female offspring don't happen."

I kneaded my forehead with my fingertips. "That's a lot to take in."

"We can stop if you're overwhelmed," he said gently.

I took in the rigidity of his posture as he sat on the edge of my bed and the stark concern in his eyes. No one had ever looked at me like this before. No one had given me their attention so fully or been so invested in my reactions. It was a little addicting. "I need to know how all of this affects me."

His chest rose and fell as he took a breath to consider. "You are not human, as I mentioned once."

"What am I?"

"A ley socium," he replied. His eyes crinkled a little at the corners. "You hold more ley in your body than even the fae. You were born under a constellation of powerful ley lines, both above you and below you. Your star chart matches mine."

"Is this my Hogwarts acceptance letter?" I asked hopefully. "Can I kick ass like you did?"

He snorted. "I'm not sure any socium has ever wanted to… kick ass. Mostly the ley inside of you is meant to keep you alive so our lifetimes continue on in tandem."

"But *could* I?" I pressed.

He thought about that. "You could. But I don't know what kind of training that would involve. A long time ago, a woman did it. She killed herself in the process, though."

That strangely made sense. "Because it was the same energy that kept her alive."

"Correct." He swished a hand through the air. "Her vampire mate was a fool. He died with her, and their child mourns the loss to this day."

"How long do you—we—usually live?"

Silas held my gaze steadily. "Forever."

I started in surprise. "What do you mean 'forever?'"

"Our oldest being, our most ancient elder, has been alive for more than four thousand years. He looks like he's in his seventies," Silas said with some wryness. "A healthy seventy-something, at that."

My brain could barely comprehend that. "How is that possible?"

"Exponentially decreasing aging model." He shrugged off his jacket and folded it on the bed neatly. "We age at a decreasing rate rather than an increasing one."

I looked up in thought. "That's got to be one hell of a math equation."

"We have a lot of years to learn it," he admitted.

I returned my gaze to his, captivated by their forest hue. "How many years for you?"

"I was born in 1442." He watched me closely for my reaction.

I gave him what he was looking for, sitting up and flaring my lashes in shock. "Shut up."

He chuckled again. "I was a baby for almost a hundred years, if that helps."

"Not really," I squeaked. "Wait, vampire babies take an entire human lifetime to grow up?"

"Vampire mothers are incredibly patient," he replied seriously.

"Jesus," I muttered, looking away. I didn't want to consider my role in that statement. That made me intensely uncomfortable to think about on a serious level. I shifted, looking down at my blanket as I adjusted it needlessly. "And, you say I'm this socium. I'm linked to you."

I sensed him leaning forward even before I looked up again. His body was so long, so enormous on my twin bed, he barely had to reach out to tilt my chin up with a gentle nudge. "I can't sleep or eat until you are safe, Sage. Look at my face and tell me I'm lying."

I did, running my eyes over his haggard features. My throat slid as I swallowed nervously. "Why am I not worrying about you the same way, then?"

"Because I'm the one who does the ass-kicking," he said with a rueful half-smile. "That's kind of the way it works."

My lip curled slightly. "That's not very gender equal."

"Nothing in life is equal," he argued, sitting back. "Many human women can, do, and will kick ass. Many human men prefer to care and nurture. We can choose our paths to an extent, but when you are a socium, and I am a vampire…" he shrugged. "Our fates are written in the ley lines."

Well, it wasn't like I was a superhero on the front lines

somewhere. I loved looking at the stars. And I craved safety more than I craved adventure, just by nature. "Hm."

"If it makes you feel better," he added, a touch rueful, "all witches are females. They're our polar opposite. First born daughters inherit their power, and their mates are always male."

"Badass," I smiled hesitantly.

"Pain in the ass," he corrected, his sharp features still gentle. "When you meet one, you'll agree with me."

When, he said. I looked down again, plucking at a loose thread on the linen comforter. "What do your brothers think about all of this?"

"They're ecstatic," he replied without hesitation. "To have our cohort be the first in so long to find a mate to love and protect? It's wonderful."

"Wait," I lifted my head swiftly. "You don't mean they *all*—"

"No," Silas said firmly. "No, you're mine. Only mine. But they will be like brothers to you."

Only mine. My heart sang, and I told it to shut the hell up. "Silas, I have a life."

He didn't respond to that, looking away in thought instead. Finally, he shifted a bit closer to me, and his hand rested near my foot as he leaned back on it. This close, I could detect his masculine scent and see the pores on his nose and the length of his lashes. He looked so very human. So tangible. "May I ask you questions now?"

Chapter Eleven

SAGE

I hadn't expected him to care about my mundane life. I blinked. "There isn't much to know."

Undaunted, he pressed on. "Who are your parents?"

I searched for my phone, and when I found it, I brought up a picture of my mom. "My mom is Malon Herriman. You've probably seen her on the news."

He dipped his head, confirming that. "Yes, I've seen her. Your father?"

I shrugged. "They split when my mom was young. She just says I shouldn't worry about him."

Silas squinted a speculative eye. "And she lives in New York?"

"Yeah."

"What's your major?"

I gave him an incredulous look. "You can't actually be interested in any of this. Not when you live with mind readers and fight shadow dudes."

"I assure you," he said seriously, "I'm very interested in you."

Blood tinted my cheeks. "Media relations."

"So, you're following in your mother's footsteps?"

"Mhm." I tried not to hesitate when I said that. It would be beyond embarrassing to admit to this clearly intelligent, practically ancient god that I had spent four years of my life earning a degree I didn't want.

Silas saw through me. "You don't enjoy it."

"That wasn't a question."

He leaned closer to me. How had we drifted so near? I'd long left the corner of the bed, and he'd managed to get so close, I could feel the heat from his arm against my leg. "That's because I heard your conversation in the cafeteria."

I started in surprise. "You did? How?"

He ignored my question. "Why are you majoring in that when you hate it?"

"Because of my mom," I admitted. "She wants me to."

"Your life might not be short anymore, but don't waste your time on pursuits that don't bring you joy." He moved again, this time pressing his side against my shins and reaching up to lightly stroke my bare arm. "You are far too beautiful to spend your days frowning, Dulcis."

Goosebumps rippled along my arms and down my legs. I stared at him in the darkened bedroom, transfixed. "I don't want to be a reporter or a news anchor," I admitted.

Silas took my hand in his, and as he balanced it on my knees, we both stared at our fingers, joined and sharing warmth. "Your dreams are yours to fulfill, Sage. But you don't have to do it alone anymore."

My throat tightened, and I couldn't seem to take my eyes off his large hand as it enveloped mine. "This is all really crazy. You know that, right?"

His thumb caressed the back of my hand gently. "It would be if we did not both feel the ley connection between us. But I do. And I know you feel something as well, or you would not have sat idly by as I invaded your personal space."

My lips twisted wryly, and I flicked a look back to his intense features. "Aren't you a predator? Maybe that's what you do. You lull me into complacency before you strike."

Silas moved so quickly, I couldn't track the motion. Suddenly his arms were on either side of my body, supporting his weight as he hovered his lips over my neck. I gasped, leaning back, but his enormous body had covered mine, and I was lost in his scent and his strength. His warm breath skimmed across my sensitive skin, and he whispered, "I am a predator. You think I would be this careful with your feelings if I was snacky?"

"Are you?" I squeezed out. "Snacky, I mean?"

"A little," he murmured, and his tongue caressed the side of my neck in a way that sent heat coiling between my legs. "Are you offering?"

Yes, take me! "I'm not sure that's wise," I said, my voice strained.

"Probably not," he demurred, but the tip of his nose continued up the side of my throat, following the line his tongue had started. He inhaled softly. "You smell like heaven, Sage. You have no idea."

I had a bit of an idea. He smelled like paradise, like safety and cozy winter nights. I wanted to curl into him and lose myself in this momentary feeling that I belonged. I tilted my head back, letting my hair hang and my pulse lay exposed for him. "You could show me. What if I'm just a really horny virgin? Maybe the connection is imagined."

He reached my jawline, and his lips skimmed it, the chapped texture of his lips chafing my skin. "Should we test that? I'm happy to pleasure your body until your mind catches up."

My core throbbed, suddenly more needy than I could ever remember. Moisture gathered between my legs, and my nipples hardened at the thought of this man showing me what pleasure could be. What was the worst that could happen, really? He wanted to fuck me. I wanted to be fucked. No one had so much as looked twice at me my entire life, let alone showed an interest in having sex with me. So, I had a crazy vampire stalker, and he wanted to pleasure me. Was that really so wrong? *It's weird. But it's not wrong.* "Sounds scientifically sound," I whispered, and my eyes fluttered closed as his lips grazed mine.

Silas kissed me, his warm lips capturing mine like he intended to never let go. He molded his mouth to mine effortlessly, coaxing my lips apart and then sliding his tongue in a suggestive rhythm that had me pressing my thighs together tightly. I arched into him, and his free hand traced the deep, lacy V of my tank top. My skin thrummed under his touch, pulsing and warming, and I suddenly wanted that touch everywhere. I wanted his skin on mine, his body joined to mine, his very essence one with me. I wanted to be filled by him and used by him, drained and sated and boneless with fulfilled desire.

For once, my thoughts quieted. They faded away, lost to the heat spreading through my body, beginning low in my belly and fanning up to my breasts and deep between my pulsing sex. Suddenly, I couldn't stand feeling so empty, and I lifted my hips, searching for pressure. Silas slipped a finger under the neckline of the silky top, and he moved it back and forth, teasing my sensitive skin as he drew closer to my nipple. I moaned softly, and I felt his smile against my lips.

"Dulcis," he whispered into my panting mouth. "I was

only half serious. I won't take advantage of your sexual desire if your mind and heart don't agree."

I wasn't sure where my mind began and my body ended anymore. Every part of me screamed for him. "I want," I began, but then I hesitated. What did I want? The last two days had been nothing but struggle, fear, and confusing desire mixed together to form a muddy palette in my brain. But I knew what my body sighed for now. I knew what my heart longed for. "I just want to feel whole."

He hummed against my skin, kissing me again before moving his lips down my throat. "Be specific, Dulcis Mea."

"I want you here," I whispered, moving his hand to my breast. I slid my left hand under the blankets and between my legs. "And here."

His strong hand kneaded my breast through the thin, chocolate silk that almost perfectly matched my eyes. When he skimmed his palm lightly over my nipple, rolling the sensitive bud, I gasped as intense need throbbed at the apex of my sex. His mouth kissed a searing path to my breasts, and as he pressed the tip of one finger to the peak of my left nipple, his other hand slipped the straps of my top down my arms. Then my breasts were bare to the cool spring air, and his warm breath caressed the tip of one nipple as his fingers lightly pinched the other.

I moaned louder, lifting my hips to find his thigh there between my legs. It was just enough pressure, and yet, not nearly enough. I writhed over the pillows, flat on my back now and at the mercy of the delicious sensations he was eliciting through every nerve ending in my heated body. I'd felt desire before, and I'd even enjoyed a handful of decent orgasms on my own but nothing like this. Nothing this intense. I bucked against his thigh in a needy rhythm, applying pressure to my aching clit as he slid his tongue against my nipple. The sensation rocked my fucking world. I groaned, lifting my breasts and silently begging him for more.

Silas teased my left nipple with his fingers and gently bit the other, swirling his tongue in a circle around the most sensitive part of the peak. My face grew branding-iron hot, and I breathed hard, rocking against his leg and giving myself over to his assault. The tightening climb to an orgasm at my core felt both electrifying and terrifying at the same time. I didn't know what it would be like to crash into this release, but I knew it would shatter me inside and out.

Silas moved his lips to the other breast, and he paused before dropping a kiss just below the gauze that had been taped to my wound. It was only then I realized it hadn't hurt since Silas had been with me. "I am sorry, Dulcis."

"It's fine," I breathed out. "Just please," I huffed. "Please don't stop."

He released a breathy laugh, kissing around the tender wound again. "I will not stop until you ask me to." He helped me to sit up, but it was only so he could carefully remove my top.

Still panting, I grasped his white T-shirt, tilting my face up to his. "You don't ever seem ashamed that you're a vampire. Where's the 'stay away from me; I'm a monster' speech?"

His lips curved into another smile, and he leaned down to kiss me softly. "I will never apologize for being a monster. I will not apologize for knowing the exact scent of your blood." He inhaled, moving to my neck again while his large hands settled on my bare waist. "I will not apologize for having the strength to move your soft body in ways that bring you pleasure." He lifted me so seamlessly, so suddenly, I found myself on my hands and knees in an instant. Silas bent to drop a kiss along my spine, his hands smoothing up my hips to my ass. "I will not apologize for hearing the flutter of your frantic heartbeat as I make you come so hard, you see stars."

I moaned, leaning forward and lifting my ass. He bracketed it with his warm palms, sliding them over the silk of my shorts. "I will not apologize, Dulcis. Because I was made for you, and you for me."

Did this man have any flaws? Perhaps that was evidence of his claims in its own right. I'd never been touched like this by another man. I'd never been pleasured and aroused to the point where my pussy throbbed and my whole being begged for release. But Silas seemed to know what I wanted, and as he kissed my back, following the valley of my spine downward, his right hand slipped under the sliver of fabric that covered my soaked sex. The tips of his fingers swirled through my slick folds, and I moaned loudly, pressing my face into the mattress.

"Gods, you're perfect," he rasped, dipping one finger into my pussy and then swirling up to my aching clit. "So wet and begging for my cock."

I wanted his cock. His mouth. His fingers. I'd take anything he gave me. "Please," I whispered harshly, gripping the sheets.

"Touch yourself," he commanded gently. "Show me how you pleasure yourself."

I hesitated, lifting my head. Shyly, I peeked over one shoulder where he was kneeling behind me. "I… don't. Not much," I admitted.

His eyes had gone from stormy to tempestuous sea, and although he seemed to be thinking, watching my blushing reaction, his finger entered me again, stretching me slowly. I lost focus, eyes fluttering closed, and I leaned my forehead against the mattress.

"Hm," he hummed thoughtfully. "Shall we discover your favorites together then, Dulcis? Tell me; do you like this?" He slid his first two fingers back to my clit where he pinched it gently between them, rubbing up and down slowly.

I jumped, and my core clenched in the most gratifying way. "Oh," I moaned.

His fingers shifted, pressing hard against my clit and moving in delicious circles. "*Oh*," I moaned again, this time a little louder. "Fuck," I hissed.

"Getting somewhere," he murmured. "Use your words, Sage. Yes or no?"

"Yes, yes, please don't stop," I begged. But he changed his technique again, rubbing back and forth across my clit, and I gasped. "Oh yes. Yes, that. That. Please, *please*, Silas."

While his right hand worked my clit, his left hooked the slit of my silk shorts and tugged hard. The fabric ripped like it was nothing more than tissue paper, and I couldn't even find it in my dazed mind to care. He slipped one large finger into my tight heat, and slowly, steadily, pushed until I stretched around him. I let out a high-pitched, wordless sound, smashing my face into the mattress and pushing back on his finger.

I was so close, now. I surged high, clenching and tightening close to an orgasm. But Silas slowed his right hand over my clit, massaging along the side of it as he eased a second finger inside of me. He groaned. "Fuck, you feel so tight."

I moaned again, clutching the sheets. "I'm so close. Please."

"I love the sound of you begging," he said, his voice husky. "You are so gorgeous, Dulcis. So soft and perfect.

Arch your back for me." I obliged, arching my back and pressing him deeper into my soaked pussy. He twisted his fingers inside of me, and I swore that white dots danced across my closed eyes.

"Oh my God," I panted.

Then he was pumping his fingers in and out of me, slowly at first and in time with the rhythm he worked over my clit. Then he picked up the pace, and soon he was fucking me hard with his fingers, filling me and igniting hidden nerves of desire that jettisoned me straight to the top of the orgasmic stratosphere. I couldn't hold back my release any more than I could keep from pulling in my next desperate breath. As he bent to kiss the valley of my lower back, murmuring praise and encouraging me to let go, I broke around his fingers. The orgasm clenched and then snapped through me, sending me into blissful waves of euphoric release.

I expelled a shocked breath and a gratified moan, my hands relaxing as I melted into a puddle of muscle and tissue, completely boneless while I came down from my high. Silas didn't move me, but he did remove his hands so he could support my hips while I gave into the longest, most intense orgasm I'd never even dreamed of.

When my breathing had calmed, and I slumped onto my stomach, Silas held his weight over me, kissing my cheek tenderly. "Are you alright?"

I slid a side look his way. "No. I think you killed me."

A rueful grin tugged his lips up. "Death by orgasm would be a rather embarrassing failure on my part, I think."

"Or an incredible flex," I challenged, lifting a lazy finger.

He smoothed his hand up the back of my thigh and over my ass. "If you felt that was a flex, then I look forward to the sounds you make when I actually," he bent to kiss my shoulder and move his lips against my skin, "take you."

I shivered happily at the prospect. That had been so mind-blowing, I had a hard time imagining it feeling better. My eyes began to close, but then Silas lifted me off the mattress and into his arms. It was only then I realized I was fully naked, my tattered shorts and flimsy top long gone, and Silas was still dressed in his white T-shirt and jeans. I looked between us as he lifted me into his arms. "Uh," I began.

"'Uh,' what?" he teased, walking across the room like I weighed nothing. "You're just now realizing I fucked you naked?"

"Does that count as fucking?" I mused, letting go of the issue of my nudity for the time being. Or forever. I was finding that there were things I probably *should* feel a certain way about, but around Silas, those concerns melted like cotton candy on my tongue.

"A part of me was fully inside of you," he said dryly. "Yes."

"So… am I a virgin?" I challenged. He was headed for the bathroom, and I leaned my head on his shoulder, riding the wave of whatever this was and just enjoying how I felt in his arms.

His mouth pulled to the side. "I suppose you are… arbitrarily." He hooked me with a stern glare. "But I'm only acquiescing to that because our kind makes that distinction for breeding purposes."

My face went chili pepper red. "Breeding?"

He shrugged, unaffected by my embarrassment. "That is the way the elders view things. My parents' generation is a little more romantic."

"How charming," I drawled.

Silas seemed to find that amusing, and as he set me on the laminate bathroom countertop, he took my face in his hands. This felt somehow more intimate than what we'd just done, staring straight into his green eyes and looking up at him while I was fully naked on the bathroom sink. He held my gaze seriously. "We are what you say we are. Nothing more. Nothing less. I will find a way to make this what *you* desire, Dulcis. You have my word."

My throat clogged with emotion, but I managed to choke out, "Okay."

"Now." He released me and stepped away. "I'll leave you alone to shower." He glanced around our small, three-piece bathroom with its boring beige color scheme and somewhat outdated bathtub and vanity. "Would you like me to leave or to stay?"

I angled my face away from him, cinching one eye. "Will you be right below my window refusing to sleep if I send you away?"

"Yes," he said with deadpan honesty.

I couldn't help the smile that crinkled the corners of my eyes. "Then… I guess… stay."

I didn't know what we were, yet. But I knew how Silas made me feel, and I knew I wanted more of that right now. Maybe that was all that needed to matter at the moment.

He kissed my forehead before backing out. "Then I will be with you."

Chapter Twelve

SILAS

I slept curled around Sage like a cat. She'd put on a large nightshirt after her shower, and the combination of her tea tree oil shampoo and natural, earthy scent had made my mouth water in the worst way. But I wanted to hold her so much more than I wanted to taste her, so when she stumbled back to bed like a half-asleep zombie, I had pulled her into my arms and curved my body around her small one. We'd both fallen asleep so fast, I was surprised I remembered it.

Now dawn had crept through the bedroom window, and I sat up slowly, propping my head on my hand to get a better view of Sage's features while she slept. She had turned so she faced my chest, and her knees were drawn up and hands under her chin. Her long, wavy hair streamed over her shoulders and fanned out behind her in a chestnut spread, and I gave into the temptation to slide a strand of it between my fingers. She was perfect. Every expression, every thought that crossed her features so plainly, every inquisitive question and shrewd defiance—perfect.

Even the comical way she scrunched her nose as she dreamed seemed too good to be true. What was the catch, exactly? I was supposed to believe that the ley magic had matched me to this flawless angel with pink lips and long lashes, no questions asked? Never had the ley felt more magical than it did now as I stared down at Sage, warm and safe in my arms.

Gradually, as the morning brightened and Sage continued to sleep, the latent fire in my throat grew to an inferno. Bloodthirst was the worst kind of discomfort imaginable. It coated my windpipe with burning ash and caused my gums to ache. Eventually, the burn would spread to my stomach, and then my intestines, scorching me from the inside. If a sanguis ignored their thirst long enough, it would wither their body to embers. I was nowhere near that now, of course, but the discomfort had intensified, and if I didn't have more to drink than the mouthful of Sage's blood I'd swallowed yesterday, I knew I would pay for it for weeks to come. It was like an athlete training for marathons for three days with no water. There were usually unpleasant consequences.

Sage stirred finally, her long lashes sweeping up and flaring as she realized who was in her bed. She really had the most remarkable eyes, expressive and wide, and a rich hue like polished mahogany that only deepened as her pupils dilated and she scanned me from head to torso and then back again. I had no issue remaining still while she processed what she was seeing; when someone lived for as many years as I had, time felt different. When time was limitless, it lost value, and when it lost value, the need to use it efficiently dissipated. I could have stayed like this in her bed for hours if not for the thirst that clawed open wounds along the inside of my trachea.

Finally, she licked her lips, and I tracked the movement like a hungry predator. "I thought maybe I dreamed all of that," she rasped out at last.

Her voice was so rich and rough first thing in the morning, like a warm, wool sweater, and I took a moment to let it settle on my skin. I resisted the urge to reach for her in case I disturbed that still moment between dreams and daylight, where the impossible still hung on the scales in balance with the possible. "Dream or reality, do you feel safe?"

She considered that. Finally, she admitted, "I do."

I tightened my hold on her, drawing her closer to me. She willingly obliged, sighing contentedly and melting into me. "Then, let's enjoy it either way."

Her breath warmed my shirt, reminding me that I had yet to really *feel* her against me, and the possessive animal that had awakened inside of me grumbled unhappily at that. I hadn't had impatient instincts like this since the seventeenth century. Sage's fingers tightened on my shirt, and then she lifted her face to mine again. "I have to work," she mumbled unhappily.

"Ah, so it is reality," I smiled.

"Unfortunately." As she pulled away from me, I swallowed another scratchy, fiery lump in my throat and forced air into my lungs. It was like standing over a bed of coals and breathing in the heat. Christ, I couldn't remember my thirst being this bad.

I gave Sage some room as she awkwardly crawled out of the bed and tugged her nightshirt to her thighs. She glanced around momentarily. "Um, so, I don't think I've ever…" She winced, like her words pained her. "I'm not sure what the protocol is, here. Do you want coffee? Or something?" Her grimace deepened, and I knew she likely had a dozen self-deprecating thoughts hammering away in her head.

I resisted the urge to laugh, keeping my features smooth instead. "I know," I assured her. "We've been over the virgin thing. Coffee sounds great."

Sage ran a hand through her thick hair. "I'm sorry. It's just that no one even looks at me, normally. I don't really have friends who do this either."

My eyes fell a touch, sagging with worry. "That would be the wards that were placed around you at birth. It was to keep you… safe."

"Safe?" She echoed, dropping her hand and tilting her head. "From what? That thing like Marcus? And what's a ward?"

I slid out of the bed, rolling my shoulders and sighing. "I'll tell you more, but if I may be candid?"

She choked, swallowing a laugh. "Your age is showing."

Americans. Like the English language wasn't the garbage disposal of etymology anyway. "Let me real," I drawled, leveling a stern look her way, but it only made her shoulders hunch with another laugh. "Coffee is nice, but if I don't drink some blood, I'm going to get 'hangry' before we make it to lunch."

Her eyes widened again, owlish with curiosity. "What happens when you're hangry?"

I couldn't resist messing with her just a *little*. I leaned forward, expecting her to shy away, but she drifted into me, pulled by the same invisible tether that continually urged me to close the distance between us. So, I bent and kissed the curve of her neck. Her blood thrummed through her carotid artery, fluttering with a delicious, steady tempo that made my gums itch. Schooling myself, and drawing on what was thankfully centuries of experience, I straightened again and gave her a dark half-smile. "I speak like an old guy."

She breathed a laugh out her nose, but her eyes traveled

over my face, searching for the signs that I was as ravenous as I'd told her. She wouldn't find any. I wouldn't let her. "Well, you should go, then. No hurt feelings if you don't drink my coffee that may or may not be stale, actually."

"Whether or not I stay for coffee isn't the issue—" I began. But then I heard footsteps coming from the living room to the hallway outside her bedroom, and I sighed. "Your roommate needs her work uniform."

"How do you know?" Sage asked with a healthy dose of suspicion.

I tapped my ear. "These work ten times better than yours."

"Oh." Sage shifted her eyes, clearly perplexed.

"She came into the bedroom late last night and then made a hasty retreat after she realized I was with you."

Sage's cheeks went peony pink. "Aren't you even a little embarrassed you got caught in my bed?"

I lifted an eyebrow. "Is there something embarrassing about having your naked body wrapped around mine, Dulcis?"

Through clenched teeth, she muttered, "Scud bucket."

"What is a scud bucket?" I asked with serious concern about her mental stability.

Then there was a tentative knock at the door, and Sage called out a breezy "Come in!" like that might mitigate her clear discomfort at this situation.

Her roommate entered, heavy eyeliner smudged and silk bonnet askew on her head from where she'd slept on the couch. The roommate gave me a slow once-over. "Oh. He's still here."

"Who, him?" Sage asked, hooking a thumb to me as hysteria crept into her tone. "He's just… like a security guard. For me."

The roommate gave me a deadpan glare. "What's he protecting, your pussy?"

If I am, I'm not doing a very good job, I thought with way too much satisfaction. Sage choked out something between a laugh and a sound of distress. "He's just—" She gave up. "Yeah, he might be here... sometimes."

That animal inside of me purred happily. She hadn't *quite* grasped the situation, but at least she'd accepted that I wasn't going anywhere.

"Cool," the roommate intoned, shooting me another distrustful glare. "Can I use our bathroom now?"

"Yes," Sage said quickly, taking a step back. "Go ahead. We were just going."

"You should get dressed," I advised as her roommate went to the bathroom and shut the door.

Sage glanced down at her nightshirt. "I mean, yeah, I have work in like two hours. I'll get dressed as soon as Zoe is out of the bathroom."

"No, now," I clarified. "That's what I was trying to tell you. I do need to go home, but I'm not leaving you here alone."

Sage let her hands fall to her sides again, and this time, her inquisitive look took on a scalpel's edge. "Sorry, what?"

She was a smart girl. I knew she understood what I was implying. "Sage, I'm doing my best to be patient, but you can't just—"

She backed away a step, glaring. "I told you, I'm not dropping my entire life, even if this," she motioned between us "is real."

Well, if that wasn't humanity in a nutshell, I didn't know what was. *"I acknowledge the truth of what you're saying, and yet, I refuse to comply."* I rubbed my face. "Let me try to explain this a better way. If I do not drink, I will be in pain. I *am* in pain.

It's extremely uncomfortable to go this long with bloodthirst. But as desperate as I am to solve that issue, I also cannot leave you. I've tried to have my brothers come instead. My instincts won't allow it."

She blinked once, folding her arms. "Is that supposed to guilt me?"

God's blood, she was stubborn. Normally, I liked that in a woman—I liked pleasuring them with punishments over it, too—but at this moment, I could have throttled her. "I'm merely illustrating to you the gravity of what I'm saying. If it was simply a matter of *liking you* and wanting to be near you, I could certainly leave for a few hours and see you another time. But that isn't what we have between us. And you are in danger, as you witnessed yesterday." *You were also terrified last night even if you didn't want to admit it.*

Panic crawled over her features, and I watched as her thoughts played out in real-time in her micro-expressions. Realization, stubbornness, fear, and finally, anger. "If you were just going to carry through with the kidnapping bit, then you might as well have done it back at the stadium. I have not changed my mind."

And I was out of time. So, we were at an impasse, and although I had made some strides with my lovely bride-to-be, the societal norms ingrained in her from birth about what relationships were, what was healthy, and what was normal were still overriding her intuition. I didn't bother arguing with her about it anymore. She'd made her wishes clear, despite the facts laid before her, and I didn't have the patience or well-fed decision-making skills to come up with anything better.

Before she could protest, I had her over my shoulder and out the bedroom door. She inhaled sharply, her hands bracing her body against my back, and then we were outside the apartment, my fast, powerful legs carrying us both impossibly far before she could even get out a word of protest. "You have *got* to be kidding me," she seethed.

She was likely disoriented at the speed I was going, and no one would fully register what they had seen, either. So, I didn't pause to explain to Sage why I was *actually* kidnapping her this time. I had a feeling that her deeply entrenched ideas about what she should be making a priority would override the facts about her being in danger. Also, I hadn't told her about my parents, yet. We had twenty-four hours, maybe less, before they summoned us, and I needed time to prepare Sage for this world she was entering.

It wasn't much of a courtship, one day of stalking and a night of finger fucking… but, hell, it was what I had.

"Silas," Sage gasped, trying to lift herself off of me. She was so soft and small, so perfectly lush in my arms, and her nightshirt had ridden up, exposing her underwear. I tried not to think about it. I failed. It was hard to school my thoughts when my whole being sang a chorus of longing for her.

We reached my car just as she came to enough awareness to really fight me, but I gently hefted her off my shoulder and deposited her into the passenger seat of the white SUV. She pushed at me, her features clearly livid. "Get off me. You cannot be serious right now."

I buckled her in, shut the door, and had myself in the driver's side in half a breath. The doors were already locked when she tried the handle, and then I started the car. "I wish I wasn't. I'm sorry, Dulcis."

"Don't you dare call me that," she hissed.

She undid her seatbelt, but I smoothly pulled it back down and buckled it again. "We're already driving, and you are still mortal enough to fly through that windshield." I spared her a glare. "Do not make me tie you to the seat."

Sage glanced out of the windshield to find me already driving safely through the parking lot. "How did we get here?"

"I walked," I replied honestly. Alright, a little smugly.

She stared ahead for a few seconds in silence. Finally, she said, "I'm officially rejecting this reality."

"Not allowed," I countered lightly. "Let me show you my world, first. Let me show you *your* world instead of explaining the parts of it that don't fit into the mortal reality. Then, I swear on my mother's own blood, I will allow you to choose your fate."

Sage flicked a look down to my hand on her seatbelt and back to me meaningfully. "Something is telling me that's a load of chicken shit."

"I promise," I reiterated, looking away from the road long enough to hold her gaze. "You will have plenty of time to acclimate and decide how to go forward. But not when your life is in danger out here. I'm taking you to a place I know you'll be safe, and we can figure the rest out later."

"And where is that? The Pentagon?" she asked caustically.

I scoffed, returning my eyes to the road. "Don't insult our wards. Human structures are plywood. Hollowhall is tungsten in comparison. Metaphorically." I glanced at her again. "It's actually just a house. But the magical wards around it make it the safest place on the Eastern Seaboard."

"What's the safest place on the *West* Coast?" she challenged, folding her arms.

Cheeky. "Stormridge," I replied easily. "The cohort there is young, but they take safety seriously." I grinned, mostly to myself. "They are going to hate me for matching when they didn't."

"Yes, we're all very lucky," she glared, arms still folded tightly and gaze shredding me to paper ribbons.

She would forgive me eventually. Maybe. I drove west, skirting around Kingston proper and taking winding, shaded roads that sank deeper into forested acres. As we climbed in altitude, I glanced at Sage again. She had sat back in her seat, arms under her breasts and pointer finger tapping her bicep like the twitch of an irritated cat's tail. Had I completely fucked this up? I scrubbed my hand over my jaw, swallowing hard against the burning chunk of bloodthirst lodged in my throat.

Eventually, the suburban developments melted away, and we climbed up a ridge that overlooked the Catskill Mountains to the west. Sage sat forward in her seat as we drove up the long driveway to Hollowhall, stretching out her neck to peer at the modern construction home that rose into view as we crested the hill.

The driveway curved in front of the house, which had three floors and a cedar shingle exterior. It was essentially the modern equivalent of a split level, with an entrance to the bottom floor next to a one-car garage out front. Stairs along the right-hand side of the home led directly to a living room on the second floor. I knew there was a larger, five-car garage along the back of the mansion, but I tapped an app on my forearm projection and opened the smaller, one-car garage at the front of the house.

"It looks like a storybook house on roids," Sage commented in a thin voice.

My lips twitched up, and I pulled the SUV into the pristinely clean garage. I didn't have a mechanical hobby, so there were no tools, and I preferred to keep things minimalist if I could. As I shut off the car, Sage's fingers went back to tapping her biceps in irritation. I turned in my seat to rest my cheekbone on my fist. "Let's hear it."

Sage's gaze flitted subtly as she thought. It hadn't taken me long, but already, I had figured how Sage operated—she would think before speaking. She would organize the words into coherent sentences like she was writing a newspaper article. For someone who didn't enjoy the field, she was clearly skilled at it. Finally, she hooked me with a steely glare. "I may be bound to you, but I should be free to choose what that looks like."

Sucker punch to the gut. I rubbed my two-day beard growth, and the scraping sound joined with her nervous breaths in the quiet car. "That is true," I admitted.

"So, *abducting me*," she went on, gradually losing her contemplative cool, "doesn't at all fit with what I want this to look like."

I chewed the inside of my lip, considering the best way to impart the gravity of our situation to Sage without completely freaking her out. I didn't know how fragile human psyches were anymore. I sometimes had sex with human women, but I usually compelled them to forget it had ever happened afterward as a protection. It had been a long time since I'd introduced someone non-vampire to our way of life.

"What you saw yesterday was one small, isolated example of what might be coming for you, Dulcis. The fae do not like vampire matches. They seek to consume them, to end their lives and empty the ley back into their ley pools," I said.

Sage's lips went pale. "They want to kill me?"

"They find you to be the very worst kind of threat—you hold more ley in your body than any other creature on earth. And you have the potential to add to their enemies' numbers. They will take you at any cost."

She blanched. "Why didn't you just lead with that?"

I traced a circle around her face. "Because of that. You look like you're going to pass out."

"Better unconscious than dead," she snapped back. "How many of those… how many are there?"

"Many," I replied calmly. "And not to add to your distress, but the fae are not the only ones who know about your existence now. My parents will want to meet you. The leader of my house, Sanguis, will wish to see you."

Her throat bobbed. "Oh."

The stark fear in her eyes brought me no pleasure, but at least she had a better understanding of our circumstances. Clearly, I needed to stop underestimating her. "So, that said, you are safe here. I would much rather you be safe and angry with me than pleased with your freedom and dead."

Her lips flattened, and she looked out of the windshield at the darkened garage. "I see."

Unfortunately, I believed that she did. "Sage," I said quietly. She slid a reluctant look back to me. "I know you didn't choose this, but I want you to. Eventually."

"Well," she replied with a hint of a whip strike in her voice, "the ley can't control how I feel. So, here we are."

Fair enough. Nodding again, I opened the driver's side door. "Maybe we'll both feel a little differently when we've had something to eat."

Sage opened her door with a little more force than necessary. "As long as I'm not breakfast."

God damn, but I wished she would be.

Chapter Thirteen

SAGE

It had to be the most ironic cosmic joke in history that I had spent my entire life invisible and alone, only to become the main attraction for a bunch of supernatural monsters.

Honestly, it pissed me right off. I hadn't asked for much from this life—I'd kept my head down, I'd worked hard to excel, I'd taken the pittance of acknowledgment I'd been handed, I'd followed in my narcissistic mother's footsteps even though my feet bled and my conscience fought me every step of the way. I'd been kind and friendly, despite never being recognized, and above all, I had *hoped*. I had *believed* that my hard work would pay off, that I would reach my goals and find a place where I truly belonged. Karma and all that.

And now, not only had I found out that my loneliness had been *caused* by this freak-of-nature bond, but I had absolutely no say in what happened from here on out. It was beyond cruel. It was sadistic.

As I followed Silas through the garage door into his home, I noted through my angry haze that it was one of the most unique, eloquently masculine houses I'd ever seen. The garage door led to a mudroom of sorts, only it was a tasteful space with a padded bench, hooks for coats, and a narrow linen closet directly across from the doorway. To the left, a door led to what looked like a powder room, and then the right opened directly into a main living space. Although this was the first floor of the house, it was a modern split level, so this room felt almost like a nicely appointed basement with enormous sliding glass doors that led to the front patio and a wet bar on the far side of the living space. A black leather sectional faced a gigantic projector screen setup, and then a set of stairs led up to the next floor.

I took off my shoes in the foyer area, and my eyes danced over little details of the space. Other than the fact that there was a couch, TV, and wet bar, one might think this was a collector's room. A suspiciously old-looking tapestry had been hung on the wall to the right of the staircase, a wooden display holding medieval weaponry had been set up to the left where the wet bar wrapped around with muted lighting at its base, and along either side of a fireplace between the tapestry and TV, matching marble busts had been placed on wood pedestals. There were other collectible-type things, like a glass case of cracked Venetian vases and a yellowed sheet of parchment with Japanese script faded into the cracks of the paper hanging in the mudroom.

I rotated a slow look to Silas. He scanned the room, like he was trying to see it through my eyes and then met my questioning gaze. "Yes," he said, his low voice reverberating through the quiet space. "I collected these over… many years."

Nearly six hundred years, more than likely. "So homey," I quipped unfairly. Actually, it was rather inviting. The lighting was low, other than the sunlight that streamed through the glass doors to my right, and there were knitted throws and pillows on the couch that looked comfy.

Silas ignored my jibe and put a hand to the small of my back, leading me into the living room. "I live down here with my brother, Art. The other three live upstairs."

Well, if my wrath over the situation hadn't been a wet blanket to the fires of our newfound passion, that certainly was. I hadn't been planning on being intimate with Silas again—not after the kidnapping stunt—but I *definitely* wasn't going to go near that possibility if his twin brother was in a bedroom nearby. There was no way I could focus on *that* when I knew a vampire stranger was on the other side of the wall… *listening*.

Silas pointed to the left, past the wrap-around wet bar. "Our rooms are right there."

"Sharing a wall," I confirmed warily.

Silas cleared his throat. "My bathroom is between our rooms, but," he shrugged. "Yes."

"Cool," I intoned.

A knowing smile slid up one side of Silas' handsome features. He angled toward me, hands in his pockets and head tipping with interest. "That upsets you."

"Why would it?" I deflected.

He pressed into my space, one hand sliding out of his pocket and steadying my elbow when I took an instinctual step back. "Why would it?" he challenged softly.

I stared into a pair of smoldering, green eyes, and the blush of warmth in my cheeks trickled south through my body. "Uh…"

Feet thundered down the stairs just before Silas' twin appeared. It was strange, but his finer bone structure, lithe body, and even his shorter hair weren't what set him apart from Silas. It was a look in his eyes, a devilment that spoke volumes about his mischievous character even before I could get to know him. "Holy shit, you brought her."

Silas sighed, almost soundlessly, and he faced his brother. "Sort of."

"Sort of?" The brother echoed, holding out a steaming mug to his brother as he crossed the room with oddly fluid, fast strides.

Silas glanced at me briefly before reaching out to take the mug. I glimpsed a dark maroon substance in the gold mug as Silas accepted it from his brother, and my stomach flipped uncomfortably. Silas ignored his brother and my clear discomfort, and gesturing between the two of us with the mug, he said, "Sage, this is my brother, Arthur. Arthur, this is Sage."

"Art," the brother grinned blithely. His eyes bounced to Silas and then back to me. "Shit, I'm sorry, but I can't help it. Can I hug you?"

My lips parted in surprise. I was still wearing my nightshirt with no bra, for God's sake, and here I was, standing in a mansion with vampires who wanted to hug me. And drink blood from a mug. "Er," I dithered.

"You may not," Silas glared before taking a sip of what had to be piping-hot blood. Whose blood was it? What did it taste like? Did he season it? Why did I want him to eat it with a spoon? Why was the mug thing throwing me off balance right now? Like those people who drank tomato soup out of mugs instead of eating it from a bowl like a normal person.

Art's mouth puckered sulkily. "No fair."

Silas watched me over the rim of his mug, his gaze sharp but his movements relaxed as he sipped the blood and licked it cleanly from his lips before I could so much as glimpse a drop of it. But then I had the sudden urge to watch my blood drip onto his lips, slide onto his tongue and swirl around his mouth. Out of nowhere, I felt jealous of what was in that mug. I didn't know whose blood he was allowing to slide into his body, but I didn't like it. I wanted it to be mine. Swallowing, I held his gaze. I couldn't let him see that he was affecting me as much as he was. But I was affected. And it made less sense to me than the fact that I was standing between two vampires with no fear for my safety.

Silas didn't divert his attention from me as he asked Art, "Any word from our parents?"

Art volleyed a look between Silas and me, clearly in a fantastic mood about this whole coerced guest situation. "Yes, but Alvaro wants to talk to you about something first, apparently."

Silas flicked a look his brother's way, finally breaking our eye contact and allowing me to breathe. "Why?"

"If I knew, I would have just told you," Art retorted.

Silas grunted, taking another, deeper swig of blood as his gaze strayed over Art's shoulder to where three beautiful men had materialized. Apparently, all vampires could move quickly, so I logged that fact away. I also took note of the fact that my memory had not done these vampires justice—they were disgustingly handsome and each in his own way.

Silas gestured to the youngest-looking vampire first, and I remembered now how beguiling his large, brown eyes were. "This is Matteo. He is the youngest in our cohort."

"Hello," Matteo said, his smile perfectly straight and white against the smooth, olive tone of his skin. He held out a hand, and almost on instinct, I took it. He kissed the back of my hand, bending over it and giving me a devilish smile. "Pleased to meet you."

"Oh, so *he* gets to touch her?" Art groused.

Ignoring his brother again, Silas, pointed to an enormous, blond statue of a man with pale skin and soft amber eyes. "Constantine, Sage. Sage, this is Constantine."

"Hi," I waved.

Constantine wasn't what I would consider to be classically handsome, but he certainly commanded my attention. His cheekbones were so sharp, Gordon Ramsey could filet a duck with them, and his hard, straight mouth did odd things to my stomach. Constantine didn't offer his hand, but he did incline his head, his toned arms folded over a black button-down and his gaze a mixture of curiosity and amusement. "A pleasure, Sage."

"I am Alvaro," the last one said, peering at me in suspicion. Alvaro was wearing a pair of pristine, white pants, a black belt, and a black, short-sleeved shirt with ribbed fabric that looked super soft. Like he was trying to entice people to lie down on him.

"Hi," I said weakly.

Alvaro hooked Silas with an intense stare. "We need to talk."

Silas drained the last of his mug, and like it was nothing at all, took my hand in his to lead me toward the stairs. "So, talk."

I followed after him, swiveling a look behind me to find that the other four vampires were following. And watching. I'd never understood what stage fright was like because no one had ever noticed me enough to get me close to a stage, but I got it now. I froze up, completely at a loss and overwhelmed because they *saw me*. They even seemed to understand me in a silent, assessing kind of way. I caught Art's gaze, and he gave me a reassuring wink.

Alvaro glanced at me in concern. "Perhaps in private."

"Family is private," was all Silas said.

Apparently, Silas' word was more than enough, because as we started up the polished oak staircase, Alvaro said, "I need to show you some security footage."

That sounded ominous. What security footage could worry a bunch of swole vampires with supernatural abilities? The image of Marcus—or whatever creature he had been—flashed through my mind, and my hand squeezed Silas' instinctively. Silas glanced at me and then back to Alvaro. "Maybe… I'll meet you in the office."

"So wise," Alvaro monotoned sarcastically. He had a hint of an accent, and I found it oddly soothing. Alvaro had to be several hundred years old as well if what Silas had told me was true about them becoming a cohort in their youth. The fact that he chose to keep a part of his heritage in his speech was strangely… human. And therefore, grounding. Comforting.

We walked up two flights of stairs and into a bright, open-concept kitchen that had clearly been designed to be the center of the house. A U-shaped island took up much of the space, and behind it, a full, gourmet kitchen gleamed in spotless wonder. To the left, a dining area and a masculine, black table and padded chairs occupied a space designated by a designer, blue rug, and to the right, frosted glass doors hinted at an office beyond. Past the dining room to the left, a gigantic great room had been framed by walls of tall windows that overlooked the second-story balcony and lush, green forest.

Silas led me to the white marble island, his expression apologetic. "I think I had better talk to Alvaro in the office. Will you be alright for a minute?"

I rested one hand on the island counter, tapping my

fingernail on its surface. "I suppose I don't have a choice, do I?"

Four pairs of eyes fastened on me, and even from my periphery, I could tell the other vampires were surprised. Silas kept his expression neutral. Patient. Eminently passive. It was infuriating. "You always have a choice, Sage. Give me five minutes with Alvaro and Constantine, and then we can go over your options in better detail."

What options? Did I get to pick which guest bedroom I was a prisoner in? White sheets or blue? I blinked with slow irritation. "Sure."

Like Silas could read my thoughts loud and clear, he gave me a brief, hard stare, and then he motioned for Alvaro and Constantine to follow him through the French doors to the right that led to the dark office.

I rotated an uncertain look toward Art, who had already come to stand on the opposite side of the island where a cutting board with half-cut potatoes lay next to a chef's knife. He gave me a genuine smile as he picked up his knife. "Are you hungry?"

My stomach gurgled. Matteo chuckled, leaning against the island and studying me with a sparkle in his warm brown eyes. "It doesn't bode well if your mate is already neglecting you, mia cara."

Art diced a potato impossibly fast and, from what I could tell, a little more forcefully than necessary. "Se è vero, soffrirà per mano mia."

Matteo's gaze darkened as he exchanged a look with Art. "Lo stesso per me, fratello."

I bobbed a look between them, unsure if I needed to point out that they had switched to another language or not. Did that happen when you'd been alive for several centuries and probably knew every language mankind had invented?

Or were they doing it on purpose to hide something from me?

Art looked up from cutting, and another smile, this one tighter, crossed his handsome face. "Sorry, that was rude. We aren't used to having humans around—" He paused, thinking. "I'll amend that. We aren't used to *seeing* them because Constantine keeps them in his quarters so furtively."

Constantine was an incubus, and Silas said he fed on *pleasure*. Lust. My brain filled in the gaps, and I made a face like I was five and had just seen grown-ups kiss for the first time. "Oh."

Art remained clearly amused. "Forgive our poor manners. We will try to be more normal. I'm making masala dosa. Would you like some?"

Masala dosa—whatever that was—didn't scream New York normal to me, but the hollowness in my stomach had turned into a gnawing, gnashing creature, so I said, "Yes, thank you."

"I didn't know you were coming for breakfast, or I would have asked what you prefer," Art said, his tone conversational.

Matteo leaned his hand on his chin, watching me with quiet curiosity. He looked so young with his enormous eyes and soft, curly hair, and I couldn't help but think of a puppy. I returned my attention to Art, still standing in place uncertainly. "I didn't know I was coming for Pancakes with Prisoners, either, if it makes you feel better."

Matteo snorted. Art finished chopping the peeled potatoes and gave me a knowing glance. "Silas is not the most subtle creature. I'm not surprised he forced you here."

"Oh, I don't know," I ventured to tease, stupidly pushing boundaries like a dog with an invisible fence collar. "I'd say he keeps plenty of crucial information *subtly* locked up." Matteo perked up, clearly intrigued, and I tried to ignore the way he was observing me the same way kids stare at praying mantises.

Art got a look on his face like he was *going* to smile but held back. "I'm a complete deviant. You can ask me anything."

I tucked that away for later. Art was an ally. Maybe. I was just desperate enough to put that theory to the test later. "Whatever you're making, I'm sure it's fine. Thanks for making breakfast."

"It's a South Indian breakfast dish—fermented pancakes," Art said, gamely ignoring my jibe at his brother. "We love them, but I won't be offended if you want eggs and toast instead." Art flashed me a charming grin before depositing the potatoes into a pot of boiling water on the island's gas range at his elbow.

I couldn't help but note how unlike Silas his twin was. He moved with easy grace, more like a dancer than a warrior, and his smiles were quicker to flash across his leaner features than Silas. Still, he had the same dark, wavy hair, and although his eyes were blue instead of green, they were bright and long lashed like Silas'.

"It sounds interesting. I'm happy to try it," I replied politely.

Matteo cocked his head, his chin still on the heel of his hand. "What do *you* like to eat for breakfast?"

"Er," I chewed on my lip, thinking. "I guess… I don't eat breakfast much. Like… oatmeal sometimes? A bagel from the coffee shop if I have time." Art and Matteo stared. I took up tapping my nails on the marble again. "What?"

"Does your mother not feed you?" Matteo asked, almost innocently.

I snuffed out a laugh. "She didn't make me breakfast even when I was at home with her."

Art gave me an inquisitive scowl. "She didn't even try?"

"What, cooking me breakfast?" I shifted nervously. It was like being in a job interview and on a first date all at the same time, and I suddenly found myself longing for Silas to return.

"Caring for you," Art countered seriously.

My heart plummeted to my stomach. *Ouch.* I swallowed hard, gluing my gaze to the dark veins in the marble slab where my finger traced them absently. "She did try."

I felt rather than saw them exchange another look. Matteo said softly, "We didn't mean to pry."

"I did," Art responded blithely. He began chopping something else, and I glanced up to find him dicing an onion. He gave me a look full of mischief and a touch of compassion. "Otherwise, how will we care for you, now?"

My insides shouldn't have warmed at that, but I couldn't help it. People rarely looked me in the eyes, let alone offered to take care of me. It was a balm to a years-old burn that tortured me on the daily. I cleared my throat. "No offense, but I'm not sure how caring it is when it's against my will."

"The bond is against your will," Art clarified with a point of his knife before he finished dicing the yellow onion. "But to love is a choice. We have already chosen to love you, I promise you that."

That warmth in my chest flared, burning up my throat and threatening to produce tears. Dammit. "That's a pretty bold claim."

"Well," Art said, his tone dipping as he seemed to think. "To be honest, I will not likely find a match. But I do have a bond with Silas that goes beyond the usual twin phenomenon. We have a connection unlike any other vampires have ever had, and because of that, I immediately felt a kinship with you." He set his knife down, leaning his hands on the counter to give me his full attention. "It isn't bold so much as inevitable."

I could hardly find my voice, I was so lost in Art's ardent gaze. Desperate to turn his attention away from me, I asked, "Why won't you find a match?"

"Ah," Art winced, squinting one eye. "Vampires don't make twins. We're the only ones ever born, and Silas was a sanguis just like our father. He is the vampire he *should* be. I, on the other hand, ended up being an adfectus, which was unheard of with a sanguis vampire father."

"Vampires give birth to their own kind," Matteo added. "That is why we are divided into five houses with our own leaders. When Art realized he was an adfectus and not a sanguis, it made him… unusual."

"I'd be an outcast if I wasn't Silas' twin," Art said bluntly. "I'm an aberration. It wouldn't make sense for me to find a match—offspring of the House Sanguis but son of House Adfectus."

A crease formed between my brows. "Wait, so… which house do you actually belong to?"

"In the end," Art shrugged, "it was decided that I would align with Adfectus. I spent some time with them, but Silas and I missed each other so acutely, they made sure we were in the same cohort."

"And your parents?" I asked, holding my breath for him. I knew what it felt like to not *fit* with what your parents expected you to be. Or, at least, I didn't fit with my mother's idea of who I should be. She was cold, aloof, ambitious, and serenely level-headed. Her eyes never wavered from mine when she spoke to me. I, on the other hand, was capable of sprinting a half-marathon in thoughts before I realized someone had been speaking for thirty seconds.

"They love me," Art replied slowly, cautiously. "But it's hard to deny that I'm something of a freak."

"You're not a freak," Matteo scowled, straightening. He glanced at me. "He's different, but that doesn't mean he won't find a match. He's being dramatic."

"Me? Dramatic?" Art asked with mild amusement. He ignited one of the gas burners with a *click, click, whoosh.* "How dare you."

"All the same," Matteo said with a significant look my way. "We are happy to have you here. We have waited a long time to dote on you."

I choked out a laugh. "You don't even know me."

"I know that you are my brother's socium," Art swiped the onion into a bowl. "That's enough for me."

"I know you have pretty hair," Matteo grinned. "That's enough for me."

"Well, with such high standards, how can I doubt?" Despite myself, I patted the unruly waves that hung down my back.

"You will love us," Matteo said with confidence.

I tried not to laugh and failed. His smile dimpled, and I found myself at ease, completely against my will. "Is that right?"

"Well, you'll love Matteo," Art amended with another sly smile. "It's impossible not to love Matteo. He should have been an adfectus like me; the way he tugs on people's emotions is unreal."

I glanced at Matteo. "You feed on magic, right?"

"A magicae vampire, yes," Matteo confirmed with a nod.

"And you like emotions," I said to Art.

"All of them," Art grinned. He put a pan on the stove. "But no, I won't feed off of yours, even if they are delectably complicated at the moment. Fear and desire are a heady combination."

"Desire?" I asked with a touch of outrage.

Art and Matteo hooked me with matching looks that brimmed with humor. Matteo murmured, "Far finta di niente."

Art chuckled. "Couldn't have said it better myself."

Chapter Fourteen

SILAS

The creature on the CCTV feed stalked the perimeter of our wards, its shape flickering in and out of visibility disturbingly like a wraith. It moved like smoke on the wind, flitting from feed to feed, its eyes glinting like cat eyes in the shadows. Like a fae.

Alvaro stood to my left, his arms folded and eyes taking in my reaction. Constantine stood on my right side, his attention fully consumed by the not-wraith. "What," Constantine asked, his voice hard, "is that?"

"Is this current or in the past?" I asked.

"Current. It's been stalking our perimeter since you arrived. And I echo Constantine's question. What the *fuck* is that? Because it's not like any wraith I've ever seen, and yet—"

"It is wraith-like," Constantine finished.

It looked a lot like the Marcus creature I had fought yesterday. And if it was, then I had my suspicions, but to give them credence was to admit that the fae were performing forbidden rites—they were committing an atrocity our world had never seen since its inception. I leaned forward, trying to get a better look at the thing. "It is what Sage's friend became when I confronted it. It attacked her, and then it took a form very like that."

"I have never seen this thing," Constantine said, his deep baritone voice rumbling with anger.

"Me neither," I admitted, straightening. I cracked my knuckles. "But I know I can make them bleed."

"Brother." Alvaro put a hand on my arm. "Don't be rash."

"It's here for Sage," I seethed quietly. "What else would you have me do? Let it test our wards unchecked?"

Constantine grunted in agreement. Alvaro gave me an irritated scowl, his usual joie de vivre replaced by the fighter I remembered from the Siege of Vienna. His accent deepened as he said, "It is too much of a risk. You are the first mated brother of our kind for eighty years. Do not be a fool."

"Hence the reason my mate needs to be protected," I retorted, pointing to the computer monitor, "and that thing needs to die."

"We don't even know what *it* is," Alvaro argued. The way his voice was rising, I could tell he was getting hot. This was why we usually brought Constantine with us.

"We should alert the Dominus," Constantine suggested calmly. "Perhaps they have received reports of these creatures elsewhere."

"Obviously, we will alert the houses," I grouched. "And I already asked around about these… abnormalities. I told Art about it yesterday, and he sniffed around. So far, no one else has seen them."

"You two never tell us anything," Alvaro muttered irritably.

"I forgot to fill you in," I admitted. "But regardless, what are we doing about *that one*?"

Constantine studied the screen for a moment, and then he murmured, "Send Matteo." Alvaro and I scoffed, rolling our eyes in tandem. Constantine ignored us. "He proved himself admirably during the Blood Wars of '87. He can drain one supernatural creature of its ley without you there to coddle him, Silas."

Constantine was referring to the Blood Wars between vampires and fae in the late eighteenth century. We had fought as a cohort one hundred years strong and ready to prove our worth to our houses. Matteo had been the youngest and had barely managed to get a hold of his impetuousness at that age, but Constantine was right. He had proved himself worthy in his own right back then. Since the Blood Wars had ended, we had only fought in human altercations here and there, but Matteo rarely joined us—there was little ley magic to drain in a human battle.

Nevertheless, he was capable, even if he was not bloodthirsty. "Fine," I agreed reluctantly. "But I want someone with him just in case."

"I will go," Alvaro assured me quickly. "Guns are of little use against wraiths, but this thing?" He shrugged, glancing at the shadow thing stalking our perimeter. "If it bleeds as you say, then perhaps."

"Its form was corporeal, too," I offered. I didn't say that I thought it was half-fae. There was no need to raise the alarms without more proof.

Alvaro's smile took on a steel edge. "Perfect." As marksmen went, Alvaro had always been the best. It didn't matter if it was with a military-grade SSG 69 or a sixteenth-century musket. He hit his mark every time.

Constantine turned to me, his gold eyes sharp. I was the

leader of our cohort, both because I had been born into the House Sanguis and doubly so because my father was the Dominus of that house. But Constantine was the oldest, and we deferred to his wisdom more often than not. At the moment, he was giving me his "I'm way older than you" face. "Take care of your socium. Times are different now than when the last socium was matched. You will need a delicate hand with her."

"She's made me painfully aware of that," I muttered, glancing at the French doors that led to the kitchen. I could hear her speaking with Art and Matteo, her tone softening with every sentence, and the smell of her fear had abated some. I needed to find a way to help her ease into this life, but it felt like we'd had no time since that ley line had exploded between us. How were mates supposed to connect when the socium was in imminent danger right away?

"I'll speak with Matteo and go to the perimeter right now." Alvaro went to a large safe off to the left of the sunny office and punched a code into the keypad before turning the crank and opening it. "Constantine, will you observe from inside? I don't want us all past the inner wards in case there are more waiting."

"I will," Constantine nodded once.

Alvaro unhooked a utility belt from the door of the safe and fastened it around his hips. I glanced up at the ceiling in frustration, pacing and glaring at the monitor where the wraith creature prowled our perimeter. "I don't like this. I should be there with you."

"I know you are used to being our strength," Constantine replied calmly, his stoic expression unchanged, as usual. It took a lot to ruffle towering Constantine's composure. His arms were still folded over his black button-down, but his forearms flexed, the only indication that he was uncomfortable with the situation, too. "But right now, that girl is your priority."

Fuck that. My job was to *protect* that girl. And instead, while my brothers were out fighting monsters we knew nothing about, I would stay inside and make her tea. Or whatever. "And if I say no?" I challenged. I was the leader of our cohort, after all.

Alvaro twisted, giving me a speculative look over his shoulder. He slid a Glock into a holster on his right hip. "What would you tell me, Caudillo?"

Caudillo. Images of a bloody battlefield in France flashed before my eyes, and with one word, Alvaro had taken me back centuries in time to our first battle together. He had called me *Caudillo* then because I had been his leader in battle. He sometimes pulled out the term when we were at odds, and it had the right effect now. As *Caudillo*, as his strategic leader, I would have told him to stay with his ley mate. Sighing in defeat, I shoved my hands into my canvas jacket pockets. "Point taken."

Constantine glanced at the doors like I had, like he could see Sage. "She appears to be wearing pajamas. Did you bring other articles of clothing for her?"

We really needed to work on Constantine's modern vernacular. "No time. She… wasn't exactly thrilled to go with me."

"You kidnapped her?" Alvaro asked with a hint of amusement, pulling a semi-automatic rifle from the safe.

"Not exactly," I muttered, rubbing the back of my neck.

Constantine looked pained. He would; the man was literally supernatural when it came to wooing his lovers. "I'll send down some clothing."

"Appreciate it." I swiped a laptop from the large, curved

desk in the center of the office. "I'll have her shop online for more things. I didn't have a lot of time to plan this shit out."

"Unusual for you," Alvaro mused, his accent thick.

"Cállate," I shot back, a hint of a smile tugging at my mouth. *Shut up*. "I'll go see that Sage gets settled in. I'll watch the feed from here," I added holding up the laptop. "Are you leaving now?"

Alvaro shoved a magazine into the rifle and loaded a round in the chamber. "Fuck yes. I've been dying of boredom. Let's kill something."

I rolled my eyes, despite agreeing with him. Modern society *was* a little tame for my taste. I opened the door and immediately found Sage where she sat at the island chatting with Art and Matteo. Art was making a masala dosa pancake in the frying pan, and his eyes sparkled as Sage told him about the first time she'd tried weed.

"... think he forgot about me after he passed me his joint, because an hour later, I found myself having a *very* serious conversation with the beta fish above his sink," she grinned.

"Gods, I wish weed worked on me," Art chuckled. "I would be such a fun stoner."

"What did you talk to the fish about?" Matteo wanted to know.

"I don't know." Sage squinted as she thought, her chin on her hand. "Probably politics. I was a bit of a campaigner in my freshman year." Her hair swirled down her shoulders to mid-back, and the way her back was arched as she sat forward on the stool sent a tingle through my body.

The briefest taste I'd had of her last night hadn't been nearly enough. The way I wanted her was primal. Painful. Still, I pushed those instincts aside and came to join them with slow, careful movements so I didn't startle Sage. She glanced at me her, dark brows raised. "Everything okay?"

"All good," I lied, smiling.

Art gave me an arch look, flipping the pancake with a loud *smack.* He would have heard everything we said in there. "I'm nearly done with Sage's breakfast if you'd like to show her around our space downstairs. You can take her down there to eat so it's quiet."

So she is safe, I filled in for him. Message received, buddy. "Oh, can I?" I challenged, giving him a hard look. I could tell Art thought I was neglecting Sage already.

Art kept his expression innocently neutral. "If that's alright with you, Sage. You are the guest."

Sage looked put out by the reminder that she was a forced guest here. "Right. Sure."

Matteo watched all of this with a quiet kind of glee. He'd always been something of a voyeur. Art flipped the pancake onto a blue plate before handing it to Sage with a fork. "We have drinks downstairs."

"Matteo," Constantine called from the office. Matteo turned, and Constantine indicated with his head for our magicae brother to join him.

Matteo waved to Sage. "See you later."

Sage took the plate from Art and waved back. "See you."

Art pierced me with a twin look, one of those "read my thoughts or else" kinds of looks. And whether I wanted to understand him or not, the message came across loud and clear. It was the same message Constantine and Alvaro had clubbed me in the balls with. *Take care of her. Help her adjust. Focus on the small picture and let us handle the big picture.*

I'd never been in such a seam-splitting situation before, with one end of me tied to Sage's dainty ankle, and the other tied to a dangerous, runaway train that looked like it might hurl my family off a cliff. I'd always had an innate need to protect, to defend. I'd never encountered a situation where they had been split, the need to defend my border at war with my need to protect Sage both physically and emotionally. It was so unpleasant, it caused the blood in my stomach to churn.

Sage gave me a searching look, both keen and completely lost all at once. I picked up the electric mug from its spot over by the coffee maker, and I was glad to find it full again. Art might be irritated with me, but he would still do anything for me, and I for him. I took a sip of tangy, coppery blood, and its strength rushed through me, feeding the ley well inside of me.

Compared to the taste of Sage's blood, it was like drinking liquified wood chips in lieu of a five-course meal. Still, feeling less weak, I offered my hand to Sage, low at our sides and without expectations. I could give her more choices. It was a small thing, but my brothers were right. She needed me to put her first. I could do that.

Sage took it, her expression almost sheepish, but then seemed to tuck away her trepidation, and her spine straightened. "Lead the way."

Over my shoulder, I sent Art my own silent message. *Stop making pancakes and get in that office.* Art shoved a savory potato pancake into his mouth with a cheeky wink before disappearing into the office. I returned my attention to Sage, leading her back down the stairs and wondering how the hell I was supposed to mend the rift I'd created between us. Especially because it was probably named Kidnap Canyon.

I led her to the bar where Art and I sometimes ate our dinners when we wanted some solitude from our other brothers, and Sage took a seat on the leather barstool. I set the laptop on the bar counter and opened it, pulling up the security footage so I could keep an eye on the situation beyond our borders. I faced it away from Sage, but I wasn't surprised when she gave me a knowing look. Sage wasn't stupid—she knew something untoward was happening out there. Her eyes followed me as I went to a fridge behind the bar.

"What do you want to drink?" I asked, opening the fridge door. "I have water, soda, iced tea—"

"Blood?" Sage guessed savagely.

I straightened and hooked her with a half-lidded glare. Slowly I sipped the warm blood in my mug. "Yep."

I could tell she was fighting not to be grossed out. And she was losing. "I'll take some water."

"Very sensible."

She took the glass bottle of water from me, and then with some wariness, she cut into the masala dosa and popped a piece in her mouth. Her eyes lit up. "Whoa."

"Art is an incredibly accomplished chef. We're all grateful for him." I swallowed the rest of the tangy blood in three pulls, glancing at the screen. Matteo and Alvaro were already leaving the inner wards and slowly making their way to the outer border where the creature stalked the perimeter. I tried to ignore the twist in my stomach and went to rinse my mug in the sink, stealing a few furtive glances at Sage while she ate. She looked around the space quietly, taking in all the invaluable collectibles on the walls.

"We have to move every ten years or so. It's not easy keeping all our little trinkets safe, so these will stay in this house, and when we move to our next location, you'll get to see new ones."

She stopped chewing, surprised. "Why do you move every ten years?"

"The ley lines shift," I explained. "Just as the Earth turns on its axis, the seasons change, and our view of the stars shifts, the ley lines shift the balance of power about every ten years." Alvaro and Matteo bounded, moving from tree cover to tree cover as they approached the not-wraith.

Sage considered what I had said, her long lashes flicking up as she thought. "Like proper motion?"

I shifted my full attention to her again, smiling slowly. Fuck, she was smart. "Yes, like universal proper motion. Only much faster, of course." She agreed with a lift of her hands, like that was obvious. The proper motion of galaxies far from us happened over thousands of years, but the universe was not static. Stars, galaxies, and whole star systems did shift. "The ley lines follow a certain kind of flow, like streams that trickle down from mountains. The concentration of ley shifts slowly over a decade, and we follow that flow across a latitudinal line."

Sage stared at me hard. "You're trying to find your ley mates that match the star charts."

I nodded. "We have witches called augurs who watch certain signs to give us clues as to where our ley mates will be. But if we move along the latitude of where each of us was born, then there's a greater chance we will come across her."

"Like me," she guessed.

"Like you."

Sage cut another section of her pancake. "Sounds complicated."

"It is. But when you're nearly ageless, I suppose that's a fair evolutionary balance." I glanced at the security feed, only to find Alvaro already taking shots at the creature. It twitched, falling to its knees. Matteo leaped forward, too fast for the camera to follow, and then his mouth was on the creature's mouth, sucking the ley from its body.

Sage gave me a piercing look. Her eyes were warm chestnut, but the sharpness in them shot through me like a deep winter freeze. "Something wrong on your computer?"

"Just… monitoring a virus," I slightly lied. She didn't believe me. The creature slumped over, and Matteo and Alvaro stood over it. I breathed a sigh of relief. "Sorry. What were we saying?"

"You were saying that vampires can't mate often. Otherwise, if you had babies as often as humans did, we'd probably be overrun with vampires who never die." I didn't need to be a mentem to enjoy Sage's thoughts, or at least, the evidence of them. I'd never been so captivated by the microexpressions on someone's face as her thoughts broadcast themselves across her features. Right now, hers were a mix of curious and disapproving. She ate another bite, chewed, swallowed, and then met my gaze again. "Still, eighty years is a long time. Surely, your death rate would still be much higher than your birth rate when accounting for accidents or untimely deaths."

"You would make an excellent augur," I grinned. I came around the bar counter and took the seat next to hers, our knees brushing briefly. "It is an unprecedented gap. Our house leaders are slightly panicking."

"Why the gap?"

I stole one of her red pepper pieces and chewed it while I considered my answer. "We aren't sure—the fae control the ley lines. They feed them and monitor their strength, whereas we, in true vampire fashion, simply feed from and benefit from the lines. We have tried to level with the fae, to find a truce, but they view us as monstrosities. We are a parasite that feeds on *their* magic. They aren't willing to share their knowledge with us."

Sage grimaced. "I can't say I blame them."

"Nor I," I agreed cautiously. "But their brutality in the name of keeping ley magic to themselves does cross boundaries that even monsters wouldn't cross."

"Like what?" she asked, eyes wide.

I wasn't sure I was ready to dump that on her. "Suffice to say, we have both made our mistakes." She shrugged, looking down at her pancake to cut it into pieces with the side of her fork.

A shouted curse from Constantine in the office upstairs drew my attention. Sage wouldn't have heard it, but I did, loud and clear. He and Art rushed from their place where they had been observing in the office to run out into the woods. I spun the laptop around to find the worst-case scenario in this defense plan of ours.

Matteo was on the ground, besieged by three grotesque creatures with gnarled limbs that wisped in and out of sight. Alvaro had his gun wedged between the sharp teeth of one of them, and he fell to the ground as two more swarmed him. They were being ambushed.

I slapped the laptop closed before Sage had time to look up from her pancake to see it. She stared at me, alarmed, and her pulse picked up a tick. "What is it?"

"I have to go," I breathed out. "Sage… stay here. Please, can you promise me to stay here?"

She blinked, looking around. "Are we in danger? What's going on?"

"I told you just now that the fae are dangerous," I said quickly, my mind agonizing over the time it was taking me to get to my brothers. Even though I worried about them and felt a pull to run and protect them, something stronger that burned in my chest demanded I ensure Sage was safe first. "They want you. I need to deal with our perimeter. Can you *please* swear to me you will stay here?"

Sage nodded woodenly. "I'll stay."

I pulled her to me, inhaling her pine and cinnamon scent, tinged with fear that pumped through her veins. I kissed her temple with a fleeting press of my lips to her cool skin, and then I jogged to the sliding glass doors that led directly outside. I spared Sage one last glance, and my anxiety forced me to add, "You're safe here. But only if you don't leave the house."

Sage's fear flooded her system, tinging the air with a pine sharpness that made my heart ache. Her fingers gripped the counter edge, but she dipped her head in understanding. "I believe you."

Praying that Sage would be safe without me, that I would make it in time to save my brothers, I opened the door and closed it with a firm *snap*. If my brothers died, I would never forgive myself.

Chapter Fifteen

SAGE

I could taste my fear. It washed away the savory, spicy flavor of the masala dosa and replaced it with a metallic tang on my tongue. Silas disappeared from view—one second, he had been there, gazing at me with clear concern, and then he had been gone. My brain still had a hard time processing what he was capable of, physically. But surely, if he was that fast or that strong, whatever they were dealing with outside their "wards" could be handled. What if they didn't handle it, though?

I should have been terrified for my safety, but as my legs took me on autopilot to the sliding glass door, I found that only one thought circulated through my head. *Please be safe. Please be safe. Please, I'm begging you, be safe.* I pressed my palm against the glass, staring at the gentle slope of the gravel driveway that led downhill and into the thick trees. I watched a breeze ruffle the lush maples and towering pines, and even through the door, I could hear the psithurism. It looked peaceful. Safe.

My heart galloped in my chest, a runaway mare terrified

for her life and blind to the dangers behind her. How could I feel truly safe when I didn't know what was out there? I forced myself away from the door, and crossing my arms over my chest, I looked around the enormous space uncertainly.

It didn't feel real, the possibility of staying here. It defied logic that the life—however pitiful—I had built up to this point would fall in second place to a destiny I hadn't known about until two days ago.

I glanced at a distinctly phallic artifact in a glass case, and I ground the heel of my hand against my forehead. And there was *that*, I supposed. I had let Silas finger fuck me last night. Out of the blue. Completely randomly. "Stupid," I hissed, turning away and going back to the bar. "You are so pathetic, Sage," I muttered out loud to myself. I twisted the wide lid off the glass water bottle and took a few cooling swigs to clear my head. *Wash away the stupid. I baptize you in the name of feminist sensibility. Do not let a handsome guy take over your entire existence, Sage… Amen.*

From the corner of my eye, a shadow between the bar counter and the wall moved. *Slithered.* I choked on the water, bending forward and leaning on the granite countertop as my gaze fixed itself to that corner. The shadow stretched between a gap in the counter and the wall that sectioned it off from a hallway behind it. I stared hard. The shadow… shadowed. Benignly.

The crease between my brows deepened, and I wiped water off my mouth with a shaking hand. Did I need to get my eyes checked? This was the third time I'd sworn I'd seen shadows moving. I'd watched a solar eclipse in middle school once, and at its zenith, our teacher had instructed us to look at the ground to observe the shadows that had appeared at our feet. They had slithered back and forth like snakes, creating an effect of alternating light and dark bands that moved across the ground in an unearthly pattern. These tricks of light that were haunting me reminded me of those shadow bands. Only, this time, it wasn't caused by a natural phenomenon I could look to a science book to explain.

The insidious feeling in my stomach defied explanation.

I was just about to turn away from the shadow and maybe curl myself into a ball on the couch when it moved again. No, it flickered. Like a flame instead of a harmless pocket of darkness, it sputtered and came to life. I backed up a step, and as I did, the shadow vibrated, skipping and growing in a way that hurt my eyes to follow. I blinked once, twice, and then that shadow had a shape. It had a form that I recognized.

Marcus stepped out of the gap like a shadow walker, his features serene and totally unbothered that he had managed to sneak into a vampire house. "I finally have you alone, Sage."

My back hit a barstool, and I stumbled, grasping the counter for balance. "Marcus?"

"I have only borrowed your friend's likeness. My real name is Cysgadyn, my Felltgwen. And you do not need to fear me." He took one step toward me, confident and at ease, as though he expected me to fall into his arms in gratitude.

I pressed back against the chair, my legs frozen and my heart in my throat. "What are you—why are you—"

"I am here to offer you a deal," he replied calmly.

I remembered how fast this *thing* could move. I remembered how his hand had felt around my throat, so strong he could crush my windpipe like it was a packing peanut. There was probably no use outrunning him. Could Silas hear me if I screamed? Unlikely. It was up to my own wits, then. "How did you get in here?"

Cysgadyn stalked around the bar area, putting the counter between us and running a finger along the edge of the stainless-steel sink with something akin to curiosity. "Your vampire captors are so old fashioned." His voice had changed, its tone garbled now, less "college kid" and more "eternal something." He flicked a look up to me, his dark eyes lit with a manic kind of spark one only recognized when they were face-to-face with depravity. "They ward against the known. But they did not account for the new. Not every creature is a wraith or a fae."

"What are you, then?" I didn't bother trying to back away anymore. My logical reasoning kicked in—he could catch me. He was talking in coherent sentences. Perhaps I could keep him busy long enough for Silas to come within hearing distance of my screams.

"I am all," Cysgadyn said with a flippant lift of his hand. He still looked so beautiful, so handsome like this. His skin was so soft, I still had a strong desire to smooth my hands over his cheeks. He was wearing the same thing I'd seen him in on the soccer field, a sweatshirt and loose jeans, and his braids were perfectly cinched in tidy rows without a single hair out of place; he looked like an innocent college student.

"All what?" I asked.

"Wraith," he listed, holding my gaze patiently and with the arrogant assurance that he had his prey well and truly cornered, "fae, and human."

I didn't even really know what the fae and wraith were. "Is that… good?"

His brow lowered a touch, and he glanced away. "Good? Interesting word choice. It is useful because I can slip through their wards. But is it good?" He returned his shadowed gaze to mine. Where before his eyes had been a warm oak brown, they slithered with darkness now. "No. I do not belong. But if I make a deal with you, then our Brenhmam has promised me a place at her court."

A few floating puzzle pieces clicked together. I didn't have a whole picture, but I had something to go off of. "The fae queen," I guessed.

He nodded once, one corner of his mouth tipped up. "She made me, but I do not yet belong. It is earned."

"Okay," I said slowly. "And if she made you, then why deny you a place at court?"

He rolled his eyes. "You are not in control here. Do not probe where you are not wanted, Felltgwen."

"What does that mean?"

"Cursed maiden," he said with haughty disdain.

"Ah. Yes. Cursed because I'm supposedly linked to a vampire. And you don't like vampires."

One side of his mouth lifted in a silent snarl, and he ran his tongue along his teeth like it was painful not to sink them into something. "Vile creatures. They steal those of you with the most ley in your bodies and force you to bear their children. They tether you to a life you never asked for. They feed and feed and take and take and have no care for the consequences."

Put that way, I couldn't even say I disagreed with him. I was still grappling to understand how being *mated* to someone like Silas was in my best interest, let alone whether it was fair.

For the first time, I considered the possibility that this creature might not be my enemy. I mean, he had choked me out and gone all creepy-crawly the last time I'd seen him, but setting aside the burning fear that pushed through my veins like injected alcohol, I had to weigh his words against what I knew. If this were a byline I was writing from an objective point of view, there weren't many positives in Silas' favor, here.

Except, he sees *you. He makes you feel safe. You've never felt more secure than when you've been with him.*

I shook that away. "Let's say I agree with you. What deal are you here to offer me?"

Cysgadyn stalked slowly around the counter again, this time coming to stand before me like he sensed I was less likely to bolt now. "Come with me to the fae court. You will be given protection there. You will be able to experience true love."

I chewed on my lip, folding my arms and tossing his words around in my head. Nowhere in that offer had he mentioned freedom. And Silas had mentioned that the fey wanted to drain the ley from my body into some kind of ley spring. He could have been lying, though. "What kind of life would I have at the fae court?"

Cysgadyn threw his arms out wide, his face lighting with genuine warmth. "The most wondrous life. The fae are rich—rich in wealth, rich in happiness, rich in living life to its fullest. They live in the sunshine. They drink and eat and *live.*"

He'd described the fae, not my life. "And you would earn a place in court?"

He sobered, his arms falling to his sides and his expression turning genuinely pleading. "It is the only way for me."

A pang of sympathy smacked me in the chest. I didn't know what kind of creature this Marcus—Cysgadyn—was, but I felt for him. I didn't belong, either. "That must be hard for you. I feel alone, too."

Cysgadyn cocked his head, folding his toned arms. "We could find belonging there together. Brenhmam has promised us a chance at love if we wish it. Your ley and mine—we could create a beautiful family. A new kind of family."

I only *just* managed to keep myself from recoiling. If I had been unsure before that statement, it now solidified my theory about the fae queen's offer to me. I would be trading one prison for another, and it sounded like she wanted me for the same reason the vampires did. To be a vessel, to bear children for them. Disgust roiled through me, and I sent it down through my toes, willing it to poison the ground and not discolor my features and give myself away. "That's a generous offer. Can I have time to think it over? It's a big decision." *Please, please, please don't take me. I don't know if Silas can hear me.*

Cysgadyn looked indecisive. "We won't have another chance like this." He paused, listening. "And we are out of time."

Silas was coming back, then. Thank God. "I need time, Cysgadyn. I feel for you—and I think you might be right. But I need to weigh my options. Can I have… a week? Two?"

He looked uncertain, scratching between two of his perfect, tidy braids. "I care for you, Felltgwen. I can give you time, and I hope this will prove to you that I will protect you. We will plant wild roses at the edge of your perimeter. If you wish to return to the fae queen, pluck a red rose. She will know you call for her, then."

That sounded positively phantasmagorical. "Er, sure." Holy shit, was this working? Was he actually about to leave me alone?

Cysgadyn grabbed me by the throat so quickly, I didn't have time to flinch. His strong hand closed around my neck, circling it completely and squeezing it so hard, I could barely eke out a shocked gust of breath. The darkness in his eyes swirled faster, drawing me in with a hypnotic quality that hooked my thoughts with tethers of panic. "You will tell no one of our conversation here, you will speak of nothing we discussed. I will return in two weeks' time." His hold on my throat burned like a brand, and I would have screamed if my voice hadn't been completely cut off.

Then he was gone.

I fell to my knees, gasping for breath and clutching my throat desperately. I sucked in lungfuls of fresh air, and it didn't burn like I expected it to. My skin didn't sting with an afterburn. My voice worked. I pushed myself to my feet shakily, making my way down the short hallway to the bathroom Silas had mentioned. I had to go through his bedroom to get to it, and I dimly registered the masculine, comforting warmth of it, and then I flicked on the lights in the huge bathroom, planting my hands on the slate gray counters to peer at my reflection in the mirror.

I looked harried, my eyes crazed, and my hair a tumbling, unbrushed mess down my shoulders. But as I lifted my chin one way and then the other, I noted no marks or bruising. It really was like Marcus—Cysgadyn—had been in my imagination. Fuck, maybe I had conjured him in my mind. I let my forehead fall to the cool counter. If only I could convince myself all of this was fake.

But it was real, I knew deep down in my gut.

So very, hauntingly real.

Chapter Sixteen

SILAS

These creatures were not natural. They smelled like fae and moved like wraiths, and when my daggers connected with their human-shaped throats, they sprayed blue blood like fae but then dissipated like wraiths did at their deaths. When Art, Constantine, and I reached Alvaro and Matteo, we made quick work of the creatures, breaking their necks, slicing their arteries, and in Constantine's case, ripping their heads off their necks. That guy was terrifying, objectively.

Their limbs had felt strange beneath my hands, they had flesh like humans but were gnarled and deformed. And they attempted to flit and flicker into the shadows like a wraith would. We had to be fast about ending their lives before they shifted between the planes of reality.

When the last one vanished, their smoke swirling into the air like a snuffed flame, I sheathed my daggers, and we all exchanged wary glances. Panting, Matteo buried a hand in his thick curls. In Italian, he asked, "What the hell was that?"

I shook my head, shucking off my jacket and tossing it

to the ground. It had become blood-stained, and it stank of those creatures, now. "That was the same kind of creature that attacked Sage on her campus yesterday."

"They smell like shit," Alvaro spat. He had blue blood smeared on his face and down the front of his black shirt. His white pants were probably unsalvageable, dirt-streaked and spattered with bright azure.

Well, at least I didn't need to explain my suspicions about these creatures to my brothers. Their thoughts were written on their faces—the disbelief, the disgust, and the same horrified realization I had come to that there were new terrors to face in this life. Unnatural ones. I sniffed my shirt, and finding more blood on it, I peeled it off, too. "Any theories are welcome, but I must get back to Sage."

"You shouldn't have come at all," Constantine chastised, his features hard.

Matteo looked between us uncertainly. "I'm sorry I failed. We did not expect so many of them, and it has been years since…" he trailed off.

"We don't face many physical threats anymore, do we?" Alvaro filled in. "You didn't fail, brother. Wraiths and fae are not so bold as to attack a cohort so openly."

"But these are not fae or wraiths," Constantine rumbled.

I paced away from them, my concern for Sage rising to a fever pitch. She had to be alright in the house, right? "Gather your observations and theories. We will present what we know to my father when he arrives." They all nodded solemnly, and then I wasted no time returning to the house. Our wards were only a half mile from the house, so I found myself at the sliding glass door in seconds.

When I let myself into the living space, my eyes searched the area for Sage while my other senses picked up two facts: she was in the shower, and she was absolutely terrified. As I walked slowly, my pace measured and human-like—more to get used to it around Sage than anything else—I tapped my wristband and sent a message on my forearm to Constantine, asking for women's clothing in Sage's size. He enjoyed women of all sizes, so I was certain he would have clothing for her.

I passed the bar where Sage's pancake sat half-eaten, and her water barely consumed. I caught a whiff of rotting fruit, and wrinkling my nose, I sniffed my skin. They were seeping into my pores, the sickening things. When I made it to my bedroom, I slowly opened the door, looking for anything that might be amiss, but I found Sage in the bathroom, door closed and water sliding over her body in an obvious cadence I recognized.

Sighing in relief, I sat on the edge of my bed and stared at the closed bathroom door. She was safe. For now. But that left us with an even greater challenge.

How to go forward in a way that was fair to her. She hadn't accepted it just yet, but we were stuck with each other. I had never heard of ley mates *not* being together. And besides that, I wanted to be near her. I wanted to learn every nuance of her character and become familiar with every worry in her soul. I wanted to shelter her dreams until she made them a reality. I wanted to be there to see every joy and heartache. I wanted all of it so much, it was a visceral hunger unlike any bloodthirst I could imagine.

Surely, she felt the same. But if not… what then?

Sage opened the door, her features tentative and her thick hair hanging over her shoulder as she poked her head out of the cracked door. Her gaze lighted on me, and perhaps I was imagining it, but I thought her heart slowed a bit. Her shoulders dropped just a fraction, and she drew in a long breath. "You're back."

I nodded. "I'm sorry for leaving you. My brothers needed me. It won't happen again, though. We have... it's handled, now." *That's a lie. You don't even know what those fuckers are, let alone if the wards will keep us safe.*

Sage's throat shifted as she swallowed. Even from across the room, the fact that she smelled like *my* soap mixed with her heady scent was making my throat dry. "It's okay. I'm glad you're alright. It seemed serious."

I stood, and I crossed the room slowly toward her—I couldn't help myself. "This definitely wasn't how I wanted to introduce you to my home."

A wry twist to her mouth gave away her sour feelings. "'Introduce,' huh?"

I rubbed my eyes, pausing a full two feet away from her. "Yeah. For lack of a better term."

A knock on the door revealed Constantine who stood in the doorway with an armful of women's clothing. "I brought a few things for Sage to look through."

Sage opened the bathroom door a little wider, revealing her towel-wrapped curves, and I almost lost my breath entirely. "How do you have clothing in my size already at the house?"

Constantine's pale lips twitched, and he entered the room with the same measured pace that I had been using around her. He placed the clothing on the bed gently. "I have several female friends who enjoy my company for... lengthy periods of time."

Sage stared blankly. "Friends."

"Thank you, Constantine," I said pointedly.

"My pleasure." My cohort brother left with a friendly wave to Sage. "Make yourself at home. We will do our best to make it an enjoyable transition for you."

Like hell *he* would be doing anything *enjoyable* for her. I knew how Constantine worked. Sage waved weakly as he left, and then her enormous, hickory eyes locked onto mine. "So, he has sex with a bunch of women and feeds on their satisfaction?"

"Pretty much."

Her eyes traveled over my bare torso and then back up again. "Why are you half naked?"

"Why are you?" I challenged.

A smile threatened to break through her scowl. "I smelled gross."

"So did I." I didn't mention that it was because I had drawn my blade across a monster's throat and gotten sprayed with blue mist in the process.

The amusement that had softened her eyes vanished suddenly, and she averted her gaze. "Silas, I… there was a —" she choked softly. Swallowing, she put a hand to her throat and frowned. "Shit."

I took a step nearer, already aching to hold her, to comfort her. "What's wrong?"

"There was a—" she gagged, choking.

I looked her over, wondering what I was missing. Her pulse was steady, her blood pressure even. There were no open injuries, no bruises. "Sage, what?"

She laughed in disbelief, looking away. "I literally can't tell you." The vulnerability in her gaze, coupled with her words had me closing the distance between us and hovering my hands uselessly near her arms, not wanting to touch her without her permission, but unable to stop myself from trying to shield her from whatever had cast a shadow over her thoughts.

"I know you don't trust me yet, but—"

"I do," she cut in. Her long lashes, darkened with moisture from the shower, flicked up, and she held my pleading gaze steadily. "I actually do trust you. Maybe it's the bond between us. Maybe it's because you've managed to show me that you care in the short time we've known each other. But I do trust you."

My hands landed on her arms, a physical manifestation of my emotional exhale. "You don't have to trust me all the way. I understand that it's earned. And I will earn it. I promise you that."

She regarded me steadily. "I believe you."

"I'll leave you to get dressed, and I'll use Art's bathroom to clean up." I released her, although it was an effort. "Just call for me if you need me. We're all back in the house now, so you're well protected."

Something flickered in her eyes, something knowing and hesitant at the same time. But then she backed away and squared her shoulders. "Thanks."

Did she feel unsafe because she knew something had happened? Perhaps I really did need to speak with my father sooner rather than later. As I left Sage and went into Art's bedroom, I considered the fact that I had never been in a true relationship with someone who mattered to me. Not a romantic one. I had had lovers over the years, but I'd always known that mortal lives were fleeting. It was easy to remain unattached when I knew they would pass on in the blink of an eye. And although I had understood the concept of a ley mate, I had never imagined that *I* would find one before the other cohorts or even my fellow brothers.

Art would have easily wooed her, understanding her emotions and the vast array of mortal experiences at a level I could never hope to reach. Alvaro would have used his deep understanding of thought processes and mortal motivations to ensure that she felt safe and accepted. Constantine, of course, would never struggle to lull women into complacent satisfaction, and even Matteo had a soft heart and a kind nature any woman would fall in love with.

Me? I was battle-hardened. I was clumsy and hulking and obtuse to a fault. I was not suited for love. But my father was much like me—he was a hard man lacking compromise and with even less compassion. My mother was as devoted to him now as she always had been. Surely, he would have advice for me, even if it was a few… centuries old.

I also hoped he had seen these fae-wraith creatures before. If he had not, then the vampire houses would need to unite once again and discover what abominations had been created and by whom. These sorts of things did not just appear for no reason. And the fact that they were tailing Sage tickled my intuition. The fae were involved here. I knew they had to be, but I couldn't see how, yet. I also didn't understand their motivations because the only interaction I had had with the things had been violent but unconnected. One had attacked Sage but had ranted about "having" her, and the others had drawn us to our perimeter, attacked, and without retreat, had allowed themselves to be slaughtered.

That fact stuck out in my mind. I rifled through my memories of battles won and lost, and as I dressed in jeans and a Henley from Art's closet, I had a moment of panic. I remembered a passage from *The Art of War* by Sun Tzu that matched this morning's events with startling exactness.

"Hold out baits to entice the enemy. Feign disorder, and crush him."

I barely had my shirt over my torso before I hurried back to my own bedroom and found Sage delicately inspecting a two-hundred-year-old paper fan I kept on my dresser. My room was more spacious than necessary, in my opinion, with ten-foot ceilings even though it was on the bottom floor, frosted windows all along the back wall, and a king bed against the right wall that still looked small in the cavernous space. I'd put my dressers on the left wall where a door led to my ensuite bathroom, and Sage stood there with the fan cradled in her long fingers. She'd put on jeans and a low-cut, white tank top, and she looked enticingly fresh, especially with her long waves still damp from the shower. Her cheeks blossomed with pink when she realized I was staring.

I cleared my throat. "I had a thought."

"Oh?" She replaced the fan on its stand carefully, not that I would have cared. We had acquired so much *stuff* over the years, we could buy *another* storage facility and still not have enough room. Art, in particular, had loved the 1980s a bit too much.

I made my way to her slowly, savoring her rich scent, warm and spiced like an autumn drink. "Did anyone approach the house while we were gone?"

She met me, hands clasped in front of her belly, and her pulse quickened. "They didn't approach it, but—" her throat worked convulsively. "I mean, I couldn't say."

She was hiding something. Cortisol and norepinephrine laced her blood, scenting the air with pine and only intensifying my belief that she was hiding something. "You can't say or you won't say?"

"Can't," she replied seriously. Her eyes held mine, pleading.

What the fuck was that supposed to mean? "Why? Sage, this is serious. We were attacked at our borders by things that were very similar to what Marcus was."

Sage cupped her elbows drawing in an agonized breath. "I suspected that."

"Did any of them come here?"

"I really can't say," she repeated, her eyes entreating.

This made no sense. If they had been here, I would have known. They would have taken Sage or worse. Was this some kind of human game I was missing? "If you saw *anything*, please tell me."

She closed her eyes in frustration before opening them again. "There's a—" she stopped, coughing. "God dammit," she muttered.

My eyebrows drew together. "If you need time to think something over, I'll give you time."

Sage pinched the bridge of her nose. "No, it's fine. I'll… figure this out. Somehow."

I really should just hit the restart button on this entire day. I'd bungled everything with Sage, and even now, her body language told me that she had retreated, bunched up and clearly unsure of her place here. I had to do *something* to turn things around. "I saw your telescope."

Sage relaxed, clearly glad for the change in topic. "I love the stars. I love taking pictures of them more than anything, and I've been saving up for better astrophotography equipment."

"Those pictures on your wall, those were yours?" I asked in surprise.

Her eyes fairly sparkled, and I hadn't even praised her yet. "Yes."

"They're incredible. You have a real talent for it, not that I know much about the technical aspects." I paused, realizing I might just be able to salvage this day. "Can I show you something?"

"I mean, it's your house," she said noncommittally.

I smothered a smile and held out my hand. "It's upstairs."

To my relief, she took my hand, and we went back into

the living area and up the stairs. As we walked, Sage's stomach grumbled audibly, and I glanced at her in surprise. "I might have overheard some of your conversation with Art. Even if you aren't used to elaborate breakfasts, if you could have anything you wanted, what would it be?"

Sage considered that quietly for a few moments as we emerged into the kitchen. "I had biscuits and gravy while camping with some of Mom's friends once. I think I get wet dreams about them, sometimes."

Art laughed, back at the kitchen table and looking calm and assured despite the battle we'd just fought. "Lucky biscuits."

I pointed to Art as we walked through the kitchen and to another set of stairs, which led up to the third floor. "She wants biscuits and gravy. Preferably sexy ones."

"On it," Art said, standing.

"I thought you were just making conversation," Sage hissed, glancing around.

"To be honest, I rarely do that," I confessed. "While we wait, I want to show you one of Matteo's hobbies. I think you'll find it interesting."

Sage perked up, her interest taking over whatever misgivings she had about our situation. "Alright. I'll bite. What's his hobby? Is it taxidermy?" I sent her a scrunched expression, and humor lifted her lips. "Extreme ironing?"

"That is not a hobby."

"Look it up. I've never been more enthralled."

I gave her a meaningful glance. "Never?"

She rolled her lips between her teeth, fighting a smile. "Nope."

"Challenge accepted." We reached the upper floor where the stairwell opened to a useless sitting room a decorator had filled with armchairs and beige decor, and then I led her down the right hallway to Matteo's set of rooms. He had two—one for sleeping, and one for…

"An observatory?" Sage gasped. We stood in the doorway of the tall, tower-style room, and I urged her forward with a gentle push.

"As far as I know, it's all in working condition. Have a look."

Sage took slow steps into the room, her mouth open in silent awe. A set of spiral stairs led up to the observatory dome, which at the moment was closed, but let sunlight filter in through its plexiglass windows. The observatory turret had two tables and a desk situated around the stairway, and to the right, an enormous monitor lay flat against the wall with a quiet, humming computer beneath it. Matteo had left things all over the tables—papers, notebooks, and printouts of graphs I had no interest in understanding.

Sage's eyes fixed on the enormous, black telescope at the top of the stairs, which had been mounted to some kind of electronic turntable thing that, again, I knew almost nothing about. I knew Sage liked it, though. She turned to me with starry wonder in her eyes. "This is absolutely incredible. I never imagined—I never dreamed I would *see* an at-home setup like this, let alone—are you sure he won't get angry if I just look?"

"I would be offended if you didn't use it," Matteo said behind us.

"Is that a Celestron?" Sage asked without preamble. I could see the feverish zeal inside her rising to the surface like an elephant's toothpaste reaction.

"The newest model, yes," Matteo confirmed with a laugh in his voice. He came to join us, his hands behind his back and patient features smooth as always.

"On an altazimuth mount?" she clarified eagerly.

"Of course. Would you like me to show you my TCS? It's brand new—a friend coded it, and it's, well," he paused, amused with himself. "I was going to say it's out of this world."

"Oh my God," Sage breathed out, almost pained. "Yes. Please."

I stepped aside, giving Matteo room to pull up a chair and guide Sage to sit in front of a smaller monitor that mirrored on the larger one. It didn't take long for Sage to catch onto how the software worked, and as they chatted about the moon Earth was apparently "borrowing" from Jupiter later this year, Art came into the room with hot biscuits and gravy, eggs, and pancakes.

Sage dug in, and we gently joked with her about her American food sensibilities. We shared stories about how annoying traveling by horse had been, and she shared her passion for the stars. In no time at all, an easy rhythm developed between us, and I found myself marveling at the perpetual smile on her lips, at the easy way she teased my brothers, and the way the clock spun away, but we kept company like time didn't exist at all. For the first time, I had an inkling of hope. For the first time, things felt stable. They felt almost normal. We could do this.

Everything would be fine.

Chapter Seventeen

SAGE

My vampires were shockingly endearing.

I spent the afternoon hanging out with Matteo, Art, and Silas, and they were so supportive and friendly, I wasn't sure what to do with myself. No one had *looked* at me so fully, not even my mother. It was easy to relax with them, despite the events of the past two days, and before I knew it, Constantine "made" us lunch—he took my order for a local deli to deliver—and we ate in the basement on TV trays while I forced them to watch the talent show competition I was currently hooked on.

Silas sat next to me, mostly quiet, but radiating warmth and safety in a way that managed to seep into my bones. It was nothing at all for me to lean against him as we watched our third episode, each of us making absurd predictions about the contestants. I was convinced the tightrope walker would win because we never actually got to see circus acts in these competitions, and Alvaro shrewdly picked the best singer because—and he was right—they always made it to the finals. Art chose a dog act because it made him cackle, and Matteo innocently thought the elderly knife thrower from Slovakia would win because he had spent so many years on his craft and had earned it. When I asked Constantine who his pick was, he gave me a knowing glance, and with his body sprawled lazily across the sectional curve, he said, "It will be the card magician."

This, of course, was an absurd pick, and we all teased him mercilessly over his pick. "Sleight of hand does not read on television well enough," Alvaro argued with surprising passion. "The home audience votes at the end of the season. That's what the announcer said."

"Well," I amended quickly, leaning against Silas' solid side and curled up comfortably under a plush throw, "they *did* vote. This season is already over."

"We can *finish it*?" Art clarified.

"No cheating," Silas said suddenly, hooking Matteo with a hard look. Matteo, of all people. I'd known the man less than a day, but I couldn't imagine wide-eyed, magic-eating Matteo cheating.

But Mateo smiled wide, almost guiltily. "Alright. Fair play."

"Play the next one," Alvaro said seriously.

I could practically smell the testosterone in the air. Unless vampires didn't have testosterone? Actually, Silas smelled like a mix of his cedarwood shampoo and a heady male scent. I loved it. I shouldn't, but with the easy comfort of the cohort and Silas' protective kindness, it was hard to fight my attraction to him too hard.

Constantine put a pillow behind his head, arms folded and long body taking up the entire left side of the couch. "I already rescheduled my plans."

"Ooh, bet she's mad," Art muttered with a touch of

glee. Constantine gave him a fast, amused glance, and then returned his attention to the TV.

Matteo pulled out his phone, and Silas pointed at him. "What did I just say?"

Matteo held up a food dash app innocently. "I'm getting dinner. What do you want from Chick-O-Rama?"

The room, minus me, grumbled in protest. "Again?" Alvaro grouched.

At the same time Art muttered, "*So* much grease."

"Grease?" I asked hopefully.

Everyone swiveled a look to me, and then back to Matteo who looked like Garfield with a full stomach of lasagna and stuffed crust pizza. "As I suspected."

Matteo handed me the app so I could look through the menu as the show's intro music began. Silas rubbed my arm while I swiped through the options. "Do you need anything? You haven't had much water."

I pointed at the three water bottles on the ground below us with an incredulous half-smile. "All I did was drink water today. You're wearing my bladder out."

Art snuffed out a laugh, and Silas' features softened with humor as well. "I suppose I'm not sure how humans... stay alive."

"I'll teach you," I promised him, patting his firm chest consolingly. "Starting with... *yes*. A large bucket of fried chicken with coleslaw, potato salad, mashed potatoes, *and* biscuits."

"I'm no expert, but I feel like that's going to kill her," Art said drily from where he sat on the floor to my right.

"Nonsense," I grinned.

"Oh, it's the magician!" Alvaro announced.

We tuned into the episode, our attention riveted on our favorites and the way the acts revved up their talents to continually impress the judges and audiences round after round. By the time the food was delivered, Silas' favorite, the dancing violin player, had been eliminated, and my tightrope walker was in serious danger.

I ate way too much fried chicken. I laughed more than I had in years. I played with Silas' strong fingers, marveling at how warm and stalwart he felt at my side. And I forgot.

I forgot that I was in danger.

I forgot that I was trapped.

I forgot that a monster had stolen my voice.

By the time the sun had fallen past the tree line and the final episode of our show had finished, I had forgotten entirely that my life was not friendship and camaraderie but supernatural bonds and unseen danger. I forgot it so thoroughly that I fell asleep in Silas' arms and missed Constantine's quiet gloating over the fact that his card magician had beat all our picks.

When I woke, it was because Silas had picked me up to take me to bed. I blinked myself back to awareness, groggy but suddenly anxious. "Silas?"

"It's alright," he reassured me softly, his voice barely above a whisper. The room was dark, lit only by the soft LEDs around the bar, and Silas passed it, going to his room with me in his arms. "The magician won. Damn, Constantine. I think he cheated."

I sighed, relaxing again and resting my temple against his shoulder. "He's too cocky."

"Took you all of one day to realize that, did it?" he asked with a mix of satisfaction and amusement. "Yes, we're all very bitter."

When we crossed the threshold into his room, I knew immediately that it was his, even if I couldn't see in the darkness. Silas had a fresh scent, a gentle petrichor that was both masculine and nature-born. He was fresh air, like he'd been on the earth long enough to absorb some of its arcane wildness. My body responded like an oxygen-starved bud, unfurling and waking with a greedy inhale. I pressed myself to his chest as he crossed his room to the bed. And then I hoped that he couldn't sense how my core was warming, how my thighs were unconsciously pressing together and my nipples were suddenly aching for his touch. The mate phenomenon was a hell of a thing.

Silas swallowed audibly as we reached the bed. "We haven't had much time to talk alone today."

I wiggled in his arms, trying to get him to put me down. He let me slide to my feet, but he kept an arm on my elbow as I rubbed some of the sleep from my eyes. "I know. We probably should."

He turned on a soft lamp beside his modern bed, still close to me. "We can talk more tomorrow." He hesitated, looking away. He'd put on a soft heather henley, and he tugged up the long sleeves as he seemed to think something over. There was something delightfully mussed about him, with his rich chestnut hair pushed messily to one side and five o'clock shadow sweeping along his strong jaw. "We might not have much time then, either, though."

I tilted my head in question. "Why?"

His eyes, like the stormy Atlantic, met mine. "My parents just landed in New York."

Surprise forked through my sleepy stupor, electrifying me awake. "Oh, shit."

Silas weighed his next words, his gaze flickering away from mine briefly before returning. "It's been a long time since vampires had a mate. And I'm afraid I didn't pay much attention to the last few I met. But if I remember correctly…" He seemed to be struggling to word something.

I waited, folding my arms and growing nervous. He skimmed a look up and down my body. "Don't be anxious, Dulcis. It's nothing bad."

I huffed softly. "How do you do that?"

"I can smell the chemicals in your blood," he replied, like that should have been obvious.

Great, so I couldn't get away with lying to the man. Then again, he'd tried to tell me that the day we'd met, when I'd attempted to lie about my name. I forced a breath into my lungs and told my heart not to panic. I wasn't sure how I could control the hormones my endocrine system released, though. "Okay, I'm not nervous. What are you trying to tell me?"

"They're going to expect me to have solidified the bond." Silas seemed to have decided to speak plainly, his attention fully on my reactions. "If I don't smell like your blood, and you don't smell like my... mate, then they're going to get upset."

"And what happens when your parents get upset?" I asked warily.

A wry kind of humor crossed his handsome features. "Usually, edicts are made and lives are threatened. In this case," he scratched his jaw, squinting one eye, "it might just be overbearing for you. For us."

"As in?" I prompted, tightening my crossed arms.

"Oh, for God's sake!" Art shouted from outside our room. I started, eyes jumping to the doorway. Art came to Silas' open doorway and held out his hands in frustration. "Sage, if you don't fuck our boy here, our parents will make you. That's what Silas is saying. They won't let you walk out of that assembly a virgin. And it could get very embarrassing for everyone involved."

I stared at Art, my mouth open and no air in my lungs.

Silas rubbed his forehead, looking weary. "Thank you, Art. You really have a way with words."

"I live to serve," Art said with a bow, backing out.

"Art isn't entirely correct," Silas said to me, bending to catch my stupefied stare. "Sage, look at me." When I did, forcing my mouth closed, he assured me, "You aren't going to be forced to do anything you don't want to. I'll make sure of it."

"But Art just said—" I sputtered.

"Art is being practical, and I'm being protective. We'll split the difference." Silas reached for me, sliding a lock of my heavy hair behind my ear. "I'll make it clear that you need more time, and you just stay calm when we're in there. I'm warning you now so you know what to expect." His fingers cupped the side of my face, and once again, I found myself drawn to him, greedy for his warmth and his scent. "You're strong, I know that already. Don't be intimidated by whatever happens in that stupid yacht club tomorrow."

"Yacht club?" I half laughed, half choked.

"One thing about vampires that hasn't changed for centuries," Silas explained, drawing me still closer, wrapping an arm around my waist, "is their pretentious displays of wealth."

I looked around his cavernous room with its expensive furnishings and priceless artifacts. "'Their?'"

"Our," he grinned crookedly.

My insides turned to warm fudge, and I placed my hands on his solid chest, relaxing into the safety of his casual embrace. I stared at my hands, at how small they looked against his broad body. "I think we both know that our bodies are falling victim to some kind of biology I don't understand." I lifted a hesitant look up to him and found him watching me patiently. "It's not that I *don't* want to explore that with you."

"I *do* understand the biology," he said. "But I get your meaning. Your mind isn't aligned with the carnal desires of your body."

"Put bluntly," I murmured, my lips twitching.

Silas squeezed my waist meaningfully. "Is this bothering you?"

"No." I drummed my fingers against his chest. "And I'm trying really hard to remember why I don't want you to take off my clothing and just repeat last night."

"Don't try too hard." Silas bent, skimming his lips along the line of my jaw. Goosebumps erupted along my arms, and my eyes fluttered closed, my head tilting back. Against my skin, he whispered, "There is nothing shameful about desire, Dulcis. I desire you." His nose nuzzled the sensitive spot beneath my ear before he dropped his lips to the side of my neck. "If you feel the same, it is no weakness on your part."

There was weakness, alright. In my knees. In my resolve. In my sanity, apparently. "If it's going to cause a problem," I said, my voice strained even as my hips tilted into his and my fingers tightened around his shirt, "then maybe we should just…" I groaned as he pressed a hot kiss to my pulse point. "God damn."

He exhaled against the sensitive skin, causing the flesh to rise, and a delicious shiver to trickle through me. "I'm very much at war with feeding what your body is asking me for right now… and knowing that it will torture your mind later."

"I mean, same," I managed to get out. I hooked an arm around his neck, clutching him almost desperately. I wanted him to kiss me. God, I wanted that so badly, it was making my lips ache.

Like he could read my mind, Silas scorched a path up my neck and to my mouth, hovering his lips above mine. "I can't satisfy both at the same time, darling."

And there it was. The crux of the problem. Silas couldn't honor my struggle for independence by giving me space *and* satisfy the burning need in my body. I had to pick one. Either he stopped touching me or he let loose and played my humming body like a symphony orchestra.

Fuck it.

I tightened my hold on him suddenly, pressing my lips to his and bringing our bodies flush together. Silas moaned into my mouth, lifting me against him so my legs wrapped around his torso and he could clasp me to him with unyielding strength. His mouth moved over mine, silk against velvet, warm breath against my frozen skin. My nerve endings lit up with a crackle of electricity, and my skin buzzed.

I was alive. I could feel everything—the rub of his shirt against my forearms, the lush pressure of his lips coaxing mine open, the molded strength of his hand under my ass, supporting my weight. He slipped his tongue between my lips, exploring, testing. It was so gratifying, I could cry. It was like I'd been standing on one leg all day, longing for a soft mattress to land on, longing to let go and unwind. Why had I tortured myself all day, pulling away from him, resisting his comfort?

There was a distant part of me that knew why. There was a logical reason. I just didn't care about it anymore. I kissed him with a desperate urgency, wanting him inside of me, wanting his tongue to fill me and his hands to claim me. Silas obliged, plundering my mouth and then lowering me to the black comforter. His body hovered over mine, and he let his fingers trace the shape of me, the curve of my waist and the bow of my breast. He followed the dip of my neckline, tickling my skin as he devoured my mouth.

My mind went blank, a haze of lust and need. It was almost painful, this awakening. My thighs burned, and my lower belly clamped tightly, empty and aching. Between my legs, a pulsing need tortured my nerve endings, screaming for pressure, for release. "Silas," I grated out. "I need—I need—I can't—"

"I know," he murmured. He kissed my cheek, and then my jaw, skating his lips to my neck. "I know, sweetheart. I'll take care of you. Just relax."

Relax? I laughed humorlessly, my hips bucking, seeking pressure. Silas brought his knee between my thighs like he had last night, like he knew I was going to burn up from the inside out if I didn't have something there, anything. Why was he moving so slowly? Why were his fingers teasing my neckline down so torturously? Why hadn't he torn off my clothing?

"There hasn't been time to explain," he said calmly against my throat, his fingers lowering my shirt and slowly baring my breasts. Too slowly. My temperature was skyrocketing, my breathing fast and my skin practically vibrating with need. I hurt everywhere, suddenly. Too sensitive. Too empty. Sweat gathered along my temples and the back of my neck. "Breathe slowly," he soothed. "Sage, there's... when we couple, your biology will work hard to ensure we mate."

He was saying something. Saying words. I didn't fully understand them. Why was he moving *so fucking slowly*? "Just take me," I gasped, grabbing at his shirt.

"Jesus," he murmured, his chest pushing into mine as he inhaled slowly. "Easy, Sage. Breathe."

"I'm breathing," I snapped.

"It's just your instincts taking over," he assured me, kissing my neck again, working the rest of my shirt and bra down and cupping my breast gently. I moaned, arching my back. *Finally*. God, that felt good. Silas was still talking, still trying to explain something. "We've put it off a few days, now. It's going to feel a little intense."

"You don't say," I huffed, and my fingers found his hair, tangling in the roots and gripping with punishing strength. He didn't seem to notice.

"I'm going to drink some of your blood," he went on, like that was a normal thing to say. "And my saliva will enter your bloodstream. It's called soporis. It will soothe some of the intensity. Okay?"

More biology at work. I didn't care. "Anything," I gasped. "Just—please."

I could sense that that hadn't made him happy. "I didn't want you to feel coerced. We might be past that point now, though." He kissed my throat again, licking it, and his hand moved over my breast, rolling, teasing my taut nipple. It was liquid balm over a burning wound. I groaned, gratified by the touch and needing so much more. I pressed against his thigh, riding him in a rhythm that should have embarrassed me. It didn't. My pulse thundered in my ears, and my flesh ached, too sensitive, too raw. There was a sharp pinch on my neck, a momentary prick of pain, and then Silas closed his mouth over my pulse point and sucked. My whole world went hazy white. Relief flooded my system, coursing through my blood in a gentle wave.

I sighed, relaxing into the mattress. It was that drug from before, the helium light fuzziness that made my limbs weightless. My frantic thoughts settled into a glassy pond. I still ached between my legs, still craved his hands and the pressure they would bring, but it was less frenzied, less wild. Silas sucked, and it pinched, but I didn't mind. The pain was good. It distracted me from the discomfort everywhere else. He swallowed a few times, sighing like he'd found relief the same way I had, and then he closed his lips, licking my neck once. "Gods above, you're sweet," he groaned. "You've ruined me. Anything else will taste like ash after that."

I desperately wanted him to ruin me, too. I wanted him to fill me and use me and make all the pangs of desire dissipate. Silas reached over me to the side table, opened a drawer and then pulled out a small object. I stared at his shadow-cast ceiling, my mind stuffed full of fuzzy cotton. I was a doll. A happy, buzzing, pulsing doll. Silas swiped at my neck with something rough, and then the astringent smell of something chemical filled my nose. A cold dab against the sore spot on my neck was followed by cool air blowing against it. I dragged myself from the murky depths enough to ask, "Is that… glue?"

"Yes." There was a hint of amusement in his tone. "Best way to close those kinds of wounds."

"Huh."

He replaced the super glue, and then with his weight balanced on his forearms, he stretched his body over mine. "You're calmer now. Do you want to stop?"

"No," I replied swiftly. Angrily. I had let go of his hair at some point, but I grabbed his shirt, lifting my body flush against his. I pressed my pelvis against the hard ridge of his erection, and he supported my lower back with his wide hand, grinding back. I lifted my chin, seeking his kiss. "I want more."

He kissed me softly. Patiently. "Think while my drug is in your system, Sage. Think it over a moment."

"I don't want to." I kissed him harder, deeper. I pulled at his shirt, seeking his warm skin, and when my hands met the solid rivets of his abdomen, I nearly sang with triumph.

He sighed, and it was ragged. I realized then that he might have eons of patience built up, but it only went so far. "Dio mio, mi stai uccidendo…"

I moved my lips to his strong, corded neck, kissing him like he had done to me. "English?"

"You're killing me," he whispered, rough like sandpaper.

"Can we die faster then?" I pleaded, my body getting warm again. The bliss was ebbing. "Please?"

"Fuck," he muttered.

"That's what I'm trying to say," I practically laughed.

Silas pulled back enough to look me in the eyes, and in the dark depths of his mossy gaze, I read all the heat, all the restrained passion leashed behind them. "Once we do this, there's no going back."

I stared back, and although I hadn't had time to think through the words, my soul spoke them for me. "I have nowhere to return to."

Chapter Eighteen

SILAS

Her words sliced through me, heart rending in their sadness and yet profoundly gratifying. Wherever she had come from, whatever she had been raised with, she was here now. She was mine now. There would be no delaying our bond anymore. She didn't know that once we made love, really mated, it would be sealed. If she thought the draw between us had been strong before, she had no idea. I'd seen new mates a few times before, although it had been so long ago that some of the memories were hazy. But they were more than attached, more than in love. They were bound. After this, she wouldn't think twice about being with me and leaving her old life behind. It was the death of her humanity and the birth of her new life all in one.

There wasn't time to explain this to her. She wasn't in the right frame of mind, and I had to wonder if that was by biological design in some way. Make us crave it. Make us impatient. Have it solidified and the union strong before anyone could question it.

And I sure as hell wasn't questioning it now. I let go of

my reservations, and my focus homed in on the details of Sage's arousal. Her blood churned and her lungs heaved. She had sweat gathered along her back and at her temples. Moisture had pooled between her legs, fragrant and mouth-watering. She kissed me urgently, and already, I could smell the soporis venom from my saliva burning through her system.

This was why I'd told her that she wasn't human. She wasn't. She was the ley socium, and her body was designed to crave mine. Soporis wouldn't last as long for her as it did for any other human that it was meant to calm into a stupor.

I shimmied her shirt and bra all the way down her waist and over her hips, taking her jeans with it. She didn't mind the rough tugging, didn't protest when she was quickly bare beneath me. I helped her remove my shirt next, and her eyes drank me in, almost feverish with interest. I didn't like that her instincts had taken over her prefrontal cortex like this. I hated that there was something so hormonal, so chemical about her avaricious need for me. Some part of me, lust-driven though I was, wanted her to want *me*. Silas. The man she barely knew.

It was stupid, really. There would be centuries for that. This was physical. It had to be, for now. Once she was bound to me fully, mated and truly mine, I could keep her safer. Then we'd have time to fall in love. Right now, she was staring at my pants, and some part of her logical self must have taken a gasping breath to the surface because she seemed suddenly unsure. Primal instincts or not, she was still a virgin.

I pushed up so I put my weight on my heels, straddling her hips. She sat up with me, wetting her lips and skipping a hesitant look from my face, down and back up. I made a genuine effort to not look as amused as I felt. Cradling her face like the most fragile china, I brushed my thumbs along her pale cheeks. "Close your eyes."

She obeyed but asked, "Why?"

"Feel first. One experience at a time, Dulcis." I kissed her, deep and exploratory, getting to know the fine lines along the roof of her mouth and the way her velvet tongue moved against mine. When I skimmed my hands down her body, she jumped, so sensitive that I could practically feel her vibrating for my touch. The backs of my fingers skimmed her nipples, and she let out a pained sound, pushing her breasts forward for more. I pinched lightly, and she groaned into my mouth. She was restless again, squirming on the bed and seeking pressure. It made me feral. I wanted to bury myself inside her, tight and warm and so very mortal, it was exquisite.

Still kissing her languorously, tasting her sweetness that hinted at the delectable flavor of her blood, I eased her back down against the pillows. She kept her eyes closed, and whether she realized it or not, her knees were drifting apart. I stretched out alongside her, still teasing one of her nipples until she writhed in frustration. When her arousal perfumed the air and my patience had reached its last threadbare tether, I skimmed my hand down her midsection to where her legs were already parted for me. She was soaked. Gods, was she soaked. I slicked my fingers over her clit and her warm entrance, holding back a growl of satisfaction when she whined with equal parts longing and satisfaction.

I had centuries of patience built up, each brick a lesson learned the hard way. They might as well be made of sand right now. I licked the column of her throat, and my finger began a rhythm side to side over her clit. She gasped, her hips bucking. I bit her neck softly. "Easy, Sage. I have you. It'll be better in a moment, I promise."

"I'm going crazy," she puffed. "It's so—I don't know. I've never—"

"I know," I assured her. I did know. My dick was straining hard against my pants, pulsing so hard with every heartbeat, it was painful. I'd been aroused more times than I could count throughout my lifetime. I'd never *needed* like this before. But she needed an orgasm before I attempted anything else. She'd be too frenzied otherwise, and we needed control, not unfettered passion.

"Focus on my fingers," I murmured low, kissing her neck and moving lower. I kept a steady pace, feeling her muscles tense, smelling the influx of fresh dopamine in her system like sweet cinnamon. "And relax your back, relax your legs. That's it," I encouraged as she obeyed, forcing herself to breathe, to relax into the sensations. I flicked her nipple with my tongue, and she groaned, her hands grabbing the blanket.

I watched her, fascinated. Her lashes flickered against her creamy cheeks, and her rosy lips were parted in ecstasy, her chest rising and falling with every puff of breath. Her smooth skin was dewy with perspiration, glistening in the low light from the bedside table, and as I licked her nipple, it caused a nearly undetectable tremor to travel through her writhing body. I dipped one finger into her heat, and her pussy swallowed it whole, tight and needy. "Oh," she moaned, arching.

"Oh," I laughed, strained. I moved the finger in and out of her slick heat, pressing my thumb against her clit in a way that sent her heart skittering. I loved the sound of her heartbeat. Strong and galloping, straining to escape the onslaught of desire racking her from the inside out. I picked up the pace, sensing that she was nearing her breaking point, both mentally and physically. If I pushed her too much, she would lose her restraint and probably try to beat the shit out of me. I started a rhythm with my right hand, middle finger entering and withdrawing, and thumb caressing in a strategic pattern.

Sage's gusty moans rose in pitch. "Yes, oh my God. Silas, yes."

My name on her lips was priceless currency. "Beautiful," I encouraged, speeding up. I sucked her nipple into my mouth and she cried out, her whole body tensing. *That's it,* I silently encouraged. *Give in, beautiful. Let go.*

Thirty seconds of steady rhythm, of loud, wet fucking, and she broke around me. Her pussy clenched and then released, spasming around my finger in the same moment her whole body shuddered and broke into a symphony of orgasmic reactions. Her heart immediately shuddered to a slower beat, and oxytocin flooded her system, making her sweet scent sharper and more defined, like citrus and cinnamon. Her muscles rippled before melting into the mattress, and she released a long, gratifying sigh of release.

Stunning. Truly, she had rendered me speechless with her perfection. I stared at her in awe, my own arousal nearly forgotten as I massaged her orgasm to its conclusion, and every one of my senses was engulfed with her. When she cracked her eyes open, they were accusatory. "I thought we were—"

"We are," I assured her. I wasn't sure I could survive walking away from this bed without burying myself inside of her. "This will make it easier for you."

"How?" she croaked dubiously. Her hair was splayed out behind her, a pool of spilled chocolate over my pillows.

"Close your eyes again," I instructed with a smile. "And

you'll feel." One of her dark eyebrows quirked up, but like she was too tired to fight it, she obeyed. I undid the top button of my jeans, and she stiffened at the sound. Nervous. She was nervous again. Better that than frenzied, though. I slid my pants and briefs down my legs and kicked them away, leaning over her on my side and capturing her lips in another kiss.

She hummed appreciatively. "You taste so good."

I chuckled against her lips. "And you taste addicting." I licked her bottom lip and then sucked it into my mouth. When I let go, she swallowed hard, her body already waking with desire again. "Your nipples are so sensitive," I murmured, almost inquisitive.

I brushed one with my thumb and she jumped, moaning. "It's—it's almost too much."

"That has merit," I whispered savagely. Torturing my lovers, edging them, making their desire balance on the precipice of insanity, was a definite pastime of mine. Doing it to Sage could easily become an obsession. "Another time, maybe."

"Another time, what?" she asked, already breathless as I blew on one nipple.

"Making you beg." I licked the pink bud, and she gasped.

"I *was* begging."

I laughed darkly, biting the sensitive flesh with the barest pressure. "No, you were not."

"I—oh," she sighed as my fingers found her clit again. This time, I moved slowly, teasing, using her moisture to slide over and around the bundle of nerves to bring her back to an arousal peak. She shifted under me, seeking more. "I feel empty."

"Hm, I can fix that." I moved over her, but rather than

do any such thing, I slid my erection against her clit. She gasped, closed eyes trembling.

"That feels *so* good, shit." She tentatively placed her hand against my chest where my heart banged away, beating my ribs and begging for mercy. I hadn't really been torturing Sage tonight. I was the one being slowly flayed into an incoherent mess. It took all my restraint to move slowly against her, teasing her sensitive peak with my aching dick. I twitched against her, and she wiggled under me. "Should I beg now? I can beg," she groaned.

I tweaked one of her nipples gently, causing her to inhale sharply, and then I moved lower, positioning the head of my erection at her entrance. My thumb on her clit caused her back to arch and her pelvis to rise up, practically begging me to sink into her. I gritted my teeth, moving forward a centimeter. She was so wet, so ready, it was easy. Too easy. I could plunge forward if I wanted, bury myself deep inside of her and slam, slam, slam, squeezing my dick until my release climbed…

I held still. Very still. She panted, her stomach contracting and hips bucking. "Why?" she moaned. "You're drawing this out."

"It's too good not to," I managed to grit out. "You're so beautiful, squirming beneath me, sweating and needy."

Her only response was a wordless plea, so I slowed the pace of my thumb over her clit, and then I entered her cautiously. I'd never been so careful with anyone, virgin or not. It wasn't that I thought I might break her, exactly, but she was precious. This was her first experience. I'd be damned if I mucked it up when I had so many years of practiced patience. I could make this memorable for her, at least.

But my Gods, she felt good. I sank into her heat, so

tight, it caused another sharp gasp from her, and I had to pause, letting her adjust to my size. She lifted her hips again, moving against me, taking me in. "That's it," I encouraged, not daring to move. "Take me in at your own pace. We have time." She did, lifting and retreating, pulling me into her in painstakingly small increments. I ground my molars together, my balls so tight, it was a wonder I hadn't pulled something.

When I was fully inside her, our bodies joined and my head bowed over her trembling shoulder, she opened her eyes. Deep mahogany drank me in, and her lashes flared. "You're in pain."

"No," I grinned sideways, a little ruefully. "I'm in ecstasy. You feel so damn good, Dulcis." I kissed her cheekbone, moving inside of her tentatively. "Are you alright?"

"Yes," she breathed, and she sounded almost surprised herself. Her eyes rolled closed again. "Really alright."

A tight smile pulled at my lips, and I tried a tentative rhythm inside her. Pleasure rocked through me, so acute I wasn't sure if it was physical or ley. It certainly wasn't like anything I'd ever experienced before. The gratification was transcendent. Incandescent. And Sage must have felt the same because her heart tripped into a frenzied pace, and then she was moving against me, pulling and pushing, encouraging me to do exactly what I'd been craving since I'd laid eyes on her. So, I did.

I filled her and retreated, glorifying in how right it felt. Slowly, at first, I moved in and out, a steady motion that sent me straight to the peak of my pleasure, and then I drew it out. I watched her moan and pant. I drank in the sight of her. The scent of her sharp arousal. The feel of her tight pussy around my pistoning dick. I drew it out for all I was worth, until we were both slick with sweat and our breath mingled into one desperate fog between us. When I kissed her, she broke, orgasming so hard, I felt it wring out what was left of my lingering patience.

I found my release with a guttural growl, speeding up and slamming into her. Her legs wrapped around me, pinning me to her. My back tensed and then shuddered as I finally, *finally* allowed myself to unravel in her arms. It wasn't the kind of unraveling like faded tapestries, but rather, a rend in the fabric of the universe, a tearing of everything I'd known about passion and belonging. I found myself utterly spent. And utterly enchanted. It wrapped around me like a warm ley line thread, like I could feel my unraveled soul knitting itself back together with hers. It was incredible. I'd never imagined it would feel this way.

Physically, I was weak, my bones useless pools of marrow and my muscles barely keeping my weight off my mate. Mentally, I was pretty sure a bowl of mashed potatoes had more deductive reasoning than I did at the moment.

"Atta boy," Art cheered from the next room over. Alvaro and Matteo laughed from upstairs, and I rolled my eyes.

Sage stared at me in wide-eyed wonder, her mouth still parted as she breathed hard. "What? What did I do?"

"Not you," I assured her hastily, kissing her temple. "God, not you. You're perfect, Dulcis. In every way." I kissed her twice more and then slowly pulled out of her, mindful that although her release would keep her on a high for a bit, she might be sore tomorrow.

Sage closed her eyes again, gusting out a long breath and wiping her hands down her face. "Sweet baby Jesus."

"Although babies are eventually the point," I smiled crookedly, dropping a kiss on her shoulder, "I can smell that copper implant in your arm. I assume you won't be wanting any of those for a while."

She lowered her hands, her expression stricken. "I didn't even think about it."

I'd been thinking about it every hour since I'd met her. There hadn't been any vampire infants in so long. Even the last match hadn't produced a child. The ley was too weak.

"And you still don't have to," I assured her. I stretched, my muscles unusually sore for what really amounted to very little physical exercise, and I propped myself on my side next to her.

Sage turned her head to look at me, and I noted with a whiff of amusement that she was studiously *not* glancing down. "That was really… I mean I didn't expect it to be so intense."

"Neither did I," I replied honestly, reaching out to tuck a strand of hair behind her ear. "It was beautiful. *You* are resplendent."

Her cheeks turned pink. "I feel kind of clammy."

One corner of my mouth lifted. "The shower is free."

"I won't wake Art if I take one? It's like midnight."

Art laughed in his bedroom, and I tamped down a smile. "He'll be fine."

With a groan, Sage sat up, looking down at her naked body. She crossed her arms, looking endearingly shy. "I guess I'll go wash off then."

"I'll be here," I promised.

Sage grabbed the comforter, and I slid off the bed to accommodate her, letting her wrap the blanket around her body as she gave me a sheepish look over her shoulder. "You're sure it's alright?"

I had already put on my boxers, and I came to stand close behind her. I couldn't help but want to touch her, to be near her. "Take your time. You can sleep in tomorrow."

"Tomorrow," she echoed. Her shoulders slumped. "Oh,

right. The reason we..." She touched the cut on her neck where I'd drank from her.

I covered it with mine, wrapping an arm around her from behind. "My parents aren't the reason I made love to you. I wanted you. Just you."

She seemed to relax at that. "I mean, same. I wanted you."

I knew very well how much she'd wanted me. It was impossible to miss from her scent to her longing glances, and all the way down to the cadence of her heart that even now was skipping a new rhythm when I touched her. "I'm glad."

"Maybe if I shower and go to sleep, this day will feel a little more real," she said, sounding dazed.

Yes, it had been a strange day. But a good one, when I tallied it against the innumerable ones that had come before it. "I'll remake the bed. Go shower." I pushed her toward the bathroom, and she tripped forward, giving me one last, lingering smile before she disappeared into the bathroom. When the water started in the standing, river rock shower, Art appeared in my doorway with a pile of fresh linens and a smirk for the record books.

I met him with another eye roll and took the sheets. "Why do *you* look smug?"

"No reason," he replied, his blue eyes glinting with mirth. "So happy for you. Don't hate you one bit."

"I was beginning to think he wouldn't do it," Matteo joked from the living room upstairs where he was playing Call of Duty.

"It was a fair effort," Alvaro added, and gunshots from their game punctuated their far-off voices. "Six out of ten."

Constantine barked out a laugh. "Two orgasms."

"Weak," Alvaro agreed.

My eyelids fell to half-mast. "If we're all done assessing my performance."

"All that matters is that she's happy," Art grinned. "She seemed happy."

"Debatable," all three of the other vampires said in unison.

"Fuck off," I replied loudly.

Their only response was to laugh at that. Thank God humans couldn't hear well.

Chapter Nineteen

SAGE

I couldn't write out a message about Cysgadyn on paper. I tried while I sat at the kitchen island, my pen poised over a pad of yellow legal paper Matteo had produced for me. Each time I tried to put the pen down with the intent to write out *any* part of what had occurred yesterday morning, my fingers refused. Finally, I scribbled "fuck," and pushed it away. Matteo glanced at it, lifting one thick eyebrow. "This is what you wanted paper for?"

"No," I groaned, digging my fingers into my hair roots. I let my head rest against my hands. "Never mind." It was giving me a headache, fighting the curse or spell or whatever it was Cysgadyn had branded against my throat.

Art was making food again, filling the space with bright citrus and the sweet aroma of ricotta pancakes. He had some kind of blueberry lemon compote going on the stove next to the pancakes. "Anything I can help with?"

"No," I replied dourly. When I'd woken this morning, my life hadn't felt any less surreal than it had last night. The soreness between my legs was real enough, but the memory of making love to Silas… it was potently magic. Too impossibly lovely to have been real. I'd never imagined that sex could feel so soul-altering. Perhaps it wasn't meant to, ordinarily, but for us, it had been. I'd been alchemized. I wasn't the same person now that I had been before laying with Silas, and I could sense he felt the same. We'd stared into each other's eyes so deeply this morning, neither of us speaking, just drinking in the beauty of the connection.

It was incredible. And horrible. It was out of my control entirely, and I was slowly coming to accept the reality of that. I belonged to Silas, and he to me. There was no fighting it. It had always been an inevitability. The stars would shift across the sky, the moon would wax and wane, and my soul would long for Silas. Always. And I barely knew the man—vampire. Whatever. It was mental.

"Are you missing Silas?" Matteo whispered, his endearing features crinkled with worry. He had seated himself on the barstool next to me after Silas had deposited me and told me that he, Alvaro, and Constantine needed to ensure that their video feed of the perimeter was accurate.

Yes. Desperately. "It's only been five minutes," I mumbled, straightening and staring down at the marble countertop. Art and Matteo exchanged looks. I scrunched one side of my mouth, splitting an irritated look between them. "Stop that."

"Stop what?" Matteo asked innocently, sipping his coffee.

"I wasn't reading emotions, you were reading emotions," Art added blithely.

"Non dovrebbe lasciarla sola, non ancora," Matteo said, setting his mug down.

Art shrugged. “Dovremmo fidarci del suo istinto.”

"English," I reminded them.

"That was on purpose," Matteo grinned cheekily. "More coffee?"

I glanced down at the cup I'd inhaled already. "Sure, if you don't mind."

"For you, mia cara," Matteo said with more gravitas than the moment warranted, "anything."

"Good grief," I muttered.

Silas, Alvaro, and Constantine returned quite literally out of thin air. One moment the living room was empty, and the next, they were striding across it and arguing. "... isn't like I catalogue every fucking flora around the fifty-acre parcel," Alvaro was saying, his accent deep and his thick, black hair wind-mussed.

"But that one reeks of fae and it wasn't there yesterday," Silas argued. He looked breathtaking today. I suspected he would look breathtaking every day, but today, there was so much to appreciate. He was wearing jeans again, light wash and molded to his powerful thighs in an indecently masculine way. The long-sleeved, black and gray shirt defining every rippling muscle in his torso and arms looked somewhat tactical. His belt was utilitarian, thick and black, and he had a handgun in a holster at his hip. His rich, deep brown hair looked a little long, covering his ears and falling into his eyes as he scowled at his cohort brother. He looked deliciously deadly.

"Every plant for miles smells like fae," Constantine replied evenly. Only he looked unruffled by the wind, his blond hair smooth and combed neatly into place and his cream button-down unwrinkled.

"That one smelled worse. What kind of roses bloom in April?" Silas asked, stopping just before the kitchen area and folding his arms. He'd become an immovable statue before his brothers.

And my heart had turned to stone. *Roses?*

"Many roses bloom in April," Art replied, like Silas was a little slow.

I could barely hear them. Roses. A rose bush planted at the edge of the wards for me to use. To pluck out when I wanted to see the fae queen. Cysgadyn had done as he'd promised, and he would return in two weeks, and there was *nothing* I could do about it. No way to warn them that these creatures could walk through their wards. No way to inform Silas that they would be coming for me.

Maybe we could destroy it.

"I'm burning it," Silas declared.

Hope flared in my chest. "Take me with you." I stumbled off the stool, tripping over my bare feet and barely righting myself in my haste to join him. All five vampires twitched toward me, and I imagined all of them cushioning one stupid fall at the same time. Vampire air bag system, complete with scolding, no doubt. "I want to see it," I clarified.

Silas crossed the room a little too fast to be normal, steadying me by my forearms. "It's just a rose bush."

"I know, I—" I tried to tell him that it was evil. My throat closed up, and I swallowed hard, my eyes lifting in frustration. "I want to go."

"Alright," Silas said in a placating tone, his eyes roving over me. I was wearing one of the outfits Constantine had brought down yesterday, just a simple pair of stretchy jeans and a violet T-shirt. "You can watch me… burn a bush."

It didn't solve the issue of Cysgadyn being able to breach their wards, but at least we could be rid of the link to the fae queen. "I'll get my shoes."

"I have them," Matteo said brightly. He had a fresh cup of coffee in one hand and a pair of brand new, white sneakers and socks dangling from the other. He glanced at the shoes thoughtfully. "You said 'my shoes,' but you came without shoes."

I had, in fact, come here without shoes. I slid an accusatory look toward Silas, but the Adonis of a man looked wholly unconcerned by my censure. "Those are cute."

"She's cute," Alvaro admitted, like it pained him.

"She has to eat first," Art cut in. "Cute or not."

"No, no, I'm fine. I never eat breakfast." I took the shoes and socks from Matteo's hand. Hopping on one foot, I slid a sock on. "I'll eat later." A chorus of disapproving grumbles followed that, and I scowled at the room of reproachful vampires. "Damn, guys. Come on."

"Art is right," Silas said, kneeling and taking my other foot in a gentle grip. I balanced my weight on his shoulders as he slid the sock on my foot.

"Hey, Silas," I started. He glanced up through his lashes, and I almost forgot how to breathe. "I can dress myself," I squeezed out.

He smiled, so blindingly charming I almost forgot how to think, too. "But why, when I'm here?"

"Disgusting," Alvaro said like it was anything but.

"I hate you," Art said at the same time.

Constantine looked murderously jealous. Matteo drank my coffee, eyes huge. I returned my attention to… God, my mate. There was no other way to think of him now. "You'll spoil me."

"Not possible." Silas put my shoes on and began tying the laces firmly. "And anyway, all my other hobbies are boring."

"You are much more interesting than knitting," Alvaro

agreed with obvious reluctance. "If I could read at least *some* of those disarming little thoughts—"

"He can't," Silas assured me.

"He could," Art corrected, sliding a plate over to where I'd been sitting. "But he won't."

Being in this house was truly the most dizzying experience. Silas finished with my shoes and then led me to the bar counter with a natural, light grip around my fingers. I followed without complaint, and then the sweet, lemony scent of Art's ricotta pancakes wafted around me, and my stomach growled. "Well, I don't *usually* eat breakfast," I commented, sitting. "But I've never had gourmet chefs making my meals."

"Gourmet," Art scoffed. "That's my new hobby. Introducing you to *real* food."

"Accepted," I said around an enormous bite of citrusy, sugary pancake.

Silas accepted a much bigger plate from his brother, and we both ate, stealing glances at one another but having nothing to say. Not with words, anyway. But the way Silas was watching my mouth, the way he licked his lips when I did, spoke volumes. I'd wanted him again this morning. I wanted him now. That soreness between my legs was quickly dissolving, replaced by a very different kind of ache.

Silas shook his head, leaning away from me. "Fuck."

"Ay dios mio," Alvaro grunted behind me.

"English," Art and I said in tandem.

"My fucking God," Alvaro said in a southern American accent.

I rotated an amused look at him over my shoulder. "You okay?"

"Ignore him," Silas suggested, still eating unholy

amounts of pancakes at a rate I could never hope to match. "We have a lot to do today, and Alvaro is surly."

"Everyone but you is surly," Constantine pointed out.

Silas didn't disagree with that. The wink he gave me confirmed it.

"We've been summoned to the marina," Art said as we walked through the forest.

Silas held my hand while we made our way down a leafy, twig-strewn hill, and I leaned on him, grateful for the many times he had saved me from face-planting into the dirt. I glanced at him, gauging his reaction to that. He looked, as usual, unconcerned. "For dinner, I assume."

"Sunset on the yacht," Art confirmed, painting his hand across the sky like he was revealing something wondrous.

"I mean, sunset on a yacht does sound kind of lovely," I admitted. The land evened out, and then we were walking easily through the trees.

Silas clicked his tongue and Art gave me a pitying kind of look. "I envy your naiveté."

It was just the three of us walking to the rose bush, and I was sure it would take us ten times longer to reach it because I'd insisted on going, but Silas didn't seem to mind. He was never in a hurry with me. Art carried lighter fluid and matches in a backpack, and Silas had talked to a witch about what to look for if the rose bush was magical. It was maddening that I *knew* it was magical already and I couldn't say a word about it. "Do you envy it or does it entertain you?" I asked for clarification with an eye squint.

"The latter, on closer inspection," Art grinned. He looked even less like his twin today, or perhaps, I was getting used to their differences. Other than their size disparity, which was still minimal, objectively, Art had a very different clothing aesthetic. He liked linen and breezy fabrics, and today, his loose, brown pants and cream, linen shirt were bordering on hippy.

"There it is." Silas pointed to it, about twenty yards ahead of us.

Sure enough, a lush, healthy rose bush sat between two venerable yew trees. Beautiful, red roses in full bloom lay nestled amongst dewy, green leaves, and the sun broke through the leafy cover overhead to bathe it in yellow light. I stopped short, staring hard. My heart gave a squeeze, and that pain in my temples stabbed into my eyes again.

If you wish to return to the fae queen, pluck a red rose. She will know you call for her, then.

"It does look out of place," Art commented with a misplaced look of understanding my way. He thought I was feeling nervous about the bush because it looked unnatural.

"It does," I agreed weakly. ADHD and a secret I couldn't speak wasn't going to mesh well, I could tell. My mind was already racing with implications. What kind of link was that bush to their home? Where would the rose take me? If we destroyed it, maybe the curse on my throat would disappear and I could tell Silas that he had a manic fae hybrid trying to steal me away from his borders...

Silas let go of my hand and took the backpack from Art. "Stay back here. I'll burn it and with any luck, it will be nothing."

I glanced around the empty forest nervously, suddenly cold out of the sun. Art put a warm arm around me, tucking me into his side. "No need to be nervous. Silas is very intimidating. The bush never stood a chance."

I choked out a laugh just as Silas reached the rose bush.

Unceremoniously, he squirted lighter fluid all over the plant, drenching its deep green leaves and causing the delicate petals to glisten. Then he struck a match on his thigh and tossed it. The rose bush lit up immediately, blazing to an instant inferno that forced Silas to take three steps back. I watched the crackling flames with hope clogging my throat. *Please burn. Please disappear.*

When the fire died, the rose bush remained. Unburned. Untouched.

"Well shit," Art whispered.

Panic stole the oxygen from my lungs, from my brain. While my heart leaped into a frantic cadence, my head went blurry with numb despair. Of course it hadn't burned. It had been created by fae, and those fae wanted me. They had creatures who could walk through wards, and they would return for me in two weeks' time. There was nothing I could do about it. It had been almost easy to ignore yesterday. I was so easily distracted. ADHD was like that. Problems were for future me, right?

I couldn't ignore this one anymore. I'd been cursed. They were coming for me. Silas couldn't protect me if he didn't know.

"... panicking?" Art was saying, his voice far away and his hands on my arms. "Sweetheart, it's nothing. It's just the..."

I only caught bits and pieces of what he was saying. My eyes stayed glued to the roses, to the eerily perfect furls that were red as blood and still as an omen.

"... did you say to her?" Silas was accusing.

"Nothing! She's terrified but she's just standing there."

"Sage," Silas said, and his face interrupted my line of vision. He bent down to put his eyes level with mine, his expression hard. "*Sage.* Look at me." I had no choice, really.

He cupped my face and forced me to hold his stare as he straightened. Some of the world spun back to life, grinding like rusted gears in my shell-shocked mind. I focused on the green of his eyes, so bright outdoors that they could be a rose leaf. "What's wrong?"

I opened my mouth to tell him. I would force it out. Even if my brain bled out of my ears, I would tell him. "Yesterday," I forced out. Pain seared across my forehead and down the back of my skull. I clamped my teeth together, releasing a growling sound of frustration. "I can't," I panted.

"You can't what?" Silas sounded scared, perhaps for the first time since I'd met him. "Tell me what's wrong."

"I *can't*," I shouted, pushing him away. I covered my face with my hands, fighting a wave of tears. I crouched down in the middle of the forest, gripping my hair like I had this morning. The pressure behind my eyes. The stabbing in my temples. It was unbearable. It crawled down the back of my neck and around my throat, a branding imprint of Cysgadyn's hand.

"What the hell is wrong with her?" Art asked incredulously.

"Tell me what you're sensing," Silas replied. He crouched down in front of me, surrounding me in his embrace that smelled like fresh rain and soothing cologne.

"She's petrified," Art said, his voice going still with concentration. "And angry. Frustrated."

"Stop that," I snapped, lifting a furious glance his way. "It's not going to help."

"Despair," Art added, staring me down steadily. "Utter despair over something."

"Over what, Dulcis?" Silas asked gently. "The rose

bush?" He glanced over his shoulder and then back at me. "The fae play tricks like that, but it won't hurt any of us."

"She's not confused," Art seemed to think out loud. "Just defeated."

I gave up trying to tell him to knock it off. "It's nothing," I sighed, raising my eyes to Silas'. "I'm sorry. I just got..." I laughed bitterly, more a breath than a sound. "Tongue tied."

"You're safe," Silas assured me, cupping my jaw and brushing his thumb against my cheek. "I won't let anything happen to you."

I believed he believed that. I almost believed it myself. "I trust you," I said so it wouldn't read as a lie to Art.

"Let's go back to the house." Silas pulled me up with him, and the more I was with him, the more my headache eased. I was unaccountably weak all of a sudden, though. Like I'd spent a full day studying and working and it was time to drag myself to bed. It was a long walk back to the house, and I spent it convincing myself that the curse wasn't affecting me physically and mentally. It was a lot of lying to myself.

Chapter Twenty

SILAS

Knowing something was wrong with Sage didn't help when she said nothing about it. She could barely keep herself upright on the way back to the house, and it was everything I could do to not overreact. She was human, after all, even if she held inordinate amounts of ley magic in her body. She was breakable. Exhaustible. It had been a long three days for her, and most likely, she needed sleep.

Damn my parents. If they hadn't summoned us, I would have let her stay in bed all day. It wasn't that I blamed them for wanting to meet my mate. I was certain they were thrilled in their own stoic, emotionless way. But it hadn't been a smooth match, not the way it had been between my parents. We were being hunted by fae and strange creatures with no discernable origin or motive, and Sage was still a little reluctant to leave her "old life" behind in favor of this new one. Which I wouldn't have thought possible after last night, but as usual, I realized how little I knew about the human mind.

"I have a shift tonight. But your parents want to mcct

for dinner?" Sage was standing in the kitchen with her eyes on her phone and her fingers tapping across the screen. "Oh, shit, I have an assignment due tonight too." She looked up, worried. "Can I borrow a computer? Or maybe we can go back and get mine. That would be easier, actually. I have all these files—wait," she gasped. "The article. I don't know if Cassandra approved it."

I didn't think it was possible for my patience to be tested, but Sage did an admirable job of it. Regularly. I thought through the best way to broach the topic at hand while my brothers sent me sympathetic glances from behind Sage.

Art was back in the kitchen, cleaning up after breakfast, Constantine stood with Alvaro at the counter where they were looking at security feed on a laptop, and Matteo was in the middle of stacking toothpicks into what looked like a complicated replica of the Notre-Dame Cathedral. I quieted them with a quick, hard gaze and then focused on Sage. "You're worried about your job with the movie theater."

"Well, yeah," she said like that should be obvious. "Jobs are impossible to find in our town. College kids everywhere."

Matteo lifted a pitying glance at Sage's way before returning to attention to the toothpick he placed on the structure. Art looked like he wanted to laugh. I was starting to think this house was too small for five vampires and a brand-new human mate. "So," I began carefully, picking through what phrases to use first, "security is a concern at the moment."

Sage stared at me, blinking once. "You want me to quit my job because the fae are hunting me?"

"For now," I hedged.

She scrunched her mouth to the side, thinking. "I feel weird about that."

"You don't want to rely on me," I guessed.

"I've seen what happens to women who move in with their boyfriends after one night together," she replied, pursing her lips. Alvaro blew out a raspberry of a laugh, and Constantine pinched the bridge of his nose. Sage sent them a frown over her shoulder. "What? Am I wrong?"

"You're wrong," Art chuckled.

"This isn't the same," I cut in, hoping to shut up the peanut gallery before they could make it worse. "And anyway, take a moment to ask yourself if you really think you can leave this house, leave me, and return to your apartment like nothing has happened." There. The choice was still hers.

"I know I can't," she replied immediately, calmly. "I'm not saying I will. I'm just saying we need to find my new normal."

"Do be practical, Silas," Constantine drawled to me insouciantly. I silently ordered him to shut the fuck up.

"So," she went on, eyeing me like I was an unreasonable neanderthal, "a laptop?"

I lifted a hand, unsure of how I could argue with that. She wanted to stay in school and hold onto certain parts of her life. I couldn't exactly say no. "Constantine?"

"On it." He left the kitchen to find a laptop in our office.

I checked my watch. "We're meeting my parents at the marina at seven. It takes about two hours to drive there." I gave her a speaking glance. "Two hours for human life stuff? Sound fair?"

"Fair enough," she shrugged, arms crossed but posture relaxed. She looked better now than she had in the forest. Color had returned to her cheeks, and after she'd had a sports drink and an apple, she had perked up. I still had no way to explain her unsettling behavior in the forest, but it wasn't bothering her at the moment, whatever it had been. She'd accepted so many things from me with startling equanimity, but when faced with a rose bush, she crumbled? It made no sense to me.

While she joined Constantine and Alvaro at the counter to get her laptop set up, I drifted over to where Art put the last of his dishes away. We shared a glance that held half a conversation already. She hadn't accepted her place here yet, but keeping her safe was more important. But also, we really couldn't fuck this up.Instead of talking about any of that with her in hearing distance, Art flicked his wrist and brought up his phone contacts on the inside of his forearm. He scrolled through them. "I'll call the witch again. She might know about our—" Art glanced at Sage where she was listening intently to Constantine give her instructions about how to log in to our secure server. His blue gaze shifted away. "Weeds."

"Not Eliza again. These new witches are practically useless, I swear." I leaned against the fridge, arms crossed and thinking through my options. If witches lived the same lifespans we did, I'd have a whole team of them I trusted by now, fifty times over. But they had human lifespans, and it seemed like the moment I found a competent one, she died.

Sage peeked over the computer screen, intrigued. "Why are new witches useless?"

Alvaro scoffed, waving his hands as he spoke. "They're all crystals and good intentions now. 'Throw this basil leaf into a river and hope for the best,'" he imitated with a sarcastic Disney princess voice.

From where he was concentrating on his Notre-Dame,

Matteo added, "'Stir cinnamon into your coffee for good luck.'"

Constantine snorted, fighting a smile. Sage looked at each one of us in confusion. "It's... fake?"

"Witchcraft is real," Alvaro explained. "But new witches are... gentler."

"They're weak," I corrected bluntly. "They gave up the ancient ways in favor of modern witchcraft that *feels* better. They're afraid of karma."

"Well, they did die kind of young when they were dark," Constantine defended mildly. "Karma is very real."

"We need a witch unafraid of fae *and* karma," I mused.

Art nodded in mockingly grave agreement. "So little to ask, really."

Matteo sat up like he'd had an epiphany. "You need a Slavic witch."

We all traded dubious looks. "Are there any left?" Alvaro asked uncertainly.

"One coven that I know of, but you don't want the coven." Matteo smiled mischievously. "You want the one who left."

That sounded perfectly ominous. "You have her contact information?"

"I can get it," he shrugged, hunching over the toothpicks again. "I'll have her here tomorrow."

One of Sage's eyebrows fell in consternation. "What does *that* mean?"

"One hour, forty-five minutes," I reminded her. The less Sage worried about supernatural affairs, the better. For now. She was struggling to "find her normal" as it was, we didn't need to add ancient magic from dark, Slavic witches onto her mental plate.

Resigned, she turned back to the computer and typed

something into it. I glanced at Art, and he stared back, hands on his hips. His face asked, "You ready for tonight?"

I shook my head, glancing back to my mate whose body called to me from across the room. The only reason I wasn't keeping her in our bed and exploring every niche of her body right now was because she seemed determined to carve a path for herself into this day. It was a delicate balance, giving Sage the room to have freedom but putting guardrails around her after she'd been thrust onto a precarious path teeming with supernatural monsters. I had a feeling I wasn't precisely striking the right balance yet. Maybe it would come with time.

We had time. We had all the time in the world.

Chapter Twenty-One

SAGE

When the sun dipped behind the horizon, I counted the day in my head.

Thirteen.

That was how many days I had left. Those were the number of days I'd been given to figure out how to keep myself safe from the fae and somehow alert Silas to the danger. It might be the only number of days I had left alive if the fae queen got her hands on me.

Thirteen. It was so paltry. So cruel when I had been promised eternity.

A biting wind swept over the Atlantic, raising the hair on my arms and leaving salt on my lips. I shivered, but before I could draw the sweater tighter around my black cocktail dress, Silas coaxed me into his side and wrapped his arm around me. "We won't be outside long," he assured me.

That was quite evident. Behind us, a stunning glass and metal structure glinted in the copper sunset. It had been built with the express purpose of housing anyone who was simply waiting to board the enormous yacht ahead of us.

And looking at the yacht in question, it was no wonder they'd been able to build such an overkill of a waiting room. The sleek, black exterior shimmered with orange and red highlights from the sparkling sunset behind us. Every angle of the boat was slick, almost predatory. There were three visible levels, each with wraparound balconies and polished, teak floors like pools of honey.

As we approached it, the air smelled like diesel and money, drowning out the fresh salt from the ocean. We stopped just before the gangway, and I glanced up at Silas uncertainly. He had his other hand in his black suit pocket, and his expression was unreadable. Art, on my other side, started up the gangway without hesitation. He saluted the two white-uniformed personnel at the top with mock severity. "At ease, gentlemen." They didn't move an eyelash.

Silas nudged me forward. "If you can look past the theatrics, you might like it inside. It'll be warm, at least."

Theatrics. Was that what one called a three-story superyacht that looked like a carved glass leviathan? The plank bowed slightly under my foot as I started up, and then with Silas at my back, I made my way to the second story entrance already open and inviting us in. As soon as I stepped inside, the world went quiet. The waves, engines, and gulls vanished, swallowed by the hush inside.

It was surprisingly bright. Generous windows lined each wall, and as we walked forward over plush, ivory carpets, I glimpsed the open deck beyond, adorned with white leather furniture and gauzy drapes rippling gently in the breeze. Silas and Art flanked me, and we came to a stop before a curved set of furniture. His parents were already waiting for us, already standing behind the polished, white couches like priceless statues. Lucian and Cassia stood as if the boat existed to frame them. They stood like they were worth a fortune that could not be bought or earned, that had survived empires.

I sipped in a soft breath, entranced.

"My sons," Cassia said softly. She hardly looked older than her own children, her lush lips an elegant shade of berry red and her wide, blue eyes glimmering bright in the golden hour. She wore a draped, red silk gown like poured wine, and as she came around the couch, she moved with exacting grace no dancer could ever hope to replicate. "Come. It has been so long."

"Only thirty years," Art replied with a roll of his eyes. "So dramatic." But he went to his mother and accepted her open arms willingly. He dwarfed her diminutive form, enclosing her in a warm hug. Her long, honey brown curls fell over his arms like satin.

The other figure in the room, Lucian, remained still as stone. Unlike his wife, he was hard granite and sharp angles, like whoever had chipped him into life hadn't particularly appreciated the human likeness. But although his cheekbones were too high and his mouth too hard, he was just as arresting, just as beautiful as his sons. He looked older than all three of them, with gray at his temples and fine lines around his fathomless, dark eyes. He shared Silas' build, broad and tall, barely able to fit in the well-tailored, three-piece suit. He turned his head to regard me openly, and his irises flashed garnet brown, almost red, in the dim light. "Be welcome, sons. And daughter."

My daddy issues made an internal ick face. *Daughter?* He spoke more formally than Silas, even. I was afraid to open my mouth. Silas nodded his head toward his father. "Thank you for sparing her the journey."

I hadn't even considered that these two had flown to *us* rather than the other way around. Maybe that had been some kind of vampire royalty faux pas. I should have asked for a manual before coming. *In the presence of ancient vampires, one must never present their neck or risk being drained of all—*

Cassia came to stand before us both, her luminous eyes dancing. "Silas, darling. And… Sage?"

My ADHD brain was going crazy, here. I forced it to focus and smiled. "Sage Herriman. It's nice to meet you." Yeah, that was normal. Was I supposed to curtsy or something?

"Such a fitting name for Silas' mate," she smiled tenderly.

What the fuck did that mean? "Er…"

Silas stepped forward and hugged his mother, a little stiffer than Art had been. I wondered at the disparity. Art had told me in the most gloating way possible that he was older than Silas by a few minutes, but Art acted like the younger brother of a royal family. Silas was far more serious, and his father's gaze stayed glued to him rather than Art. Was it because Art wasn't a sanguis?

"Let's sit," Cassia suggested, moving to one of the rounded, white couches. Like her words had cast a spell, Lucian walked stiffly around the couch to join his mate, and they both sat in the middle. Silas put his hand on my back and led me to the perpendicular sofa, and Art threw himself down on my right side like a teenage bro about to play Fortnite.

Cassia went still again, a picture of beauty that barely breathed. Lucian speared me with a searching glare that made the tips of my ears hot. "You will forgive any lapse in manners, Miss Herriman. It has been many years since I have spoken directly to a human."

I imagined this hulking giant of a vampire sleeping in a coffin and drinking blood by moonlight, and it was an incredible effort to not smile. I swallowed hard. "I don't mind."

Somehow, that answer surprised him. He blinked twice. "How gratifying."

"Father," Silas said smoothly, running his thumb over my knuckles, "Sage has accepted her role as my mate. I'm sure that's what you wanted to ascertain."

"I can see that," Lucian replied stoically. His garnet gaze flickered to my neck, and the pink in my ears spread to my cheeks.

Nothing made a meeting with the parents better than broadcasting our exploits to the room with a hickey and a superglued cut. No one else seemed the least bit affected by the fact that everyone had just verified that I was having sex with Silas. Cassia drank me in, quietly fascinated.

Silas reached into his lapel pocket and produced a printed picture. "If you are satisfied, then I want to make the Conexus aware of this."

Lucian leaned over and took the picture from his son, expression barely cracking to reveal a touch of wariness. He held the picture away from him like it stank. "What is it?"

"We don't know. There are creatures stalking our property, stalking Sage. They appear to be part fae and part wraith. Possibly part human."

Lucian's thick brows twitched together a millimeter. "This is not possible."

"It shouldn't be," Silas agreed. "Nevertheless, they are."

And they can get through your wards! I screamed internally. My mouth stayed shut. Art slid a contemplative look my way. *Read my emotions*, I screamed at him silently. *Danger! You're in danger. He's in danger. I'm probably going to get drained like a prize cow after a fair.* Art sat up a little, his eyes flickering over me in concern. My gaze pleaded with him.

"You've seen these things, Sage?" Cassia asked.

I forced myself to look away from Art, who was openly scanning me now, and I could practically hear him thinking. *Please figure this out*, I prayed. To Cassia, I nodded once. "It attacked me."

Lucian gave his son a withering scowl that sent fear scampering down my spine. That was the look of a killer. Silas' fingers twitched around mine. "I miscalculated."

"You never miscalculate." Lucian's voice was a whip strike, subtle but deadly.

A spring of anger bubbled to life inside of me, and whatever fear and frustration I'd been feeling a moment ago burned away in the wake of my sudden wrath. How dare he talk to Silas like that? I didn't care if he'd donated demon sperm to make him exist; Silas could—*should*—probably beat the shit out of this geezer. "I pushed him away," I argued suddenly, my chest hot. "He was giving me space."

"Space," Lucian repeated, like I'd just dropped the filthiest curse at his feet.

"Father, women in this time are different," Art said with a lazy swish of his hand. "Independent. Mates from here on out will be different than you're used to. Much has changed in eighty years."

"A fact that your father tries very hard to ignore," Cassia said with something of a conspiratorial smile. "I'm sure Silas is doing an admirable job."

Lucian didn't break eye contact with his son. "She is the first mate in eighty years. Far longer than we've ever experienced. If you cannot protect her alone, then you will return to Geneva."

Whoa, whoa, Geneva? Switzerland? "He's very protective," I hurried to assure him.

Silas looked pained. "I understand."

"He's really very overbearing," I insisted, my brows pulling together.

Slowly, Silas cupped my chin and turned me to face him. His features were a mask, iron clad and just as cold. "We understand, Dulcis."

His eyes were mesmerizing, a foggy forest in the rainy Pacific Northwest. I swallowed hard, pulse slowing the longer I stared into his verdant gaze. "Alright," I whispered.

He slid his hand along my jaw, and then around the back of my neck, massaging. He turned back to his father. "We're taking it slow. She doesn't understand everything yet, but she will. Three days is short, even for humans."

Apparently, I'd said the wrong thing. Lucian didn't look impressed. "Your sole focus is her, now. Not," he clipped, dropping the photo onto the carpet, "monster hunting. Move to a more secure location if these pests are an issue."

"Our wards are secure," Art replied confidently. He was still lounging, still a picture of repose, but I caught a glint of cunning in his eyes when he shifted a look to me. "Our cohort is strong, too. You have no need for concern. Two hundred years from now, Mother will be rocking a baby in her arms and all will be well."

Holy hell, two hundred years? My slight panic last night about baby making was clearly for nothing if that was how long it took to conceive vampire babies. I could live three or four lifetimes of my choosing before even thinking about being a mother.

Lucian remained unconvinced judging by the way his eyebrows stayed microscopically pinched inward. "Are you certain she is your mate?"

The air left the room. Cassia sent her mate a swift, incredulously questioning glance, and Silas' hand at the back of my neck stilled. His questioning hiss slithered like venom through my veins as he said, "Say that again?"

"She smells like you," Lucian stated bluntly, "and you've had her blood, but is she your *mate*?"

Cassia rounded enormous, blue eyes on all three of us, and Art let out a disbelieving croak. Silas lowered his hand from my neck and angled a look his father's way. "I don't understand your meaning. Yes, I am sure. We all saw the ley line connect us."

"I didn't feel it. Did you?" Lucian asked his mate.

Cassia volleyed an uncertain look between us and her mate, her long black lashes flickering. "It has been such a long time since we had a mate connected to our family. I couldn't begin to remember what it felt like for adjacent members."

"She's being diplomatic." Lucian returned the full pressure of his distrust to us. "We felt nothing."

Other people were supposed to have felt it? Art expelled an incredulous breath of a laugh. "We all felt it. It was impossible to miss."

Silas stared hard at his father, and although I barely knew him, I knew that look. He was strategizing. And his father was doing the same. They were playing some incomprehensible game of silent chess, and the longer they stared, the more moves they traded back and forth. The problem was, I had no idea what the goals of either of them were.

Finally, after what felt like minutes even though I knew it was mere seconds, Lucian smirked. It cracked across his marble features like he hadn't done it in millennia. "It will be better to ascertain in Geneva—"

Silas had me on his lap in one swift move. Before I'd fully registered what he was doing, before I could fix the hem of my black dress that had ridden up or get my bearings, Silas kissed me. He framed my face gently, but with an unyielding grip, and his mouth captured mine. My body responded immediately. My mouth softened, and my back arched, reaching for his touch. He coaxed my lips apart, curling his tongue and teasing the sensitive nerves in a way that doused me in red hot flames. I was too shocked to fight it, even when he trailed his knuckles down the sides of my neck, grazing the bruised flesh there and reminding my body what true ecstasy had felt like.

The fire in my blood rushed through my system, and I found myself panting, too hot and aching from breasts to pussy. I squirmed in his lap, but he didn't release me, kissing me deeply and stealing rational thoughts from my brain. There was something very off about what he was doing right now but I couldn't—

I gasped, pulling away. I steadied my weight on his shoulders, and his chest rose and fell fast like mine. His pupils were dilated, blown out wide and nearly swallowing the soft green of his irises. He looked as unsteady as I felt. Already, my panties were damp and my nipples taut, begging to be touched. I felt feverish. Wild. Silas looked past me. "Does that satisfy your doubt?"

There was resignation in Lucian's voice when he bit out, "It does."

"We'll be going then." Silas stood, carefully setting me on my feet.

This absolute *caveman.* Had he used my attraction to him to prove a point? Like a girl couldn't pretend to enjoy kissing him. How the hell did that prove I was a mate other than illustrating how easily he could manipulate me? Was that it? I was some kind of pet, and that demonstrated how pliant I was when he wanted to use me?

He held my hand, and I tried to pull away, but he held

fast. Cassia didn't look at all weirded out by the fact that her son had made out with a woman on her couch four feet from her. "I hope to see you again soon, Sage."

The fuck she would. My blood boiled. It burned in my veins, astringent and painful, but still not enough to distract me from the acute need Silas had awakened in me. My breasts felt heavy and sensitive. Every movement as we said our goodbyes and walked out of the room chafed. My underwear was driving me insane. It was too tight. Too damp. I wanted it off. I wanted all my clothing off. I tore at my sweater as we reached the gangway, and Silas helped me.

I threw it at him as we walked, breathing too hard. What was wrong with me?

"I'll see you at the house," Art said to Silas, low. He gave me a sympathetic glance, and then hooked a right, away from us. He was retreating, then. Whatever had just happened there, Art seemed uncomfortable with it.

The salty air was cool, but it didn't matter. As I stormed down the pier, my shiny pumps clunking on the weathered wood, it was all I could do not to tear off my clothing and jump in the ocean. Silas kept pace with me, and he didn't touch me until we reached the boat house. He put the barest pressure on my lower back, steering me to the left and down the pier. When he touched me, it was like being struck by lightning. My muscles seized, and before I fully comprehended what I was doing, I turned to him and grabbed his suit jacket, pulling my body against his. The pressure was good. Some of the aching eased.

"What," I hissed, "was that?" I was spilling over with emotions; arousal so intense, it was stealing my thought processes, fury, confusion. Art would have a feast with me.

"I'm sorry," he murmured, all traces of the hardened

warrior from before gone. The sunlight was nearly gone, painting his strong features in shades of violet and red. "My yacht is nearby." He smoothed a hand down the back of my head and then along my spine like he couldn't help but touch me, too. "It'll be better once we're there." He kissed the crown of my head, inhaling deeply and repeating, "I'm sorry."

"I'm so confused." I punched him half-heartedly.

"I'll talk if you walk," he promised. Reluctantly, I peeled away from him, and he took my hand, urging me down the darkening pier. There were yachts and sailboats moored at each pier, and I wondered how far we would have to walk to get to his. My shoes pinched my feet in a way they hadn't before. My cotton dress felt like Brillo pads against my skin, and I was covered in a thin sheen of sweat that made me want to claw the first layer of dermis off. "You're feeling resonance. It's the pull between us."

I stopped to take off my shoes. In a pique of fit, I chucked them into the ocean. "I feel crazy."

"You are crazy," Silas said with a hint of amusement. "It's not your fault, though." He pulled me forward again, keeping us at a quick pace that almost distracted me from the fact that I wanted to lick his neck and taste the salt on his skin. "When I kissed you, it was like tapping a tuning fork. We're connected, the tines of the fork vibrating in frequency with each other."

I could almost keep up with that, too. "What, so I can't kiss you without getting a fever?"

"It's probably a little… intense right now," he replied tightly. He'd said two tines of the same fork. Was he feeling the same way, then? Somehow it helped to know I wasn't the only one who wanted to go banshee. "It's new. We just mated to each other. It will take time to adjust."

I spied a little boat house to our right, vacant and dark and inviting. We could just dip inside and kiss each other senseless, until we felt better. He could take off my clothing and lick me all over, until I stopped itching and sweating and panting…

"Come on," he said with a laugh. "A little further."

I groaned, skipping to keep up. "Why did you do that?"

"My father was playing games." Silas hooked a left down a pier that stretched out longer than the others. At its end, another luxury yacht—black like his father's—lit the dark sea with golden light.

"Did you win?" I huffed.

Silas picked me up suddenly, kissing me ravenously. I moaned into his mouth, scrabbling at his shoulders to get closer. Against my mouth, he said, "I always win."

Chapter Twenty-Two

SAGE

We made it to the upper deck before I tore at my dress. I barely registered Silas bringing us aboard, only dimly cataloguing the refined, cherry wood furnishings and cream, leather details on the sun deck. I fought with my dress in his arms, shucking it up to my waist, and he smiled into our kiss, lowering me to a cold, leather daybed. It was padded and comfortable, and the texture soothed my heated skin. Silas helped me with the dress, slowing down my frantic clawing and carefully levering it over my head and away from my arms. When he tossed it aside, I reached around for my lacy bra clasp, but he stilled me, his large hands on mine. "Easy, Dulcis."

Breathing hard, I stared up at him from where he still stood bent over me. Silas straightened, his eyes hot coals that left burning trails over my flesh as he raked an appraising gaze over me. I lay back on the lounger, watching in fascination as he shrugged off his suit jacket, slow and methodical. He drank in the sight of me stretched out before him in my underwear, and painfully slow, he undid his cufflinks, pushing up his sleeves to his corded forearms. Saliva pooled in my mouth. I wanted to lick those flexing ridges, to feel their hard strength under my pliant tongue.

Silas unbuttoned the white shirt, pulling it out of his dress pants, and when he let it slide off his torso, I breathed out a whine, my legs clenching together. He was so magnificent, so finely hewn and taut in all the right places. I wanted him with a kind of desperation that couldn't be human. When I reached for him, he stepped back, still burning me with his gaze. "I'm taking my time with you tonight."

That was quite literally the last thing I wanted. "Pretty sure my discomfort is your fault."

"I'm pretty sure your discomfort is *your* fault," he countered. He unbuckled his belt slowly, and the clank of metal on leather thumped low in my belly and sank between my legs. I wanted him to do things with that belt. Things my brain didn't even know about yet, but my body certainly did. When he whipped the belt out of the loops, I jumped, but he didn't flinch. "You have a lesson to learn tonight."

I watched the way his forearm flexed as he held the belt looped at his hip. "What lesson? Don't date vampires?"

"Never," he said calmly, but so low, I caught the emotion behind the word, "put my welfare above yours."

My heart bounded into my throat, nearly clogging my denial. "I didn't do that."

"Yes, you did." Silas dropped the belt to the deck, and a sea breeze ruffled his chestnut hair, already darker as the sun finally slipped below the horizon. "Verbally challenging and contradicting a two-thousand-year-old vampire is quite possibly the most dangerous thing you could do."

And I'd done it in his defense. It was hard to think straight with my pulse gathering between my legs and my breasts so hot and aching, they rubbed uncomfortably against my bra. It was hard to think when his strong body was bending over mine again. I tried to formulate a reasonable response. Some part of me knew that I'd only wanted to prevent Lucian from forcing us to Geneva. All that came out was, "Wha—oh," because he had shifted to his knees, straddling me as I stretched my legs out beneath him, and he supported his weight on his forearms on either side of my head. His large body dwarfed mine, shielding me from the cool breeze I'd barely noticed and making that aching need intensify excruciatingly.

He ran his lips along the ridge of my cheekbone. "I'll hear this phrase from your lips three times tonight." He hovered his lips above mine, speaking with razor-sharp softness. "'My life is precious.'"

I pulled away, quirking one sardonic brow. "Oh, will you?"

"I will." He kissed me deeply, and every nerve cheered with delight. I lifted my breasts to brush against his chest, and it eased some of the heaviness, that pressure. He cupped the back of my head, digging his fingers into the thick waves of my soft hair and forcing my mouth to open for him. He plundered me, thrusting his tongue in and out of the warm recesses and making me dizzy with desire. The pulsing between my legs became unbearable, my blood like lava with every heartbeat. I lifted my hips, seeking him, but he was too tall, straddled over me and only touching me where he wanted to touch me.

A real pang of fear shot through me. He didn't actually mean he would take his time, did he? It had been too long from one boat to the other. It had taken a human lifetime to remove my dress and find myself between his hard arms. I made an impatient sound and wrapped my arms around his broad back, attempting to pull him down on top of me. He didn't move a fraction. Instead, he moved his lips away from mine, kissing my jaw, my pulse point, and then the wound from where he'd drank from me last night. He licked a feather-light line down to my bra, and I shuddered, twisting under him, desperate for pressure and friction.

When his mouth closed over my nipple through the padded bra, I gasped, twitching. "Yes, please," I pleaded. He nipped and sucked hard, but it wasn't enough because there was fabric between us. I loved it and I hated it. I reached for my bra strap to pull it down, but he captured my wrist and forced it down to the leather bed. His fingers were an iron manacle, utterly inescapable. He took my nipple between his teeth, biting just enough to give me sensation through the padding. He glanced up through his lashes at me, and I saw it, finally.

Deviousness. The words he expected me to say. The lesson he expected me to learn. He would use his centuries-old patience against my manic need for him. And as he'd said moments before… he always won.

I narrowed my eyes. "You—"

He bit harder, just enough to cut off my sentence, and when I moaned, he sucked the nipple into his mouth. His arm snaked around my arched back, supporting me, and he worked the other nipple with his free hand. Every squeeze and pinch went straight to my pussy, somehow intensifying the empty yearning there. I bucked under him, trying to roll away, to escape from the torture. He pressed my wrist back into the leather and sucked me back down under him, grinning devilishly. "Where are you going? This is what you wanted."

I garbled out a frustrated noise. "I'm sorry. Just *please* touch me."

"I don't think that's the right phrase," he mused. But he ran his teeth over my bra strap, and it snapped in half. When he lowered the cup and covered my breast with his rough palm, I saw red with white sparks behind my eyelids.

"Oh my God," I moaned.

His thumb circled my nipple, and sparks of pleasure flooded my system. "You smell so damn good," he whispered, lapping at my nipple and then sucking it into his mouth. My back arched hard, and the pulsing between my legs squeezed tight, pulling me unexpectedly close to an orgasm. He released me and blew on the bud, tickling and caressing in a way that made me mad.

"Fuck. Silas, please. I'm burning up." And I was. There was a furnace at my center, and he was shoveling coal into it.

"I don't think that's the phrase either." He sounded equal parts amused and unyielding, and then he swirled his tongue around the exposed nipple, tweaking the other through my bra.

I writhed, insane with desire, desperate for pressure, for release. "Silas, please."

"You're so close," he murmured with his lips against my breast. I was fighting him now, trying to escape or get closer. It was hard to tell which. But his arm around my waist held me steady, and he worked my nipples in earnest, licking and nipping one, tweaking and circling the other. The pulsing at my center grew stronger, tighter. I squeezed my thighs together.

"*Silas*," I nearly screamed.

"So very close," he encouraged. "Say it, Dulcis. Engrain it in your brain, in your soul. I will not compromise on it."

There was nothing for it. I'd known I would lose, but damn him for it anyway. With a harsh exhale, practically a growl, I bit out, "My life is precious." *But I don't believe it, and you can't make me—*

Silas slid his hand down my body and between my legs. He didn't even have to slip the finger into my underwear. He pressed against my clit and sucked my nipple deep into his mouth, and I came so hard, I screamed. The release crashed through me with cymbals and a beating bass drum that hammered from my legs to my breasts in deafening waves. Pulse after pulse, so intense, so gratifyingly inevitable, I melted against his hold.

"Good girl, even if you did lie." He kissed my breast and removed the bra entirely before nipping the other bud. I jumped, overly sensitive while waves of pleasure still rocked through me. "I'll bet your cunt tastes exquisite right now. Should I try?"

My chest squeezed. "Now?"

"I said three," he reminded me.

"Oh my God."

Silas gave me a hard smirk, his green eyes glinting with savagery, and then he slid down my body. I couldn't even fight him on it. I was a steamed green onion, floppy and boneless. When he peeled my black lace underwear down my legs, I watched in mute wonder as he kissed his way down my leg, licking and nipping and waking my sleepy senses back to life.

He was going to do this to me again. He was going to drive me wild and use the resonance against me, all while suffering himself without giving us both what we really wanted, which was his hard cock deep inside of me. To make a point? I could strangle him. When he reached my ankles and threw my underwear aside, I snapped my knees together. "Silas."

"Hm?" he ran his lips back up my leg, and a delightful shiver followed.

"I-I'll say it two times. Maybe you could just—" He reached the apex of my thighs and paused, lips near my crease and eyes flicking up to me. "Fuck me?" I finished weakly.

He smiled wickedly. "I'll hear it when you're ready to say it." He pried my knees apart, spreading my legs wide.

I swallowed thickly, suddenly entranced by the way he was staring at my pussy like it was the last glistening coconut in an endless, sandy desert. "My Gods, you smell like dessert." He licked a line from my thigh to my spread pussy, and I gasped, head falling back as a fresh wave of nearly unbearable lust rocked through me. When he ran his tongue along the edge of my folds, I saw stars again. So good. *Too* good. "So *good*," he echoed, groaning.

Silas began the most decadently torturous exploration of my cunt known to mankind. He licked and tasted, swirled and sucked, all while studiously ignoring the pulsing bundle of nerves that screamed for pressure. He dipped his tongue into my heat and then circled the entrance. He licked up one side and then down the other, groaning happily and murmuring phrases of encouragement, telling me what a beautiful goddess I was, how I tasted like heaven and felt like sin. I gripped the sides of the daybed, my hips twitching and thrusting against his mouth, begging in useless, babbling phrases for him to please, please, *please* stop. And to not stop. To stay right there but also please, for the love of God, stop the torture.

Silas knew what drove me wild already. He blew cold air on my clit for the briefest of seconds, and my whole core tightened to an almost peak. "Oh fuck," I gusted. I was panting hard already, my center empty and fluttering. "Silas, I'm really begging. I am."

"You will be," was all he said. He reached up and rolled one hard nipple between his thumb and forefinger. I cried out, twisting, and he held me still with a large hand low on my belly. "That's my good girl," he encouraged, low and humming. "You want my cock, don't you?"

"So much," I panted. "Please."

"Hm, and I want you to learn a lesson. We're at an impasse." His tongue lapped at my entrance, and I jerked, my hips reaching for more.

"I'll do what you want," I promised, opening my eyes again to watch the torment.

He circled my clit with his tongue, and it was agony. "Will you?"

"Anything," I squeezed out.

He pinched my nipple again, blowing across my clit. "Anything?"

I screeched, fighting against his firm hand. "Yes, Silas."

"Then say it. And mean it."

I saw the truth of his intent then. The intensity of his gaze. The adoration in the way he watched my reaction, in the way he handled my body with ruthless but gentle care.

Silas believed it. I could try. "My life is precious," I said with half conviction.

"Good girl," he murmured. He rewarded me with pressure on my nipple, his mouth on my clit, and a gentle sucking, licking maneuver that sent my soul straight into orbit. My limbs shuddered, my pelvis lifting, and then the tension snapped. Another orgasm rippled through me, a crashing wave that reverberated for miles. He gentled his sucking, drawing out the spasms for all they were worth, prolonging the pleasure until I shook.

I opened my eyes, and the dawning stars greeted me, a glittering blanket overhead. I released a breath of wonder, reveling in the way my whole body thrummed and tingled. Silas hadn't drunk from me, hadn't fed my blood that calming, addicting drug in his saliva, but it felt like he had. I was calm, now. Satiated.

But Silas wasn't done with me. He dipped two fingers into my sore entrance, and I sucked in a surprised breath, arching again. It wasn't possible that I could do this a third time, that I could feel a renewed surge of arousal at his touch, and yet, I was. He kissed the inside of my thigh, his fingers moving in and out of my soaked pussy, demanding nothing, like he simply wanted to feel me. I shifted, seeking more of him. Even in the aftershock of two soul-shattering orgasms, his breath on my thigh and his fingers in my heat coaxed my pulse back to life. When he withdrew, I groaned, lifting my head and giving him a pleading look. Somehow, that emptiness was worse than anything else.

He smiled, softer now and less savage than before. When he kissed up to my hip and slid his fingers to my clit, my abdomen sucked in tight. The direct contact was so good, so right. It would have been too much before, but now, it was exactly what I wanted. He kissed my navel, my ribs, my breasts, and then he was over me again, warm and solid. My shield. When he kissed me, it was slower. Controlled. I remembered then that he felt resonance, too. And yet, he'd been eternally patient with me, drawing out the pleasure for us both.

It wasn't fair, really, his perfection. How could a mere mortal hope to compare to that? But his kiss told a different story about what he thought of my humanity—about what he adored. He persuaded my lips to part, and then he filled me with his scent and mine. His fingers moved in a slow, coaxing rhythm over my clit until my breath hitched. His lips devoured mine, tasting and savoring. He kissed me in a way that went beyond pleasuring. It was more than a skilled kiss from an adoring lover. It was worship.

When he had me panting for him again, squirming beneath his solid body and moaning pleas, he stripped off the rest of his clothing and positioned himself between my legs. With the utmost care, with languid passion, he brought me back to the precipice of pleasure, back to that tipping point where the only way down was a sheer plummet into ecstasy. And when he entered me, I was soft and slick, ready for him to fill me to the breaking point.

This time my eyes were open and my mind alert. He held my gaze as he filled me and retreated. He didn't have to utter a single word to convey the depth of his feelings—he didn't demand the phrase from me because he'd made it clear with every loving gesture, every careful caress. With his gaze soldered to mine, he drove the message into me with relentless strokes.

As we reached our zenith together, I had no choice but to accept it. "My life is precious," I whispered. *But so is yours.*

Chapter Twenty-Three

SILAS

Sage was in pain again. I couldn't pinpoint where, and she wouldn't admit to hurting when I probed, but I could tell from the cortisol and lactic acid release in her blood stream. I wasn't an adfectus, though. I couldn't read her moods or understand her emotions. I took her to Art the moment we were back home the next morning.

Art scanned her with his eyes and his dark brows pulled together. "She's annoyed with you, mostly." We were standing in the downstairs living room, and Art had been waiting for us by the wet bar. I could hear and smell the random female companion he had in his room, so I was surprised to find him fully dressed in a white T-shirt and black joggers.

"Because you keep letting him read my emotions," Sage accused. She was dressed in a matching jersey loungewear set that looked as cozy as it did rippable. Probably because she looked eminently *fuck*able. Her long, untamed waves hung down her back, and her lips were still swollen from the kiss we'd shared before coming inside. I'd held back from drinking her blood last night, but now my gums were aching and the scent of her was doing insane things to my brain. Wild things that made me feel like a young, bloodthirsty vampire again.

"She's in pain," I said to Art, ignoring her dismissal.

"Are you?" he asked her.

Sage hesitated. "Not exactly."

Art's tongue rolled in his cheek as he thought. "I sensed something really off from you last night, Sage. While our father was speaking." She stared at Art, her doe eyes wide but not saying anything. Her heart picked up, too, but that was all I could sense from her. "Yeah, that," Art frowned in thought. "It's really intense, whatever it is." He glanced at me uncertainly. "If I fed on her, I could—"

"No." I met his annoyed glance with unflinching steel in mine.

"Yeah, well, then I can't tell you what's going on." He gave Sage a speculative eyebrow tilt. "You're being really weird, though. Even for a human."

"I'm aware," she sighed, almost dejected.

"Hm," Art thought out loud.

"I need to do some research," Sage said, looking between us. "Maybe I can figure something out on my own. Would it be safe to go get my stuff now?"

"Already did," Art assured her. "Constantine gathered the things from your room and brought them here."

"I don't understand," I frowned, taking in Sage's beautiful, healthy appearance in confusion. There was nothing *wrong* with her, but clearly something was off. "What do you need to research?"

"Let me read her," Alvaro said from the staircase. He scrubbed the beard growth he'd allowed to grow in, looking quietly confident as he came down the last of the stairs.

Unlike Art, Alvaro wasn't fully dressed. He'd had the presence of mind to put on a pair of jeans, but his upper half was obnoxiously bare.

Sage suddenly looked enlightened. "Yes," she agreed quickly. "Yes, do that."

What the hell? "Why?" I asked them both.

"If she feels a certain way but can't name it," Alvaro replied in his patient, lilting accent, "then let me try."

I did not like my brothers getting anywhere near feeding on Sage. "I don't know."

"I won't consume the thought," Alvaro promised, like I was daft for even thinking he would. He came to stand close to my mate, and all my instincts told me to drain his worthless body.

I ground my molars together, leaning back against the wet bar. "Fine."

Alvaro motioned for Sage to sit on one of the padded bar-height chairs, and when she did, he leaned one hand on the granite counter to peer at her. Sage stared back, a little line between her brows while she clearly concentrated on something. Alvaro's features grew increasingly concerned. He lifted his eyes to mine. "I cannot hear her."

"What?" I hissed.

"I mean, I can hear her now. She's thinking how frustrated she is and how she really hoped this would work. But then she goes in and out." Alvaro gestured vaguely with his hand. "Like static."

Sage sighed, rubbing her face with both hands. "Yeah. Figures."

"Also, she wants me to put a shirt on," Alvaro grinned crookedly.

"We all want that," Art drawled.

Constantine appeared at the foot of the stairs, too,

thankfully clothed in his usual, well-pressed button-down and chinos. "Matteo has returned with the witch."

Sage suddenly looked intensely exhausted, like she'd crossed the finish line of a 500 meter sprint. She winced, rubbing her eyes. I went to her, standing between her legs and cupping her face to look at mine. "What do you need?"

She shrugged and shook her head dismissively. "Nothing. Maybe the witch can help."

"With what?" I enunciated with frustration. Humans were supposed to be easy and a ley socium even easier. They lived a long time with all the ley in their bodies, and as long as they were protected by us, they flourished with their mates. What could possibly cause Sage to suffer internally that couldn't be read by any vampire?

She covered my hands with hers, smiling wearily. "I don't know, really."

This was going to drive me insane. I was a problem solver, not a problem endurer. "Let's get you some coffee and food."

"You fed me breakfast already," she pointed out with some amusement, but she didn't protest when I took her by the hand and led her to the stairs. My brothers were already up there, and I could smell the witch as she crossed my threshold. Ley had an interesting scent to it, like the air high in the stratosphere and a cold winter morning. This witch was full to brimming with it, and I was surprised that Matteo had the resilience to travel with her and not feed on her. I didn't even drink ley and I found myself enamored with her power.

As we entered the kitchen from the stairwell, I heard Matteo say, "This is Isabeau Rusalka from the Embervein line."

"Beau," a young female voice corrected almost in monotone.

We walked through the kitchen to the open, brightly lit living space. They had all gathered around the front entrance area, and as Sage and I came to join them, I found a diminutive, almost fae-like girl standing next to Matteo and staring down the vampires with admirable bravery. She had silky, black hair cut into a sharp bob with bangs, pale, almost translucent skin, and enormous, expressive, blue eyes. She didn't look older than seventeen, if that, and the baggy T-shirt and shorts that disappeared under the hem didn't help the impression that she was quite literally a child. Neither did her stature, which put her at maybe five feet with her platform sneakers on. That explained why Matteo hadn't fed on her ley.

Art pointed to the witch, sliding an incredulous look my way. "That's a child."

"Why did you bring a kid into this house?" Constantine wanted to know, folding his arms in consternation.

Matteo gestured up and down Beau's body like he was pointing out an invisible figure. "You needed a powerful Slavic witch. She's the strongest."

"She's a baby," Alvaro scowled.

"So is Sage," Matteo shrugged, looking confused.

Art assessed Sage, like he was just now realizing how young she was. "Huh."

Beau chewed gum with lazy indifference, hooking a thumb over her shoulder. "You want me to go back?"

"No," Matteo assured her. "We want you here."

Beau rolled a disbelieving look his way. "M'kay."

"This is Alvaro," Matteo said, gesturing to the shirtless, bearded brother, "Constantine, Art, and Silas. And this is Sage, his new ley socium."

Beau gave Sage a once-over, blowing out a bubble. When it popped, she said, "Cool."

Witches. They ran the gamut from impudent to fanatical, but they were *always* a pain in the ass. "Has Matteo explained the situation to you?"

"Yeah," Beau said, twirling her hand nonchalantly. "Fae rose bush, tried to burn it, reeks of ley, et cetera."

"Can you destroy it?" I asked.

She shrugged one shoulder, still insolently bored even surrounded by five dangerous vampires. Witches and vampires didn't mix—we avoided each other whenever possible, and when forced to interact, witches usually viewed us with wary distaste. Beau seemed unconcerned about the situation. Perhaps that was why she'd left her coven. She was clearly a little different. "I'll look at ley line maps and let you know."

I didn't have the foggiest idea how witch magic worked, let alone how the Slavs did it. "What do you need from us?"

"I don't know, some coffee would be nice," she said, moving past us and into the house. "Your boy here witch-napped me in the middle of the fucking night."

We all rounded incredulous glares on Matteo. The young vampire shrugged, palms up. "What? You asked me to bring her."

"I'll make coffee," Constantine sighed, beleaguered. If there was one thing Constantine couldn't stand, it was mishandling women. The man had made pleasing the fairer sex a religion.

Sage tracked the witch's movement with obvious interest, her long lashes flickering as she took her in. I tried to imagine all of this from Sage's point of view, how strange it had to be to meet vampires and witches and fae in the space of mere days. I had never lived without the knowledge of these things, but she had to learn it all with merciless rapidity.

Beau walked past the sectional and the chairs in the living room and to the curved island in the kitchen. Sitting on a barstool, she said, "I need your ley line maps for the area. And then someone will need to mark where the bush is. Be as exact as possible."

"Digital or paper maps?" Constantine asked, pulling down the French press from a shelf over the counter.

Beau leaned her chin on her hand and made a flourishing motion with the other. "Whatever is easier. Tell me about the bush. Has it been growing for a while or did it pop up over night?"

"The latter," I said, coming to the counter to join her. Sage took a seat at the island, and Alvaro, Art, and Matteo gathered together on the other side, facing Beau. "It appeared after a group of unknown creatures attempted to breach our ward perimeter."

"Creatures?" Beau asked with a skeptical lift of her eyebrow.

"We're unclear on what they are," Alvaro admitted. "Some sort of cross between fae, wraith, and human."

Beau lifted her head, finally moderately interested. "Huh."

"You don't seem surprised by that," Art observed.

She made a thinking noise. "My coven suspected something like this had happened. It was a long time ago, but there was a surge of massive ley energy from somewhere and then the immediate opposite. The ley practically ran dry ever since. We called it 'The Flare.'" Her short fingernails, bitten almost to the quick, drummed on the island counter. "Running theory was that there was a power surge for a ritual. Like tripping a breaker."

"A lot of ley funneled into one thing that siphoned the whole system," I thought out loud, following her logic.

"A ritual that could have *created* something," she agreed. "So, no, I'm not surprised to hear that the fae made some kind of new species for a tediously evil reason. The covens have been speculating for years. The ley magic has been weak since well before I was born."

So, the fae had created these things on purpose, which meant they'd been working on a scheme for some time. Whatever informants we had watching the fae either weren't doing their job, or the fae were keeping this tightly under wraps. Sage looked like she was in pain again, and her heart slammed against her ribs suddenly. I moved closer to her, rubbing her back and hating that I had no idea what was causing these mini panic attacks.

Constantine brought over a mug of coffee and a stack of maps we kept in our office. "After they tested our wards and lost—"

"Abysmally," Art grinned.

"—the rose bush showed up." He placed the coffee and maps in front of Beau and then slid over the black caddy filled with creamer, sugars, and spoons. "Silas tried burning it, but as you've heard, it didn't work."

"Fae," Beau muttered, reaching for the creamer and sugar. "Eliana is so high drama. And predictable. I can wither the plant, but it will take some time." After she made up her coffee and took a sip, she spread out the first map of our property marked with blue ley lines. "Where is it?"

Art came to stand next to her and pointed on the map to the edge of our northern wards. "Right here."

"On a ley line, of course," Beau mumbled almost to herself. She sipped the coffee as her eyes ran over the map, tracing the blue lines. "Do you have a broader map? This might be an intersection, actually. It might be to our benefit."

Art handed her another folded packet of paper, and she unfurled it, holding it in front of her with a squint. This map was more of an atlas, a broad view of the major ley lines across the world. They had been printed in blue, and they connected to one another through wellsprings, the ritual points where the fae renewed their power, usually during sabbats or planetary events. Sage sat up straighter, leaning forward on her stool to peer at the map.

"Yeah, you're at an intersection," Beau said with some satisfaction. "This will be child's play."

"You are a child," Matteo reminded her. "Wait, should we be giving her coffee?"

She lowered the map and hooked Matteo with an irritated glower. "Any witch could have done this, I mean. And take my coffee at your own risk."

Matteo remained unrepentant. "You certainly can do it, and you're here now, so…"

Beau made a disgusted sound in the back of her throat and lifted the map again. Sage lowered herself off the barstool, her hazelnut eyes wide and fixed on the spread map. Like she was in a trance, she came to stand behind Beau. "I know that pattern."

"You should," Beau replied absently, comparing the two maps. "Everyone knows the wellsprings and connected—"

"No, I've *seen* that pattern," Sage breathed, running her finger along one of the blue lines. "In the sky."

Chapter Twenty-Four

SAGE

Blue streaked across my vision, blindingly bright. The patterns practically glowed, rising off the map and fitting themselves to my memory like a skeleton key. I'd charted those lines. I had identical shapes in my notebook. No one spoke, but I could feel the surprise of six sets of eyes locking onto me. I tore my gaze away from the map and to Art. "Where did you put my things?"

"In Silas' room," Art replied vacantly.

"Silas, is she—" Matteo started to ask.

"Stop," Silas interrupted. "Sage, you mean the constellations?"

"No—yes—I mean kind of. Sorry, excuse me." I turned and jogged to the staircase, heading down to Silas' room. How many of the patterns in the sky matched the ones on the earth? I had to compare them. I hurried down the stairs and swung right, heading past the wet bar and to Silas' door.

He remained my shadow, my shield, following me with ease. "Where are you going?"

"My stuff," I explained, suddenly unaccountably excited. "I've drawn those patterns before. When I was star gazing."

"You mean you've charted the constellations," he clarified again, slowly, like he was hoping the words were true.

"Not the constellations. The blue lines." I opened his door and went inside. They had brought my things into the enormous room and set them up neatly on a new desk across from the bed. My books, my telescope, my pictures... even my used pencils and pens were there in the same cup. They'd gone to great lengths to recreate where I had everything in my room at home, which was oddly touching.

I found my notebook easily and flipped through it. As I did, Silas looked over my shoulder. "Fuck," he hissed.

"What?" I found the page I was looking for. The pattern I recognized over North America and had charted in the sky. "Look, it matches."

Silas stared at the page like it might come alive and eat him. And then he gave me a stricken look. "You can see these lines? Between the stars?"

"Yeah, not that I knew what they were." I went to return upstairs, but he stopped me with a hand on my arm.

"Have you shown anyone else those sketches?" Silas almost always looked serious, I was discovering, but he looked downright grave at the moment, and worry flattened his lips.

"No," I replied slowly, uncertainly. "Why?"

"No one has been able to see lines since before even my father was born," he said, his grip on my arm drawing me closer to him. "Star weaving is a lost art. Or it was."

My brow crinkled in surprise. "Seriously?"

"I think we've covered how serious I always am." He

turned away, his eyes searching the dim room for invisible answers. "But does she know that?"

"Does who know what?" I divided a look between my notebook and his profile. "Wait, is this a problem? I thought you said that mates found each other with matching star charts."

"Yes, star charts that any human or witch can track easily. Although we know that ley connects the universe, that it feeds our planet through matching ley points, we cannot see those connections." Silas sighed, looking down. "Fuck. I mean, of course, you would be a star weaver." He slanted a sardonic glance my way. "We wouldn't want this to be too easy, right?"

"Is this… bad?" I closed the notebook. "Should I not have said anything?"

"I don't know yet." Silas was lost in thought, clearly, giving me distracted answers. "I need time to consider the ramifications of this discovery."

I was itching to compare my charts to the maps upstairs. It would be so satisfying to fit the patterns together. I lowered a pointed look to his hand around my upper arm. "Do I need to put the notebook away? Or can I see if my theory is right?"

He released me reluctantly but stayed close. "You can. We will need to swear the witch to secrecy, though."

"Something tells me that she's not overly interested in the drama of subterfuge," I replied pragmatically, leaving his bedroom and going back to the kitchen.

He grunted in assent but didn't add anything else. When we were back at the counter, the other five people in the room stared at me like I'd sprouted snakes for hair. That really was all I needed. One more thing to make the spotlight over my head brighter, to make me more of a freak than I already was.

I hurried to the island where Beau had already laid out all the ley line maps, like she'd anticipated what I wanted to do. She watched me with quiet interest, sipping her coffee. I opened my notebook to the page that matched North America and set it flat on the map. With my fingers, I traced the lines and dots in unison. Perfect match.

"I thought I was crazy," I whispered in awe.

"Dear fucking God," Art said baldly.

"She's a star weaver," Matteo said with some wonder in his voice.

"Silas told me it's rare, I know," I replied absently, flipping to another page to see if I could find its match on the other maps.

"We know," Matteo and Alvaro said at once.

Right. Vampire hearing. One of my sketches looked like a crown with two points on either side of a taller, triangular configuration. It was so distinct, I found it immediately. "Here." I pointed to Europe where the ley lines on the map matched. Almost. I frowned, my left finger tracing the ley lines on the map until it stopped and my right finger continuing up on my paper. The very top of the crown, the tallest point, wasn't on the map. "What happened to this one?"

All five vampires and Beau crowded around me, all peering at the map. I had my finger resting where the point should have been, roughly; in France. "Heol," Art whispered, and I guessed it was a word from another language.

I craned my neck to look at him from where he towered over me. "Do you know where this is?"

"It's Monaco. Where Eliana keeps the fae court," Constantine rumbled.

I turned to stare at my finger again, frowning. "Why do the points match everywhere but here?"

"I don't know," Silas admitted, but I could hear the gears turning in his head as he answered. "The main points that match the stars on your chart, those are wellsprings on Earth. According to your diagram, there should be one in Monaco."

"A big one," I added. "That's Venus, not a star."

"A missing wellspring?" Art asked dubiously.

"Or a blocked one," Beau spoke finally. She pursed her lips, her eyes flitting from my drawings to the maps, no doubt matching them herself. "Yeah, that should be a huge wellspring there."

"Why would they block a wellspring?" I frowned.

"Oh my God," Alvaro said, walking away and running a hand through his hair in agitation. The other vampires all gave me space, too, each one wearing various expressions of horrified realization.

"She's been controlling the power flow," Constantine said.

"Blocking the main celestial power source," Alvaro went on, rubbing his mouth.

"To control the ley-feeding species," Silas finished. Unlike his brothers, he didn't seem as shocked. A muscle ticked in his jaw, and he glared at the map. He was pissed.

"She's performing rituals to feed small amounts of cosmic ley into lesser springs," Art went on. "But she's blocked a major one. A connecting one."

"To keep us from overpowering her species," Beau nodded. She took another sip of coffee, admitting, "Otherwise, your kind would have wiped them out or put them under your heel long ago. This makes them relevant—needed. Smart."

"It's been so long since we had a star weaver. She had to have known that," Silas said, crossing his arms and leaning his hip against the counter. "The lost knowledge worked to her advantage. Without a star weaver, there would be no one to identify the connection."

"Until now." Matteo gave me a concerned look. "She cannot find out."

"Obviously," Beau replied with a roll of her eyes. "Sage, hide those drawings somewhere safe in case she sends spies. I suggest you pretend you never even saw these."

"But we can open the wellspring," I argued, pushing my drawing over the point on the map. "We know where it is, now. You could unblock all that ley. It might help you all find your mates."

"Someday," Silas agreed, reaching around me to close the notebook. "But that isn't important right now."

"Are you crazy? This is a huge discovery. Your vampire government or whatever should know about this so they can fix it." I reached for the notebook, but Silas pulled it out of reach. "Stop that."

"Sage," he replied evenly, unruffled as usual. "If we tell anyone what you discovered, including the Conexus, we would have to reveal what you are."

"It will put you in tremendous danger," Matteo agreed. "It isn't worth it."

"Kind of sounds like it's worth it," I shot back, getting really irritated now. "What's more important to you all than finding your own mates? Or ensuring that the fae aren't controlling the ley like a bunch of greedy billionaires?"

"You are," Silas said, close behind me now and wrapping an arm around my waist. He kissed my temple gently. "My brothers will agree with that."

"We do," Constantine agreed. The other three nodded seriously when I sent them questioning looks.

Beau looked bored again and popped a piece of gum in her mouth. "Man, I got to skip school today *and* we found a star weaver. My abundance spells are putting out."

I was getting *really* tired of knowing things and being silenced anyway. I knew that the fae queen had created the creatures like Cysgadyn with the intent to do something terrible with the ley socium. I knew her plan was to abscond with me and find a way to use me to hurt the vampires. And now I knew that there was a rose bush at the edge of our property that would take us right to that dammed up wellspring. I knew she had found a way to block it from feeding the veins that ran through the earth, and if we could unblock it, it could help literally every ley-based creature on the planet.

And I couldn't do anything with that information. I tried to speak, tried again to tell them what I'd witnessed, but my throat seized up and I choked. I dropped my forehead to my hands, growling in frustration. Silas was watchful, as always. "Why do you keep doing that? Starting to say something and then stopping?"

I lifted an agonized look to him. I gestured to my throat. The other four vampires in the room exchanged worried glances, and Beau cocked her head at me. "You're trying to say something but you can't?"

I couldn't even nod yes or no. I just stared. She pursed her lips. "Leywork?" She looked at Silas. "Has Sage been anywhere near the fae?"

Silas shook his head. "She's been here with us since—" he paused, thinking. "There was an attack. But I know what leywork looks like. He didn't perform any on her."

My heart skyrocketed. *Yes,* I thought with a trill of elation. *Fates bless the goth witch. She's going to figure this out!*

Beau snapped her gum speculatively, looking me up and down. "Well, there's one way to check for sure. I mean, I'm not fae, but all leywork has a source, and that always leaves a trace behind."

Relief collapsed all the stress inside of me, and I breathed evenly, unable to nod or even help her get closer to the answer. "You could check," I suggested carefully.

"I need sage, two candles, a bowl of well water, and your hair," Beau said in deadpan.

"I'll get it," Matteo offered. He paused. "Wait, which sage? This Sage? Or sage, sage?"

"Sage, sage," Beau said, like he was stupid.

"Right." Matteo disappeared to go find the necessary items, and I shifted my weight from foot to foot nervously. This could work. I didn't know anything about actual witchcraft, but this had to work, right?

Beau held out her hand, palm up. "I need your hair."

I combed my fingers through the thick mass of it, dislodging a few loose strands. "Is this okay?"

Beau gagged but took the hair. "Yeah. Sorry. I hate hair."

I looked at her short cut bob and pulled a face. "Oh, sorry."

Matteo returned suspiciously fast with everything, setting two white candles on the counter along with a bundle of white sage. Art filled a blue bowl with water. "We use well water anyway."

"M'kay," Beau said like she didn't care. Which she likely didn't. She took my hair, and pulling another face, she wrapped the strands between the candles. Then she placed the bowl in front of the candles and gestured for me to join her. "Put your hand in the water."

I obeyed, sending Silas a nervous look. He nodded, his verdant gaze pinched at the corners with worry. When she found the leywork, they would be able to undo it, and then I could tell him everything. We'd be safe. It would be just fine. I placed my hand in the cool water.

Beau touched both wicks, lighting them instantly. It was the first time I'd seen something *actually* magical. My eyes rounded, but she ignored me, chanting in another language. "Mat' ognya, mat' zemli,

pod pepelom dyshi…"

My hand tingled a little. The hair between the flames caught fire, burning brightly and illuminating Beau's razor sharp, defined features. The light from the fire seemed to spread, dousing the bowl of water in warmth like a ray of sun. Beau continued her chant, watching the bowl. Then, suddenly the fire died, and curling smoke rose above the candles.

Beau blinked at me. "No source."

My eyes bugged. *What?* That had to be wrong. If Cysgadyn hadn't leyworked me, then what the Hell had he done?

Silas released a sigh of frustration. "There's no leywork?"

As Alvaro handed me a towel, Beau shrugged, folding her arms. "Leywork doesn't exist without a source, so no."

But it did. Somehow it did, but I didn't have the faintest idea how. I dried my hand and threw the towel on the counter, frustrated beyond measure. My only hope was for them to make a move on the fae queen first, before she came for me. "Let's free the wellspring," I suggested. "Focus on that."

Silas put his hands on my arms gently, his expression concerned. “I’m having a hard time tracking your thoughts, Dulcis. And your frustration.”

Because I couldn’t fucking tell him. I wanted to scream. “I think it’s important.”

“Not as important as your safety,” he argued gently.

"You're seriously going to ignore this,” I glowered.

"For now." Silas released me and began folding up the maps with methodical care. "We can strategize how to approach a blocked wellspring another time. Maybe if we bring it to the Conexus after you've had a few hundred years to become stronger—"

"A few hundred?" I repeated, aghast.

"Damn, I'll be dead," Beau mused, her gum clicking between her teeth. "Bummer."

"You can come to me when you're older," Matteo suggested. "Ley donors live longer when they stay with magicae vampires."

Beau's lip curled, and she shrank away from him as she returned to her coffee. "I wouldn't feed a vampire to save my life, let alone prolong it. Creepy old geezers."

Matteo lifted his hands like she was missing out, and Silas stacked the maps on top of each other neatly. "Do you have what you need, Isabeau? To shrivel the bush?"

"No." Beau finished off her coffee. "I need one of you to go get me a young pepper plant. A seedling preferably. I'll plant it so its roots touch the rose bush, and then we'll drive silver rods into the ground around the bush. The rods will draw ley into the plants, and the spell will slowly siphon the bush's ley into the pepper plant. Once the peppers grow, the bush will wither."

"Withering spell," Constantine nodded thoughtfully. "I remember that one. It's archaic, isn't it?"

"And a little evil," Beau smiled viciously. "It works with humans, too."

"You wither humans?" I asked in surprise.

Beau gave me a deadpan stare. "If they deserve it."

Jesus. Something occurred to me, suddenly. "Wait, wait, what do the silver rods do?"

"The bush is on a ley line, but you already discovered for yourself that ley flows down to us from the universal lines," Beau said, pointing a lazy finger upward, "and it also enters us from below. Utilizing both will strengthen the spell."

I was getting an inkling of an idea here. "So, if we happened to put a *bunch* of silver rods where this wellspring is blocked—"

"Stop," all five vampires said in unison.

Art added, "I know that humans are precocious little things, but you have to let this one go, Sage."

"We can deal with it later," Alvaro chided.

I didn't have later. I didn't have the luxury of hoping they would figure out what the fae queen wanted with me and how the wellspring was connected. "Wait, how long does this spell take?"

"With the ley speeding up the growing process?" Beau seemed to tally in her head. "Four weeks, maybe five."

I didn't have four or five weeks. I had twelve days. Twelve days and then Cysgadyn would come take me away. I didn't know what kind of force the fae queen planned on sending to retrieve me, but I knew the vampires would be caught off guard when they walked right through their wards. There was a good chance I'd stay safe with Silas. There was a fair chance I wouldn't.

The headache started behind my eyes again, and my throat burned. Every time I thought about that damn silencing spell, my body wigged out. I had to stop thinking about it.

Constantine brought me a mug of hot coffee, his icy eyes strangely warm. "This has been a lot for you to take in."

"A bit," I admitted.

"Does it ever occur to you oafs that you don't *have* to snatch these girls up? So what if a ley line fritzed around them?" Beau asked sourly. "You could just leave them alone instead of dragging them into all this shit."

"The minute we match," Silas replied evenly, "she becomes a target. It's us or the fae."

"Same fucking thing," Beau muttered. Matteo glared at her. She gave him the middle finger.

"I'll find the necessary plant," Constantine said, like he was quelling an argument between toddlers. "Beau, I have guest quarters on my floor that are currently vacant. You're welcome to stay there."

"You would offer," Alvaro snorted.

"She's like five minutes old," Constantine shot back with a look of disgust.

Beau rolled her eyes and hopped off the barstool. "Yeah, whatever. If it has a shower, then fine. I like breakfast burritos, in case you were going to bring me something to eat."

"Oh, 'in case,' huh?" Matteo asked with a dollop of amusement. "This witch."

"You're paying me for doing this, too," she added, following Constantine to the floating, modern stairs that led to the third floor.

"Naturally," he agreed, and I caught the hint of humor in his tone, too.

When they were gone, I rotated to face Silas and pointedly plucked my notebook from his hand. "I'm going to figure out how they blocked the wellspring."

His eyelids fell in irritation. "I told you not to worry about it."

"Yeah, well," I shrugged walking past him, "humans never do what they're told."

"That's the fucking truth," Alvaro agreed in his heavy accent.

"Matteo, can I use your observatory?" I smiled sweetly.

Matteo's puppy dog features brightened considerably. "Of course."

"Traitor," Silas growled.

Matteo ignored him, gesturing for me to follow him upstairs. "Vampires don't do as they're told either," he winked.

Chapter Twenty-Five

SAGE

Eleven days.

Beau planted the pepper, staked silver spikes around it, and cast her spell before being returned home. I did my schoolwork from the safety of Hollowhall, which I learned was the name of their home. Two days passed and I felt like I had the flu, which only validated my suspicions that this silencing spell was affecting me physically. I couldn't offer any concrete evidence for it, but my intuition seemed to have puzzled it out. The spell was a device, and my body was the battery.

As Silas walked beside me back on campus, I squinted up at the cloudy sky speculatively. "What makes me different from witches if I carry ley like they do?"

Silas glanced down at me briefly before resuming his scan of the sparse crowd to catch possible threats. I'd had a test I needed to take in person today, and there was nothing for it but to return to campus. After conferring, my little vampire security detail had agreed that since there hadn't been any threats since the attack that first day, the fae weren't going to do anything crazy. They didn't know that the fae were patiently waiting two weeks for my answer. "Why do you ask?" he asked finally.

"I'm just curious." I adjusted the strap on my shoulder. "Matteo said Beau had almost as much ley in her as me, and it got me wondering." *Also, I think this spell might be draining my ley.*

"Witches are like," he paused, thinking, "garden hoses, I guess. Ley flows through them from the earth and they release it into spells. They're conduits. You are a bucket. You're filled to the brim with ley, but you can't channel more of it. Theirs is use and renew. Yours is use it or lose it."

"But there's enough to keep me alive forever?"

"Yes." He glanced back down to me with warmth in his mossy eyes. "Forever."

Or eleven days. It was anyone's guess at this point. "Can I hold more ley if it's given to me?"

That seemed to puzzle him. "I've never heard of it. I'm not sure."

"And spells use ley, right? To cast them? Or maintain them?"

Silas' expression sharpened with suspicion. "Yes."

"Hm." I stared forward again. The pain behind my eyes was getting worse. It was hard to sleep through it, and I felt sapped of energy faster than I should have. I'd just taken a test—an easy one—and I wanted to curl up in the sun and take a nap.

"I'm this close," Silas said, pinching his thumb and forefinger together, "to employing medieval torture methods on you. What are you hiding?"

"Nothing intentionally," I sighed. We'd had this conversation several times. Silas knew there was something wrong with me, but I couldn't tell him, and he took it as intentional deception.

Silas opened his mouth to interrogate me for more information, but a shout cut him off. "Sage!" My roommate, Mila, waved to me from across the grassy commons, her light blond curls bouncing. She hurried to reach us and called out, "Hold up!"

Silas and I stopped, and I stared at her in dazed detachment. I imagined this was what middle-aged adults felt like, seeing their classmates from twenty years ago. Mila felt like a whole other lifetime ago. A world that didn't fit into the reality I was currently walking. I waved back. "Hi Mila."

"Where have you been?" Mila demanded, her pretty features pouting as she caught up to us. She eyed Silas with wary surprise, then looked at me again. "You moved out."

"Oh, yeah," I hedged, fiddling with the straps of my backpack. "I, uh, well I have that internship with my mom soon, so..." I wasn't sure where I was going with that.

Mila filled in the blanks. "Oh, so you got a new place already. That's so cool." She gave me a dainty waive. "So grown up."

I breathed out a laugh. "Yeah, I guess so."

Mila ran her fingers through her hair, glancing at Silas again, this time with interest. "Are you still coming to the alignment party next week?" She paused. "Both of you?"

"This is Silas," I said, shaking myself out of some of my stupor. It was so strange that the world had continued on as normal. My roommate was flirting with my vampire boyfriend, and the observatory club was still throwing a silly party for the planetary alignment event. "And, uh, I don't know. I'm kind of focused on getting my schoolwork done."

"Aw." Mila's blue eyes turned down at the corners. "Yeah, I get it. You just disappeared, you know? Crazy."

You didn't even know I existed, I thought somewhat caustically. "Yeah, it was sudden. Sorry."

"Okay, well, I hope you come to the party," Mila said, angling to walk away again. "The planets don't align every day, you know."

"Okay, yeah. Thanks Mila." She left after another wave, and I exhaled in relief, walking down the paved path toward the parking lot again. "I forgot all about my clubs and stuff."

"I find it amusing that humans celebrate powerful cosmic events with a club party," Silas replied, shaking his head. "Like it's a football game."

"Is it… actually a big deal?" Silas pulled me into his side, dragged us to the left, and a sprinkler turned on right where I'd been walking.

"It is for the witches and fae. We call it the Confluence. It only happens every few hundred years, and it triggers a surge in the ley lines. Mates have been known to find each other during these events." He smiled wistfully. "Fortuitous, actually. It might be good for my brothers."

Fortuitous. If my memory served me right, it would be happening in exactly eleven days. My mind whirred, picking up possibilities and setting them back down again rapidly. This wasn't a coincidence. Silas didn't know about the deadline. He didn't know that the fae queen wanted me with her the same day as this Confluence. She was planning something. Something more dangerous than wanting to mate a ley socium with her wraith hybrids. I had to try and warn him. "Silas, this—" I stopped, choking.

"Sage?" Silas pulled me to him, looking me over. "What's wrong?"

I squeezed my throat, gritting my teeth. My neck burned. My vision swirled. I kept trying anyway. "There's…

The C-Confluence, it's—" Pain streaked through my head and down my throat. I groaned, falling into him.

He wrapped his arms around me. "You're in pain. This is driving me mad, Sage. Please, for the love of the Gods, just *tell me*."

"I can't!" I shouted angrily. I gripped his soft cashmere sweater, pulling my face into it and swallowing back tears. He smelled safe, like a warm room on a rainy day. My body reacted, yearning for him even though the rest of me was too tired to act on it. "I can't, Silas."

His arms tightened, and he kissed the crown of my head, breathing me in. "I can feel you getting weaker."

I had no answer for that. It was too frustrating. I had to find a way to show him. "Take me home. Please."

He did, keeping a secure arm around my waist and leading me through the campus and to his white SUV. When we were in the car, I closed my eyes, too tired to even look at what I knew would be a worried, searching expression on Silas' face. He took off back to Hollowhall, his silence taut. I didn't know what to say to him, what reassurances to offer him.

When I felt the shadow of trees passing over my closed eyes, felt the forest enveloping us in her depths, Silas said, "We're meant to be happy, Sage." I cracked my eyes open. Silas was watching me, still driving perfectly between the lines but holding my gaze intently. "It's meant to be happily ever after, now."

Emotion welled up in my throat, clawing at my eyes and bringing beads of tears to their corners. "I'm so sorry."

"I don't understand," he gritted out, looking through the windshield again finally. "What am I doing wrong?"

"You are quite literally perfect," I told him honestly. "There's nothing more you can do for me right now."

"Why do you keep talking like you've received some terminal diagnosis?" Silas' hands went white-knuckled around the steering wheel. "You can't die, Sage. You're safe."

I exhaled a humorless laugh. "I know." I had to hide this better. It was eating him up from the inside out. I had to pretend better, to lie better, to ignore the banging in my head and the searing, phantom fingerprints around my neck. I pulled in a bracing breath, smiling and straightening. "You're right. This is our happily ever after. We're meant to be getting to know one another. Having fun." I smiled softly. "I'm really, truly looking forward to that. Your brothers are fun. Hollowhall feels like home already."

"You can't lie to me," he reminded me tightly.

Damn. "Well, none of that was a lie."

"You said it like a lie." He glanced at me before fixing his attention on the grand house as we pulled up to it.

The only lie was that I wasn't sure I would actually get to have those things. I'd waited so long to be seen, I'd worked hard and sacrificed all my life to be noticed, to be loved for who I really was. And now that I finally had it, there was an expiration date on it. There had to be a better way than this. Surely, if Silas was with me and his brothers were, too, then the fae queen couldn't just snatch me to her home. Maybe I didn't need to worry so much. "I think I'm just worrying about nonsense things," I said finally. "Maybes. What-ifs."

Silas parked the car in his quiet, clean garage and killed the engine. The leather creaked as he turned to me and fitted my chin between his thumb and forefinger. "Let me handle the what-ifs. You handle the here-nows."

I smiled at that. "Like how I want ice cream here, now?"

"Like that." He tipped my chin up and kissed me softly,

igniting that little flame that always burned low in my belly for him. "I like problems I can solve. That's solvable."

I really felt like my problem was solvable, too, if I could just have some time to work on it. There had to be something to the Confluence, the fae queen's ultimatum, and that hidden wellspring that fit together correctly. There had to be some reason all these threads were connected to me. If I could just research, just look it up for a while, maybe I could figure it out.

But I had to get Silas on board with that first. "Actually." I opened the car door and stepped out, keeping my tone neutral and words carefully chosen so there was no deceit in them. "Charting the stars is my comfort hobby. Maybe I could have a few hours to sit in the observatory?"

Silas angled a shrewd look my way as he joined me at the garage door. "Really."

"Yes. It would really help." I meant that. I was the only one who had an idea of what the fae queen was planning, so I was the only one who could research the implications. If I did nothing, it would drive me insane.

"If it makes you happy," he yielded with obvious reluctance. "But ice cream first."

"Deal."

Blue swept between the planets, brighter now that I had confidence in what I was seeing. I couldn't believe I hadn't looked for my weird blue lines between the aligning planets before now. Probably because every astronomer in the world was watching the phenomenon already. Textbooks had plenty to say about it, about the rarity of the event, about how our orbits brought all the planets together in the perfect way for one brief night. But the astronomers couldn't see ley in the sky. And what I was seeing took my breath away.

"It's directly tied to that wellspring," I whispered in awe. The blue fell in a waterfall across the night sky, pouring into Venus. I pulled away from the eyepiece in Matteo's observatory to add lines to the star chart he'd printed off for me. "Here and here." I shifted along the table to where the map of France had been laid out. "Which means all that energy—"

"Will go nowhere," Matteo finished for me. He was sitting in a rolling chair by the table, watching me chart the stars for the fifth hour, now. Silas had given up out of frustration, too angry with me for wanting to work when I was fatigued but too doting to make me stop. "If that wellspring has been dammed off for whatever reason, it will go nowhere. Odd choice, to be honest. I see why you're intrigued by it."

"Unless…" I frowned in thought, staring at the chart. Surely, the fae queen wouldn't let all that ley go to waste. She would want it for herself. That was why she'd blocked that wellspring to begin with, wasn't it?

You're like a bucket.

I gasped, rounding a horrified look to Matteo. "She—she—" My throat closed up again, and pure agony spread through my throat and chest like wildfire. I gasped pitching forward.

Matteo caught me, his voice suddenly full of worry. "Sage?"

She was going to pour it into me. Into her experiment. Whatever she had planned for creating fae children, for using the ley socium and her odd creations, she needed the energy surge from this planetary alignment. She would ensure she had me, then. It wasn't *if* she could get me. It was how. She'd put all her resources into it, I was sure of it. Silas and the others had no idea what was coming for them. She would unleash her entire army on five vampires. She would destroy them all to have me. I could see our inevitable fate, but I couldn't warn them. I couldn't stop it from happening.

I choked, forcing down tears as Matteo held me upright. He smelled different, like a calm summer morning, and his body was warm and solid, if somewhat leaner than Silas'. But then Silas was there, taking me from Matteo and murmuring, "I have you."

I forced the agony back inside, swallowing my fear and gulping in lungfuls of air to clear away the aftereffects of the spell. "I'm sorry." I cleared my throat, finding my feet again. I still clung to Silas, my limbs shaking.

"We're taking you to a doctor," Silas said with finality, and I knew there was no use arguing. It would be pointless, though. No human doctor would be able to diagnose a weird wraith-human-fae spell.

"That's fine," I panted, straightening. Sweat had broken out along my forehead, and I could feel how bloodless my lips must look. "But Silas, you need to open the wellspring during the alignment." If we focused on the wellspring, if we opened it up, then the fae queen wouldn't be able to pour all that energy into me. It would go where it belonged. I couldn't tell them about what she had planned for me, about her coming to get me, but I could tell them about the wellspring. "You have to do it then. That's when the connection will be the strongest."

"Is this a star weaver thing?" Matteo asked, rubbing the back of his curly mop of hair.

"Yes," I lied. *Sure. It's a star weaver thing. Just please, do as I ask.*

"She's lying. Again," Silas bit out. He had me cradled against his chest, his arms securely around my torso, but his words stung. Because for the first time, I heard disappointment in his voice. I'd let him down.

God, that smarted. We'd only barely begun to know each other. I craved him. I dreamed of him. Even when he had his arms around me at night, I searched for him in my subconscious. Maybe some part of me knew that we were owed centuries together, and it was raging against the unfairness of our reality.

"The Confluence only happens once every, what, three hundred years?" I bit out.

"Three hundred and twenty-eight," Silas said. "What of it? I told you, Sage, we have more pressing matters to attend to than whatever the fae queen's games are. She will play them for our entire lifetimes. I will deal with her when I have you settled."

"There is *nothing* more important than this," I argued through gritted teeth. I pushed Silas away, but he didn't budge. It was like trying to move a Greek pillar. I craned my head back to stare into his stormy green eyes instead. "You can't wait another three hundred years for this. You have to do it now."

He shook his head, his handsome features painted with sorrow. "Not when your wellbeing is at risk. You don't have an accurate grasp on time yet, Dulcis. It feels urgent to you, but I assure you, three hundred years is the perfect amount of time to strategize a move against an ancient, powerful fae queen. It's almost not enough time."

This was going to make me insane. It was. I was going to be a babbling, pleading mess by the end of the eleven days, and Silas would have me committed if the fae queen didn't get to me first. I reined in my panic through sheer force of will. "It could mean matches for your brothers."

"I can wait three hundred years, mia cara," Matteo chuckled. "I don't mind. You're plenty of work for all five of us as is, anyway."

I let my forehead fall against Silas' chest. It was no use. "Right." I realized then that even surrounded by five fussy, overprotective vampires, I was on my own.

They would try to protect me when the siege came. The fae queen would have all the advantages. I had a sinking feeling that she would succeed. She'd probably been waiting for this, planning her moves years and years in advance for the moment the ley socium arrived at the right time. So, I would have to fight back myself. If I charted the stars exactly, coordinates and equations, numerical certainties, then I could find the exact coordinates of the wellspring, too.

I didn't know the first thing about true astronomical calculations, about coordinates and how to match the stars to the earth so precisely that I could pinpoint a location within a five-hundred -meter radius. But I could try. I had eleven days to learn it. And then when I found the location of the wellspring, I would free it. She could take me, but I would have to use it to my advantage. I would make a move of my own first. And I would save Silas and his brothers in the process.

My life is precious. But so is yours.

Chapter Twenty-Six

SAGE

Six days. I had six days left.

Rain pattered against my umbrella, sliding off the edges and dripping down my back. I barely noticed it, crouched in the damp forest and breathing in fresh petrichor.

The rose bush swayed in the wind, its lush flowers dewy with moisture. A large raindrop plopped off a velvet petal, bounced on a leaf, and slid to the earth. Some of the droplets had gathered on the silver rods, too. They were long and thin, like incense sticks, and they surrounded the bush and pepper plant in what looked like a strategic arrangement. I leaned my cheek on my arms, crouched in a ball and letting mud seep into my damp sneakers. Behind me, Art stood patiently under his own umbrella.

I'd been here long enough that the rain was bleeding through my jacket and sticking to my skin. I needed to think away from Silas and his coaxing touches, his intoxicating warmth. Because when he was near me, I lost focus. When he kissed me, I didn't want to learn complex mathematical equations that were, at best, theoretical when matching ley lines in the universe to wellsprings on Earth. When he held me, I didn't want to chart lines and compare longitude and latitude. I wanted to love him. I wanted to rest. And God, did I need to rest. I was so weak already, Art had carried me halfway here. I'd never worked harder in my life, dragging myself out of bed in the morning, keeping myself from Silas' tempting embraces, keeping my mind alert and dedicated to finding the missing wellspring.

Silas got a thunderous expression when he found me in that observatory day after day. The other four weren't much happier about it, either. But I ate the food they made me and drank the water they insisted I consume. I rested when they demanded it and I cajoled when I couldn't stand being away from my calculations anymore.

I was close, now. I'd figured out what I thought was a mathematical correspondence between the stars and the wellsprings. I just needed to plug in the right measurements and coordinates to locate the exact place in Monaco the fae queen had been hiding that power source. Hoarding it. If I could find it, then I would at least have a goal to reach for when I gave myself to her.

A shudder of fear ran through me, and I stared at the roses hard, hating them. I hated that I would pluck one of them on my own in five days. Six days until she sent an army to retrieve me. Five until I chose to go first. To protect them, to stop a war, I would be brave.

Art joined me, crouching with his sneakers scraping against rocks and soil. "I've only sensed this kind of terror three times in my life." His voice broke the silence with silky softness. "One of those times, a woman was walking to her death at the guillotine. She had four children she was leaving behind." He turned to look at me, and reluctantly, I met his deep blue gaze. "What guillotine are you approaching?"

I sniffed, glancing back at the roses. "One I'm choosing, at least."

"If something happens to you, Sage," he grated out, "I will lose my brother. You understand that, don't you?"

I did. Every embrace, every kiss, every longing touch told me that story. "I'll protect him," I promised. "You have my word."

He shook his head, staring at the roses. "The one mystery we were born to solve, the one life we were destined to protect, and we are all powerless, the five of us."

It really was the most unfair outcome, admittedly. My phone rang, saving me from answering. My thighs were burning from crouching for so long, so I stood, balancing the umbrella so I could slide my phone from my sweatshirt pocket. It was my mom. "Hey, Mom."

"Sage, honey," she said brightly. "I'm so sorry I haven't called. The election coverage is getting out of control. How are you, baby?" She sounded busy, still. The hum of a crowd buzzed in the background, and she had that energetic, breathless quality to her voice that told me she was working as she talked.

"I'm good," I smiled. I turned my back on the bush and began to make my way slowly back to the house. My legs shook and my breath sawed in and out of my lungs, burning up to my throat. The spell was getting worse, greedier. It took more of me every day. I was starting to wonder if I'd even make it five days.

"I just wanted to check in. Your landlord said you'd moved out? No, John, the other one. Yes, that one."

I smiled, shaking my head. "Uh, yeah. I met someone and we decided to move in together. Sorry I didn't tell you."

A pregnant pause followed that. "What do you mean you met someone?"

There was no use in lying to her more than necessary. "Yeah, I figured you wouldn't approve. He's really nice, though. You'll like him." *If you ever meet him.*

My mom made an unintelligible, garbled sound, and suddenly the background noise died down. "Sage, are you crazy? You can't just move in with some stranger."

"He's not a stranger," I sighed, making my way slowly up a slick hill. Art walked beside me, eyes watchful and mouth downturned. "He's a CEO, actually. It's been good for me."

"But you're still in school," Mom clarified, clearly trying to moderate her tone.

I hated letting her down, but with everything else going on, my agony over wanting to follow in her footsteps seemed like a paltry issue. It was something the old me had worried about and the new me couldn't be bothered to consider. "I am, and I'll graduate," I promised. I'd done all my work ahead of time. I'd pass my classes even if it was posthumously. "But if I'm honest, Mom, I don't want to be a journalist like you."

"What?" she asked in outrage.

"I know, you really want me to. You got me a wicked internship, and anyone would be lucky for that opportunity. But I don't find joy in it." I stared up at the trees as I walked, past the black umbrella canvas and to the clouded sky. "I'm sorry it took me this long to be honest with you."

"This is completely unacceptable, Sage. You can't just throw your whole life away like this. Is it the boy you're with? You're confused." She sounded just as desperate as she was angry. She'd probably bragged about me to all her colleagues. She'd built this picture in her head of us, a duo, an unstoppable journalistic force. The first mother-daughter news anchor team. That kind of shit went viral.

She never had factored the real image of me into her picture-perfect future, though. "I love the stars. Astronomy. The math aspect isn't even terrible, either. If I get the chance, that's what I'll pursue."

"If?" Art hissed. "Sage, I swear to God, it sounds like you're saying goodbyes."

I ignored him while my mom spluttered, "You've lost your mind."

"A little," I smiled wearily. My feet slipped on wet leaves and Art caught me by the elbow.

His expression was fire and ice, the burn of dry ice on bare skin. "Stop. I'll carry you."

I did stop, panting. "I know I've disappointed you." I wasn't sure who that was for—Art or my mom.

"You have," my mother said, her tone clipped. She wasn't known as a badass bitch for no reason. She'd be angry with me, but I couldn't go to my end without having been honest with her, without having shared one real moment, at least.

"I'm sorry, Mom." I paused, pulling in a ragged breath. "I love you."

"I can love you and still be disappointed," she bit out. "We'll talk about this later. I have to get back to work."

"Okay." My heart tugged painfully. "Talk to you later."

She hung up, and as I inhaled, I found that it snagged on a sob. Art pulled me against him, throwing my umbrella aside and sheltering me under his. He smoothed his hand down the back of my head. "Whatever it is, I'm so sorry Sage."

I nodded, sniffling. He was wearing a rigid jean jacket that scraped against my nose. I pulled away a little, not wanting to smell like Art when we came back to the house. It would only frustrate Silas more. "It's alright. I just hate letting people down."

"The only one let down here is you, Sage. Your mother is selfish. You know that." He shifted so he crouched in front of me, and then he patted his shoulders. "Come on. I'll give you a ride and then we can make Mexican chocolate. Have you ever had it?" I wrapped my arms around his neck and let him heft me onto his back. "It has chili pepper in it."

"Sounds gross," I said with half a laugh.

"No, no, you have to trust me," he insisted, walking forward. "It'll blow your mind. Okay, here we go. Close your eyes so you don't get motion sick."

I obeyed, pressing my face into his shoulder, and then seconds later, he slowed and gently placed me back on my feet. I wobbled a little, shaking the dizziness from my foggy brain. "Thanks."

He'd managed to keep the umbrella over us both, and we stood in the overhang that sheltered the bottom floor's glass door entrance. I rotated, taking in the rainy forest, how the mist clung to the ground and filled the spaces between trees. Art stood with me, closing his umbrella and then sliding his hands in his pockets.

"How long before the guillotine?"

My stomach clenched. Could I answer that? "Six," I choked out. Pain lanced through my brain and down to my chest, searing the delicate tissue like a hot iron. I threw out a hand to catch my fall, aiming for the redwood post. I hit solid muscle instead.

Silas pulled me into him, enveloping me in his warmth. "Six what?"

I shook my head. I couldn't say more than that. I'd managed to get the number out, but it was costing me dearly. I could actually feel my life force swirling down an invisible drain, disappearing into the spell that locked my throat.

"Silas, we might have no choice," Art said. I couldn't see them, could only lean against Silas and keep my eyes shut until the churning in my stomach and the ringing in my ears subsided.

"Not yet. I'm not ready for that," Silas replied tightly.

Art said nothing, but in his silence, I could have been an adfectus myself. I felt his censure just as plainly as if it had been mine. Finally, Art turned to leave. "If it's days, then you'd better figure it out now."

"I will," Silas said. It sounded like a vow.

He didn't know it was an impossibility.

Chapter Twenty-Seven

SILAS

Sage was withering away before my eyes. Like she'd become the target of a Slavic witch's pepper plant spell, she deteriorated faster than I could comprehend it happening. But Beau had assured me that no witch could cast such a spell on Sage when she was within our warded borders, and anyway, who would want to? The witches would never dare to hurt a ley socium and hope to survive the attack. There were no spells she recognized that were connected to Sage.

I took her to a human doctor who ran a gamut of tests: blood tests, X-rays, a CT scan, and a biophysical profile. Sage sat through the ordeal patiently, and when they declared her healthy and fit, Sage didn't look the least bit surprised. The shadows under her eyes and the sluggish pace of her blood disagreed with that diagnosis. She'd given me a small smile and asked if we could go home.

And then she'd worked. I tried to stop her, but she used every wile in the book against me. And they worked.

"It distracts me."

I'd acquiesced then.

"I think it's part of my nature."

I'd relented.

"I need this," she'd whispered as her eyes glassed over with tears. I'd have torn out my own beating heart before making her cry.

But she was fading even as she wrote out numbers on star charts and watched videos about astrodynamics. Art made her food every two hours, if not more. Savory dishes that made my mouth water and sweet dishes that filled the house with confectionary aromas. Sage ate them all, infinitely tolerant with our fussing. She drank water and tea and coffee when Constantine brought them to her. She became skeletal anyway.

I climbed up to Matteo's conservatory with my heart already in the soles of my bare feet. Sage was with Matteo and Art, and already, I could hear the ragged pull of her labored breathing. Her pencil scratched feverishly against paper. Her heart skipped a few beats, a murmur she hadn't had a week ago.

Matteo was pacing anxiously. Art's anger was palpable even before I opened the door. When I did, Matteo and Art looked at me, but Sage did not. The observatory looked pristinely clean. All Matteo could do to help was clean, so the spacious room had been swept, mopped, and dusted to within an inch of its life. The equipment gleamed. The computer screens all had smudgeless reports and charts piled up on the desk. Sage was working on the map of France again, whispering mathematical equations under her breath as she matched coordinates to the map. Her shoulder blades jutted out sharply even though she wore a soft, oversized sweatsuit. Her hair still hung heavy and thick down her back, curtaining her pale face.

I could physically pull her away, but I knew it wouldn't

do any good. Not while we were still in Hollowhall. She would cry while she sat on my lap and plead for me to take her back. And I'd give in because I was powerless to do anything else. I locked eyes with my twin, and he communicated his feelings to me clearly. *Do something, or I will.*

There was only one recourse left to me at this point. "Sage."

She sat up quickly, looking over her shoulder. As soon as she saw me, a wave of happiness swept over her, and I could have wept over the intensity of the longing in her gaze. Her cheekbones were sharper now, her eyes smudged with blue beneath their luminous oak brown but no less radiant for it. "Silas, I found it."

Matteo and Art had a beleaguered sort of patience on their faces, like they'd already heard this and tried to reason with her. I'd been away for only an hour, but it had been necessary to make preparations. I came to where she was sitting and crouched down in front of her so that our eyes were almost level. "What did you find, Dulcis?"

"I found the wellspring." She pulled up a satellite image with exact coordinates plugged into the search bar. The fuzzy picture showed a crumbling piece of Roman architecture I'd seen many times before. "It's the—" she paused to read her notes, "Trophy of Augustus? It's in Monaco, obviously."

She'd made herself out of breath just talking, and her lips were turning blue. I took her frail hands in mine, rubbing my thumbs over the backs of her hands. "You matched the star coordinates to the ones on Earth."

"Yes," she smiled proudly, and her cracked lips sent a fissure of pain through my whole being. "I know, I know. You don't want to do anything during this Confluence. But I thought you should know. I think she built that structure a long time ago and dammed it up. Back when the last star weaver was alive." She paused frowning. "Or when the last star weaver died, maybe."

It was the latter, I was sure. The fae queen would not allow a star weaver to live if she wanted to hide a major wellspring. Which put Sage in very real danger even beyond what was happening to her body. "Art, Matteo, may I speak to Sage alone, please?"

"We'll check the perimeter," Matteo agreed readily.

Art backed out slower, his hands in his gray, linen pants pockets and his blue eyes matching wells of sorrow. "I'm sorry, Sage."

"Sorry?" She stared at the spot Art had been, and then back down to me. "Why is he sorry?"

"Dulcis." I brought her hands to my lips, kissing them softly. "I am out of options."

Dread pulled her mouth into a tight line. "What do you mean?"

"We must go to Geneva."

She tore her hands from mine, leaning away from me. "*No.* Silas, no. You can't—we can't leave."

"Sweetheart," I begged, on my knees now and gripping her arms in a careful hold. "You are dying. You are dying and no one can figure out why. I cannot let it happen."

"It's not—" Her throat worked convulsively, and she winced, eyes screwing shut. "Silas this," she jabbed the paper, "is the answer." But then she cried out in pain, and every life-saving hormone in her system flooded her blood, trying to trigger her fight or flight. She was numb to it, though. She ignored it, kneading her forehead. And I held her. Helpless. Powerless.

"This is a distraction from your pain," I argued gently. Gods, this was tearing me apart. It wasn't supposed to be this way. I'd found my mate. I'd found my ley match, and we were meant to spend endless years of bliss together. My reward for lifelong dedication to our people and our ways. Instead, my soulmate was dying a little more every day, and there was nothing I could do about it.

Sage framed my face with her hands, butterfly wings against my hardened shell. Tears lined her bottom lashes, and she sobbed out a breath, pulling me to her. I went willingly, laying my head in her lap and allowing her to cradle me. "Silas I'm so sorry. I'm so, so sorry. You deserve better."

I clung to her, arms around her hips and heart breaking with every beat. "I deserve *you*. I was promised *you*."

"I know," she whispered brokenly.

When I lifted my head, it was to find myself dangerously close to something I hadn't indulged in hardly ever in my long life. Tears. I swallowed them down and nearly choked on the brimstone. "In Geneva they have witches. Doctors. Specialists. We'll make you well again."

"And will your father ever let us out of his sight?" she challenged. Her heart was going crazy now, a rollicking, chaotic flutter that sent my panic into overdrive. "You'll be forced to leave your cohort. You'll have to leave Art."

"I don't care," I snapped. There it was. My patience had finally met its match. The brimstone tears lodged in my throat fanned to life, burning my organs, my muscles, my marrow. "I will. Not. Lose. You." I took her arms in mine again, shaking her softly with every word. "Do you understand me, Sage? I will not do it. I cannot bear it."

Her throat worked as she stared at me. A tear dropped to her cheek. "I do," she managed to get out.

"I've made preparations. In your weakened state, the travel will be hard enough on you, but if we take a helicopter to my jet, and we bring medical equipment—"

Sage placed her hand on my cheek again, smiling sadly. "Alright. It's okay, Silas. I'll do what you want. When do we leave?"

"Tomorrow morning. It takes a little time to charter flights." I covered her hand with mine, caressing the delicate skin. "I know you don't want to. I'm sorry."

She shook her head, hiccupping back the rest of her tears and smiling gamely. "No, it's really okay. I'm really such a burden, aren't I? Like you said, it was never meant to be this way."

"You are not a burden." I leaned forward and kissed her forehead, breathing in the scent of her, relishing in how she smelled like a mix of me, of my home, and of her. "Your life is precious. The most precious life in my family. Ask any of them and they will tell you."

"I know," she strangled out. "It's crazy—it's only been what, a week and a half? And they already feel like family." Her lips tilted into a wan curve. "Matteo taught me how to play Call of Duty. And Art is determined to introduce me to cuisine from every country around the world. I think Lu Rou Fan is my favorite. Constantine is like a mother, I swear. He even has the mom voice down." She imitated him, pulling a serious face. "'Don't walk outside without shoes on.'"

I snuffed out a laugh reluctantly. "Yes, he always has been."

"Alvaro probably thinks I'm the sign of the apocalypse, but he's trying to teach me chess. I think mostly he likes the excuse to beat me."

I rolled my eyes. "Also true."

"Matteo has been with me in here for hours." She looked around the observatory fondly. "He shares my love of the stars." She returned her gaze to me and pushed my dark hair away from my forehead, smoothing the ruffled locks. "And you."

"I know. Overbearing prick."

She kissed my eyelashes, first one eye, and then the other, so delicate, she could have been a passing dandelion seed. "You are my whole world. It's a little shocking how quickly I have come to need you. I *should* be shocked, anyway."

I opened my eyes, letting her talk if it helped her to process leaving. "It will seem less strange in three hundred years when we storm Monaco for you," I grinned crookedly.

She choked out a laugh. "That's the weirdest thought. Will it still be there three hundred years from now?"

"It's lasted this long," I shrugged and then sobered, taking her hands in mine again. "I know this isn't what you wanted."

"It does alter my plan," she agreed with sadness tugging at the corners of her eyes.

"But we will make this right. I promise. You'll see." I stood, helping her to join me by holding her upright. "You'll love Geneva. It's a beautiful oasis from the terrors of the real world. That's why my parents never leave it."

"I'm sure it's amazing," she agreed weakly. I hated how many of her bones I could feel between my arms. Humans didn't lose weight this quickly. It didn't make scientific or logical sense. Something was burning her up. Unaware of how stricken I was by the feel of her, she leaned her head back and searched my face. "You stopped touching me days ago."

I'd stopped because she couldn't afford to waste any of her energy on me. "Again, plenty of years for that later."

She huffed, her eyes already growing heated. "But I want you now."

Kryptonite. Those words were my one true weakness. "Sage, I…" I hesitated, cradling her against me.

"Please," she begged. She pushed up on tiptoes and placed a delicate kiss on my lips. My whole body tightened like a coiled spring.

"Sage," I groaned.

She kissed my jaw. My neck. "Please, Silas. For me. One more time… I mean here. At Hollowhall."

Biology was working against me. My erection pushed against the seam of my pants, and I inhaled the scent of her hair, of her skin, of her blood beneath the translucent surface of her skin. She was ambrosial in every way. "You need to rest."

"I need you," she whispered back urgently. Vaguely I could make out that she was trying to turn me. I let her. She sat me in the chair she'd just occupied, and then she straddled my lap, pressing her warm, wet heat against my erection. "Please, please, Silas."

I was clay in her dainty hands. I groaned, running my nose up the column of her neck and tasting the salty tang on her skin. She sighed in pleasure, her head falling back and her hair swishing gracefully.

I could ignore the physical response of the resonance if I wanted. I had been for days. But I couldn't ignore my love for her. My desire for Sage went deeper than physical craving. It had dug down deep to my core, to the heart of everything. I loved her gentleness. Her intelligence. I loved her laugh and her ready teases, the way they deepened her bond with me and with my brothers. I loved her caring heart, how she thought of others before herself, even if that drove me crazy. I loved that Sage was all the good things about mortality and all the beautiful promises of immortality.

I didn't want her because we were fated. I wanted her because I'd chosen her, and she was *mine*.

I kissed her softly, so very careful of her fragile state. She kissed me back hungrily, and I tempered the rising passion inside of me, urging my brute of a body to treat her with care even if she refused to.

I could sense Sage's mounting arousal. It perfumed the air and surged through her blood, spurring her to claw at my black T-shirt. I removed it willingly, and she did the same, struggling with the sweatshirt, her limbs weak. I helped her, and then we were skin to skin, warmth to warmth. She moved her hips against me in a familiar rhythm, and my pulse turned percussive in my ears.

Slowly. Gently. This would expend too much of her energy this way. I wrapped an arm under her bottom and the other behind her back, lifting her and then setting her on the stupid map of France. She didn't even protest, so I pushed the papers and notebooks aside. She kissed me like it was her last breath, desperate and needy. I kissed her like she was made of breakable things, of porcelain and trust. I refused to let this drain what was left of her. Mindful of her head, I lay her back on the table, and while computer monitors hummed on the desk to my left, I caged her between my arms and brought my erection between her legs. She moaned, eyes closing.

"Just relax, Dulcis," I soothed, kissing her neck, her jutting collarbones. "I have you."

"I know," she sighed. But her heart was going far too fast, and her skin had flushed. The resonance was pulling at her energy, siphoning what was left. I slid her sweatpants down her hips and then her legs, only briefly remembering that she'd abandoned wearing underwear days ago because it was too much effort added onto getting dressed in the morning. She smelled like sin and sweets, like the most intoxicating cocktail never invented. I kissed her thighs, and she spread them for me, her back arching.

"I'm going to give you soporis," I murmured against the sensitive skin of her inner thigh. "Just enough that you won't have to work so hard."

Her fingers dove into my hair, and I shuddered with pleasure. "Anything you want."

I wanted her to be well. I wanted her to be healthy enough that I could fuck her in every position and on every continent in the goddamn world, but I didn't get what I wanted. Not today. But I *would*. The alternative simply wasn't an option.

"Relax for me." She did, and I nuzzled her inner thigh before making a small incision with my teeth. She gasped, not in pain, but in renewed arousal, and I swore her body hummed for me. I closed my lips over the wound and sucked gently. Her blood was indescribably good. Sweet and salty, warm and coating my tongue and throat in a decadent layer. I swallowed twice and then stopped, damming her wound with my tongue.

Her muscles unraveled. Her pulse slowed. She sighed happily, kneading my scalp with her fingers until I thought I might pass out from the sheer gratification of it. When the bleeding had mostly stopped, I pulled away from her wound, tore away really, and then brought myself back over top of her. Licking the last traces of her blood from my lips, I bent to fog my breath over one taut nipple. "Feel better?"

"Almost," she mumbled. "I want you."

I wasn't going to draw this out any more than we needed. I undid the zipper of my pants, freeing my aching cock and positioning it at her center. She was still so tight, so new to this, but we didn't have the luxury of time. I entered her as quickly as I dared, and she was wet and inviting, practically sucking me deep within her. I took her nipple into my mouth until she arched into it, moaning loudly. And then I moved inside of her, in and out slowly, savoring the feel of her warm cunt around my hard cock.

She writhed beneath me, breathing fast and bringing her hips up to meet me. We went slow at first, her panting out little sounds of pleasure with every thrust. And then she begged for more. She wrapped her legs around my hips and dug her fingers into my sides, seeking a quicker tempo. I gave her what she wanted, marveling at how her throat looked with her head thrown back, how her mouth parted with ecstasy as I slammed into her hard and fast, how her breasts bounced with every impact.

And then she came around me and I was undone. In every way, she had peeled me to the bone. She had undone my DNA, stitched it back together, and rearranged the genetic sequence to read SAGE. As we breathed together, gripping one another tightly and coming down from the aftershocks of pleasure, I couldn't help but feel like I was holding a frail farewell. I couldn't shake the instinct that she was leaving me.

No, I wouldn't let her. I had chosen her and she was mine.

Chapter Twenty-Eight

SAGE

I had to leave tonight. It was cruelly unfair to lose my last two days with Silas, but we couldn't go to Geneva. The fae queen would come for me no matter where I was. And the more vampires I was around, the bigger the conflict would be. I didn't know the implications of such an act of war firsthand, but the others had mentioned the last one. The Blood Wars in the seventeen hundreds. It had been brutal, apparently. Humans died, the vampire population lost a sixteenth of their numbers—I couldn't be responsible for another one. Not when I had a plan to open the wellspring.

There were so many unknowns, but there were a few facts I had at my disposal. The wellspring was hidden under a crumbling monument built during the Roman Empire. It had cracks and weaknesses—structural issues. One snippet about the Trophy of Augustus had stuck with me in particular.

Recent surveys reveal more than surface weathering. Reports mention that hairline fractures have widened fissures in the Trophy's limestone core. Past attempts to repair this damage have eroded with time, leading to the discovery of drainage cavities that now open to the cliff face. Conservation teams warn that these internal gaps compromise the foundation's load paths.

If there were gaps, then there was room to shove something thin, long, and conductive into the weak points. It was the only plan I had—steal the silver rods, stash them in my pockets, and hope that my theory about being taken to the Trophy of Augustus during the Confluence was right. If that was the point at which the cosmic ley line would pour open, and the fae queen hoped that *I* would be the vessel to accept it, then it stood to reason that I would be right where I needed to be.

There was also a good chance that even if I did manage to hold onto these rods, I would shove them in a crack and be laughed at. Or worse.

I hadn't had enough time to plan, to research. All I had was a harebrained scheme and more determination than was healthy for me. Also, I had the pity card, and I planned to use it judiciously.

Silas hadn't let me go since we'd made love in the observatory. He carried me or held me on his lap. He kept one hand on me at all times, like he knew I was planning to slip away. He couldn't know it—he'd have solved the problem if he had. But some part of him must have sensed it. Which meant I had to get cunning.

As we sat downstairs in the informal living space, we all pretended to watch a new Jurassic Park movie. I didn't think any of us were paying attention. Silas was twirling an unruly lock of my hair around his fingers, staring into the middle distance. Art had his eyes on a cookbook, Constantine had his eyes on the screen, but they were glazed, Alvaro had fallen asleep, and Matteo kept glancing at me, at Art, and at Silas in turns. I'd been turning over my plans in my head the whole movie.

Finally, halfway through, I asked, "Do we have apples?"

They all perked up. I hadn't asked for anything specific in days. "Apples?" Art echoed. "We did… I think I used them."

I knew he'd used them, of course. "I don't know, I'm kind of feeling apple turnovers. Do you know what those are?"

"Yes," Art said immediately. "I'll go get ingredients."

"Wait, don't you have to make the dough first?" I asked. It was downright evil, this plan of mine. I knew very well how they would all react based on the patterns I'd picked up on since living with them.

"True," he frowned.

"I'll get the apples," Matteo offered. Right on cue. Because where Matteo went, since he was the younger brother, then inevitably…

"I'll go with him," Constantine offered. "He'll probably get the wrong ones, anyway."

"You guys don't have to go right now," I pointed out. It wasn't a lie. My pulse stayed steady.

"We're happy to," Constantine replied like I was ridiculous.

I hated myself for knowing them so well that I could manipulate them. They all got to their feet, finding shoes and stretching. Alvaro yawned, checking his watch and then letting his gaze stray to the darkened windows. He sighed. "If they're going, we should do a—"

Perimeter check, I thought in tandem with his statement. *Yes, do a perimeter check. Once you do, Silas will insist that you have someone with you.*

"Let's do a quick one," Silas said, glancing at me. "Art, will you…?"

"Sage, it's time you pull your weight around here," Art said with mock solemnity. "I insist you learn how to make pie dough."

"I can see this is incredibly integral to the house's working order," I replied, making my best attempt at humor. "Fine. Let's go to the kitchen."

Silas twined his fingers with mine while we walked upstairs together, playing with them idly. I let a shiver course through me, wondering if this would be the last time I would touch him. And then I immediately schooled those thoughts into a box because if Art was reading me, it would give everything away. Silas went to the office with Alvaro, and when they emerged again, outfitted with holsters and weapons, my heart lurched. What if plucking the rose didn't stop the fae queen from attacking them? What if she did it preemptively to stop them from coming after me?

I couldn't warn them and I nearly allowed the despair of it to swallow me. Art glanced at me as he reached for a glass cannister of flour. "Stop worrying about them. They're brutes, seriously."

I was thankful I had a logical reason for feeling the stab of pain. "I'm sure you're right," I breathed, steeling my emotions again.

Silas pulled me away from the marble countertops and into an easy embrace. "I'll be right back. Art is right—I won't have a scratch on me."

If I did my job right, he wouldn't. I ran my finger over the leather shoulder holster holding up his gun. "I believe you."

Silas crooked his finger under my chin and tipped it up. Pine forest green swallowed my emotions, engulfing me in a love so palpable, I could have sworn it fed the dwindling ley inside of me. "I'll be right back." It was a promise. It was a threat. I struggled to contain the onslaught of anguish and fear that threatened to drown me.

"Okay," I choked.

Silas kissed my forehead, and then he was gone. And my time was up. I stared at the shadowed living room where he'd disappeared into, my thoughts blissfully vacant for one moment. But that was all I could allow myself. One last moment to yearn for him, to be in his home, safe and cherished. I hadn't had nearly long enough to appreciate the poignant gift these men had given me. Whatever happened next, I would have these two weeks with me to hold in my memories and cherish in my heart.

Art tossed sticks of butter on the counter. "First of all, if you tell me to make this dough with shortening, I'm going to put you in time out."

"I need a favor." I turned to him, steeling myself. I'd already gotten dressed in more practical clothing after Silas had taken me to the shower this afternoon. Sneakers, soft jeans, a Rolling Stones graphic tee, and most importantly, a canvas jacket I'd found amongst Constantine's donations. It had a zipper pocket on the inside just deep enough for incense-sized silver rods.

Art raised his dark eyebrows, already wary. "Sage, I swear to God, if you do that thing with the puppy dog eyes—"

I looked up through my lashes, my gaze pleading. "It's a small thing."

Art closed his eyes, clearly in pain. "No, Sage. I'm not taking you to the Goddamn fae bush again."

"Just one more time," I implored. "I have some calculations." I pulled out a smaller notebook with nonsense equations scribbled on the pages. "I think I found our ley line in the sky. But I need to tag the exact coordinates with my phone."

"Sage," he groaned, his face scrunched. He didn't want to look at me because he knew he was a sucker for the puppy dog eyes thing. I'd gotten disgustingly good at it the last few days.

"Please, Art? Silas won't do it. And it—it makes me feel better."

Art's eyebrows tipped up with indecision. "We can't keep visiting the stupid thing. It makes Silas edgy."

"Just one more time," I promised. I meant that. I sent my whole soul into the emotion. I let him feel my longing, my desperation to see it.

He tipped his head back and groaned. "Fine."

"Really fast," I promised. "I'll tag the coordinates and we can come right back."

"You just want to see Silas give me a black eye," he accused, coming around the island to crouch down in front of me.

I smiled as I twined my arms around him, pressing our cheeks together. "I just like the feeling of knowing you care."

"That is patently obvious to me," he drawled. "Close your eyes."

I did, and I felt his body move beneath mine, so strangely smooth and strong for how fast he was undoubtedly moving. The cold air rushed past me, dotting my arms and neck with goosebumps. When he stopped, he lowered me carefully until my feet touched the damp earth. It was dark enough that I squinted and blinked, trying to make out where we were. "Is this the right place?"

Art turned on his phone's flashlight, illuminating the

bush and the rapidly growing pepper plant beneath it. The silver rods winked in the soft glow. My pulse skyrocketed, and a cold sweat broke out down my spine. This was it, then. There was no hesitating now. I had to go through with this right now, right here, and I couldn't let Art sense what I was about to do. With my hand shaking, I pulled out my phone and unlocked it. "Okay, one sec."

My feet crunched over leaves and dead twigs. Art scanned the forest, preoccupied with keeping me safe from a threat he had no idea I was reaching for. I bent down in front of the bush and plucked out the silver rods quickly, *one, two, three, four, five.* Fumbling a little, I stashed them in the zipper pocket and closed it before standing again. Art leaned over. "What are you doing?"

I rotated to face him, finally allowing the dam to break, allowing the torment to flow from my aching heart and into his awareness. "Tell him I love him." I grabbed a thorny rose, ignoring the way the punishing spikes dug into my skin. I yanked.

"Sage, no!" Art yelled.

The world went blinding white.

Chapter Twenty-Nine

SAGE

"Ms. Herriman, what made you take the fae queen's offer?"

"Ms. Herriman, over here! Have the vampires been feeding on you?"

"Give us a smile!"

Click, click, click. Flashes of white and clamoring questions stuffed my disoriented senses, and I put up a hand, shielding myself.

I'd expected to find myself in a lot of places. A dungeon. A forest. Maybe the ruins themselves. I had not remotely prepared to find myself in the middle of a jostling crowd, besieged by camera flashes and peppered with questions. As far as I could tell, I was in front of a luxury apartment building or hotel. And I wasn't alone. The moment I appeared there, a crowd of paparazzi had surrounded me, hollering for my attention.

"Ms. Herriman, is it true you're escaping the vampire cohort in fear for your life?"

I covered my face with my arms, ducking down. What

the actual fuck? I backed up several steps, hoping to find refuge through the elegant, glowing entrance. But then the doors were thrown open wide, and the crowd behind me gasped to a hush. I lowered my arms, peeking through them.

A woman and her entourage strutted out of the building's opulent entrance, walking down the marble steps like they were on the runway. The woman in front swayed with confidence, her leather pants practically sewn on to her luscious body and her silver jacket hanging off her shoulders. She removed a pair of sunglasses, coming to a stop at the bottom of the stairway, and the small group of gorgeous, fashion-studded people behind her did the same, all of them adopting matching poses of careless confidence.

The woman's bright green eyes, an unnatural shade of lime, fixed on me, and her brown-tinted, glossy lips pulled into a smirk. "I knew you'd come."

The crowd behind me went crazy.

"Your Highness, did you orchestrate this?"

"Your Highness, please, is this the end of the vampire line?"

"How did you convince the ley socium to join you?"

"Your Highness, over here! A picture!"

The woman waved at her admirers with long, pointed nails, and her sleek, black ponytail swished like silk over her shoulder. "You animals. Never a moment's peace." Despite her words, she posed, jutting out a hip, pursing her lips, smiling for the many cameras that flashed and clicked. I stood there, five feet from her, bedraggled and clutching a blood-stained rose.

Was this… a joke? Had I been brought here as some kind of prank?

Hope unfurled, a tentative bud emerging from a freshly

dug grave. I took a few tentative steps backward, wondering if I could escape into the crowd. Someone shoved me forward, and I stumbled, put right back where I'd been. The woman turned the full force of her attention on me again. "My little ley socium. The fae have been waiting for you."

I saw him, then, Cysgadyn among the throng of beautiful people. He looked different, though. More stylish, more put together. His pristinely white sneakers, slick, black suit, and gloating smirk quashed the burgeoning hope in my chest that I might escape this. He didn't seem at all surprised to see me. When I rotated my gaze to the woman, I saw her for what she was. A queen. I dropped the rose, straightening.

"How did you know she would come?" a reporter asked.

"Was she forced here, Your Highness?"

"Your Highness, are we at war with the vampires?"

Queen Eliana rolled her eyes, flourishing her long nails with annoyance. "Bring the socium inside. She looks half dead." A little louder, to the paparazzi and reporters she said, "This is what vampires do. Do you see this poor girl? She's skeletal."

"Have the vampires lost control?" The reporters started up with their questions again, and I found myself flanked by a pretty woman with a blond pixie cut and a thug of a man with a shiny bald head and menacing expression. I couldn't have fought off a sleepy four-year-old, let alone these two, so I let them lead me up the marble steps.

My mind buzzed with questions. The portal had taken me to the fae queen after all, then. But it was her… apartment? Her hotel? And she had paparazzi outside the building, following her around. But I'd never seen her on TV before. I didn't think she was famous.

We went through double glass doors into a lavish lobby,

and I found myself surrounded on all sides by expensive perfumes, clacking, designer shoes, and excited titters. It was a hotel, I realized, as we passed sitting areas and tables, an enormous lobby desk manned by red-uniformed hosts, and expensive vases on Grecian columns. Sparkling champagne chandeliers overhead lit the space with garish light, and the retinue moved en masse across the empty lobby and toward a long room at the back. The whole area had been walled off by frosted glass, and my guess, as we went through the door, was that it was an event space.

It was, but it wasn't just any ballroom or conference area. Every wall had been made of ceiling-length glass, and on the opposite side, it overlooked the Mediterranean from a high cliffside. Chairs had been arranged throughout the room strategically. They were oddly reminiscent of what I'd *expected* to find when transported to the fae queen; a court. An elegant, cream armchair had been set to face the dark ocean, and around it, smaller, less ornate chairs were set slightly behind. The Italian tile clanked under my sneakers as they led me past dining tables set with white tablecloths and over to the makeshift… well, it was a throne. There was no denying it as Queen Eliana took a seat and crossed her legs, still smirking.

As she did, the fae's appearances shifted suddenly, and their true forms were revealed. Most of them took on a bluish appearance, their skin like moonlight and their hair varying shades of brighter colors. Their teeth elongated, pointy and snarling, and their ears grew long tips. Many of them had claws like Eliana's. Some were smaller in stature, and others freakishly tall. I recoiled as the pixie cut blonde hissed in my ear, circling me and grinning with a serpentine tongue licking the dagger points of her teeth.

Most of the entourage sat on either side of the throne, but guards stood near the entrances and at my back. In case I tried to bolt, probably. Eliana regarded me with smug indifference. She, too, had changed, although not as dramatically. Her teeth, sharp but white, grinned maliciously, and her skin glowed like shallow sea water in the sun. "You really have let them suck you dry."

The assembly watched me, all apparently eager for what I had to say. "It wasn't them," I rasped, surprised my voice even worked. At least I hadn't been put in chains or immediately hung upside-down and drained like a pig.

Eliana lifted a perfectly manicured, black eyebrow. "What, are you on a juice cleanse? Is it a good one?" She looked me over. "Looks effective."

I pointed to Cysgadyn where he was watching me with rapt interest. He looked wraith-like again, his form shifting and slithering like mist on water. He looked even less human than the others, part shadow and part fae with his long ears and jagged teeth. "Ask him." I still couldn't tell anyone about what he'd done to me, even if they were fae.

Eliana turned in her chair, giving her wraith creation a questioning glance. He started, like he'd forgotten. "I used silencing leywork so she couldn't tell the vampires about our deal."

Eliana pinched the bridge of her nose, and her bracelets clanked. "Did you give it a power source, you bawling infant?"

"No," Marcus hedged. "What—what power source?"

"For *fuck's* sake," she screeched suddenly. Everyone jumped, clearly nervous. Eliana stood, and her silver jacket fell off her shoulders. "Come here, *cum cake*, so I can instruct you in the correct use of leywork."

The room practically quaked with fear, silent as a mausoleum. Cysgadyn stood unsteadily, three chairs down from her and shuffling past the other courtiers, who all ducked to avoid their queen's wrath. "H-here?"

"Right here," Eliana snapped, her pointed nail like an arrow to the carpet.

Cysgadyn fell to his knees. "I-I didn't know. I mean I just..." he swallowed convulsively.

"'I just,'" Eliana mimicked in a nasally voice. She lashed out suddenly, grabbing Marcus by the throat with so much strength, I heard something vital crack. "*This* is how you perform effective leywork on humans. You cast your intent, *to make this fucker shut the hell up for the rest of his miserable life*," she hissed, and the wind picked up around us even though the windows and doors were shut.

Cysgadyn choked, scrabbling uselessly at her hold. She looked like a movie star but clearly, she was far stronger than she appeared. I took two stumbling steps back, only to be met by pixie and thug.

"And you give it," she started out low, increasing her volume in wrath, "*a fucking power source*." She reached her other hand out to the side, aiming for a courtier with bright green hair and several piercings on her face. The girl screamed, shriveling almost instantly, a husk of a corpse. Bright blue flashed from Eliana's hand and into Cysgadyn.

He fell over gasping, and the green-haired corpse slumped to the tiles with a soft *plunk*. I gasped, falling back against my captors, but other than my ragged breathing and Marcus' pained wheezing, the room didn't make a sound.

Eliana turned to me, perfectly composed, and twirling her long nails. "That's how you do it. Otherwise, you little *shit bag*," she hissed, kicking Cysgadyn in the ribs with her platform heels, "the target dies. If she hadn't been a ley socium with ample ley in her body, you would have killed her in a day. Stupid little shit," she hissed again.

I barely restrained a whimper of fear, leaning heavily against my captors. Eliana turned a sympathetic look to me. "Poor love. I'm so sorry I sent half a brain to handle that. I should have known better." She approached me, and I flinched. "Shh, no, no, love. You're not in trouble." When she reached me, cloying perfume clogged my nose, and one long, black nail dragged down my cheek. "You're a guest. You're wanted. I'll prove it. Be still, darling. Hush, no, don't struggle."

The two fae behind me held me still despite my sudden struggle to escape. Fear consumed me, every instinct driving me to escape. But Eliana wrapped her long fingers around my neck in a gentle grip. Her unnatural green eyes glowed with a flash of blue. "I release you."

I'd been wearing fifty-pound chains, and Eliana had turned the padlock. A weight suddenly fell from my body, from my soul, and with a gasp, I inhaled frosty air, a mentholated rush of pure ley. It flowed back into my body once the spell was released, and my skin tingled and tightened, filling out to the healthy size I had been before. My jeans were suddenly a little too tight, and pure energy flowed through my veins. I drew in a clear breath of air for the first time in days.

The room released a collective, appreciative sigh. Eliana looked pleased with herself. "There you are. We wouldn't want that ley to go to waste on a half-assed leywork would we?"

I put a hand to my throat, swallowing. "Thank you."

"You came to the right place," Eliana smiled, like she

hadn't just sacrificed one of her own people for a demonstration.

Cysgadyn had pulled himself to his feet, his half-shadow, half-corporeal form hunched in pain. I felt another pang of sympathy for him just like I had when he'd cursed me. How new was he? When had Eliana created him?

Eliana sneered at him as she walked back to her throne. "We don't need you to speak to play your part, do we? That will teach you to perform leywork before you are asked."

It wasn't that I liked Cysgadyn. He'd been responsible for some of the worst days of my life. He'd been the reason I'd had to choose between the cohort's safety and mine. But it was difficult to watch him suffer, to watch the sorrow in his coal black, haunted eyes, to watch him slink back into the ranks when he'd been so fervent about winning her favor. I did my best not to look resentful to the fae queen. If I played along, I would have a better chance at planting the silver rods in place. If I fought it, they might tie me up, or worse, knock me out altogether. I didn't know what she actually planned to do, after all.

Eliana considered me from her chair again, her long black nails tapping elegantly against her sharp jaw. "How long before the vampires come for her, do you think?"

The fae directly to her right, a hauntingly beautiful woman with long, silver hair and mercury eyes spoke like she was thinking out loud. "Half a day if they come alone. Two days if they assemble."

No, I thought in despair, suddenly. *Don't start a war, Silas. Please.*

"We should have her ready in either case, then," the fae queen smiled mirthlessly. What did that mean, have me ready? Ready for what? But she didn't answer my silent questions. Instead, she gestured vaguely to the guards behind me. "Take her to her room. See that she is dressed appropriately." Eliana angled a look full of cunning malice my way. "Do rest, pet. You have much to accomplish."

I might as well have been silenced by leywork, still. My throat refused to work even as my mind screamed for answers.

Chapter Thirty

SILAS

My brain shifted into neutral, spinning uselessly on its axes.

Art's words barely penetrated my mind. I briefly took in the withered rose bush and missing ley rods. I inhaled the absence of her. Still, my brain stalled, unable to shift back into motion, to make sense of what my brother was trying to tell me. Some part of my gray matter catalogued all his words for later use even if I wasn't able to fully comprehend the enormity of what they meant.

"She plucked the rose and just vanished…"

"… said she loves you."

A breeze rustled through the decayed branches, rattling them like bones. Alvaro, Matteo, and Constantine stood behind me, still as rooted pines. Art waited three feet from me, his body tense, like he was waiting for a blow. I didn't give him the satisfaction. I breathed in deeply again, making sure that my finely tuned senses weren't lying to me. She wasn't here. Her scent was gone. Her heartbeat wasn't within a mile of the house. Our connection had been spread thin, stretched over an impossible distance. Sage was gone.

Wisely, none of my brothers said a word.

A timer started in my soul, and I finally realized that I didn't have twenty years to stand here and absorb the anguish of my reality. I checked my watch. 9:04. She'd left two minutes ago. For two minutes she'd been with the fae queen. Every second counted now. Wars were won by decisive action and strategic command, not by the emotional disintegration my whole being wanted to surrender to.

I indexed every detail available to me. The rose bush had died, its magical source dried up, which meant that it had been leywork, a magical device tuned into existence by fae. Which meant something had triggered it.

She plucked the rose…

Sage had triggered the mechanism. On purpose or on accident?

She said she loves you.

On purpose, then. She'd known. And it hadn't been something Alvaro or Art had been able to read from her, which made even less sense than Sage willingly putting herself in harm's way. I set that puzzle aside. The ley rods were gone. "Did you remove the witch's silver rods?"

Art shook his head. "She took them and put them in her pocket before she plucked the rose."

Forethought. Strategy on Sage's part. But why? The air didn't smell like decaying fruit, so the fae had not been here. The pepper plant hadn't died, but I didn't understand the significance of that. "Matteo, I want that witch here within the hour."

Matteo left without another word, running unnaturally fast to our helipad. Beau lived somewhere in Pennsylvania, I knew, but he'd make it happen all the same. I thought back to the Blood Wars, to the leyworks they'd created, and I knew they were capable of transporting living creatures along ley lines. It was a secret they patently refused to share with any other species, and they would count on how long it would take me to react to Sage's abduction.

I flicked my wrist, bringing up the projected phone display on my inner forearm and scrolling through the contacts. "Constantine, we need to parley with the vertos." There weren't many vampires who had communicated openly with the shapeshifting vertos, but Constantine's house attended occasional parleys with the species, ensuring that borders were maintained and disputes handled discreetly. The last thing anyone needed in the digital age was an all-out brawl between vampires and vertos.

Unlike Matteo, Constantine hesitated. "They will ask if we are at war."

"I'd say taking a ley socium is an act of war," I replied icily, turning to face him.

Constantine remained unperturbed as usual. "The vertos will have conditions." There would be a price to pay, of course. I didn't know what the vertos would ask of us—ask of House Incubus—but I was certain that Constantine would pay it if they asked.

"We have to," was all I said.

"Understood." Constantine was gone, then, already calling his house.

Alvaro was on his phone, too. "She'll broadcast it on her network." We weren't supposed to have access to the fae-only, heavily contrived "network" that aired whatever Queen Eliana wanted. We had a direct feed to it anyway, of course. Alvaro watched his screen, his forehead creasing. "Yes, she's there."

I joined him, looking over his shoulder at his phone screen. Cameras captured a confused, frightened image of Sage. On screen, she looked smaller than I remembered. Frail. She clutched the rose to her chest, shrinking away from the reporters peppering her with questions. I saw red. "Drain every fae's mind within a fifty-mile radius until they're brain-dead. I want something, *anything*, about Eliana's plans."

"Happily." Alvaro handed me the phone so I could continue watching and disappeared.

I didn't have time to watch this farce of a news network engineered to feed Eliana's vanity. I watched anyway. As I walked back to the house at a human pace, I took in as many details as I could through the camera lens. The number of reporters outside the hotel in Monaco. How many were in Eliana's retinue when she arrived. The wraith-like creature who seemed to have been elevated to Eliana's personal court when it usually took hundreds of years to earn that spot. He'd done something critical to her plans, then.

Sage didn't say a word, clearly too fatigued to find her bearings. When they took her inside, the feed switched to a hired news anchor—likely given a script ahead of time—and I pocketed the phone. Alvaro certainly already had his house watching the network for information.

As I walked, Art kept pace with me, watching me. I knew my brother like I knew myself. His guilt would be eating him alive right now, gnawing at his thoughts like rat torture. I didn't care. He stared forward again, easily keeping up with me when I ran at my full speed and made it back to the house in the next instant. "She's been planning this for days."

"No shit." I threw open the glass door, only just

managing to catch myself from ripping it off its hinges and shattering the glass.

He caught it carefully and closed it. "She said something about the bush matching a celestial ley line. I don't know. She managed to keep this from us when we should all be able to read her like front page news."

"No. Shit." I reiterated, running full tilt again and appearing in the office with its camera feeds and ward surveillance. I pulled up the feed on the rose bush, needing to see her disappear for myself. I didn't have to rewind it far. Sage and Art appeared at the edge of the wards on the black and white, night-vision feed. Sage barely hesitated. She went right for the silver rods, picked them up, and put her hand on the rose. She said something to Art, plucked, and vanished. That was it. It had happened literally minutes ago, and I still couldn't believe it was real.

"Silas." Art snapped the laptop closed and stared at me from the other side of the desk. "I'm telling you, we're missing something crucial. We can't go charging in unless we know what was going on with her."

My rage, which I'd thought well contained, suddenly erupted through layers of continental crust with a fiery explosion. I didn't even blink fully before I'd vaulted over the desk, grabbed the front of his shirt, and slammed him into the glass wall. The window cracked, webbing out from Art's body as the shatter-proof glass absorbed the impact. "No *fucking shit.*"

Art grunted, his airway closed and his features cracking with morose humor. "There... he is."

"If you didn't have boiled shrimp between your ears instead of a *fucking brain*, I'd eviscerate you here and now. But you're clearly brain-dead, brother, so I don't see a point." I slammed him into the window again, and Art winced as cuts opened on his scalp only to immediately heal before much blood could coat the surface.

He coughed. "Boiled shrimp is a new one."

If he could quip, then he wasn't hurting enough. I crushed his windpipe and pinned his head to the window. "What were you thinking?"

It took Art a full five seconds to heal and regain his voice before he rasped out, "Wasn't."

I shoved him, letting him fall forward to his knees where he gasped and choked while his body finished healing. "I'd kill you, but let's be real—father will end my life if we lose her, and then House Sanguis would have no heir."

Art laughed harshly, finding his feet and wiping blood splatter from his mouth. "We both know I'll never be his heir."

"*It's not funny*," I seethed.

Art sobered, standing there in the darkness, bathed in moonlight and withering under his own guilt. "No, it's not."

I ran a hand through my hair, nearly breaking under the weight of my panic finally. "This cannot happen."

"We'll get her back," Art promised. "I'll break through wards myself if I have to."

We both knew that Eliana had planned this out decades before this night. We were at a strategic disadvantage with little intel and even less time. "Sage tried to tell me that her charting, that the wellspring was the answer."

"Why wouldn't she tell us the rest of it?" Art paced. "What reason could she have to keep secrets? And how? Alvaro read her."

We looked up at the same time, gazes locking. "He couldn't read her."

Art rubbed his face. "She *was* leyworked. We shouldn't

have trusted the word of one witch. We should have asked elsewhere."

"But how was she leyworked? I was with her every moment since we matched." It didn't make sense. She'd been safe with me. I'd made sure of it. "Of course we didn't think she would be leyworked. There was no evidence of it."

Art shook his head, clearly as disturbed as I was. "I don't know what we're missing."

Constantine appeared in the doorway, and his gaze landed on the window before blinking over to Art. "You're alive."

"Three hundred years ago, I wouldn't have been," Art winced, brushing glass from his hair. "He's getting old."

My fury flared again, heating my neck. "If neither of you takes this seriously, I swear to God—"

"The vertos have agreed that the ley socium in fae hands during a Confluence would be bad for everyone involved," Constantine said evenly. "But they want to redraw some boundaries."

Of course, they would want more land in exchange. "Your house agrees?"

"Readily," Constantine said.

I glanced at my watch. Fifteen minutes. She'd been gone fifteen minutes. "We need to know what Eliana wants with Sage, specifically."

"Sage was obsessed with the wellspring," Constantine pointed out. "We thought she was trying to distract herself or perhaps acting on her star weaver nature, but there must be more to it."

I thought back to all my conversations with her. She'd said she *couldn't* tell me, and if she'd somehow been leyworked into silence, then it was no wonder that she had been frustrated. "Sage said that the Confluence would pour a ley line into the closed-off spring, and she was insistent that we open it."

Art frowned, rolling his shoulders and glancing up like he could see the observatory through the ceiling. "Matteo said if it was closed, it would pour into nothing. And she had a surge of pure fear when he said that."

I suddenly remembered a question she had asked. *Can I hold more ley if it's given to me?*

Surely, it wouldn't be that. It wasn't possible. Like Sage had been handing me ripped scraps of the same picture, I began placing them together in my mind. The wraith-like creature screeching about having been promised the ley socium, the one-time attack from scientifically created, magical aberrations, her deterioration, her obsession with the Confluence. It began to bleed together, a swirl of paint and pixels. The image was horrific.

"I think I know what she wants Sage for." My voice sounded far away in my ears. It echoed down a tunnel, another realm where the impossible had suddenly become inevitable. "I know Eliana's plan."

Chapter Thirty-One

SAGE

Song: Blood Guts & Pixie Dust by Neoni

Cysgadyn pulled me into a dance in the middle of the ballroom, his inky eyes slithering over me. His hand came to rest low on my back, and he tucked me into his lean body, coaxing me into a slow sway. I went rigid in his hold, torn between the fact that he looked human again, and therefore, like a friend, and the fact that he was the reason I'd been forced to attend this ball. He still couldn't speak, but I'd been placed next to him all evening after being allowed to fitfully rest in the hotel room through the night and most of the day.

Dancers swirled around us, elegant and perfectly graceful in their coordinated dance moves. It was like I'd been plopped in the middle of a Victorian movie set, with swishing gowns, smiling faces, and pristine actors. Up close, I saw the fear behind their eyes. I read the terror in their perfect movements, their gazes that didn't meet one another.

Eliana watched from her wingback chair, dazzlingly

happy for the cameras around us. She giggled and answered questions from interviewers behind the camera crew. She drank and *appeared* to converse with her companions. It looked rehearsed. It reminded me of when my friends and I had pretended to be pop stars in elementary school. We'd each been given roles and told that they had to follow around the "pop star" like paparazzi.

The more I was with the fae court, the more I understood what drove them. For vampires, it appeared to be power. For fae, it was fame. Only, I had to imagine that fae weren't necessarily allowed to be overtly themselves before the whole world. The fae queen wasn't allowed to be admired by the whole world, so maybe she had dictated that her people do it instead. Which meant that smartphones and a digitized civilization were probably hell for the fae. I wondered if Queen Eliana had an app yet…

Marcus steered us to the front of the ballroom near the queen. To our right, the Mediterranean sparkled with sunset bokeh, and to our left, a row of fae soldiers guarded the wall connected to the rest of the hotel. A disco ball turned slowly, and it really only solidified my theory that Queen Eliana was playing out a childish mimicry of what fame looked like from the outside looking in. We twirled where the cameras could catch us, and they rounded on us in synchronized harmony.

"Here, we have the ley socium and her new mate, Cysgadyn! Aren't they a beautiful couple?"

I gritted my teeth, glaring up at Cysgadyn. He stared above my head, stoically unfeeling since the queen had silenced him. He held me just the way he ought to, his palm on my bare lower back and his hold on my hand outstretched and perfectly aligned. My white, silk gown swished around his shiny dress shoes, and to anyone watching this scene from the outside, we could have been the bride and groom. I'd tried to fight the dress, tried to insist on keeping my jacket with me, but the fae had been much stronger than me even with my ley returned. I had bruises on my arms and legs from the scuffle we'd had over the damn gown, but in the end, I'd ended up here in this ballroom again and paraded on Marcus' arm. I silently seethed over it.

Silas could see this. I was sure of it. Somewhere, he would have figured out that I had gone to the fae and would have found access to their phony network. I fought a wave of tears, stumbling in my pearly white heels. Would he be sad? Or angry? I hoped he was angry. I hoped he hated me.

I missed him. I missed him so keenly, my chest hurt. I missed him so much, my bones creaked and my head pounded. I'd been ejected into space, deprived of oxygen and adrift in an endless sea of shadows. My only hope was to finish what I'd started. Maybe some good would come of this. Maybe I would make a difference. The others could find mates. Would Silas be able to find a new mate if I failed?

The live orchestra below Eliana's dais brought the song to a close, and Cysgadyn halted us before the queen. I rolled a sardonic look his way. Did they rehearse this while I was tossing in my swanky king bed upstairs? Eliana stood, and her transparent, mesh dress barely shifted on her curves as she did. "Is it just me, or does this feel like a fucking *wedding*?"

The crowd of fae behind us clapped, and the cameras zoomed in on the queen's grinning features. She held up her hand to halt the applause, which stopped immediately, and then her neon green gaze fixed on me. "I don't think it's any surprise that EL! Network has *record views* at the moment. We have quite a guest."

The crowd clapped again, and I tried not to curl in on myself, uncomfortable with the many pairs of multi-colored eyes that pinned me to the ballroom floor. *She's right. Silas is watching. Be strong.* I kept my spine straight and my face neutral.

"It's easy to forget about the fae, isn't it?" Eliana asked the crowd. An actual teleprompter had been set up for her, and it was a massive effort on my part not to roll my eyes. "We feed the ley lines. We give power to literally everyone else." The crowd clapped again, this time a little more enthusiastically. "We give and give and *give*," she practically shouted, her filter-perfect features beginning to snarl.

"And what are we told? We must hide. We are the best singers on this miserable planet." The crowd cheered a little louder. Eliana shouted, "The best artists!" They agreed with her, enthusiastic now. "The best entertainers! And only now does the world tune in to our performance."

I got a sinking feeling in the pit of my stomach. The Confluence wasn't until tomorrow, but this spectacle felt eerie in its premeditation. I ventured a look around the ballroom and found the fae all in their natural states, now. Bright hair, pointed ears, and varying sizes from unnaturally tall to impossibly petit. The feel of Cysgadyn's arm through mine shifted too, and I found him in his shadow state, his body sifting and swirling in and out of corporeal substance. His eyes swam with writhing shadows and he rotated a haunted, empty look down to me. I recoiled, but he held me tight against his side.

"It's time we give the world something worth watching. It's time we unleash our true power for *all* to behold," Eliana shouted. The crowd agreed with raucous support, apparently abandoning their rigid roles for ones of wild enthusiasm. "Allow me to introduce you to the future of the fae." Eliana brandished her arm to the right, and on cue, smoke machines filled the air with choking smoke.

Cysgadyn left my side, walking almost robotically to where a crowd of bodies was emerging from behind the raised dais. The orchestra began to play a rendition of "Applause" by Lady Gaga. I would have cringed if I hadn't been genuinely horrified. Cysgadyn joined a throng of shadow-slick, flickering forms exactly like him. Most of them bared their fae-like, piercing teeth, drooling blue and grinning with manic pride. The fae crowd fell into a shocked hush. The collection of creatures gathered at the base of the dais, three dozen of them, nearly identical in their male form and eerily silent.

"I present to you, the Elianthi," Eliana grinned widely. "A new species of fae. Our future."

I could practically feel the bug-eyed stares behind me. Clearly, these fae had not been properly introduced to what Cysgadyn was, and they hadn't known that there were more of them. That sinking feeling in the pit of my stomach hardened to lead, weighing me down with dread. The reporters began their questions right on cue. "What are they, Your Majesty?"

"They are hope," Eliana recited with unconvincing solemnity. "My own creations. With the advance of technology and our unparalleled skill with ley magic, I have managed to create the very first fae capable of *siring fae.*"

The crowd gasped, and for once, I was pretty sure it was genuine. Whispers broke out amongst the crowd, and even the camera crew lifted their heads from their eye pieces to stare with open mouths. I rubbed my bare arms, covered in chills. I knew what was coming next. I'd already guessed it.

Cysgadyn had said I "belonged to him." They needed to pour ley into me, to change me, so I could help them bear fae children.

Eliana confirmed it, gesturing to me with an open palm and a sadistic gleam in her heavily lined eyes. "With ley socium."

The whispers turned to shocked murmurs, and the onlookers buzzed, most of them sounding intrigued rather than horrified. I felt empty inside. A shell. The vessel they believed me to be. Whether or not this experiment of Eliana's worked, I did not plan to survive long enough to let them impregnate me with whatever spawn Eliana envisioned.

"Why should these fertile, ley-blessed goddesses be hoarded by the vampires?" Eliana demanded, and true anger broke through her veneer of perfection. "Why should we not fill the earth with talented fae from continent to continent? Why *not*, my brave people?"

The astonished conversations turned to cheers once again, and I found myself drowning in a sea of eager applause. "Why not?" someone shouted behind me.

"They steal everything!" another one added.

"When the planets align," Eliana shouted, her expression growing increasingly crazed as her people fell for her plan in lockstep, "everything will change. The stars themselves will bear witness as we sever her false bond to the ley suckers and forge a truer one. A fae bond. She will be mated to one of the Elianthi, and through their union, the ley cosmos will be made whole again. Under perfect symmetry, a new age will dawn—an age of the fae, reborn in my image!"

The crowd went wild, and my heart refused to beat. They cheered and beat their feet on the dance floor. Eliana threw her jeweled hands out to her adoring subjects, drunk on success. I felt my dying star of hope approaching a black hole. A handful of silver sticks didn't stand a chance against this.

Eliana was confident. She was so assured, she had broadcast her entire plan to the world, bragging for all the vampires, all the witches, all the shifters to see. Because she knew she'd already won.

My lips trembled, and amidst the chaos, jostled left and right by moon-skinned fae, my resolve crumbled. Tears dampened my cheeks, and I clasped my hands together so tightly, they lost all color. A glance at Eliana told me that she'd hoped for my tears. She reveled in them from her throne, smirking cruelly as I stood alone in an ocean of glee.

I swallowed hard and tore my gaze from the stoic Elianthi and reveling fae. The sun had nearly fallen past the horizon, and I let my feet carry me to the glass wall. The lambency reminded me of that day with Silas on his ship. The breathless ecstasy of a promise whispered.

My life is precious.

I stared at the glittering sea through a wash of tears, and as my fingers met cool glass, I made out five shapes against the falling sun. On a jutting cliff below us, five figures stood still as monuments. I gasped, pressing closer.

Silas.

I could barely make them out from this high and with the light failing fast, but I was sure of it. All five of them stood on the sandrock, their postures as familiar to me as my own palm lines. Silas, at their head, stared at me with shadowed features and his hand in one pocket. Carelessly handsome. I blinked hard, wiping the tears from my eyes. Was my mind playing tricks on me? When I opened them again, the figures were gone.

I gasped out a sob, wrapping my arms around my middle. I had imagined them, then. I wanted so badly for them to come for me that I had conjured a waking dream. I had no one to blame but myself. I'd chosen this. To keep Eliana's army from starting a war, I had chosen to go gently into my fate. There was no use wishing for something different now.

I risked another glance over my shoulder. Eliana stared out of the windows where the figures had disappeared. Her mask cracked, and one deep line formed between her brows.

Chapter Thirty-Two

SAGE

I couldn't stop watching the cliffs. I had *probably* imagined the cohort. Maybe. I'd run through the memory in my head all day, watching the waves break against the cliffs from my hotel room. I'd seen five figures, I thought. One had looked just like Silas from afar. But then again, I'd blinked, and they'd been gone. Vampires could move quickly, but would Eliana have just let that go? Surely, she would have locked me down if she'd known Silas was here.

I went through that thought process one too many times, questioning myself, convincing myself it had been real and allowing hope to blossom, only to quash it under rigid sensibility, ad nauseam. That was how I'd spent my last day. No one forced me into any dresses as the afternoon sun drifted toward the horizon again. Eliana had sent up a black spandex jumpsuit and jean jacket with white sneakers for me to wear. I'd put it on but swapped the jean jacket for my canvas one, and as I stood at the window, my mind racing, I'd played with the silver rods in the pocket. I had hours left.

By the time I was bundled into a car, and it made its

way through the vibrant streets of Monaco, the sun had fallen. The stars winked into existence, weakened by the city lights, until we approached the familiar landmark on a hill.

In essence, the Trophy of Augustus was little more than the ruins of a once-grand monument, with most of its construction lost to time. What was left consisted of a rounded wall some hundred feet high and four and a half columns remaining on one side. It wasn't anything spectacular to behold, even as we approached it, backlit by the city lights and high on a hill. But as the last vestiges of pale-yellow evening slipped into shadows, it suddenly glowed.

Like a beacon, the Trophy blazed blue, and I stared at it in silent wonder in the back of the SUV. At least I was by myself, other than the driver, and I didn't have to hide my reaction. The planetary alignment overhead was trying to pour ley into the wellspring, and if I was the only one who could see the light between stars, then it was possible I was the only one who could make out the blue light on the Trophy. Which would account for why no one had known about this wellspring for, I assumed, hundreds of years, possibly more. The last thing I needed right now was to have Eliana find out that I was a star weaver. Although, that would serve her right—her precious ley socium brood mare being the *one* thing she couldn't afford to keep alive.

The SUV made its way up the hill, past a visitor's center which sat dark and empty, and to a parking lot at the base of the monument. Six other cars parked around mine, their headlights illuminating lush shrubbery and wild plant growth untamed by landscapers the way I imagined Americans would have done. I stared up at the dark monolith, my breathing too loud in the quiet space, and my fingers gripped the silver from inside my pocket.

It was now or never. Either I would succeed and survive,

or I would fail and… I couldn't face the outcome if I failed. I couldn't fail.

As a fae opened the door for me, his bright red hair stood out against the blue night. It was strange, this mix of relief and sorrow that churned inside of me. Like baking soda and vinegar, my relief that Silas hadn't stormed the hotel, hadn't started a war, reacted angrily with the sorrow that I would never see him again. The concoction fizzed and popped inside my stomach, distracting me, at least, from the all-consuming terror that should have ruled my emotions.

All dozen of the fae who surrounded me looked like they shopped exclusively on Rodeo Drive and told the salesclerks to "put it on my tab." Rather than looking like guests at a sadistic, archaic ritual, they looked like they were waiting to walk on the set of a talk show.

Two of them took my arms in a firm grip, like I was going to bother to run, and then we climbed. Stairs had been built leading up to the Trophy, and the fae's heels and boots clicked and shuffled as we climbed. I didn't think the fae could move fast like my vampires, they'd all walked at human-like speeds, even as we made our way up the dark stairway. I would have bet one of my silver rods that they could see well in the dark, though. I kept tripping on my feet, and the fae on either side of me dragged me forward unceremoniously, anyway.

As we neared the top where the columns rounded the wall, my brain followed my feet and tripped all over itself, trying to understand what I was seeing. It looked like a movie set. There were cameras on dollies, lighting rigs angled at the columns, and a cluster of crewmembers huddled around a monitor. On the other side of the cameras, between the enormous columns, a breezy archway had been set up. White, gauzy fabric stirred in the wind, and lush, fragrant flowers curved along the arch. Beneath it, a white chair with padded arms had been placed on display. It looked like they were about to film a perfume commercial. What the actual fuck?

My entourage brought me to the edge of the well-lit set, and Eliana turned to me from where she stood by the arch. "Our leading lady has arrived." In her tailored, black suit, metallic, wide belt, and silk shirt in a deep hue of claret, the fae queen looked more like a movie director than a tyrannical monarch. Which, I assumed, had been her point. Maybe she'd never had a childhood five billion years ago and felt the need to play pretend every day to compensate. The whole thing was strange, and it was made even more off-putting by the fact that the camera crew and onlookers all had light blue skin, sharp, dagger-like teeth, and inky black eyes.

As I was pushed toward the spotlights, I realized two things. One, Silas would witness this entire atrocity, and however he felt about me after I'd left, I knew he'd watch it. I knew it would wound him in some way. And second, there would be no sneaky planting of silver rods in the cracks below my feet. Although there were several gaps in the foundation, I didn't see how I would get away with shoving them in there with lights and cameras pointed at me.

My heart went wild in my chest as I was guided to the chair. Bright lights blinded me. Belatedly, I thought to fight back, but the fae were still far stronger than I was, even if they were nothing like Silas or his brothers. They shoved me into the padded chair, and Eliana sang, "Will you stay or should we tie you?"

If they tied me down, I really wouldn't get a chance to

escape or reroute the ley into the foundation instead of my body. I shook my head. "I'll stay."

"Good pet," Eliana crooned.

I could barely see her past the lights. As my eyes adjusted, I made out an excited throng of fae around us, three cameras aimed at me, and tables along each side with what looked like—

My stomach gave a nauseated slosh. Medical equipment. What did they need medical equipment for?

"Are we all here?" Eliana asked brightly, clacking across the ancient stone in her stilettos to stand by the monitor with the camera crew. "Alright little dove, you just look pretty and scream on cue. Okay?"

Scream on cue? My ribs practically rattled with the force of my heartbeat as it slammed in my chest. My breathing grew erratic as a male fae with long, jet black hair and chiseled features took his place on set, a little in front of me and to the side, and then a clapperboard snapped through the hushed set. "Good evening, EL! Network! Thank you for joining us for our star-studded ball last night. It was a gala to remember. Here, tonight, we have a spectacular event lined up for you..."

The ringing in my ears drowned out the rest of his spiel. They were actually making a spectacle of this. Whatever ritual Eliana had planned, she was going to share it with anyone who would watch because she was proud. She had created a new supernatural species, and now, she would accomplish something that had probably eluded the fae since their inception. To her, this was a historic demonstration. And I was just a beaker in her experiment.

I didn't know if it was my fear or something else, but my body began to vibrate, humming uncomfortably like tires on a rumble strip. I glanced down at my hands and found them glowing. I was blue. I jerked a look up to the sky, and a despairing, whispered "No," escaped me. The Confluence. Already, the ley was seeping into me, filling my body with tingling warmth.

"… joined with our very own Elianthi, Cysgadyn. You are witnessing history in the making, folks. This is a new dawn for our people—fae who can eventually recreate with one another. Isn't that incredible?"

It was vomitous. I watched Cysgadyn in his shadow form approach the well-lit area, and the vibration in my head grew louder. Like I had been submerged under water, sounds went muffled and my lungs stopped working. He was holding a syringe in his hand, which the host was explaining had been filled with some of Cysgadyn's essence and human blood. He said something about an initial trial being promising, and I remembered the black goo in my heart. I remembered Silas sucking it out of a wound above my breast and spitting it to the floor like viscous slime.

I couldn't let this happen. But if I moved, they would restrain me. Panic clawed at my senses, immobilizing me just as surely as if they had tied my arms to the chair. Cysgadyn approached me, and then fast as a bullet, his hand closed around my throat. I choked, fighting him on instinct. A sharp stab in my chest tore a gasp from my cinched airway, and then burning liquid pushed into my chest cavity. I convulsed, gagging and losing myself to murky black for several heart-stopping moments. I barely registered the syringe exiting, and then Cysgadyn released me. I slumped in the chair, clutching my heart and gasping in pain as a red-hot spiderweb crackled through my torso.

"… will break the bond while connecting the ley socium to her new mate…"

Saccharine rot filled my mouth, and I retched, crumpling forward. No one said a word when I fell from the chair, bruising my shoulder and inhaling dusty stone as I clutched the ground in desperation. *Make it stop*, I begged, swallowing my screams.

Scream on cue.

I wouldn't do it. I refused. For Silas, who was forced to watch from a distance. For the queen, who thought to make my suffering a performance. I ground my teeth together until my jaw trembled, and then I endured. I could endure this. The buzzing along my skin like a thousand wasps. The burning in my chest like white, molten silver. I forced my eyes open, focusing on a crack in the stone as wide as my finger. The cameras rolled on. The host kept talking, playing out his scripted role, describing the experiment to the fae people while Eliana watched with smug satisfaction.

"... mate bond is fully broken, if our socium survives, you will all have the privilege of bearing witness of their first union. The first mating of fae and socium for all the world to see."

"No," I choked. I really had failed. I kept hoping I'd have a chance to reverse this, a moment to slip away and channel the ley into the wellspring. It wasn't going to happen. I'd been an utter fool, but then again, I had been alive for twenty-one years. Eliana had been plotting this for decades. Maybe it had always been doomed, the inevitable fate of the star weaver socium.

My nose started to bleed, dripping to the ground in steady plops. Somehow, it was comforting. This was what my body did, after all. I was stressed. Possibly dying here on the stones of the Trophee D'Augustus, and so naturally, my nose bled. I would have laughed if my entire focus hadn't been on containing the agonized screams raking at my throat.

The blood pattered to the stone, and with bleary eyes, I realized it wasn't just red. Like me, it glowed blue. Not for anyone but me, though. Only I knew that the planetary alignment was gushing ley over my head, filling my body with stardust and turning my blood into pearlescent magic. It slid into the crack.

I snapped to awareness with a tortured gasp.

My blood was draining into the wellspring. It would take more than a nosebleed to make it all the way down into the foundation, though. I lifted a look to the cameras and Eliana, and finally, *finally*, I had my opening. All three cameras had been rotated to Eliana, who stood with her Elianthi creatures, waxing prosaic about the incredible blessings of the leysprings on the fae. I wasn't going to bother with the silver rods in the ground. Everyone would see them if I tried that now. But they might not see a ley socium bleed herself into a crack in the floor.

With a shaking hand, and moving slowly, I fought the pain in my chest to reach my pocket. I retrieved one of the rods, and hilariously, it wasn't the pure silver I needed right now. I needed the tiny, sharpened stake made of crude metal at the bottom of it. Surreptitiously, keeping my eyes on the fae who seemed mostly absorbed with what their queen was saying, I tucked my hands against my stomach. It was nothing to slice a vertical line from my wrist to my elbow under the canvas jacket. Nothing compared the wild-fire burning my insides to charred remains. I wondered if I would live long enough to keep the flow of my blood open for the wellspring to absorb.

What would happen when my blood connected the cosmic ley with the wellspring? How much was needed to awaken it? I curled in on myself, watching my blood flow freely now. It pooled on the rough, gray stone, and I shifted so I wrapped my convulsing body around the open crack. My blood coursed into the crack freely. Blue radiated from my body and into the crack, illuminating the dark recesses of the foundation. Hope unfurled its cautious petals in my chest.

A fae crewmember in a black polo and baseball cap turned to look at me with curiosity. His onyx eyes narrowed at me in suspicion. I tried to curl around myself tighter, to hide the stream of blood trickling past the cuff of my jacket. Cysgadyn caught the crewmember looking and glanced my way. He looked so unnaturally beautiful, the Cysgadyn-Marcus creature. An Elianthi. His shadowy eyes fixed on me, and then I knew he knew. He sniffed, his nostrils flaring, and then his expression tightened in fear. He couldn't speak but he could give me away all the same.

I pleaded with him silently. *Do nothing. Please, Cysgadyn. Let me die before we are forced to do this.*

But why would he? He had been *promised* this. It was his honor to start a new species with a ley socium, to gain the favor of the queen again and perhaps buy back his voice. Cysgadyn's features settled, and I assumed he had made his decision. He glanced at the crewmember, who still seemed confused, and then he… turned away. He shifted where he'd been standing, backing up closer to me and cutting off the line of sight from the crewmember. The other fae glanced at Cysgadyn, seemed to lose interest, and returned his attention to Eliana.

I remembered how to breathe again. Cysgadyn still faced away from me, shielding me from view. I couldn't believe it. Was it possible that Cysgadyn saw me as a victim in this, too?

"What do you mean *dead*?" Eliana snarled loudly. I hazarded another glance toward her and found the camera crew and several other smartly dressed fae gathering worriedly around a laptop.

"Your Highness, the network died just before she was injected. We're doing everything we can to—" the girl's voice cut off with a gargled, wet crunch, and then she slumped over, taking the laptop with her.

"Get us live *now*," Eliana roared.

A flurry of movement erupted around me, and I despaired silently. *Please, no. Don't notice me. Don't find it.*

They had forgotten about me completely. Someone who sounded like a producer snapped at technicians. Eliana raged, throwing things off tables that landed on the ground with metal clangs, and fae shrieked as they were caught in her warpath.

I bled. I focused on the glittering liquid, my eyes growing heavy as it trickled into the earth. How much longer? Or had I done it? I still glowed like an LED lantern, but maybe enough of it had seeped into the wellspring to make a difference, to reconnect the leylines and feed enough power into the earth to help everyone thrive. Maybe Silas would find a new mate. I hoped he would, and I hoped that she was boring. Sweet. That she cradled his head when he was sad and took care of herself so he didn't worry for her.

Eliana bellowed, and the ground shook. The group went dead quiet again. "Did you feel that?" someone hissed.

The ground trembled again, rattling my teeth and shaking equipment. "What is going on?" Eliana demanded.

"There could be a ley disturbance interfering with our connection," another fae suggested.

My head had gone fuzzy, and I realized I was running out of time—out of blood. Eliana snapped, "Well, fix it." Another quake shook the stones, and that time, a bit of dust sifted down on our heads. "Is this a fucking earthquake? Like *now* of all times?" the queen demanded.

"I don't know but I—" someone replied but stopped with a sharp gasp, and then the air filled with tension, a bloated balloon poised to burst.

I lifted my head wearily, and two things happened in rapid succession. A bullet lodged itself between Eliana's eyes. And the ground exploded.

Chapter Thirty-Three

SILAS

We all visibly flinched when Sage cut her arm. Hanging from the cliffs in blackout tactical gear and waiting for Matteo's signal, all four of us exchanged horrified looks. She'd cut herself severely, and even from below, I could smell her blood. So much blood. It poured out of her body in sickening gushes, and my fingers tightened on the rocks. The cliff creaked.

"Easy," Constantine warned.

The wind carried our voices away from where we hid on the other side of the Trophy. I had no choice but to be "easy." We were waiting on Matteo and the witches to disable Eliana's wards. Alvaro shifted, rolling his shoulders. To outsiders, our position would look perilous. Rock climbers in heavy tactical gear hanging off a cliffside without ropes or harnesses. For vampires, it was so easy, I couldn't believe Eliana had only posted four fae at the base of the cliff as a precaution. She always had been cocky.

I brought my wrist to my mouth. "Matteo, she's wounded."

"I can only eat so many fae," Matteo bit back.

"Don't care how many," I whispered back. Sage's heartbeat slowed dramatically. "Just do it faster."

"It's appropriately horrific," Beau said from her line. She'd already done her part, drawing some of the cosmic ley into a breaking spell that would trigger the moment Matteo had disposed of the fae acting as batteries to the wards.

"I can't believe he brought a teenager here," Art muttered.

Alvaro beat his head against the rock wall. "I cannot believe our socium is killing herself."

"She's not going to die," I ground out. "Art, do you have blood in that med kit?"

"O negative," he confirmed.

"They're down," Matteo panted in my ear. He'd had to suck the ley out of every fae and witch feeding Eliana's wards. Eliana had *a lot* of living batteries at her disposal. Matteo would probably be puking, wherever he was.

We climbed fast, finding handholds and vaulting up the cliff face so rapidly, we could have been passing shadows. Eliana started to lose her shit over the severed network connection, courtesy of a few tech-savvy vertos. There would also be a team of highly trained vertos, already shifted into their animal forms, slithering up the other side of the Trophy, poised to sandwich the panicking fae.

We reached the top of the cliff, and I slid my knife across the throat of a startled fae soldier. Constantine ripped the head off of one, and Art blew past us all, heading for Sage with the med bag. It wasn't far, now. We were on the opposite side of the monument, but we'd be around it in thirty seconds tops.

The ground shook beneath our feet as we advanced

through young trees and wild plant growth. I stopped and shared a worried look with Alvaro. "What was that?" he voiced.

"No time," I bit out. Sage's heart fluttered weakly and her breathing slowed. My instincts screamed at me to go faster, but we had to be just as methodical as we were quick. We couldn't afford to miss hidden soldiers in the foliage, to leave anyone living.

The ground trembled again, rolling under our boots as we ran up the steep monument. Slick, ancient stone pounded under my feet. A tremor rumbled so menacingly, a crack whipped from the base of the monument to the very top and down the other side.

"What the fuck?" Alvaro hissed, his rifle out and ready.

No time. There was no time to wonder what was happening with the Earth's crust. All four of us came around the curve of the massive monument at the same time, all four with weapons trained on our top four targets. I only had a quarter of a second to take in the scene, to absorb the movie set charade that had been erected under the Trophee D'Augustus' columns. A quarter of a second to find Sage curled in a ball around a pool of her own blood. The other three quarters I gave to putting a bullet square between Eliana's mint green eyes. It landed, shocking her. I ran for Sage.

And then the ground exploded.

I watched in horror as pure ley erupted from the ground, breaking the stone into shrapnel, launching everyone on the Trophy to their deaths. I had already been moving for Sage when the gray slab beneath her launched into the air. A millisecond later, and I wouldn't have made it. A millisecond wasted on the cliff, slitting a fae's throat, waiting for Matteo, and I would have failed her. But as her body catapulted into the air, propelled by blinding ley and aged limestone, my arm looped around her middle. Mid-air, I pulled her to me, and unable to fight the savage force of the explosion, I did the only thing I could. I wrapped myself around her and prayed.

Cool ley mixed with battering, percussive shrapnel, and I braced myself as Sage and I were hurled away from the Trophy and down the slope. I managed to half-temper our descent by grabbing a cypress tree trunk. It slowed us enough that when I landed hard on my side, it didn't break every bone on impact. I broke enough, though. I grunted, tightening my hold around Sage and skidding to a stop on the hill. Debris rained down on us, and I stayed crouched over Sage while the ground quaked and the Trophy of Augustus crumbled back up the hill. My bones knitted themselves back together painfully.

If I hadn't seen the ley, I would have accused someone of hitting our target with a missile.

Art landed hard twenty feet from me, groaning. He'd broken several somethings, too. While his bones healed rapidly, he dragged himself over to us with the med bag. It wasn't dark anymore. Bright blue bathed the rocky slope like starlight, and I glanced at the Trophy with a strong suspicion leading my gaze. The Trophy had exploded. The wellspring was open. Somehow, Sage had done it.

She breathed weakly between my arms, groaning. Art reached us and then we both got to work on her, our focus solely on her failing, mortal body. Alvaro, Matteo, and Constantine would have our backs. The main targets would be down. The remaining fae who had survived that blast would be eliminated swiftly. With their wards down, they were nothing more than spiders to quash.

Art established a line in her arm while I put pressure on

her arm wound, packing the abused tissue and wrapping it tightly. Art started a bag of blood and pushed morphine and two other meds I knew nothing about. I held her arm tightly to staunch the bleeding, willing her heart to pick up. "What else?"

"You really have no excuse for not having a medical degree," Art chastised. "Is she still bleeding through that wound?"

"No, it's clotting." I looked her over. "What about the shit they injected her with? I can still smell it in her blood."

"A lot of it bled out," Art replied, uncapping a syringe with his teeth and injecting it into her thigh. "She may have accidentally saved her own life, much as it galls me to say. Can you suck out the stuff closest to her heart?"

I tore the black fabric away from her chest, revealing the puncture site, which had webbed with black along her veins. I did the same thing I'd done the first time, making an incision with my teeth and then sucking hard. Foul, sickly-sweet rot filled my mouth, and I let her blood and the poison fill my mouth before spitting. "You have enough blood?"

"Yeah, keep going." Art squeezed the blood bag. "Her vitals are picking up."

I knew that, of course. Her pulse grew stronger and her blood cleaner with every mouthful. When I felt confident that I was drawing mostly a mixture of her blood and the donor swill into my mouth, I stopped and put pressure on the wound I'd created. "Now what?"

"She'll be fine, Si. Again, no excuse," Art muttered.

In my defense, computers and video game consoles had been invented around the time I thought to learn modern medicine. Sage moaned in pain, and my head fell against her shoulder in relief. She was alive. We were filthy, covered in debris from a magically induced explosion, and my ley socium was teetering on the brink of death on the side of a hill... but she was alive. I gathered her to me, kissing her temple, breathing her in. She smelled all wrong and felt too cold, but she was mine and she was here.

"Eliana will be up any minute," Art reminded me.

A bullet wasn't enough to stop the immortal fae queen. We'd all known that going into this. It was meant to be a retrieval mission—disable the fae, grab Sage, get out. We weren't interested in starting an all-out war with the fae again, and even this much put the Conexus at risk of being pulled into a conflict. Not that they minded. Every house had made it clear that saving the ley socium was a priority, and we'd started far worse disputes over far less. But, of course, Sage had managed to find a way to blow the dam to smithereens. Eliana would be livid over this, and I didn't foresee her letting it go now.

"Can she be moved?" I asked, already taking her in my arms carefully, mindful of the abrasions on her back.

"Yeah, let's get out of here," Art said right as Alvaro and Constantine skidded to a halt on the hill next to us.

"We have to go," Constantine said, looking over his shoulder. The ground rumbled again, but this time, I knew it was Eliana.

Art and I took off running, knowing that the other three would have our cover, and we went as far as we dared at full speed this close to the city. The last thing we needed with the wards down and glamours disabled were humans catching a whiff of what was going on. Although... we'd blown up their historical monument. No glamour could hide that.

In my arms, Sage stirred, groaning and then clutching my tactical vest. Still breathing. Still alive. I held onto that fact, held onto my mate while we slowed our pace as we entered the city, heading for our safe house which was warded to the gills and stocked with a hospital's worth of medical supplies.

Fae followed us, but Constantine and Alvaro dispatched them efficiently. We ran through the city, through dark alleys and under neon signs, garnering a few interested looks as we went but making sure to run fast enough that any human would question what they had seen and forget about it.

The neighborhood we stopped in was vampire territory. Similar rows of stucco homes with clay tile roofs made up the seaside community, and we barely broke stride going through the bright pink front door and inside the three-story apartment unit.

The safe house had been cobbled together this morning, warded by any witch we could find—or drag from their beds, in Beau's case—and Art had acquired all the medical supplies in preparation for whatever shape we might find Sage in. Somehow, she was still worse off than my panicked brain had expected. Maybe because I'd seen her last night in the window, draped in white silk and healthier than she had been before she'd disappeared. It was only then that I'd realized the leywork on her had used *her* as a source. Cruel and risky. She could have died.

She still could.

We entered a clean, modern lower floor with vacation-friendly furniture all chosen for Mediterranean flair, I assumed, but I hardly looked. I followed Art up the narrow stairs to the third floor, where the converted attic space had been made into a generous bedroom suite with windows overlooking the aquamarine water and quaint stucco buildings. Around the white king bed, medical equipment waited on rolling dollies and tables, ready to go. As I set Sage down and Art washed his hands and pulled on gloves, Matteo stumbled into the room.

"Silas, you need to see this."

"Not now." I ripped Sage's jacket down the middle, prepping her for whatever Art would need.

"Silas, really, Art can help her. You need to see this." Matteo actually put a hand on my shoulder, which was bold of him. He was holding a tablet, and on it, Eliana's blood-streaked features shrieked into a camera.

I watched it with half an eye, still undressing Sage so Art would be unimpeded with his life-saving measures. Eliana's bullet wound had already healed, but she hadn't bothered to rinse off the blue blood or fix her appearance. "The vampires want war."

"Oh, for fuck's sake," I muttered.

"My people, you have seen the tyranny of the leeches first-hand. They stole our future and destroyed our legacy." The camera panned to the destruction that Sage caused. The Trophy of Augustus had not survived the ley explosion. It lay in total ruins, a crumbling mass of stone above a gaping pit that would draw ley into the earth the way it was meant to. Any magical framework that had been built over that ancient structure would be gone, now. And Eliana wouldn't be allowed to re-work it. Not with the whole supernatural world knowing what she'd done. So now, she was lashing out, and it wasn't going to be pretty.

Sage moaned again, twisting in the bed with her eyes closed and her heart sluggish. Art was already hooking her up to an IV bag of saline and had two more units of blood at the ready. "Put the BP cuff on her other arm, Silas."

I did as he asked, and Eliana continued in my peripheral vision. "Do you see the destruction, my children? The *hatred* of the Conexus must come to an end. They will tell you this was warranted. They will tell you that it was fair, but they have *stolen* our power for themselves. The final wellspring has been unearthed, and with it, will come the extermination of the fae."

"She's so dramatic," Matteo drawled. "Do you think her people buy this?"

"They eat it for breakfast, lunch, and dinner," I said. Sage's BP blipped on the monitor, low and still falling. Art hung a unit of O neg, his features pinched.

"Hell is empty," Eliana said, eyes gleaming, "and all the devils are here. Let them come. Let them crawl from their marble towers and call us monsters. Let them bare their fangs. We are older than their hunger. We will prevail through blood and hellfire; we will rise from the ashes."

My father was going to kill me. But if Sage didn't pull through this, I'd do it myself.

Chapter Thirty-Four

SAGE

There was no gradual ascent into awareness. I opened my eyes, calm but alert. I'd fallen asleep on the stones of the Trophy, releasing myself into a bed of my own blood and the knowledge that I would never wake again. I'd closed my eyes, expecting the Trophy to be my grave, and to my utter confusion, they were open again. There had been no near-death experience, either—no tunnels of light or departed loved ones calling me from beyond the veil. With my eyes blinking several times in bewilderment, I found only a wood beam ceiling and the distant sound of a television playing in the background somewhere.

And then I sensed him. Like a marionette string tugging my head with inexorable force, I rotated a look to my left with hope fluttering manically in my chest. Silas was there. He sat in a chair, backlit by the bright sunlight and watching me with silent intensity. He had his chin on his bent fingers, leaning to one side in the armchair, and his tight, black T-shirt looked dusty, ripped along the shoulders and hem like something had shredded it. I stared at him in mute awe, not trusting my own eyes.

"Yes, you're alive," he said softly, reading my mind.

"How?" I croaked. My last moments landed in the forefront of my mind, shocking me with their brutality. The movie set, the injected poison, the jagged cut down my forearm and the creek of blood that disappeared into an ancient crag. And then an explosion. I'd thought for sure that had been it for me.

"Nothing short of divine intervention, I'm convinced," Silas replied, his voice a tranquil cove.

Suddenly, I didn't care how I was here and he was there. Silas was *there*. Tears blurred my vision and dammed my throat, forcing a hiccup. Somehow, Silas and I were in the same room together. His eyes flared, and he leaned forward. He had me in his arms before I fully realized it, encircling me gingerly and holding me upright against his hard chest. "Dulcis," he murmured, stroking my damp cheeks.

"You're here," I forced out.

"You're not allowed to cry," he replied gruffly. "The Hell you put us through precludes you from tears, you impetuous, foolish little—"

I launched myself at him, throwing my arms around his neck and ignoring the painful tug on my arms. "If I'm hallucinating, I'm not letting you go," I rushed out. He *felt* real. He smelled real too, like cedarwood and ocean breeze, but also something darker, something dusty and labored. "I thought I saw you, and then I didn't, and when she had me at the Trophy, I knew it was the end and I'd never see you again."

"Sage, easy, easy." He unlinked my arms from around his neck and pinned them back down, wrapping me in an inescapable but gentle hold. "You can't just—fuck, your IV."

I looked down to find an IV line dislodged from the inside of my elbow and weeping blood. Silas kept his arms around me as he fixed it, carefully repositioning the line and then reaching around me for medical tape and gauze on a side table. I realized for the first time that I was in a bedroom I didn't recognize but there were hospital room medical supplies by my bed. A heart monitor sent a soft, steady tone through the room, and there were wires attached to me. Silas fixed the IV line with slow, sure movements, like he was afraid anything too rapid would disturb me.

I craned my head around to look at him, leaning my head against his shoulder. "I really almost died, then?"

"Almost," he agreed stiffly. God, he was beautiful. I drank him in, slaking my thirst, following the sharp angle of his jaw and the way it ticked angrily, his stormy eyes fixated on readjusting the cuff and monitors that I'd shaken loose. I wanted so desperately to lift my lips to the underside of his jaw and press a kiss there, to inhale his warmth and savor the fact that he was real. "Stop ogling me. You're in trouble."

Holy shit, I really was alive. I was alive and Silas had me in his arms, and he was palpably furious with me. My crumpled, tear-streaked features wobbled into a smile. "You're angry with me."

"Livid." He finished with the wires and then misty pine green met my searching gaze. "What were you thinking?"

I twisted my left wrist, confirming that, yes, it burned. I had a long cut there that I had no doubt he'd already managed to stitch up. "I couldn't tell you," I whispered back.

"I know that, but to *leave*," he seethed softly. "What were you *thinking*?"

I swallowed, sobering a touch but too grateful to be truly repentant. "Marcus made it through your wards the first day I came to Hollowhall. When you went to save your brothers."

"I deduced that much," Silas replied calmly. "I'd suspected it the day of, but you had looked unharmed and there'd been no evidence. I should have thought it through all the way, knowing that those things wouldn't be affected by our wards."

"I tried so hard to tell you, but he forced me into silence." I frowned, thinking. "And I found out later that Marcus didn't know what he was doing, so he made me its power source."

"It was an *accident*?" Silas asked, dumbfounded.

"Yes. But it worked well enough. I got weaker every time I tried to tell you. But he could walk through your wards, Silas," I said, determined to get it all out now. Every torturous thought I'd carried with me for weeks poured out of me. "They gave me two weeks, and they would have come for me no matter what. And then I realized what Eliana wanted with me, to use the Confluence to make me a vessel for her messed-up fae-hybrid baby things, and I knew she would do anything to get me."

I twisted in his arms, trying to see him better, but Silas didn't let me move far. "They would have killed you. Or maybe they would have failed, and you told me about the Blood Wars, and there would have been so much death," I rambled. "I didn't know what else to do because I was gagged, and you were in danger, and she would have taken me no matter what I did."

Silas closed his eyes briefly, like that had caused him mental pain. "Sage. You did this to avoid a war?"

"And your death," I defended with a touch of ire. "What if you had died?"

"Do I look dead?" he shot back. "I infiltrated their wards on their own fucking turf to get you back and I barely broke a sweat."

"She would have sent an army," I argued.

Silas' jaw worked back and forth, and he seemed to be schooling his emotions into that placid flatline. "I really thought you understood. You said it back to me."

"My life is precious, I know," I assured him. I couldn't move my arms or cup his infuriated features. "But so is yours."

"Hah!" someone barked from downstairs.

I startled, glancing around the room with its peaked ceiling and bright windows. "Is… is someone else here?"

"They're all here," Silas replied impatiently. "Sage, I can't survive another detour in our life together like this. I swear to God, I thought I was going to have the world's first vampire heart attack."

Detour. Because we had forever, and this was a detour. I struggled to fathom the implications of that realization; it was too wonderful. "I'm sorry." I nuzzled my cheek against his shoulder. "I'm really sorry. I tried to tell you. I tried to fix it."

Wryly, Silas admitted, "Oh, you fixed it. Your blood hit that wellspring and the entire monument exploded."

My eyes widened. "Is that what happened?"

"Yes, you terrorist," he squinted with dark amusement.

"Oh my God."

"That's what you get for meddling with magic you

barely understand," he said with a little venom in his tone. "You don't run off and fix problems by yourself. That's how you get killed and take your anguished mate with you."

I wriggled in his hold, trying to escape, but he didn't budge. "You wouldn't have died."

"I'm telling you this so you never, *never* do something like this again," Silas said with such intensity, it stabbed my heart to a stall. "I will die if you die. There is no 'maybe' about it. There is no future without you. I won't bother."

My brow fell into a glower. "Don't say that."

"I'm not being dramatic. I'm telling you a fact. Do with it what you will."

"Silas," I reprimanded. How could he say such a thing? His implication there was that he would end his own life, which was absurd.

He stared back, his expression neutral. "It's a fact. Keep it in mind. I should have told you sooner, but I never considered that you could be quite so…" he paused, thinking. And then he rolled his eyes. "Art just said, 'goosey.'"

"Goosey," I repeated blankly.

"I feel it's quite a bit more serious than 'goosey,' but I think you take my meaning." He held my gaze steadily. "Yes?"

I nodded, swallowing against a dry throat. "Okay." Silas reached over to a hospital-style side table and picked up a cup with a straw. He held it in front of my lips, and I glared. "Can I have my hands back now?"

"No."

"Why?" I demanded, suspicious and irritated in equal measure.

"Because I don't trust you."

"I'm not going to go leaping after another rose bush,

Silas. We're both alive now, and I'm pretty sure I remember Eliana getting a bullet between the eyes." Talking really was starting to grate on my dry throat, so I took a disgruntled sip of water.

Silas put the cup down, settling back against the bed and keeping me in a comfortable straight jacket. "She's not dead. At best, we gave ourselves two minutes while she healed, just to stabilize you and get you out of there."

"Oh." A little blip of fear peaked in my heartbeat.

Silas' thumb stroked the top of my uninjured forearm. "She won't hurt you. Her plan failed and the whole world knows that she's been keeping the ley lines suppressed. She's going to be strongly regulated by the other species for a while."

"So, it *did* help that I freed the wellspring," I said slyly.

"I'm not giving that to you. It was beyond reckless," he growled.

"I did what I thought was right," I sighed wearily. "It seemed like the best choice at the time. I didn't know you were coming for me—I thought I was going to be—" I choked on the words. *Raped. Impregnated. Used.*

Silas hugged me tighter, pressing the side of his face to mine. "Alright, Dulcis. Alright. Don't distress yourself. You're safe now, and we won't let anything like this happen to you again."

"We," I huffed out with a laugh.

"We," Art agreed, standing in the doorway with his arms folded and dark eyebrows raised. "Silas, I know you've been dying to fuse yourself to her skin but let me check her vitals while she's awake."

Silas grumbled something about sharing but finally released me, shifting so he sat closer to the edge of the wide bed. Art shoved him aside, forcing his brother to sit in his chair again, and I felt the distance like a strained bowstring. Art checked the readings on the monitor to my left, fiddled with the saline bag flow, and started the blood pressure cuff. I watched him with deep skepticism. "Since when are you a doctor?"

"Since nineteen seventy…" he paused, squinting in thought, "two?"

"I guess medical school was something to do," I thought out loud, watching him warily as he checked my bandaged arm and then ran a thermometer over my forehead.

"Most of us have at least had *some* medical training," Art said with a reproving look over his shoulder for Silas.

"Most ley socium don't need emergent, life-saving care," Silas drawled back, tossing the censure back to me.

"True," Art said, and then I had two half-lidded reprovals pointed my way, and I rolled my eyes.

"How long are you two going to hold this over my head?"

"At least a century," Art replied automatically.

"Is there a limit?" Silas wondered.

Art checked a bandaged spot on my chest, and I remembered something else. Cysgadyn. His pitying look. How he'd helped me. "Is Cysgadyn…?"

"Dead," Silas confirmed heartlessly. "As is every Elianthi. The vertos were not keen on mutated supernatural creatures lurking through wards."

My face fell. I shouldn't have felt sorry for them. I should have felt safer. I felt empty inside. "Cysgadyn tried to help me in the end," I offered.

"Sweetheart," Art said with brisk rationality in his tone, "they never should have existed. Eliana knew it was wrong, and she knew they would ultimately become sacrifices in the long run. Nothing you did could have prevented this."

How many lives were lost, then? Dozens? I stared at my hands on the pristinely white comforter, and I realized they'd cleaned all the blood and dirt from my skin, but there was blue blood on my hands. I had caused an explosion with the wellspring.

Silas dipped one brow. "Stop upsetting her."

"Okay, Mr. I'll-Off-Myself-If-You-Die," Art drawled. He checked the blood pressure reading on the screen, which blinked red, and I was pretty sure it was low. But he didn't look concerned. "You're much better than you were last night. We had to give you four liters of blood, and I'm certain you can thank all that extra ley in your body for the fact that you're alive."

"Divine intervention," Silas repeated, shaking his head.

I didn't care what it was. I just wanted to crawl back into Silas' lap and remind myself again and again that we were together now. When Art had finished and seemed satisfied that I was doing better, I shifted impatiently, staring at Silas. He smiled faintly, leaning his cheek against this fist again. I glanced at the wires on my arms and electrodes on my torso and wondered if they would reach.

Silas breathed out a laugh before joining me on the bed again. I lifted myself onto his lap, careful with the lines this time so he wouldn't trap my hands. I framed his face, my fingernails scratching against a day of beard growth. "I really thought I'd never see you again."

"More fool you," he teased, leaning into my touch. "You don't get to flash into my life and then waltz back out again."

"I am a very bad dancer, I discovered."

Silas' expression darkened. "Yes, I saw. With the right partner, you wouldn't be."

I glanced around the bedroom. "You want to?"

He clicked his tongue and then pulled me against him, tucking me into his chest and pressing my head down. "I want you to rest and heal, and when you're marginally better, I want to punish the absolute fuck out of your perfect body. How does that sound?"

"Better than dancing," I eked out. My tired body responded to his words, warming in all the best places.

Silas sighed, kissing the top of my head. "In reality, I think I'm going to hold you for a long, long time. And we'll watch reruns of your talent show thing, and I'll feed you until your blood smells like yours again and the color is back in your cheeks."

That sounded like heaven, actually. "I really hope this is real."

"It's very real," Silas promised, rubbing my arm. "I'm real, and you're real. And my paranoia about your safety is real, and I hope you don't plan on leaving my sight for a few hundred years."

I smiled lopsidedly. "I love how you all make jokes in hundreds of years."

"Sanity and immortality don't usually mix, as you can see from Eliana's brand of mania. We do what we can to stay sane." Silas tilted my chin, turning my head so that I leaned back against his arm and he could gaze into my eyes. "Having you will help immeasurably."

"I'm having a hard time wrapping my head around a lifetime that long." I smiled softly. "But then again, there are a lot of stars to chart."

"And so many ways to chart the star weaver's body with my tongue," he murmured. My cheeks warmed, but I matched his growing smile, and then he lowered his lips to mine, capturing my whole soul in a gentle kiss. As he stoked the fire at my center with his tongue, and my blood warmed for the first time in days, I let myself feel something that had been denied to me for longer than I could remember.

This love we shared was precious.

Chapter Thirty-Five

SILAS

"Which century had the best clothing?" Sage asked, her warm brown eyes sparkling with interest. She had my comforter wrapped around her naked body, and she sat in my lap, legs straddling my hips and long, unruly hair cascading down her shoulders.

One chestnut lock fell across her cheekbone, and I smoothed it behind her ear. "Elizabethan era. Men were allowed more colors, and the women showed off their breasts more. Then again, I was a very young, very… randy vampire then."

"Didn't everyone smell?" she asked with a wrinkle of her nose.

My attention had fixed on her cheekbone where I'd skimmed it with my fingers. I loved that spot on her body. I loved everything about her body. "Humans smell bad regardless of century," I replied, bending down to skim my lips up the ridge of her cheek. "Except you. You perpetually smell delicious."

"Not when I had donor blood in my system," she

pointed out, tickling her fingers down my shoulder absently. "You complained *so much.*"

"Because humans stink," I reminded her with a wry smile.

"Except me."

"Except you," I agreed, straightening again. It was an impossible choice to make—to drink in the sight of her with greedy gulps or taste her incessantly. With her trapped in my bed for the last three weeks, I'd simply alternated between the two.

"Best food," she grilled.

"You," I grinned.

She gasped, but her open mouth curled upward despite it. "I didn't mean people."

"Oh, apologies," I continued, loving every gasp of outrage I could manage to elicit from her. "Korean barbeque usually makes my eyes roll in satisfaction."

Her expression softened with simmering warmth. "Anything else that does that?"

My body reacted immediately, and although my dick had been hard already, it stiffened painfully. "That thing you did with your tongue two hours ago."

Her gaze dropped down my bare torso and back up. "We should try it. For science. We'll get Korean barbeque and then I'll do that thing with my tongue while you eat it, and you tell me which one is better."

"I already know the answer to that." I cupped her ass and sucked her up against me, fitting my dick between her legs with perfect congruity. "Anything to do with you is my favorite."

She exhaled a sound of arousal, and her long lashes dropped. "We should just get a head start on it. We can get barbeque later."

Her stomach growled angrily, undermining that statement. There weren't many things that could derail my insatiable lust for Sage Herriman, but her own wellbeing was one of them. I kissed her lips slowly, luxuriating in the satin slide of them, and then I murmured, "It's lunch time."

She moaned, wrapping her arms around my neck. "You said I was your favorite food."

I disentangled her and then reached behind her for her shirt. "You are. And I can't very well enjoy you if you aren't healthy, can I?"

"I think our definitions of healthy vary vastly," she intoned, but slid her shirt on obligingly.

I heard Art go to the kitchen and grab pans from the cupboard, and I smiled to myself. Art was just as devoted to Sage as I was, even if it was in a brotherly capacity. They had grown close over the last month, spending almost as much time together as she and I did. When I had business to attend to for the multitude of companies that were run under my name, Art took her on hikes or learned a new board game with her.

Alvaro and Matteo were getting jealous, really, glaring at Art every time he managed to steal her away. One mate in a household of overprotective vampires was definitely an unbalanced situation. At least Constantine had an excuse to escape, having been called away to territory re-negotiations with the vertos. It weakened our wards to have him gone, so I hoped they would finish soon.

When Sage had dressed in a T-shirt and shorts, and she'd wrangled her thick hair into a messy bun, we made our way upstairs. Art had already started on what looked like a risotto, Matteo seated himself at the island, and Alvaro sounded busy in the study as he talked in low tones to Constantine. Our incubus brother must have called with an update, which was intriguing.

It wasn't that we didn't get along with the shifters, per se. It was more that we were vastly different creatures with different ambitions. Vampires wanted power and solitude with a heavy dose of privacy. Vertos ran in packs. They wanted mushy things—families, safety, love, and freedom. All things I would have scoffed at before I'd found Sage. Now, I understood them a fraction better.

"...new leypoints that emerged after the Trophy incident, and one of them runs between our territories. They want us to visit and draw a new boundary," Constantine was saying.

Interesting. It was true that in the weeks following the "gas line incident" at the Trophy—humans were so gullible, it was almost disappointing—the ley lines had been strange. Flares were erupting all over the globe, and new wellsprings and leypoints had emerged since the full force of cosmic ley was able to pour into our planet again. There was a portentous feel to the air, a sign of changes to come. What those changes would be, I couldn't guess, but they were clearly already affecting our family and alliances.

"In what way will you be educating my palate today, Art?" Sage took a seat at the bar, propping her chin on the heel of her hand.

"We're going to try a chanterelle risotto with—brace yourself—truffle." Art tossed the risotto mixture in the pan with a bounce of his eyebrows.

Sage pulled a skeptical face. "Hm."

"You'll love it," he said with annoying confidence, turning back to the food preparation.

I sat next to Sage, taking her hand in mine but keeping

my ears mostly on the conversation between Alvaro and Constantine. "Where?" Alvaro wanted to know.

"It opened up under a bed and breakfast in the Adirondacks. I'll head there tomorrow with some of the vertos envoys." Constantine sounded bored. And a little hungry. He hadn't been feeding as often lately, and I wasn't sure if it was because Sage was in the house or because of something else.

"Do you want me to join you?" Alvaro asked, almost absently as I heard him typing something into a computer.

"No, I have it. Thanks, though."

"Be safe," Alvaro said, and then they hung up. We hadn't had much to do with the vertos since World War II, so this was an interesting development for us. From what I understood, the newer generation of vertos were more welcoming than past ones, and they had an active interest in collaborating with us. I'd gotten wind of a cohort in Denver that had buddied up with a vertos pack to defend their territories against an attempted fae takeover of a critical wellspring. They'd been wildly successful and actually lived as neighbors. The horror.

Sage slid a knowing look my way. "What's going on in the office?"

A smile touched my lips. "Constantine is shaking hands and making deals with the mutts. Imagine his repulsion."

"You're not very nice to the other species," Sage frowned. "You're all ley blessed. I don't see why you have to have rivalries."

"They tried to eradicate us in the nineteenth century," Matteo said. "I almost got my heart ripped out by a coyote shifter."

Sage blanched. "Oh."

"We're on better terms now," I promised her, squeezing her hand.

Alvaro came to the doorway of the office, hanging out of it casually. Once again, the man wasn't wearing a shirt, and I despaired at ever teaching him the value of clothing in this current millennium. "Package being dropped off at the ward line."

"I'll get it," Sage said brightly.

We got *a lot* of packages now that Sage lived with us. She hadn't been shy about the idea that my brothers and I had endless wealth available to us. Her new favorite hobby was finding obscure charities she thought no one would care about and donating disgusting amounts of money to them. Also buying board games and photography equipment. I stood with her, keeping her hand in mine. "Going for a walk, then."

"Why do you make it sound like you're walking your cute little Maltese?" Sage asked suspiciously.

Given that I never let her out of my sight and would absolutely put a leash on her if she'd let me, it was disconcertingly accurate. "Nonsense."

She slipped on a pair of black clogs at the front door, and I shoved my feet into a pair of sneakers before opening the door for her. Fresh summer growth scented the air, mingled with damp soil. Sage breathed deeply, closing her eyes before blinking a sheepish look up to me. "I really love it here."

"You'd better," I chuckled. And then I sobered a little because we moved every ten years to chase the ley flow. I didn't know yet how she would feel about leaving.

But was that still necessary? The ley lines had changed completely, and so had the pulsing flow beneath our feet. I would need to consult with an augur. Of course, I wanted my brothers to find their mates, too, if possible. It seemed more likely with a stronger magical connection at work. But would we need to continue moving all over the globe? There were cohorts who refused to move anymore, like the one in Denver. They didn't have mates, or perhaps they'd found one or two, and they were content with that. We would need to discuss as a family what our best strategy would be going forward.

We took our time walking down the driveway, our feet crunching over gravel and arms swinging loosely. Sage finally looked healthy again, her face filled out and cheeks pink under the noonday sun. Her hair had regained its shine, and her eyes sparkled more every day even if she had had to acquiesce to being confined to our home for a while.

I still woke in the middle of the night with panic clawing at my chest and urging me to save my mate. Those two days had tortured my psyche more surely than any gory inquisition could have accomplished. She had her own nightmares, I knew.

But we were safe now, and Sage was healthy. Everything had settled the way it was meant to.

We reached the end of the driveway, and I stepped past the wards to gather the small pile of packages for her. On the top, a telltale document envelope drew Sage's attention. Her lashes flared, and she reached for it, handling the cardboard envelope with obvious trepidation.

"What is it?" I asked, already guessing as I juggled the stack of awkward boxes.

She ripped it up and slid out a thick sheet of paper. Her eyes ran over it before lifting to mine. "My diploma."

I set down the boxes again, unsure why she'd bitten her

lower lip uncertainly. "You look unsure about that. Are you unhappy?"

Sage breathed around a wry laugh. "It's just funny. It says 'Media Relations' and… I hate it." She stretched her mouth to the side guiltily. "Which is stupid."

I came to stand behind her, wrapping my arms around her waist and resting my cheek on the top of her head. Sure enough, she held a diploma with fancy script that declared her Bachelor of Art in Media Relations. "You did it, though. I wanted to strangle you when you insisted on writing papers while we gave you *another* blood infusion in the safe house."

"I guess it's worth it," she sighed. "I couldn't leave it unfinished."

"I'm proud of you." I kissed her cheek. "And you have a long time to get as many degrees as you want."

"Should we go to med school together?" she smirked, twisting in my arms to look at me.

The idea had merit. I'd have an excuse to be with her even more incessantly than I already was, and when one of my brothers found their human mate too, we'd both be able to keep her safe with Art. "I will go anywhere with you," I said, kissing her luscious mouth.

She sighed, smiling into the kiss. "I'm not going anywhere."

"Forever," I prompted.

"Forever," she grinned. "Unless I hate truffles, and then I might have to walk out."

I turned her in my arms, pinning her to me and skimming my nose up the beautiful curve of her neck. "Do you want me to kick my brother out? Just say the word."

She shook her head, snuggling into me closer and

making my ancient heart squeeze. "They're my brothers, too. You all belong to me, now."

I was hers and she was mine, and of all the cosmic connections in the universe, that was the one that mattered to me the most. The vampire and his star weaver.

Also by Devon Atwood

vinci-books.com/FaieAndFury

Fate bound her to a king she cannot trust.

Anwen escapes an enchantment—and the man who isn't real—only to fall into the hands of a Faie king who claims her by fate. With her family in danger, she must choose: trust him, or watch both worlds burn.

Turn the page for a free preview...

Faie and Fury: Prologue

Molten earth spewed from a fissure in the ground, illuminating the shrouded form of a desperate mother clutching her child to her breast. The explosion sent them both sprawling into the ash. The mother cradled her boy closer to her as she absorbed the impact.

An alarmed cry rang out from a small, robed figure behind her. The girl struggled to keep her balance, but helped to right the mother and child. "Your Majesty, please. We cannot outrun it."

Pulling herself to her knees, the mother gathered her child closer. She inhaled fiery ash, her lungs shuddering on a sob of despair.

The figure knelt beside her, glancing anxiously around. "Your Majesty…"

"I know," the woman whispered, voice hoarse.

The boy in her arms was quiet, watching with terrified green eyes as his world collapsed around him.

"We must find a way to hide," the figure insisted. "Perhaps…the sea?"

"No," the mother ground out, her eyes focused before her on nothing. They grew more vacant, hazing over with a white film as the future stretched out before her mind's eye. Cracks in the earth split and hissed around them.

The figure glanced uneasily at the tendrils of darkness in the distance that burned the *Faievale* in an unstoppable force of carnage. Destroying, yes, but seeking. Searching. She held her silence, prepared to wrench the boy from the mother's arms and fly them to the sea if need be.

"It will find him in the sea," the mother said at last. "It will find him in the earth, in the trees, in the air, and in every stone he touches."

The figure kept her silence once more. It was true.

The mother looked down at her boy, their eyes meeting. With tears streaking a path through the soot on her cheeks, she kissed her small child on the forehead. She buried her face in his black hair and said, "I must summon Elaine."

"Elaine?" the figure asked. "With the humans?"

"Yes." The mother raised her face, resolve forming in her features.

"We must take *Moros* from him. We can hide it. We can hide him. Until he is strong enough to reclaim what was lost."

The figure shook her head, "Hide it with a human across the vale? Surely not."

"Listen to me," the mother said, frenetic energy overtaking her. "Take him deep into a vale of the *Faiewood.* Raise him there." Her hands fastened upon her son's upper arms with a vice grip. White began to creep through her veins, bulging along her temples, standing up from her skin along her arms and up her neck. The boy cried out, his body going rigid.

The mother's eyes glazed over white once more. "*Moros*

taken, *Moros* given. Upon the name of given, take. Taken, given, mind of one. To the worthy, *Moros* bound. Two of one restore the ground."

Around the boy, a dark blue light began to glow, and his pained cries suddenly stopped as he flopped backward into the other figure's arms. The mother then cradled the dark light within a sphere of white brilliance emanating from her hands. "Take him," she commanded.

"But where will you hide it?" the figure asked, gathering the unconscious boy to her breast. "How will we know?"

Eyes still white, voice hollow, and conscious thought lost to her magic, the mother stood with the light held carefully between her hands. "*Creatio ex nihilo.*"

"No," the figure breathed. "No! You'll die."

The ground trembled beneath them. Tendrils of black smog began to thicken in their lungs.

"There's no time," the mother said, her body already shimmering as she summoned her corporeal form to another place. "Go now," she commanded. Her voice echoed with the voices of the thousands of *Faie* before her.

Swallowing her fears and her sorrow, the figure took the boy and ran.

Faie and Fury: Chapter One

I am certain to lose. With my knights demolished and the king in jeopardy, there is little hope of survival. One well-aimed blow, and…

"Hah!" my betrothed bellowed in triumph.

I gave him an exaggerated glower of contempt. Wooden blocks dropped from my hands. "I had only one of your knights to topple, Gresham, and you know very well I could have beaten you."

"But you didn't," he grinned from across the lawn and waved one of his wooden blocks my way. "Pay up, princess. It is an unbecoming trait to sulk."

"Oh, very well," I grumbled.

Before us, the scene of a completed game of *Faie* Chess sprawled out with toppled blocks and one defeated king in the center. It was not a complicated game–seven knights on each side of the lawn with one "king" block in the center. We had only to throw blocks at the knights on our opponent's side and topple each of them before finally knocking the king in the center to claim victory.

"Well?" Gresham prodded, impatience sharpening the edge of his words.

I hesitated, a sense of foreboding coloring the happy scene with a sooty film of doubt.

Gresham huffed, smiling tightly. "If you want, of course."

His words wove through the air, thick with something intangible that confused my mind and left a flicker of sourness on my tongue. "Yes, yes," I relented, smiling. The sour taste dissipated, and a warm complacency settled over my bones. "A kiss for the dashing conqueror."

He reached me, hooking an arm around my waist and pulling me close. "That's more like it," he said softly. So close, I could just about drown in the spring-green depths of his eyes, which stood in such stark contrast to his raven black hair. His face was round above a well-built, solid frame.

"You earned it, of course," I said, hoping to banish the strange pang of worry that had accompanied his impatience.

"I did," he agreed, his voice smooth again.

We had been here before. Close to one another, only a breath away, and by all appearances, a happy couple. I should have wanted to fling myself at him, kiss him until we were flushed and breathless, and vow that my heart would be his forever and ever.

And yet, every time, I hesitated.

Then a breeze blew past, and eerily, like so many times before, it seemed to carry words with it. *To the woods.* A shiver tapped up my spine like icy fingers, but I drew a breath and smiled. I stood on tiptoe and kissed his smooth cheek.

"Well earned."

A guarded anger crept into his eyes, but it was only for a moment. As ever, Gresham recovered quickly and grabbed my chin with a playful shake. "Soon enough."

"Anwen!" My sister ran, skipped, and then attempted to moderate her speed to a more stately walk before giving in to a run across the lawn again.

I pulled away from Gresham to face her. "You'll never marry if you gallop through the grounds like a filly," I said in mock scolding.

Stopping before me, slightly breathless and pushing blond tendrils away from her red face, Emma waved a hand dismissively. "My beauty far exceeds my ungainly run. Hello, Gresh."

Gresham gave a half bow to my younger sister. "A good day to you, Princess Emma."

"Anyway," Emma said, still catching her breath, "Matth wants you in the throne room."

I resisted the urge to roll my eyes. My brother, the king, took himself far too seriously. *The throne room? Really?* "I'll be along shortly, then," I said.

"He's very cross," she mock whispered, so loudly that anyone within ten paces could have heard her.

"He usually is," I mumbled.

"Go," Gresham said with a wave of his hand. "The sooner you go, the sooner you can return to me."

I followed Emma back across the gardens to our sprawling estate at the edge of Ironvale. With the keep and castle situated at the top of a hill, the gardens flowed down in tiers, connected by stone stairs and paths, and punctuated with glistening, domed follies and vine-shrouded archways. Beyond the gardens, past the impossibly high, stone walls, the farmlands gave way to forests that were better off ignored. Why our predecessors had chosen to build their keep so close to dangerous *Faie* vales, I could not possibly guess. Strange events plagued our farmers so often that my father had created a branch of his militia solely devoted to handling them. Not that they were of much use. *Faie* magic was as tangible to us as the wind. We could feel it, we could see its effects, but never could we control it. Looking over the wall at the light green treetops, I heard a whisper rustle through the branches. *To the woods.*

After climbing through the gardens, a guard opened the iron, double doors that served as the only entrance, and we entered the darkly-lit halls at the base of the castle. We passed by the apothecary room, now abandoned, but still smelling of dried herbs. The herbalist had left sometime in the last year. Many of our staff had. Matth hadn't bothered to replace them.

Emma chattered on about an art contest she wanted to host for the surrounding provinces of Ironvale. At seventeen, she was finding her purpose through art and beauty, leading the charge for progressive ideals she hoped would make our world a little brighter. I admired her greatly.

At twenty, I had no purpose whatsoever. Like a hollow shell, I waited for some meaning to make me whole. Deep inside I felt the echo of something more, as if I had dreamed another me. It was as if a twilight version of the Princess of Ironvale existed, living out the ghost of her purpose under the starry quilt of sleep, and in those moments, I knew who I was. I remembered things that drifted through my subconscious like the wail of something long ago buried. If I tried to grasp it, the shadow flitted away, dissipating behind an iron door that felt as if it had always existed. There were things I should have known but did not. Details I should grab hold of but could not find purchase.

Some nights I closed my eyes and wondered what I had done that day as the hazy memories evaporated through the fingers of my mind like mist. It was like each day passed and disappeared, floating around in my mind but never settling into a memory.

I should have worried. I should have wondered. But then, just as the thoughts of concern arose, they were replaced with sedate, comfortable security in my surroundings. Even as I walked the halls of Ironvale with Emma, I noted the disconcerting emptiness of our stone halls. *Where are all the servants? Why is there so much dust in the wall sconces? Is there no one to light them?* But then, like the flutter of a raven's wing, my worries flashed away as I remembered that Matth had asked to see me.

Matth had always been destined to rule Ironvale. He was only ten months my senior, but his soul was probably eighty. Crotchety old man.

After our father's death, he hadn't even bothered to update the throne room. Situated near the front entrance of the castle, it was a long, dark room hung with grotesque tapestries depicting battles won, usurpers beheaded, and hunts that stuffy old kings had found particularly memorable. *Nothing sets the mood like an embroidered hog squirting blood.*

We entered the hall and made the long walk down the green carpet to where my brother stood at the head of a gilded round table. It was tradition for the king to rule with his council surrounding him. Today, the table was empty, and Matth was sitting with his fingers steepled on the table before him. I wasn't sure where he got that stately pose from. Probably a manual on kingly poise, or something.

He narrowed his eyes at Emma. "I believe I instructed you to send a servant after Anwen."

She shrugged. "I like the gardens."

"Princesses do not deliver messages."

She folded her arms, jutting out a hip. "Then why did you ask me in the first place?"

He speared her with a blue-eyed gaze. She glared back.

I cleared my throat. "What is it I can help you with, brother?"

His gaze shifted to me. "Emma, you may leave us."

She huffed, throwing her hands in the air. "Your communication skills are *abysmal*, Matth. I walked *all the way here–*"

"Emma!" he barked.

Grumbling, Emma stomped from the throne room, but not before grabbing one of the ancient tapestries near the entrance and yanking it full force off the wall. "These are horrid!" she shouted.

I sucked in my lips to keep from laughing. Matth had only been on the throne three months, and Emma had been hounding him about the ancient furnishings every day of them. The loud echo of the metal bar that had tethered the tapestry to the wall clanged through the long hall as it fell to the floor.

Matth stared at me above his steepled fingers.

I blinked back.

Finally, he drew a breath and held up a letter. "This appeared on my pillow this morning."

"Appeared?"

"Yes. Appeared. None of the servants claim to have left it. It was addressed to me by our father. Sorry," he amended, eyes darkening. "*My* father."

I tilted my head slightly, scowling. "What does that mean?"

"It means," he said, standing slowly from his winged throne, "he claims that you are not his daughter."

My heart dropped to my stomach.

Matth continued, and only then did I notice that his blond hair was in disarray, his eyes red. He wasn't angry. He was devastated. "As you know, our mother's death was quite sudden. There were things, Father claims, that she wanted you to know. It fell to him to relay them to us. Namely, that you are not the king's daughter."

I swallowed, but my throat felt dry. How could it be? Had Mother been unfaithful?

"A bastard sister I can stomach," he said, beginning to come around the table toward me. "But there is more. He has left me very specific instructions regarding your…future. And Anwen, I cannot deny it. I am concerned. I am a new king. To have any of this information leave this room would be…" he paused, apparently unsure of how to continue.

"Disaster," I whispered.

He nodded.

"What else is there?" I asked.

"He says you are never to marry. Or…*be* with…anyone. In any way."

My frown deepened. "What? But he betrothed me to Gresham himself."

"It is a curious contradiction. And while our mother insisted that you be harbored here indefinitely, it is Father's wish that you be removed from the castle and taken away from the family as soon as possible."

My head reeled. None of this made any sense. It couldn't be.

"You are never to give your name to anyone," he added, this time looking puzzled. "Whatever that might mean."

My shock was quickly igniting into anger. "Everyone in Ironvale knows my name." Where had this letter come from, so full of riddles and determined to ruin my easy existence? A dark thing inside of me began to writhe with anger as my perfectly assembled reality burned at the edges like a paper over a flame.

He shook his head. "I don't understand it. But it was his writing, his seal…his writing voice. I know it was him."

"But none of that makes any sense. Matth, are you saying you believe those things? That Father would ever have said any of that?"

Uncertainty crossed his sharp features. Matth had the appearance of a downy hawk with sharp angles and feathery, blond hair that stuck out at all angles. He could look intimidating when he needed to, but to me, he would always be a gangly, awkward fledgling. At that moment, he was more a distant king than ever before. There was concern in his eyes, but also a steely resolve that made my insides feel like iron.

"Matth," I pleaded.

He shook his head, "Anwen, I don't know what any of this means, but I must tell you that I felt something when I read this letter." His blue eyes went unfocused, looking past me. "It was like an omen. It felt dangerous."

My breaths were coming faster now, shaking in my chest as my heart beat furiously. "You're sending me away?"

He blinked, returning to the present. "No. I haven't decided anything yet. But I felt you should know; I did not want you to be left in the dark. And…there's the issue of Gresham."

"Wait, you want to end my betrothal? I thought I *had* to marry him, that it was my duty or whatever it was that Father spouted off when Gresham arrived. Isn't he a…" I paused, my thoughts turning murky. "Well he's important somehow, isn't he?"

Matth looked as uncertain as I did. "Yes, he…is. He is a lord, I think."

We both stood there in silence, trying to remember something that remained out of reach in our memories.

"In any case," Matth said, shaking himself from his thoughts, "we should hold off on these things. I will try to verify some of this information if I can. Surely, Mother left something to indicate Father's claims are valid."

"Surely," I echoed, feeling more numb than usual.

Matth closed the distance between us, and put a hand on my shoulder, his eyes full of pity. "I pondered this letter all day, Anwen. I can only imagine how you are feeling. Go and rest, and we can discuss this further tomorrow."

"Right." My voice had no emotion to it. No feeling. I bowed my head, something I never would have done before that moment, and then turned to leave the throne room. My legs carried me through dark hallways, past my bedroom, and to the back of the castle. I needed air.

Faie and Fury: Chapter Two

That night, I ran.

Emma found me on the veranda, hands pressed against the railing and eyes turned to the emerging stars. I wanted my eyes to fill with tears, but they wouldn't. I wanted to cry, but I couldn't. Rage boiled beneath the surface, but never broke free. I had been this way for ages. I longed to feel something, but it remained out of reach. The dark thing inside of me had clamped around my feelings, and the moment they rose up, they were drowned back to the darkest depths of my being.

Emma wrapped her arms around me. "I don't know what Matth said, but I'm here."

"Thank you," I whispered.

With her face pressed into my shoulder, she looked over at me. "Let's run."

I nodded, and we headed to our shared rooms to change into soft doeskin breeches, flowing white shirts, and soft-soled boots. And then we ran.

Through the countryside, along the border of strange,

dark trees, past the shadows that lurked beyond, and then back through the countryside. We ran until our lungs felt like they would burst, and the wind burned away the dark, heavy feeling inside of me. *To the woods, to the woods*, the wind seemed to scream then. Louder than ever before, it called to me.

I ignored it. Instead, I ran as I so often did with Emma, and we spent our bodies of energy.

When we returned to the courtyard, we slumped against a water barrel, taking turns sipping the cool water that the early spring air had turned icy. She leaned her head against a wooden support, watching me drink. "What happened?" she asked.

I tossed the ladle back into the barrel. "I can't tell you."

"Well, I know that," she said, rolling her eyes. "But how bad? I mean, is someone dying? Are we in trouble? Can I help?"

I shook my head. "No...to all three. It's just something about me. I really can't explain. I promised Matth." *And I wouldn't tell you, anyway*, I thought, remembering how she had cried for days after Mother's death. If she thought I might not stay with her, it would unravel the stitches we had sewn over her broken heart.

"Bully," she muttered. "He's been a right ass since he took that throne. He didn't even grieve father's passing."

"He did," I said with a weary smile. "And it's not him. He was just relaying information. I think I need to break off my engagement with Gresham, though."

Her blue eyes went round. "No."

I shrugged. "It seems that way."

She stared ahead, silent.

My mind felt a little clearer after our run. Some of Matth's words–his father's words, in truth–had found a place in my mind instead of bouncing around like fireflies on a summer night. If I was, in fact, a bastard child, then the question of my legitimacy as an heir to Ironvale would undoubtedly cast questions on Matth's claim as well. He had done well to keep it a secret between us. But the rest of it? They were such strange stipulations about my future.

Baseless. I needed more information.

I stood, and Emma stood with me, her eyes still round and watching me warily. I motioned for her to follow me. "Come with me to Mother's apartments. We need to look for something."

"Look for what?" she asked, breathless.

"I don't know yet. Something…secretive."

"Well, that clears that up."

We hurried through the quiet halls. Most of the castle had gone to bed already. I'd missed dinner and hadn't seen Gresham since our game on the lawn, but that was for the best. I needed some answers before I went and broke off an important engagement. At least, I was pretty sure it was important. And I did love him…right?

Shaking my head, I pulled my focus back to our task. Mother's rooms were the prettiest wing of the castle. And the newest. While pregnant with me, she had gone into a flurry of activity, ordering a new wing to be built that spilled out from the main keep and was made almost entirely of glass and iridescent, semi-precious jewels. Marble columns supported the semi-circle wing, where glass domed over top like a greenhouse. No one had touched her rooms since her death.

"Aren't they locked?" Emma asked as we approached the bronze, double doors.

"Maybe," I said. Something told me it wouldn't be a problem. I pressed my hand against the beveled surface of the door, and an audible *click* sounded through the hallways. Emma and I exchanged surprised glances, and then I pushed.

The door gave way, and we entered a tiny kingdom of sparkling moonlight. Bathed in a soft, blue glow, her quiet apartment felt cold and still, as if it too had become a corpse. I smelled fresh air, crisp and pure. From the entryway, I could see that Mother had left windows open the day she had died, and vines had grown through them. Her bed, built low to the ground and piled high with soft, white, downy pillows, looked yellow and aged. The wind rattled the windows, rasping, *to the woods, to the woods.*

I swallowed hard and moved forward, cautious and fearful, but I didn't know why. Emma followed suit, her hand on my arm. I tried not to sound nervous. "I'm sure it's fine. Start looking through her books. A diary. A letter. Anything that seems out of place."

"Alright," she said, but there was a tremor in her voice.

While Emma moved off to the bookshelf in a cove tented with gauzy material, I found Mother's white oak writing desk. Her elegant scrawl was on so many papers on the desk. Letters to friends, orders for dresses and furnishings, and even letters to her husband. Loving letters. They had so much love between them. How could she have been unfaithful? I opened every drawer and searched the seams for hidden compartments, but I didn't find any evidence of a lover. And nothing out of the ordinary.

Behind me, Emma shook books, looking for loose papers. I moved on to her nightstand, which was in the middle of the vast wing along with her bed. Strange of her to want to sleep in the middle of such an open space. It felt so exposed. I opened drawers and found a velvet pouch, but it held only a pearl necklace. With a furtive glance at

Emma, I shoved the necklace in the pocket of my trousers while she was occupied. *Why did I just do that?* I looked down at my pocket. The necklace seemed to burn in my pocket as if I had plucked it from the fire. I patted it, strangely comforted, and turned to join Emma.

She had gone through most of the books and stood studying one of them with furrowed brows.

"What did you find?"

She showed me. It was just an ordinary book. I couldn't see the title with it open, but it was open to boring-looking text. I gave her a puzzled look.

Emma ran her finger over the pages. "There's kind of an indent here. And the book has a natural gap. Like there was something in here."

I took it from her, and sure enough, when I closed the book, there remained a gap where the pages had been pressed down together for a long time. The title *Herbology for the Modern Ages* was embossed in gold. "Huh."

"Yeah." Emma stepped back and looked around the glassy room. "I never realized how…unique mother was when she was alive. This is odd, though, isn't it?"

"Very," I agreed. But none of it explained the king's instructions to Matth. Frustration bubbled beneath the surface of my emotions, which were anchored down once more by a weight I couldn't name. Suddenly, I was exhausted. My arms were heavy, and my eyelids felt like metal visors crashing down over my eyes with every blink. "Let's go to bed," I suggested. "I don't think there's anything in here."

Emma crossed her arms over her torso with a shiver. "Good. I don't think I like it here."

Doubtless, it would be less eerie in the morning. But I

had to agree with Emma. My mother's soul gave the space a haunted feeling of unrest.

That night, I dreamed fitfully. My mother's voice sang to me, soft and lilting, carrying a tune that resonated in my bones. Somehow, the words *were* me. But I couldn't call them to mind. I was so close. I could see her, sable hair flowing in waves down her back, singing to a baby as a midnight blue aura surrounded them both. I could see the words forming on her pale lips. Had she always looked so gaunt?

Green eyes swam before me. They glowed, sucking me into their depths. I had been so close, but I saw nothing but green. Spring green. Sickly green. Poison green.

I opened my eyes with a gasp, and to my horror, the green eyes remained. Framed by dark lashes and blinking in surprise. "Wh–"

"Sorry," Gresham said, pulling away from me a bit. "Did I startle you?"

I blinked rapidly. "I-I-no." My unease grew to a fever pitch, and then, suddenly, leached away and was replaced with a comfortable complacency.

Gresham lounged beside me in bed. He was fully clothed and on top of my pink quilt, his elbow propped against my pillows and head lounging on his hand. "You're in my bed," I said.

"Of course," he smiled warmly. "I always lay with you in the mornings."

Something smoothed over my uncertainty. "Right. You do."

His smile sobered. "Emma said you'd had a difficult evening. I wanted to make sure you're alright."

I was flooded with memories. Everything felt surreal like I was processing it through a thick muff of cotton. I wasn't a princess. And something was strange about me—the king wanted me to leave. Last night, in the moonlight, I had felt something, but I couldn't quite grasp it.

Gresham shifted his leg against mine, reminding me of the pearls in my pocket. They still burned with a comforting warmth. He lifted a hand to brush a wavy strand of brown hair off my face. "You can tell me, you know."

Something tugged at me to get up. To put some distance between us. And then another part wanted to lean into him. I wanted to close the space between us and ensure we were one. *Never apart. Bonded.*

I blinked. "I will," I said, feeling as if my voice was underwater. "I'll dress first."

"Of course," he kissed the back of my hand and rolled off the bed. His snug black breeches and black shirt gave the perfect backdrop to his intricately detailed silver vest. "I'll wait for you outside."

Groggily, I pulled myself from my bed. I was still in my breeches and loose shirt. I didn't even remember falling into bed. With stiff muscles, I went to the bathing room where a tub of steaming water waited for me. It was there every morning, whether I asked the servants for it or not.

I bathed and then dressed in a green cotton dress embroidered with gold details from the bodice to the hem. The sleeves were fitted past my elbows, where sheer fabric fell away in a bell to float around my wrists. Gresham liked green. He liked me in green, specifically. A gold clip held most of my hair away from my face.

I glanced down at the upholstered chair in my bathing

room where I had thrown my running clothes. The pearls called to me. I fished them out of the pocket and instead of putting them around my neck, where they would be easily seen above the heart-shaped cut of my bodice, I wrapped them four times around my wrist. The clatter when I lifted my hand was comforting. As I stared at them, I felt the sensation of an invisible mantle sliding off my body. In some way, it was like a film of ice had been covering my eyes, had been blinding me. The more I stared at the pearls, the more clear-headed I felt. Blinking rapidly, I dropped my arm and covered the pearls with my sleeve.

As I left my rooms, and sunlight streamed through open glass windows along the corridor, my head cleared. I pulled in a breath of fresh air as I made my way to the dining parlor. It was a smaller room than the dining hall, and our family took most of our meals in the breezy space, where a pair of double doors opened to the veranda I had fled to the night before.

At the table, Gresham and Emma sat with plates already piled with food, both laughing over a joke. I started to smile, and then it faltered. Something about their laugh sounded all wrong. The whole scene wasn't right. I stared at them both, even as their laughs faded and they turned my way, eyeing me suspiciously as my gaze bounced between them and around the delicately decorated sitting room. Emma's hand had been at work in this room. It was all light and life and relaxation with greens and blues and breezy drapes.

"Anwen?" Gresham asked, concern furrowing his brow.

I pasted a smile on my face. "I must be hungrier than I thought."

They both relaxed, and Gresham began to pile my plate with sweet rolls, sausage, and fresh greens. I stared at the plate as I sat beside Gresham. "I don't think I like sausage,"

I said. As I said it, the thought solidified in my mind. I hated sausage, actually.

"Yes you do," he said with a slight laugh. "You eat it every morning."

"I know I do," I said, spearing the greens with my fork. "But I can't imagine why."

Again, Emma and Gresham were silent. Staring.

I looked up and caught Gresham frowning down at me. "What?" I asked. "Why are you looking at me like that?"

"Nothing," he murmured.

Emma looked between us both, and then with an airy grace, stood from her chair and flounced her pink dress around her. "I have things to do. Anwen, meet me where we were last night. I had an idea."

My interest piqued, I nodded eagerly. "Alright. I'll see you then."

With a wink at me, she floated out of the room, leaving Gresham and me alone. I looked over at him, and with a fluttery, anxious feeling, I realized that I would need to tell him about our engagement. At the very least, we needed to put a halt to the betrothal for now.

As I looked at him, something else dawned on me. I didn't like him, either. At all.

He caught me staring, and concern darkened his beautiful features. "Anwen, are you alright? What did Matth say to you yesterday? You don't seem like yourself."

"I don't know," I confessed. "I feel *more* like myself today than I have in a long time. Maybe being in Mother's room helped me to accept my fa–the king's passing. I don't know. I've been strange these past few months, haven't I?"

He cocked his head. "Really?"

I nodded, taking another satisfying bite of the crunchy greens on my plate. "I'm pretty sure I feel more energetic. I mean, when did we dismiss so many servants? When did we let the hallways become so shabby? I used to be in control of all of that. I've been floating around like a ghost or something." I set down my fork.

"And, actually, I do have something I need to talk to you about, Gresh. It's not great," I admitted, sobering my tone as much as I could. But there was an indescribable glee about what I needed to tell him. "I think we need to put a hold on our betrothal. Just for now," I assured him as his face darkened further. "Matth told me some things that make it… difficult for us to go forward with our union."

"What things?" Gresham asked, turning his body to me and balling his hands into fists on the table.

My eyes flickered to his hands. "Just… well… I don't know if I'm allowed to tell you. But I might not be who you think I am."

"I know exactly who you are," he said, his voice dark. "I know everything about you. We've been betrothed for years. We love each other."

No, I don't! My mind screamed. On the outside, I took his hand. "I know. It's nothing permanent. We just need to take a moment to figure out some state business first."

"State business," he repeated.

I nodded, taking a bite of the sweet roll. "Matth is hoping you'll understand. I know you've been a part of our lives for a long time." I paused, frowning again. "Or… wait. How long has it been?"

For the first time, Gresham looked truly angry. "We've been destined to be together since you were born, Anwen."

My brows went up in surprise. My quickly clearing mind told me that was probably a lie. Since when did Gresham lie to me? *All the time!* my inner voice shouted. I gave him a placating smile. "Well, that might still be the case. Just give Matth and me some time to work out a few details, okay?"

Gresham blinked, staring at me hard.

Suddenly weary of dealing with Gresham, I stood wiping my lips with a soft napkin. "We can talk again later, alright?"

He didn't respond. He just scowled.

Unease crept in. "Gresham, I'll talk to you later. I promise." With that, I left the room, more aware of my surroundings than ever before. The hallways really were looking dilapidated. And where were all the servants? I should get an updated list of our staff and set them to cleaning the blackened walls above sconces and cobwebs up in the corners. If I could get to my apothecary, I could—

I stopped in the middle of the hallway. The apothecary. *My* apothecary. It had been so long since I set foot in it, and yet… it was part of me. I made tinctures and potions. I gathered herbs and studied medicinal uses for them.

Or I had.

My heart began to beat twice as fast. Something like panic began to creep in around the edges of my emotions. Where there was a bubbling energy before, now there was a kind of urgency. Something was very wrong.

About the Author

Devon lives in the mountains of Wyoming with her family, and when she's not writing her next romantic adventure, she can be found snuggled up with Mr. Grumpy, playing a raucous game with her kids, or playing a video game with no skill whatsoever.

www.ingramcontent.com/pod-product-compliance
Lightning Source LLC
LaVergne TN
LVHW030915080826
845145LV00013B/2902